THIS CRUEL DESIGN

EMILY SUVADA

PENGUIN BOOKS

PENGUIN BOOKS

UK | USA | Canada | Ireland | Australia
India | New Zealand | South Africa

Penguin Books is part of the Penguin Random House group of companies
whose addresses can be found at global.penguinrandomhouse.com.

www.penguin.co.uk
www.puffin.co.uk
www.ladybird.co.uk

First published 2018

001

Set in 11/15.5 pt Dante MT Std
Typeset by Jouve (UK), Milton Keynes
Printed and bound in Great Britain by Clays Ltd, Elcograf S.p.A.

A CIP catalogue record for this book is available from the British Library

ISBN: 978–0–141–37928–9

All correspondence to:
Penguin Books
Penguin Random House Children's
80 Strand, London WC2R 0RL

For Lora Beth Johnson.
You are my favourite.

CHAPTER 1

It's midnight, but the sunset is still fading into darkness, the day stretched late by our northern latitude and the Earth's axial tilt. A million-strong flock of passenger pigeons soars above me, the tips of their feathers glowing faintly, like a swarm of fireflies. They swoop and dart between the trees, their movements sharp and agile, a constellation of pinprick lights against the darkening sky. The sound of their calls echoes from the steep mountain slopes, filling the crisp night air with a hurricane of sound.

This flock is nothing like those I remember from the cabin. These birds are a new strain, with their own mutations and quirks. Their cries are shrill, punctuated with complex streams of whirs and clicks. They're getting smarter with each new generation.

It's almost like they're learning how to speak.

'Lighter on your feet. Eyes on me,' Leoben says, prowling in a slow circle around me.

I lift the weight from my heels, dropping my eyes from the flock. My fists are raised, my hair hanging tangled about my shoulders. We're deep in the forest, the grass around us tracked with muddy footprints. There's blood in my mouth, dirt streaked across my skin, and bruises rising on what feels like every inch of my body.

'Keep that guard up, squid.'

I tighten my stance. 'Did you just call me *squid*?'

A low smile tugs at Leoben's lips, and my stomach clenches. He's going to come at me again – I can see it in his eyes. He's unarmed, and I know he won't really hurt me, but he's still a black-out agent. A tower of finely crafted Cartaxus weaponry, trained to fight since he was a child. His every movement is precise and lethal, corded muscles flexing beneath the tattooed skin of his arms. He tilts his head, his smile growing into a grin, then pushes off his rear foot and streaks forward in a blur.

There's no time to think. I lurch to the side, dodging the fist he's aiming at my ribs, but his other hand goes straight for my throat. I bring up a knee, sending out an elbow that connects with his jaw, but by the time I can draw back for another strike, his foot is planted behind mine.

That's all he needs. A simple lever to tilt me off balance. Even though I know he's sending me flying, I can't help but marvel at his grace. His fingers stay locked on my neck, guiding my descent as I tip backwards and hit the ground hard enough to knock the air from my lungs.

He steps back, rubbing his jaw as I wheeze, curling up on my side in the grass.

'Good,' he says, nodding.

I roll to my knees, choking in a breath. 'Good? I barely touched you.'

He reaches down a hand to help me up. 'You're getting better, but you need to be more aggressive. You have to try to bring me down too.'

I stand unsteadily, trying to blink away the flecks of silver at the edges of my vision. We've been at this for days, and every session makes me feel like I've been hit by a car, but he's right – I'm getting better. My reaction times are being whittled down, my senses growing sharper, and there are fresh, slender muscles in my shoulders and forearms. I've never felt as powerless as I do when I fight Leoben, but this training is the only thing in my life right now that makes me feel like I'm in control.

'You OK?' Leoben asks, peering at me. 'You don't look so good.'

I rub my eyes, swaying. 'Yeah, I'm fine.'

He shakes his head, the streaks of iridescent blue eyeliner traced above his lashes catching the sunset's dying light. 'You're a bad liar is what you are. Come on, Cole'll be back from lookout soon. We should stop for the night or he'll kick my ass for beating you up.'

'I disabled his protective protocol.'

'I know,' Leoben says. 'But he'll still kick my ass.'

He slings an arm round my shoulders, walking me back into our makeshift camp. Our two jeeps are parked in a muddy clearing, a camouflage-printed tarpaulin stretched between them. The trees around us are tall and thick, their trunks coated with moss, the ground at their bases bursting with ferns. We've been here for a week, hidden deep in the forest, an hour's hike from the Zarathustra lab. We camped in its parking lot the first night after I blew up the genkits, but a troop of Cartaxus soldiers arrived and sent us fleeing into the woods. None of us wanted to stay near the prison we spent our childhoods in, but we were too hurt to get on the road, and we had nowhere else to go anyway.

So we've stayed here, resting and healing, eating freeze-dried rations and sleeping in our jeeps. There are still soldiers at the lab, and it probably isn't smart to stay this close to them, but the jeeps' black dome chips are hiding our location. Besides, this flock of pigeons has been growing larger by the day, their cries filling the air, their glowing plumage providing more than enough cover to hide us from the prying eyes of drones.

Leoben swings open the rear doors of his jeep, pulling out two metal flasks. 'I mean it. You need to rest. You're not looking so great, squid.'

'You can't call me squid,' I say.

He tosses me one of the flasks. 'So many rules with you. Can't call you "squid", can't call you "potato". You're my sister, and you're getting a nickname.'

'Cole doesn't have a nickname.'

He rolls his eyes. 'That's because his name is *Cole*.'

I unscrew the flask and take a swig of water, swishing it around my mouth to clear out the blood, then spit it into the grass. 'And where did you get "squid"?'

'They can change the expression of their genes, kind of like you. Cephalopods. I read about it.'

'Wow.' I take another swig, fighting a rush of dizziness as I tip my head back. 'I don't know whether to be offended or impressed.'

He crosses his arms proudly, a grin spreading across his face. 'Definitely impressed.'

I snort, lifting the flask to pour water over my face. Leoben and I have spent most of the week together while Cole has been recovering from his injuries. Lee braided my hair when the gunshot wound in my shoulder was healing, and I've woken him from his nightmares, but after a week of living as brother and sister, he still can't call me *Cat*.

Honestly, I don't really mind, though I'm not so keen on squid. The three of us are all coping with my identity in our own ways. Cole's been quiet, Lee's cracking jokes, and I'm doing what I always do – building carefully constructed fortresses of distraction and denial.

That's how I made it through the outbreak – I spent my days hacking Cartaxus, helping Novak's rebel group, the Skies, distribute medical code to the survivors on the surface. The harder I worked, and the longer I locked myself away in the cabin's basement lab, the less it hurt when I heard people detonating in the distance or had to choke down doses for immunity.

This week I've had no shortage of ways to occupy my time. Cole's tech has needed constant attention while it's regenerated. I've been training with Leoben and reading through the paper files that Cole and I brought from the cabin – barely sleeping, barely eating, barely letting myself think. I'm probably headed for a crash, but it's working so far. I've managed to bend my thoughts away from what's been hurting me the most.

I've barely thought about the green-eyed child with scars curling across her chest.

Jun Bei.

She is a shadow on the edge of my senses, a puzzle left unsolved. All week I've been waiting for more of my childhood memories to return, but they're still blurry and scattered. I don't know if that's all I'll ever remember, or if I'm just afraid of seeing more. My childhood feels like a black hole I'm locked in an orbit around – I can't escape it, but if I drift too close, it could tear me apart. I might spend a lifetime recovering from what's been done to me.

But right now, I have to stay focused. I have too much work to do.

From what we've been able to tell, there haven't been any attacks since Sunnyvale. No more orange panels, no more crowds of people turned into mindless killers by the toxic code that was added to the Hydra vaccine. Cartaxus has hidden the truth about what happened – they're still sending out daily broadcasts from the joint satellite network they set up with the Skies. Every morning, Dax and Novak splash on to the jeeps' dashboards, talking about the success of the vaccine, promising that we're getting closer to a new, unified world. Everyone is still celebrating the end of the plague – there are parties raging in the bunkers and in every survivor camp on the surface.

None of them know that there's a threat hidden inside their panels, and that the real enemy is still out there.

Dr Lachlan Agatta. The world's greatest gentech coder, and the man I once called Father.

Three years I loved him, waiting desperately for him to come home after Cartaxus took him from the cabin. I still wear his features on my face and his DNA inside my cells. From what he told me when I faced him at the lab, the patterns of his thoughts are carved into my very *mind*.

I don't really know what that means yet, or why he chose to do it, but I know that Lachlan's plan didn't end with changing me. The daemon code he added to the vaccine gave him access to every panel on the planet, and his goal is far worse than turning crowds of people into monsters.

Lachlan's work on Cole showed him the link between genes and instincts, and it let him isolate the gene that controls the Wrath – the instinctive rage that lurks inside all of us, coded into our DNA. A single whiff of the sharp scent of the infected can be enough to trigger it, turning a crowd of people into mindless, bloodthirsty killers. Lachlan thinks he can use the vaccine to make humanity *better*. He wants to permanently recode everyone's minds by forcibly erasing the Wrath from our DNA.

But we won't let him. I know better than anyone how it feels to learn that your mind is not your own, and every minute since I found out the truth I've been researching, planning and learning to fight.

Because once we're ready, we're going to track Lachlan down.

And then we're going to kill him.

I screw the cap back on the flask and toss it into the back of the jeep. There's a creek a short walk from our camp, and I should go and wash this mud off me before I try to sleep. Not that I have anything clean to change into. We're almost out of soap, food and healing tech. We'll need to get on the road again soon, but we still don't know where Lachlan is. The best lead I have is the comm message Agnes sent me after the vaccine's decryption saying that she'd tracked him to Nevada. I've tried contacting her every day since then, hoping to hear her voice or just find out if she's OK, but I haven't been able to get through.

I know we'll find Lachlan, though. He told me he needs my help to finish his plan. He can use the vaccine to suppress or trigger instincts like he did with the crowd at Sunnyvale, but he still can't alter them *permanently*. I'm the only person whose natural DNA can be recoded without killing them, and now he wants to use me to recode everyone else – to change their minds in the same way he changed mine. Going after him is dangerous, but as long as he's alive, I'll just be another pawn on his chessboard.

I have no choice but to face him, and I know he'll give me a way to find him. He *wants* me to go to him. He thinks I'll actually join him, though the thought is ridiculous.

We just have to make sure that when we're hunting him down, we're not walking into another trap.

'How's your tech today?' Leoben asks, tugging off his dirty tank top. The brown, scarred skin on his chest gleams in the soft light from the pigeons.

I look down at my dirt-smeared arm. The backup node in my spine has unspooled into a brand-new panel – a blazing stripe of cobalt light that stretches from my elbow to my wrist. I spent the last three years believing that I had hypergenesis, an allergy to the nanites that run most gentech code. I survived the outbreak with six measly apps, but now I have thousands: reflex enhancers, built-in painkillers, even eyebrow management. I should be able to code without a screen or keyboard, and my VR chip is powerful enough to launch me into fully rendered virtual worlds.

But I still can't get any of it to work.

My panel's automated apps are running – my healing tech, sensory filters, even a standard aesthetic suite – but it won't *listen* to me. There's a net of four million nanoelectrodes coiled inside my skull to record the electrical impulses that flit through my brain, so I should be able to *think* about my comm-link and have it pop into my vision, but my panel still hasn't learned the patterns of my thoughts. It can't tell if I'm thinking *comm*, or *night vision*. It was learning faster while I was injured, but now that I'm healed the installation has slowed to a crawl. At the pace it's going, it could be weeks until I have full control over my tech . . .

Unless I find a way to speed up the installation again.

'It's still not working properly,' I say, reaching into the back of the jeep, searching under the piles of clothes.

'I was thinking of deleting your healing tech,' Leoben says. 'If we freak your panel out, it might speed up again.'

'I had a similar thought,' I say, sliding out a black handgun, 'but my plan was a little more direct.'

Leoben's eyes drop to the gun, narrowing. It's a Cartaxus model – silencer screwed into the barrel, a hacked targeting chip wired into the stock. It's loaded with custom ammo – hollow resin bullets filled with beads of healing tech that should cause superficial injuries.

At least, they *should* be superficial if my calculations are correct. I haven't tested them yet.

Leoben just stares at me. 'Are you serious?'

'It's totally safe.'

He snorts, shaking his head. 'Those sound like last words to me.'

He takes the gun and turns it in his hands, his eyes fixed on an empty space in the air beside it. His tech will be showing him data from the targeting chip. Muzzle velocity, recoil, impact simulations, all displayed in a virtual interface sketched into his vision. I'd be able to see it too if my panel was working, but when I try to focus on the gun, all I see is a burst of static. My tech has been like that all week – glitchy and strange, messing with my vision. I need to get it running again soon, though. We've been waiting here for Cole's injuries to heal, but now he's better, and I'm the one we're waiting on. There's no point in us going after Lachlan until my panel is running and I'm able to *code*.

Leoben checks the gun's chamber. 'What's the plan?'

'Thigh,' I say, propping my leg up on the jeep's tailgate. 'Close range, more accurate that way.' I pull up the hem of my black leggings, pointing to a scarlet targeting glyph drawn on my skin. 'I marked a site already – no arteries, no bone. Just muscle fibres and at least five days of recovery. That should be enough to kick my tech's installation into emergency mode again.'

Leoben taps the gun's barrel against his palm. 'This seems risky, even for you.'

'Do you have a better idea?'

He tilts his head, considering. 'Actually, yeah. I could shoot you in the hand.'

'What?' I step back, pulling my hands to my chest instinctively.

'It's safer,' he says. 'If this bullet fragments in your leg, it could nick an artery, but your hand will be fine. Those bones heal fast, and your tech will shut down a bleed like that in seconds. Come on, hold out your hand.'

I look down at my clenched fists, hesitating. This seemed a lot less reckless when I was planning on getting shot in the leg. An injury in my hand should still speed up my panel's installation, but it feels more frightening, and definitely more painful. Leoben could change his mind any minute, though, and I don't want to have to do this myself.

'OK,' I say, holding out my left arm, the light of my panel washing over the creases in my palm as I unfurl my fingers. 'Give me a five-second warn–'

Leoben pulls the trigger.

The shot through the silencer sounds like glass breaking, startling the pigeons in the trees above us. They erupt in frantic spirals of light, their cries filling the air like a hailstorm. I double over, clutching my hand to my chest. The pain hasn't hit me yet, but I can feel it coming. Scarlet emergency messages scroll wildly across my vision. Blood pressure readings, injury monitors, healing tech levels. My tech is kicking into gear, sending a jolt of adrenaline into my muscles, making my vision flicker as it draws in and out of focus. I suck in a breath through gritted teeth, then look down at my hand to survey the damage.

But there's no wound.

Leoben throws his head back, laughing. 'You should have seen your face!'

I look up, shaking. 'What the hell, Lee?'

'There's no way I was going to shoot you, squid.'

I lunge forward to punch him in the arm, but a *crack* echoes in the distance, and the air rushes from my lungs.

Leoben doesn't react, but I stand frozen, listening to the sound as it echoes off the hills. Someone else might mistake it for a gunshot, but I've heard that sound so many times that it's burned into my memory.

It was faint and muffled, mixed with the cries of the pigeons, but it sounded a *lot* like a Hydra cloud.

'What's wrong?' Leoben asks.

'I thought I heard something. Didn't you?'

'These birds are messing with my audio filters. What did you hear?'

'An explosion.'

Leoben's smile fades. His eyes glaze, scanning the trees, and another *crack* sounds in the distance.

'I heard that one,' he breathes, and I turn and bolt into the trees.

My vision flashes as I race through the woods and up a muddy hill, my tech spinning up emergency filters automatically, trying to brighten the trail ahead of me. Leoben follows close behind, catching up as I reach a switchback, both of us heading for a lookout on the crest of the hill. I've run up this trail a dozen times searching the sky for Cartaxus copters, worried they'd found us, but never to look for a *blower*.

The vaccine is out. The virus is dead.

Nobody should be detonating any more.

We burst together through a line of trees at the top of the hill and stumble out on to the edge of a cliff. The last rays of sunlight are disappearing over the horizon. From up here I can see the sawtooth silhouette of the three-peaked mountains in the distance, the infinite stretch of spruce forest to the south. I shove the loose hair back from my face, searching for a plume. The flock of pigeons forms a writhing, swirling blanket of light through the tufted canopy, but there's no sign of a cloud.

My vision flickers, and I rub my eyes, willing my tech to switch back to standby, but it doesn't respond. My panel is only listening to my adrenaline levels, not my thoughts. It still thinks I'm in danger.

And maybe I am.

If those explosions were blowers, the victims probably had the vaccine. I gave Cartaxus code to force it into every panel on the planet. There are a few survivors on the surface without panels in their arms, but the likelihood of *two* of them blowing near our camp is low. If those explosions were blowers, it could mean the vaccine isn't working any more.

But I don't even want to think about that possibility.

'I can't see anything,' I say, rubbing my eyes again. 'I don't know if it's my tech or not. It still isn't responding to me.'

Leoben steps to the edge of the cliff, scanning the horizon. He'll be checking for heat signatures, anomalous air patterns. If there's a cloud, his tech will find it. 'Nothing,' he says. 'That was a detonation, though. Seemed smaller than a blower. Could have been a bomb.'

'Why would two be going off right now?'

We turn to each other at the same time.

'Shit,' I breathe. 'Cole.'

Leoben turns so fast he's barely more than a blur, bolting back through the trees and down the trail. I race after him, my heart kicking, fresh adrenaline alerts blinking in my vision. I couldn't tell from the sound where those explosions were coming from – they could have been in a nearby camp, or they could have been at the lab. Cole could be hurt. The thought wrenches at something inside me, as real and painful as a wound.

I try to summon my comm-link to call Cole, but all I get is a burst of static. 'Can you call him?' I yell to Leoben.

'He's gone dark,' he shouts back, racing into camp. 'You drive to the meeting point!' He wrenches the tarpaulin away from his jeep, slamming the rear doors shut. 'I'll run the trail in case he's there.'

'No,' I gasp, skidding down the last stretch of the hill. 'I'll run. My panel's still freaking out. I won't be able to control the jeep. You take it.'

Leoben's brow furrows, but he nods, climbing into the driver's seat. 'He'll be OK, squid. Be safe.'

'You too,' I say. He pulls the jeep across the clearing and down the muddy tyre tracks that lead to the road that loops around the lab. There's a meeting point we set up there, where if anything happened, if there was any hint of danger, we'd meet.

Cole will have heard the blasts, and he'll be waiting there for us. He *has* to be.

I race across the crumpled tarpaulin, heading for a gap in the trees that marks the trail to our lookout point. Leoben and Cole have been taking turns to hike to it every day and watch the lab in case Lachlan shows up. The trail drops sharply once it leaves camp, zigzagging down a rocky, tree-covered slope. I take the switchbacks fast, bolting through the trees, spotting a figure at the bottom of the hill.

A person, kneeling on the ground. Dark hair, black jacket.

'Cole!' I scream, racing for him. He's on the ground. I should have brought a medkit. 'Cole, are you OK?'

I skid to a stop as the figure stands and turns to me.

It isn't Cole. It's Jun Bei.

CHAPTER 2

The forest seems to fall silent, time slowing to a crawl. Jun Bei's eyes lock on mine, and suddenly I can't breathe. It's *her*. Green eyes, black hair, her shoulders slender and hunched in a man's black jacket that hangs halfway to her knees. She takes a step closer and I stumble back, stunned by the intensity of her gaze. Her eyes are as keen and sharp as a razor's gleaming edge. She looks past me, her brow creasing as she scans the trees . . .

And suddenly she's gone.

The spot in the clearing where she was standing is empty. I spin round, staring, but there's no sign of her. No footsteps pressed into the grass, no tracks in the mud. Nothing but trees, grass and mossy rocks stretching into the rain-drenched darkness of the forest.

'Holy shit,' I gasp, doubling over, bracing my hands on my knees. I feel more shaken than I did when I hit the ground during my training session with Leoben. That must have been a VR glitch. My ocular tech has been glitching all week, but that was *different*. That wasn't just a misfiring loop of night-vision code or a broken filter. It was a three-dimensional *person* standing right in front of me. Every detail was perfect. Her hair was loose around her shoulders, her skin pale, a flush colouring her cheeks.

She looked so *real*.

I press the heels of my hands into my eyes until neon spots burn across my vision. A rush of broken memories is rolling back to me – the lab, the forest, the other children. Wires and scalpels, restraints and itching grey blankets. I force the memories away, driving the fingernails of my left hand into my palm. I don't care if it's a trick that Lachlan taught me – all I care about is the pain that slices through the storm inside me, dragging back my self-control. Footsteps sound in the forest behind me, and I spin round, reaching for my gun as a figure pushes through the trees.

Black jacket, a backpack with a rifle strapped to its side. Sparkling ice-blue eyes meet mine, and the adrenaline coursing through me fades into relief.

'Cole,' I gasp, running to him. He opens his arms, confused as I launch myself at him, wrapping my arms around his neck.

'Hey,' he murmurs, swaying with my weight. 'Are you OK?'

I just nod, tightening my grip on him. He's spent the day on lookout duty in the woods and he smells like earth and rain, but the hint I catch of his own unique scent is like a lighthouse in a storm. Home. We've barely talked for days, let alone touched. I've slept in Leoben's jeep most nights to avoid disturbing Cole during his healing cycles, but now that feels like a mistake. Just holding him like this makes my racing thoughts slow.

He pulls away, looking down at me. 'What are you doing here?'

'We heard the blasts. I thought you were hurt.'

'Oh, of course,' he says, his voice softening. 'They were south of here, near that survivor camp. I thought they were fireworks from the celebrations.'

Fireworks. I let out a choked laugh. 'I can't believe we didn't think of that. We were coming to save you.'

'Well,' he says, stepping back to look me up and down, taking in my bruised arms, the space at my side where my holster should be, 'it sure looks like you're prepared.'

I roll my eyes, swatting his arm. He grins, driving a hand back through his dark, tousled hair. It's long enough to fall into his eyes, its rapid growth propelled by the tech that's been regenerating his cells. He's spent most of the week in a series of tech comas recovering from the injuries he took in the explosion in the lab, and he's only just starting to regain the weight he's lost, but his eyes look exactly the same. The colour of the sky on a clear midsummer day. Just looking at them now, I feel a tug in my chest.

'You sure you're OK?' he asks.

I glance back at the spot where I saw the VR glitch of Jun Bei. I want to be honest with Cole, but I'm still reeling. I don't even know what I *saw*, let alone how I feel about it.

'I'm fine,' I force myself to say. 'Lee's probably worried. He drove to the meeting point.'

Cole nods, his eyes glazing. 'I'll comm him. I picked up a new signal coming from the lab tonight but I don't know what it was. Lee's better with that stuff. I'll tell him to check it out.'

From what we've been able to tell, the Cartaxus troops at the lab have been clearing out its equipment to study it. They sent off the broken pieces of the genkit I blew up, as well as the body of the puppet I thought was Lachlan. We've been hiding from them, but they're not really our enemy. We all want to stop Lachlan, and there's a chance we'll need to work together to do it. Lee and I even talked about turning ourselves in one night when Cole's tech was struggling, but we don't know how they'll respond if they find out who I am, or that Lachlan needs me for his plan. They might lock me up and never let me go.

Or maybe they'll just kill me. It would be the most logical way to stop Lachlan.

'Lee says he'll check it out,' Cole says.

'Should we go too?' I ask. 'If there's a new signal at the lab –'

'It's fine,' he says, blinking out of his session. 'I think it was just the AC.'

I frown. 'Then why did you tell Lee to check it out?'

Cole grins, pushing the hair back from my face. 'I figured we could have some time alone.'

Heat prickles at my cheeks. 'Cole, we have so much to do.'

He leans in, pressing a kiss to the side of my neck. 'Like what?'

I push him away, smiling. 'Like reading through Lachlan's files, making a checklist of supplies we need to go after him. You know, saving the world.'

His eyes travel down to my lips. 'The world can wait.'

I open my mouth to argue but pull him to me instead.

It isn't a perfect kiss. We're just two people in tired bodies with a million things we should be thinking about instead of this. I have so much to do, and so much confusion hovering in the back of my mind, but the feeling of Cole's lips on mine washes it all away. My shoulders drop, my breathing hitching as his hand slides to my waist. He tilts me backwards, deepening the kiss, and I clutch a fistful of his dark, curled locks to pull him closer, dragging a growl from low in his throat. He drops his backpack to the ground and walks me up against a tree until my shoulder blades hit the bark.

'I've been going crazy being so close to you,' he whispers, his mouth moving to my neck. He drops his hands to my thighs, lifting me in one smooth motion, pushing me against the tree. Heat coils through me, my legs wrapping instinctively around him as he presses his weight into me. 'I want to take you away when this is over. I don't want to be disturbed for about a month.'

'Oh yeah?' I ask, grinning as his lips move down my throat. 'Where are you going to take me?'

'A beach,' he says without hesitating. His lips pause on the hollow in my throat. 'Somewhere far away and warm. I've been thinking about Australia.'

I shy away as his mouth moves back up the other side of my neck, his stubble tickling my skin. 'You seem to have given this some thought.'

'I have,' he breathes, kissing the corner of my jaw. 'I can already see it. A little place, just the two of us. We can disappear. There'll be plenty of people doing it once they open the bunkers. It won't be hard to blend in with them.'

I look down at him. 'Is that what you want to do after this? Disappear?'

He leans back to look up at me. 'Of course. I don't want to work for Cartaxus any more, not now that I've found you.'

'Yeah, I know,' I say, unwrapping my legs from his waist. He lowers me to the ground, his cheeks flushed. 'But that doesn't mean we have to *hide*.'

A crease forms between his brows. 'They'll want us, Cat. We're valuable whether or not there's a virus to fight. I'm not going to let them turn me into an experiment again.'

'No, of course not . . .' I murmur, trailing off. I hadn't really thought about it like that. I hadn't thought about *anything* beyond stopping Lachlan. But Cole is right – of course Cartaxus will want us. My natural DNA can *change*. My body, my cells, even my mind can be altered in a way that's unique to me. Gentech code is like a mask – it can change the way your DNA works, but it can't change who you really are underneath, and that means it's limited. There's only so much that a mask can do to change your appearance. The ability to change your underlying, natural DNA would revolutionize gentech completely.

And that ability is hidden inside my cells. Of course Cartaxus will want to study me. I'll have to spend every moment of my life hiding, running, and being afraid of them.

But I never imagined a life like that.

'I'm sorry,' Cole says. 'I shouldn't have said that.'

I scratch my neck. 'No, you're right. We'll have to hide. We'll never be free.'

He reaches for my cheek. 'We'll build a life, I promise. Where do you want to go when this is over?'

'I . . . I don't even know. I guess I'd like a lab. I want to keep coding.'

Even though the last three years of my life were based on a lie, they still hold some of my favourite memories – working together with Lachlan and Dax in the cabin. Collaborating, talking about code. I always thought I'd find that again one day after the outbreak.

But if Cole and I are going to disappear, I won't be looking for new coding partners. I might never have that kind of life again. The thought tugs at me, low and deep and surprisingly painful.

'We'll get you a lab,' Cole says.

I nod, chewing my thumbnail, but my eyes drift past Cole's shoulder to the clearing, and the air freezes.

A metal structure is jutting from the trees. I don't know how I could have missed it before. It looks like a pylon used to transport electricity. Twenty feet tall, constructed with steel and rivets. Something about its shape flickers in my memory, and it hits me.

I didn't see the pylon before because it wasn't *there*.

It's another glitch from my VR chip.

'What's wrong?' Cole asks. His eyes glaze, following mine, and he stiffens as he looks towards the pylon.

'Wait, you're seeing this too?' I ask.

He shoots me a cautious look. 'It's a public feed from your panel. What is this?'

'I don't know. I think my tech is glitching. It just did this a minute ago too.'

I try to summon my panel's menu, but my vision just flickers. The pylon is still standing, an electric hum rising in the air. I know it isn't real, but that doesn't stop the jolt of fear that runs through me when a pale figure appears at my side.

I turn round, bracing myself, but I already know who I'll see.

Jun Bei is back, standing in the middle of the clearing, a gust of wind ruffling her long black hair. She's wearing the same oversize jacket over a white hospital gown, her feet in scuffed black boots. There's a stray eyelash on her cheek, a fine dusting of dark hairs on her legs. The jacket's sleeve slips back as she lifts her hand to push a lock of hair from her face, and the cobalt glow of her panel lights up the curve of her jaw.

She looks so *alive*.

Cole is frozen beside me, his eyes wide. Jun Bei is shivering, her hands clutching the jacket tight around her shoulders. Flecks of white drift across her face, settling on her glossy hair. Snow. It swirls through the air, spreading as I watch until it's falling around us too. A dusting stretches across the clearing, and Jun Bei shivers, dragging the back of her hand across her nose, then scrunches up her face and lets out a high-pitched sneeze.

My heart clenches. She's just a *kid*.

She must be fourteen, maybe fifteen. Frightened and alone. She suddenly looks so fragile. There are red scars curling up from the neck of her gown, a bandage wrapped around her wrist.

Lachlan did that to her. He hurt her. He cut her open.

What kind of a monster could do that to a child?

'Why are you showing me this?' Cole asks, his voice wavering. The expression on his face is like an open wound.

'I . . . I'm not,' I say. 'I don't know what's happening.'

Jun Bei crosses her arms over her chest, huddling in the jacket. She lifts her head to scan the trees behind us, and I turn, following her eyes. Something is moving in the forest, back towards the trail. Shadows flicker in the branches, footsteps carrying on the wind. A gust of snow swirls through the trees, clearing to reveal a troop of guards marching through the forest, dressed in black Cartaxus uniforms. Cole reaches for my hand as a figure strides through the trees behind them.

Lachlan.

The light is dim, but I still recognize him instantly. His eyes, his chin, the sweep of his hair. The same features that are etched into my bones and my DNA. My breath catches as he steps into view. This is the man who took my life from me – he fed me lies, changed my face, and ripped my identity into jagged pieces. We've been talking about killing him all week, and I thought that seeing him would have me itching for a gun. I thought the first thing I'd feel would be *rage*.

But it isn't as simple as that.

Lachlan scans the clearing, his grey eyes sharp, his left hand twitching as he sees Jun Bei. It's a nervous tic I recognize from our time in the cabin. He only ever did it when he was upset, and seeing it now tugs at something inside me. I'm angry, but there's a low, deep ache spreading through me too.

Lachlan hasn't just taken away my identity.

He's taken away the *father* I loved.

'It's OK, he isn't real,' Cole says, pulling me against him. His body is like rock, his eyes blazing as Lachlan walks past us.

All Cole is feeling right now is fury – I can sense it rolling from him, humming in the air. I know he wants to kill him. There's nothing that could hold him back if Lachlan were really here. That's the natural, reasonable reaction, and I thought I'd feel it too, but it's only been a week since I called this man my father. I spent three years loving him, idolizing him, proud of the resemblance I bore to the great Dr Lachlan Agatta. I know he's a threat, and I *hate* him for what he's done to me.

But I don't know if I can kill him.

'Running again?' Lachlan asks, marching through the grass. The guards fan out in a semicircle behind him, their rifles gripped in their hands.

I don't understand why Jun Bei isn't running, but suddenly slender cords of what looks like smoke puff from the metal pylon, billowing out in brilliant blue jets, crackling with electricity. *Triphase*. Clouds of magnetically controlled nanites, designed to chew biological matter into ash. It's the same weapon Novak used to force us to come to Sunnyvale, but I've never seen a version that looks quite like this. The glowing ropes flow out from the pylon, stretching through the trees, linking to more pylons that blink into view as my eyes move across the forest. They form a continuous, wavering river of light.

It's a *fence*. This is the barrier they kept around the lab to stop us from running away.

Jun Bei is standing with her back to it, several feet away, flyaway hairs rising in a halo around her head in the electrically charged air. The guards and Lachlan stop beside us, watching her, and Cole's grip tightens on me.

'Tell them to turn off the fence,' Lachlan says to one of the guards. A beat of silence passes, and the flowing ropes of smoke die away. The ground beneath them is left scorched and smoking, a line of black cut through the snow. Jun Bei turns to stare across the perimeter, but she doesn't run.

'Come back,' Lachlan says. 'You have nowhere to go.'

'I'll figure it out,' she murmurs.

'No, you won't,' he says. 'There are people out there who would do terrible things to gain control of your gifts. You'll be a prisoner anywhere you go. I know you don't really want to run, or you'd already be gone. You're safer in here.'

She lets out a soft, bitter laugh, turning back towards Lachlan. Her hand lifts to tug down the collar of her hospital gown, revealing a mess of red and purple scars. 'You think I'm *safe* here?'

'Our work is important, darling,' Lachlan says. 'I know you understand that.'

She shakes her head. 'You don't know anything about me.' Her voice trembles, her glossy hair slipping across her forehead. 'You don't know me. None of you do. Nobody knows me.'

'Jun Bei –' Lachlan starts, his voice growing thick, but she lifts up a hand.

'You're right about one thing,' she says. 'I don't want to run. I came out here tonight because I wanted you to watch this.'

Her eyes glaze, and the glowing ropes rush back into place behind her. I stare, confused, as she blinks out of her session. It seemed like she turned the fence *on* again, but that wouldn't make any sense. Surely she's trying to get away. She must have a plan, a weapon. Some way to fight past these guards. But instead, she balls her hands into fists and turns to the rippling cords of light. Cole's grip tightens on me, and it hits me with a low, sickening thud.

She didn't come out here to escape. She came out here to die.

'Stop her!' Lachlan roars, and the guards surge forward, but Jun Bei is already running.

Her eyes are scrunched shut, her black hair streaming out behind her. She's fast, but she's small, and the guards are on her in moments. Gloved hands stretch for her arms, for her hair, yanking her off her feet.

'Let me go!' she screams, writhing in their grip. She sends a kick into the side of a guard's helmet, an elbow to another's throat, but there are too many of them. One stumbles and topples into the fence, half his torso disintegrating into a wafting pile of ash. The others wrestle Jun Bei to the ground, dragging her away from the rippling blue fence, and she lets out a strangled cry of rage.

'Sedate her!' Lachlan shouts. 'Hurry!' The guards tighten their grip on her, one of them sliding a vial from his pocket.

But she stops fighting suddenly.

Her eyes glaze. Her lips move silently, as though she's coding, and the hair on the back of my neck rises. I don't know what she's doing, but I can feel something – a shadow descending across my memory. Something cold and violent. Something profound.

Jun Bei stares into Lachlan's eyes, whispering a command, and the soldiers fall to the ground.

CHAPTER 3

I scrunch my eyes shut, my hands pressed to my face. Memories slam into me like meteors to earth. The fence. The guards. The attack on their panels. The footage of Jun Bei is gone, but the images are still racing through my mind.

Cole's arms lock around me as my legs buckle, a wash of silver rising in my vision. 'Look at me,' he urges. 'Look at my eyes. I'm here. I'm *real.*'

I clutch his shirt, trying to drag in a breath, but my lungs won't respond. I've been trying all week to keep my past locked away, but seeing Jun Bei like this has shattered something inside me. A door to my childhood unlocked, a barricade forced open. My chest shudders, images of scalpels and wires racing through my mind like a flock of panicked birds.

'It's not *real.*' Cole's voice is shaking. He takes my face in his hands, pressing his forehead to mine. '*Cat*, please. Come back to me.'

I blink through the mess of silver in my vision to look up at him, the sound of my name on his lips like a beacon in a storm. His ice-blue eyes are locked on mine, and somehow I'm able to breathe as long as I'm looking into them. The hurricane of memories subsides, my focus clearing. I look back at the grass where I saw Jun Bei, shaking, and a single thought rises through me:

That wasn't *me*.

The thought sends a flare of horror through me. The girl I just saw in the clearing didn't look like another *version* of me – she looked like a completely different person. I could see it in the expressions on her face, in her stance, the pursing of her lips. I thought I was keeping my past at a distance out of fear of the pain in my memories, but now I'm not so sure.

Maybe what I've been frightened of is the thought that my memories aren't really *mine* at all.

'I'm not . . . *her*,' I whisper, looking up at Cole. I know he sees it too – the truth I've been telling myself that I didn't need to face. I thought I could put my past aside to focus on stopping Lachlan, but it was madness to think I could keep ignoring this. Lachlan told me that he gave me his mind – he overwrote my brain with his – but I haven't really let myself believe it.

I can feel it now though – a divide rising inside me.

A wall between *her* past and *my* present.

'I know you're not her,' Cole whispers. His hand trembles as it slides to the back of my head, pulling me against him. 'You're your own person, Cat. You need to hold on to that. You have to keep sight of who you are.'

I close my eyes, pressing my face into his shoulder. My breathing is still fast and shallow, my pulse racing. Seeing that clip must have been as hard for Cole as it was for me, and I don't know how he's holding himself together. He's giving me his strength right now, letting me lean against him, and it's the only reason that I'm still on my feet.

'Come on,' he says, pulling away, his grip tight on my arms. He shoots a glance at the dark patch of grass where the guards pulled Jun Bei down. 'Let's go down to the creek and get you cleaned off. Staying here isn't going to help either of us.'

He slings his backpack over his shoulder but keeps one hand on my arm, the feeling of his skin against mine steadying me somehow. I let him guide me away from the clearing, his presence quiet and tense beside me as we walk through the trees.

'Not what you had in mind for our time alone together, huh?' I ask.

He lets out a breath of laughter. 'Not really, no.'

We cut down a hill towards the creek. The water winding through mossy boulders, splashing down into a clear knee-deep pool. Cole's shoulders loosen as we get closer, and he drops his pack near the edge of the water, then shrugs his jacket off and folds it neatly, laying it on the rocky shore. He's wearing a tank top underneath, the white Cartaxus antlers emblazoned on his chest, scars peeking from the collar. His leylines cut across his skin, black and matte, curving up from his panel and branching into the outer corners of his eyes.

'I should have warned you about clips like that,' he says. 'That's not the only one you're going to find once your panel is finished installing.'

I kneel at the creek's edge and dip my hands into the water, splashing it over the mud on my arms. 'What *was* that we just saw?'

Cole tugs up the knees of his cargo pants, dropping to his haunches on the rocks beside me. 'It was a VR clip re-created from ocular footage. We all made them to store moments we didn't want to lose. Sometimes Lachlan would wipe our memories – we'd come back from days of experiments and not know what had happened for the last few weeks.'

I pause, looking up at him. 'That's terrible.'

He lifts a handful of water from the creek, splashing it over his face. 'Sometimes memories aren't worth the pain they hold,' he says simply. 'Anything that was important, we stored in VR and encrypted it.'

'So you have VR files like that too?' I ask.

'Not from back then, not any more. When I joined the black-out programme, they wiped my panel. Same with Lee's and Anna's.'

He means Anna Sinclair. The blonde-haired girl whose file I have in my backpack, whose face I've seen in countless memories from our childhood in the lab. 'They took your files from you? Everything?'

'I gave it up,' he says, dropping his eyes to the water.

It suddenly hits me. 'So you haven't seen Jun Bei like that for . . . years?'

He shakes his head, smiling bitterly. 'I haven't seen her since that night. That was when she escaped. I joined the black-out programme just a couple of months after that.'

I rock back on my heels, my mind rolling back to the footage of Jun Bei – the desperation in her eyes. The way the guards fell to the ground. I dip my hands back into the water and splash it over my face, scrubbing the mud off my skin. 'She killed those guards, didn't she?' I ask.

A shadow passes over Cole's face. 'Yeah, she did.'

I blow out a breath, closing my eyes. When Cole told me that Jun Bei had killed fourteen people when she escaped from the lab, I assumed she must have shot them.

But it seemed like she'd killed them with her *mind*.

I saw it in the footage – her lips were moving. She was coding. It looked like she launched a wireless attack at their panels and somehow kicked off a piece of code that killed them instantly. That kind of code is supposed to be impossible, but clearly it isn't.

Jun Bei must have written a *scythe*.

The two genehacker holy grails that have never been cracked, or at least I thought they hadn't, are scythes and ambrosia – apps to kill people, and apps to keep them from dying. The other big puzzles – cancer, ageing, dementia – all have promising work being done in hundreds of labs and genehacker camps around the world.

People don't do much testing when it comes to *death*, though. I've heard rumours of other scythes before but never believed them. There are more layers of security around gentech's biological controls than there are for nuclear weapons. There's a whole universe of firewalls built into every panel to stop lethal code like that from running.

But Jun Bei must have figured out a way to do it when she was just a kid. I just watched her kill fourteen people with what looked like a single command.

Cole reaches for his backpack and tugs a canteen from the side, dipping it into the creek to fill it. 'I didn't know she was that close to breaking. I thought she'd planned to escape, but it didn't seem like that in the footage. She must have panicked and run after she killed those soldiers. She didn't even have a bag. It was freezing. I don't know how she got away.'

I lift my hands from the water, remembering the snow on the ground in the clip. 'So it was winter when she escaped.'

'December,' Cole says, lifting the canteen from the creek.

'Right,' I murmur, my mind turning over. I've managed to piece together a rough time line of my past starting when Lachlan changed me. It matches up with the records of when he quit Cartaxus, but it starts in the middle of July. My memories get foggy then – I remember fighting him, struggling, but every flash I've seen from that time was lit with a bright midsummer sun.

Jun Bei left the lab in winter, but the next thing I remember is half a year later.

I'm missing six months of my life.

'How old am I?' I whisper.

'Eighteen,' Cole says. 'Same as all of us. You know that.'

I sway, standing from the creek, nausea rolling through me. 'No, I thought I was seventeen. The dates don't match up. I'm missing six months. I don't know what happened between Jun Bei leaving the lab and ending up in the cabin.'

Cole's eyes narrow. 'Are you sure?'

My hands tremble. 'There's nothing in my memories. I have no idea where I was.'

'Hey,' he says, reaching for me, but my vision flashes suddenly and I stumble back on the rocks. He catches my shoulder, his eyes flying wide. 'Cat, are you OK?' His face blurs in and out of focus, and his name appears beside his head, a comm icon blinking in green below it.

'Shit,' I breathe, gasping in relief. I thought I was going to see another VR clip of Jun Bei. This is what I've been waiting for, though – it looks like my tech is finally working. I try summoning my panel's menu, and it flashes cleanly across my vision, folders and files spinning out in a curved wall, hovering in the air.

'What's wrong?' Cole asks.

'Nothing's wrong. My panel is working.' I let my eyes glaze, scrolling through the files. There are photographs, videos, and hundreds of snippets of text I recognize as gentech code, labelled and dated, stretching back for years. Half of them are password protected. Breakable, but time consuming. But they're there.

Every file that Jun Bei ever wrote is stored inside my arm.

Cole starts to reply, then stops suddenly, staring at the trees behind me. I turn, following his eyes. The forest stretches out behind us, the pigeons soaring above it, but it's not dark any more. A light is cutting through the canopy, sweeping across the trees, and a low thud starts up in the distance, cutting through the cacophony of the pigeons.

It's a Comox. Cartaxus has found us.

Cole's eyes flash to black. His protective protocol isn't running any more, but he can still invoke it when he wants to. He grabs his rifle and his backpack. 'Head for the road,' he says. 'Lee's coming to get us.'

He breaks into a run, and I race to follow him, heading for the dirt road that cuts around the lab. The trees on the edges of my vision blur. A week ago, I never could have run this fast, but my legs are stronger now. Tech-enhanced, with oxygen-heavy nanites swimming in my bloodstream. We race through a grove of pines and burst out on to the road, skidding to a stop as Leoben's jeep barrels towards us, its engine whining. I run for it, but the Comox swoops closer, and Leoben flies out of the jeep.

'What are you doing?' I ask. 'We need to go!'

'They're already on to us,' he says. 'It looks worse if we run. It's only the one copter. It might just be a routine patrol.'

'They're not answering my hails,' Cole says. 'They're running dark. There's something wrong here.'

'Well, we're outgunned,' Leoben says. 'Let's play this out, OK? I have the jeep's weapons locked on it. We can handle them if they land.'

The Comox quadcopter roars over the road, its rotors sending down a gust of wind. I can see the sheen of its windscreen, the Cartaxus antlers slashed in white on its belly. Its spotlights sweep across the jeep, then swing over us and intersect in a blinding circle of light. I throw my hands over my eyes, stumbling into Cole.

'Stay calm,' he yells. 'They might just want to talk –'

He's cut off as an arc of blazing light shoots from the Comox's belly, and Leoben's jeep explodes.

CHAPTER 4

The explosion knocks me off my feet, but I don't hit the ground. Cole's arms lock around me, shielding me, clutching me to his chest. The blast sends a burst of light and pressure slamming into us, turning the night to day as a roar rips through the air. My ears whine, a wall of heat billowing over us, thick with the choking scent of smoke and burnt plastic. Cole shudders, his arms tightening on me for a second before he goes limp.

'Cole!' I scream, rolling him off me. Arcs of flaming shrapnel hurtle through the darkness, tracing orange streaks across the starlight of the pigeons. A hunk of twisted metal lands with a *crack* beside Cole's head. 'Get up, come on!'

He groans, pushing himself up unsteadily, but it's already too late.

The Comox is tilting, swinging round to circle back to us. Cole's eyes are midnight black, and he's swaying on his knees. I can't tell in this light if he's wounded or not. His back still hasn't healed completely from when I blew up the genkits in the lab, and there's only so much damage his body can take. If he took a chunk of shrapnel in his back, his tech might be too overwhelmed to heal him right now.

'Lee, I need you!' I yell, my voice ragged. He's nowhere in sight. The Comox lurches back towards us, its rotors roaring. 'Come on, Cole, you have to get up.' I slide myself under his arm and he staggers to his feet, but we only make it a few steps across the muddy road before the Comox starts to drop. Its spotlights lock on to us, and the hurricane of its descent sends a wall of black smoke rolling out from the jeep.

'Lee!' I scream, doubled over, choking. Cole stumbles and falls to his knees, almost taking me down with him. I try to lift him back up, but it's no use.

'Run,' he gasps.

'No! We can *make* it.'

But I don't know if that's true. The Comox is close, and there's no sign of Lee. Cole can't run, and I can't take enough of his weight to carry him. But I'm not leaving him behind. We promised that nothing would tear us apart again. Not Lachlan, and not Cartaxus.

We've just found each other. I can't lose him.

'I'm not leaving you.' I drop to my knees in the mud beside him and take his hands in mine. 'We're together now. Whatever happens.' His eyes are black and glassy, his brow furrowed, but I know he can hear me.

The Comox jolts, touching down, when a shadow appears at my side.

‘I’ll take him,’ Leoben says, suddenly appearing next to me. I choke out a cry of relief. A ball of orange flames bursts from the jeep, lighting up the dark streaks of blood on his face. He loops an arm round Cole’s side and heaves him up. ‘Trees, now!’ he urges, breaking into a run for the forest.

I stagger after him, hope leaping inside me. With Leoben’s help, we might just make it out of here. A voice shouts at us from the Comox, but the words are lost in the roar of the rotors. We race across the road and down a muddy path into the trees. I stumble through the grass behind Leoben and Cole, my eyes watering from the smoke, dragging my tank top over my mouth to keep from coughing. The Comox rises again, turning to chase after us.

‘This way,’ Leoben yells, charging uphill, hauling Cole with him. The forest is dark, the ground thick with ferns and bushes that tear at my leggings as I run. The pigeons are flying in circles, panicked by the explosion, their glowing feathers painting a whirlwind of light that we can use as cover. Between the birds and the canopy, there’ll be too much interference for the Comox’s systems to track us. Even the smartest targeting algorithms can’t see past millions of glowing birds in the middle of the night.

‘I pinged Cole’s jeep, but I don’t know if it can get to us through these trees,’ Leoben says, then pauses, looking up. The Comox is soaring above us, sending wind whistling through the branches, but its spotlights are sweeping wildly, passing over us. They can’t see us through the flock. ‘They should turn back soon,’ Leoben yells, but he freezes as a metallic noise starts up from above us, like the sound of a gun being cocked.

'Cover!' he shouts, hauling Cole behind a tree as a hail of bullets rains down on us.

I scramble into cover, throwing my arms over my head instinctively. Clouds of glowing feathers puff around me, the pigeons dropping like stones. The flock scatters, screeching furiously, another wave of bullets whistling through the air.

No, not bullets. Tranquillizer darts.

They slam into the ground around me, releasing sprays of yellow serum. Cartaxus doesn't want us dead – they want us captured. Tortured and interrogated. An image flashes into my mind of restraints on an operating chair under blinding white lights. I push away from the tree, racing after Leoben and Cole, when something *smacks* into my leg.

'Shit,' I gasp, staggering to a stop. A dart is jutting from my calf. I bend down and yank it out, hissing. Yellow liquid bubbles from the tip, tinged with scarlet. A blood-pressure warning flashes in the bottom of my vision.

'Come on!' Leoben yells.

'I'm hit!' I shout, limping after him.

He reaches back with his free hand to grab my waist and drag me forward as more darts slam down behind us. I lean my weight into Leoben, limping as fast as I can, my vision blurring as we veer through the trees. The cloud of pigeons parts before us, the air echoing with their cries. We stagger down a hill towards a valley with a creek winding through its centre, and the Comox's rotors grow fainter. We're not moving fast, but it looks like Leoben's plan has worked. They must have lost us in the flock.

We stumble to the bottom of the hill. The creek is only ankle-deep here, wide and rocky. Leoben sucks in a breath, scanning the trees. I don't know how he's managing to carry us both like this. 'We can't stop here,' he says.

'But they're pulling back.' I look over at Cole. His eyes are still black and half closed, his face shiny with sweat. He looks like he's getting worse. 'We need to stabilize Cole.'

Leoben shakes his head. 'If there are troops in that Comox, they're going to storm these woods. We have to keep moving. Are you OK?'

'I'm fine,' I say. My left leg is tingling and heavy, and I can feel the sedative working through my body, but I can still run with Leoben pulling me forward. We splash through the creek, the icy water jolting the nerves in my foot back to life. 'Where are we going?'

'As deep into this flock as we can get –' Leoben freezes again, lifting his head as a crashing sound echoes through the valley. The pigeons' cries pitch higher, a copse of trees shaking in the distance. It doesn't sound like the Comox, and it's definitely not troops. Leoben's eyes narrow, then he grins as Cole's jeep hurtles along the creek, bouncing over the rocks to follow the water's path.

'Holy shit,' I breathe. 'You're amazing, Lee.'

'Oh, I'm aware,' he mutters. 'I can't believe they blew up my goddamn jeep.'

Cole's jeep splashes out of the water, its autodriver pulling it to a stop beside us, the rear doors flying open. Leoben heaves Cole inside and reaches out for me, grasping my upper arms to lift me into the back. It's cleaner than Leoben's was – the clothes are packed away, and there are no piles of trash, but it's still cramped, with our backpacks, blankets, and a few boxes of files we pulled out of the lab.

'There's an antidote for that dart in the medkit,' Leoben says. 'Shouldn't take long to kick in.' He grabs Cole's shoulders, turning him so he's lying on his side.

'Won't they follow us?' I ask, crawling over Cole to get my backpack. The tingling in my left leg has dropped into numbness, stretching up the side of my back.

Leoben shakes his head, clambering between the seats to climb into the front. 'If they're smart, they'll give us some clearance now that we're in the jeep. It's too dangerous for a single copter to chase us. We could have a rocket launcher or be leading them into a trap. They'll land and call for backup and bring in drones instead. I doubt they'll spot us through these pigeons, but they might set up checkpoints on the roads. Let's get moving and see if we can beat them.'

He presses his hand to the dash, and the jeep's windows darken, its rear doors swinging shut behind me. We reverse through the creek and spin round, heading back uphill. I rip open my backpack and yank out a medkit with shaking hands. It has a row of vials strapped into one side, each marked with Cartaxus glyphs. They meant nothing to me before my panel started working, but now I can see white text hovering beside them, sketched into my vision by my VR chip. Muscle relaxant, emergency blood thinner. I slide out a vial marked as a *tranquillizer antidote* and press the needle-tipped cap to the side of my neck.

It only takes a second before I feel it burn through me, hot and sharp, countering the rising tide of numbness.

'Do you know where he's hurt?' Leoben asks, looking back at Cole.

'Not yet.' I drop the empty vial and turn to Cole. His eyes are closed, his breathing shallow, his face pale and dotted with sweat. 'Have you seen him like this before?'

Leoben nods. 'A few times. Some of our black-out code is experimental stuff – it doesn't play nicely with the rest of our tech. If we push it too far, it can glitch out and crash us. You'd better give him some healing tech, quick. He's not looking so good.'

'OK,' I murmur, yanking my backpack open again, sliding out the box of healing tech syringes. It hisses open with a puff of cold air. Only three left. Healing tech works best when it's injected right into a wound, so I need to find where Cole is hurt before I can give him one.

'Cole, can you hear me?' I lean over him, scanning his back. I sit the syringes on the floor and run my hands over his body, searching for swelling or a hint of shrapnel. The skin on his back is still silver-tinged and strangely firm from the nanomesh that grew through it when he was injured in the explosion in the lab, but it doesn't seem to have been wounded again. I grab his face in my hands, trying not to focus on how weak he looks. 'Cole, I need you to tell me where you got hit.'

He just shakes his head. We pull on to a gravel road and he groans with the movement, his face paling. Every bounce of the jeep's wheels makes his eyelids flutter, and I still can't see where he's hurt. I roll him on to his stomach, running my hand along his side, searching for a wound, and pause.

A piece of metal is jutting from his ribs.

'Shit,' I breathe.

'What?' Leoben calls back, swerving us round a corner. I grab the side of the jeep for balance, yanking my backpack open for the little genkit I've been using, but it's not there. It was in Leoben's jeep.

Which is now in a hundred pieces.

'*Shit,*' I say again.

'Getting worried here, squid.'

'He's got a puncture wound,' I say. 'I don't know how big it is inside, and I don't have a genkit.' Without a genkit, all I can really do is turn on and off the apps that are already on Cole's panel. I can't install anything new or send an emergency stream of custom-coded nanites into his body to heal him. Panels are made to interact with each other, but they aren't designed to update and override other panels. They aren't even made for *coding* – panels don't have the ability to compile and check gentech code or optimize it for a person's unique DNA. That's what genkits are for.

Leoben pulls us over the crest of a hill and on to the road. 'You got healing tech?'

'Yeah, but it won't work properly if he's got a piece of metal inside him.'

Leoben's eyes meet mine in the rear-view. 'Can you pull it out?'

'I don't want to make it worse.'

'Field medics yank, then jab,' he says. 'Healing tech'll get him back on his feet.'

I nod, doubt prickling inside me. It's true that healing tech can handle most wounds, but that doesn't mean people are indestructible. There's code to oxygenate your blood in case your heart stops, and triage code to run repairs on the body's vital organs, but if your brain activity cuts out – if that spark of life dims, even for a moment – then no amount of tech is guaranteed to bring it back. Your body could heal, your heart could even beat again, but you'll never wake up.

I press my fingers to the wound in Cole's ribs. His vitals are low, his tech is still regenerating, and I don't know how much energy his panel has left. He spent the day on lookout in the rain, so he'll be hungry and exhausted. Yanking out this shrapnel will heal him faster, but it just might kill him too.

'*Hurry*, squid,' Leoben urges me, swinging the jeep through a grove of trees.

Cole lets out a wet cough, a tremor passing through him. His eyelids flutter open. 'What . . . what are you doing?'

'Shhh,' I say. 'Just stay still. You have a piece of metal in your side.'

He groans, shifting uncomfortably. His breath is starting to stutter. If I wait much longer, he's going to die anyway. The thought feels like a hand around my throat. I grab the blood-slicked edge of the metal, hold my breath and pull it out.

It slides from his ribs with a squelch, followed by a gurgle of blood. Cole stiffens, letting out a cry, another tremor running through him. The piece of shrapnel is shaped like a knife. Cruel, sharp, the size of one of my fingers. I toss it to the floor and uncap one of the healing tech vials, shoving it deep into the wound.

'You OK back there?' Leoben snaps his head round. 'His vitals dipped. What did you . . .?' He pauses, his eyes lifting to the jeep's rear windows. 'Dammit. Hold on, this is going to get rough.'

I loop one arm around Cole, using the other to put pressure on the wound in his side, and follow Leoben's gaze. The Comox is back, soaring over the forest, its spotlights blazing.

'I thought they were supposed to land and call for backup.'

'They *should* have,' Leoben grunts, jerking the wheel. We speed off the gravel road and back into the forest, veering through the trees. 'They're not following Cartaxus's rules of engagement, and they're definitely using manual controls.'

'Maybe we should stop.' I lift my hand, looking down at Cole's ribs. He's still bleeding. 'Cole's hurt, we have nowhere to run to –'

'I haven't spent the last week living in the mud to give up now, squid,' Leoben yells back.

We lurch over the crest of a hill and bounce down a rocky slope, the movement throwing me into the side of the jeep. I grab the back of Leoben's seat to steady myself as we ram through a patch of saplings. The Comox roars above us, its lights sweeping through the darkness. Cole coughs, trying to sit up.

'Cole,' I gasp, tightening my grip on him. 'Don't move just yet. Are you OK?'

He nods, staring blearily through the rear window, and lifts his hand to a chain around his neck. 'Bait drop,' he whispers.

'Too risky,' Leoben yells, reversing to pull round a copse of trees. 'Not when we can run.'

'What does that mean?' I ask. 'What's a bait drop?'

Cole tugs at the chain. A gleaming black pendant is tucked under the collar of his shirt. Nightstick. The same weapon I used at Sunnyvale to knock out Dax. It shorts out gentech panels, knocking out anyone in a twenty-foot radius. It didn't affect me in Sunnyvale because my panel was still installing, but it'll take us all out if we set it off now.

But if we use it when the Comox is close enough, it'll also knock out the pilot.

'You said they were flying with manual controls,' I say.

Cole nods. 'We can crash it.' He pushes himself up on one elbow, grimacing against the pain from the movement. 'We need to stop the jeep somewhere clear. They'll drop down lower, then you and Lee run. I'll stay behind and set the nightstick off once the pilot's close enough, then you can come back.'

Leoben shakes his head, yanking the wheel to swing us back towards the road. 'Too dangerous. If this goes wrong, we may as well hand ourselves over to them.'

'They've chased us down twice, Lee,' Cole says, his teeth gritted. His face is still pale, slick with sweat. 'This way we might get ourselves a copter. We could get across the country tonight.'

Leoben's jaw tenses, his eyes lifting to the rear-view as the Comox roars closer, the pigeons screeching away from it. We'll never outrun them in the jeep. They'll flip us with another rocket. They could follow us for hours.

'I say we do it,' I say to Cole, 'but I'm not leaving you. They take you, they take us both.'

For a second, I think Cole is going to argue, but he nods.

'Goddammit,' Leoben says. He shakes his head but slows the jeep, veering us into a clearing. His door flies open, and he turns back to me. 'Twenty feet, OK?'

'Run,' Cole says, clutching the nightstick.

Leoben curses, then slides out of his door and races into the night.

Cole reaches for my hand, his other hand clutched around the nightstick pendant. The jeep shakes, the air roaring as the Comox descends. Forty feet, thirty. Twenty now. Close enough to make this count. Cole squeezes my hand, his eyes locked on mine.

Then he twists the pendant, and everything goes black.

CHAPTER 5

For a moment, as the darkness clears, I'm lying on Agnes's couch with one of her quilts draped over me. I can smell her lavender soap and hear her voice like she's in the next room. The clatter of pans, her footsteps soft as she moves about in her kitchen. Distantly, I know it isn't real, but the memory feels like a blanket that I want to wrap myself up in. This might have been the last time that I felt truly safe – waking in her home, knowing that she was watching over me. Cooking lentils, humming to herself, her shotgun leaning against the wall. I want to lose myself in the moment, but I can't ignore the sense that something is *wrong*.

'Wake up.'

The voice is a blade, cutting through the memory. I scrunch my eyes shut against it, struggling to slip back into Agnes's home again. Her crowded shelves of food and supplies. Her wispy grey hair, her keen eyes.

'Wake up, dammit.'

The voice returns, sharper and more insistent. I open my eyes, but there's no sign of Agnes. The air is cold, heavy with the scent of rain. I'm lying in the back of the jeep, the rear doors flung open, the cobalt glow of the pigeons streaking across a midnight sky. Leoben is beside me, blood soaked into his white-blond hair.

It all comes back in a sickening blur: the Comox, the chase, the nightstick. I gag, covering my mouth, scrambling out into the grass to throw up.

'That's the nightstick,' Leoben calls back. 'Makes some people puke. Come on, Cole's waking up. Help me carry the gear.'

I straighten, wiping my mouth. We're in a clearing at the base of a hill, tyre tracks cut into knee-high grass behind us. The Comox that was chasing us is crashed, one window shattered, one of its rotors bent. It's perched on the stump of a snapped tree that's now lying across the clearing, the grass around it strewn with leaves and broken glass.

'Holy shit,' I breathe. 'It actually worked.'

'Yeah,' Leoben says, 'but we gotta hurry. Cartaxus will be sending backup.' He slides out of the jeep and reaches back in to help Cole, slinging one of his arms round his shoulders. Cole's face is pale, his eyes glassy and unfocused, but he's awake.

'Will that thing even fly?' I ask.

Leoben grunts, looking up at it, one hand locked around Cole's wrist. 'I don't know. It should be able to compensate for a hit like this, but it might be too damaged. Either way, we don't have long until a fleet arrives, and we're not going to outrun them in the jeep.'

'What about the pilot?'

'Still knocked out,' Leoben says, helping Cole out into the grass. 'It's just one person in there. I can't tell much from my scans, but I think they're hurt.'

He shuffles towards the Comox, Cole staggering at his side. I clamber into the back of the jeep and grab my backpack, searching through the piles of blankets and files for anything we'll need. It looks like Leoben's already packed everything away, though. My black backpack is open, stuffed with the medkit, a few folders of Lachlan's paper notes, and some slender boxes marked with Cartaxus glyphs. I yank it closed and sling it over my shoulder, grabbing Cole's rifle, then run to catch up with them.

The Comox is balanced precariously on the splintered base of the tree, one landing skid buried in the dirt, the other tilted in the air at chest-height. The tiny squares of broken glass from the shattered window crunch beneath my boots, catching the swirling cobalt light of the pigeons. There's a steel cable stretched from the Comox's belly to the ground, the thickness of my forearm.

'Gonna have to cut that,' Leoben says, nodding at the cable. 'It's an anchor to stop us stealing it.'

'How the hell are we gonna cut through that much steel?'

Leoben gestures to my backpack with his free hand, the other wrapped around Cole. 'I put some flash strips in your pack. Blue box.'

I drop my backpack to the ground and rip it open, sliding out a rattling turquoise-coloured box. The glyph on its side throws a warning into my vision.

High-powered lasers. Use protective eyewear.

I blink the words away, still not used to my panel flinging text and images at me like that. 'How do I use these?'

'I'll do it,' Leoben says, shifting Cole from his side, leaning him against the Comox's raised landing skid. Cole's eyes are glassy, his breathing shallow, but there's colour in his cheeks, and his bleeding seems to have stopped. Leoben takes the box from me, pulling out a chainlike length of segmented black metal with a lever on one end and an LED battery icon on its side. He ducks beneath the Comox's raised landing skid and wraps the black strip around the cable.

'Don't watch,' he says, scrunching his eyes shut, yanking the lever. I look away just as a flash of pure white light splashes out from the strip. A sound like a gunshot echoes through the air, startling the pigeons, and Leoben jumps away, shaking one hand as though it's burned.

'What the hell was that?' I ask, blinking away a storm of neon spots in my vision. The cable is cut – one half dangling from the Comox's belly, the other lying on the ground, its severed end glowing orange.

'It's an anti-anti-theft tool,' Leoben says, ducking back out from under the Comox, sliding his arm back round Cole. 'Probably gonna have to blow the door open too. It'll be locked, and these things are built like tanks.'

I shove the box of flash strips into my backpack, looking up at the Comox's dented side. The shattered window looks like it's the same width as my shoulders. 'I might be able to get in,' I say.

Leoben eyes the broken window and looks me up and down. 'OK. Hurry, though. The pilot's still unconscious, but they won't be for long. Be careful, squid.'

I zip my backpack up and leave it on the ground, grabbing Cole's rifle. 'I thought I told you not to call me squid.'

Leoben snorts. I sling the rifle across my back and grab the landing skid, kicking at the broken tree beneath it to push myself up. The Comox groans, shifting sideways with my weight as I grab a handle on its side and clamber to the window.

'Can you get in?' Leoben asks.

'I think so.' I swing the rifle round and use the butt to knock out a jagged shard in the window's base, scraping it back and forth to clear it, then duck my head through to scan the cargo hold. It's dim, smelling of rubber and oil. The walls are a dull black metal, studded with hooks and cargo straps, a row of parachutes lined up beside the door. Two duffel bags are stowed in the cargo hold beside a box of what looks like gentech equipment, but I can't see any weapons. Still no movement from the cockpit, but there's a figure slumped over the controls. I swing Cole's rifle off and drop it through the window, then kneel against the Comox's tilted side to shimmy through, rolling when I hit the floor. The figure in the cockpit doesn't move.

'Pilot's still out,' I say, straightening.

'You see the handle?'

I grab Cole's rifle and stagger up the slanted floor, grabbing a yellow lever beneath the window. The door hisses, swinging up, a ramp extending to the landing skid. Leoben crouches to boost Cole up, and I jog down the ramp to take Cole's arm, helping him inside. 'You OK?' I ask.

He nods blearily, staggering into the hold, grabbing one of the straps on the ceiling to steady himself. He winces as he raises his arm, stretching the wound in his ribs. 'Never better.'

Leoben climbs up with my backpack and dumps it on the floor, then slides a handgun from his side. He meets my eyes meaningfully, glancing towards the pilot. I nod, lifting Cole's rifle to my shoulder, and follow him to the cockpit.

The Comox's flight controls look like the jeep's – a curved LED screen with two sets of manual controls built into it. The screen is showing a terrain map of the mountains and a scrolling log of warning messages. The pilot is slumped across it, his hand wrapped around one of the yokes.

My breath catches in my throat. It's Dax.

'Dax?' Leoben pushes into the cockpit, sliding his gun back into its holster. He takes Dax's shoulder gently, easing him away from the controls and into his seat.

Dax's head rolls back. He looks haggard, with dark shadows hanging beneath his eyes, a bruise rising on his pale, freckled cheek. A deep gash is open on his forehead from the crash, and the sight of his blood-streaked face brings the attack at Sunnyvale back to me in a wave.

I can suddenly feel Dax's hands around my throat, his bullet in my back. I can hear the screams of Sunnyvale's people as they turned on one another. I know it wasn't really *Dax* who hurt me that night – it was Lachlan's code – but it's still his face that's in my memories. His breath, his voice. My muscles tighten as I stand over him, part of me wanting to make him feel as helpless and frightened as I did on the floor of that hallway.

Leoben turns to me, his eyes wide. 'Put the gun down!'

I stiffen, looking down at the rifle. I'm still aiming it at Dax, my knuckles white on the grip. 'Shit,' I say, lowering the barrel. 'Sorry.'

'Get out of here!' Leoben says, his voice sharp. 'I'll deal with him.'

'OK,' I murmur, stepping back into the cargo hold, slinging the rifle's strap off my shoulder. My hands are shaking, my heart racing. Dax used to be my friend. My coding partner. I used to dream that we'd end up together one day after the plague was over.

Now I don't know if I can trust myself to be around him with a gun.

'Did he say Crick's in there?' Cole asks from behind me. He takes the rifle, pushing past me and into the cockpit. The Comox shifts on the splintered tree, groaning. 'What the hell is he doing here?'

'I don't know,' Leoben says, dropping into the navigator's seat, grabbing the secondary controls. He pulls a lever on the controls and the Comox's engine whines, the rotors spinning up. They sound *wrong* – their normally steady thump is syncopated, the walls shuddering with the strain. 'This thing won't take much more of a beating. We need to go before Cartaxus gets here.'

'We're not bringing him with us,' Cole snaps, grabbing the collar of Dax's lab coat.

'Cole,' Leoben says, a note of warning in his voice.

'He's not on our side, Lee,' Cole says. 'He shot at us.'

Leoben reaches out, wrapping one hand around Cole's wrist. 'He used tranquillizers. He didn't come out here to kill us, but he came here for a reason, and I think we'd better find out what it is.'

I look between the two of them, torn. Part of me agrees with Cole – Dax blew up Leoben's jeep and *shot* at us. He's clearly not here as a friend. My first instinct is to throw him out and leave him the hell behind us, maybe with a medkit if we're feeling generous.

But the horror of remembering Sunnyvale is fading, and another emotion is settling through me. It seems like it's been a lifetime since Dax and I were playing pranks on each other at the cabin, but I can't help feeling an echo of that affection when I look at him now. In the chaos of my past, Dax is one of the few people I can remember clearly – because the memories are *mine*. We were both young and naïve, but he was important to me.

Maybe he always will be.

I turn to Cole. 'I think we should see what he has to say.'

Cole lets out a growl of frustration, but he jerks Dax from his seat and drags him into the cargo hold. 'Fine, we'll bring him. But he's going in the back.'

Leoben's eyes follow Dax as Cole drags him away, then he tilts the Comox's yoke. The door hisses shut, and Cole drops Dax into one of the seats, yanking a harness over his lab coat to keep him in place. The windscreen is splattered with mud and splinters of wood, the flock forming a wild, glowing mess of light beyond it.

'Where are we going?' I ask.

'South,' Cole says. 'You said your friend tracked Lachlan to Nevada?'

'Agnes,' I say, nodding, a twinge of anxiety rippling through me at the thought of her going after Lachlan on her own. I still don't know why she left like that, or why she isn't answering her comm. But she *has* to be OK. She's the toughest person I know.

'Nevada it is,' Leoben says, turning the controls.

We lift with a screech of metal, the wind from the rotors whipping through the broken window. The roar of the rotors shifts frequency as we rise, growing smoother and more high-pitched, the syncopated thud flattening into a constant whine.

It's only been an hour since sunset, but this far north in summer, the sky doesn't stay dark for long. The horizon is already a pale shade of blue, the first hints of daylight peeking round the curve of the earth. Cole pulls a metal shade over the broken window to cut out the gale blasting in, then grabs one of the straps on the ceiling to stand beside me, glaring down at Dax.

'Maybe you should sit down,' I say. 'You weren't looking so good a few minutes ago.'

'I'm fine,' he says. 'My tech just needed to kick into gear.'

'You had a piece of metal in your side.'

'I know.' He shifts the strap of his rifle to his shoulder. 'I can handle it.'

Leoben tilts the Comox, picking up speed now that we're above the pigeons. I fold down one of the seats near the cockpit and sit down, staring at Dax. He looks awful. His hair is greasy, his clothes crinkled and stained, like he hasn't changed them in days. There's no stubble on his jaw, but he probably has an app to keep it smooth. The bruise on his cheek is dark and painful-looking, and the gash on his forehead is deep, still trickling with blood. It looks like the last week has been just as rough for him as it has for us.

He coughs, his eyelids fluttering, and blinks awake. His eyes focus on me, widening in surprise. 'Princess,' he says, his voice slurred. 'You're alive.'

Cole swings his rifle up. 'Don't call her that again if you want to stay conscious.'

Dax looks up blearily at Cole, then at Leoben in the cockpit. He sighs, leaning back against the seat. 'This has not gone as planned.'

I stand up, waving Cole's gun away. 'Why the hell did you shoot at us, Dax?'

He touches the gash on his forehead, his fingers coming away bloodied. 'The jeep was armed. I didn't want to get shot down, and I had to disable it to stop you running. I came here to help you. Cartaxus central command is searching for you all.'

Leoben looks back from the cockpit. 'Central command?'

Dax nods, squinting as though trying to clear his vision. 'Brink is sending an envoy. They're headed to the lab you were camped near.'

'Shit,' Leoben says.

'Who's Brink?' I ask.

Cole shifts uneasily. 'He's the leader of Cartaxus's central command. They run the whole organization – military division, the science group, the bunkers.'

'How come I've never heard of him?'

'That's how he wants it,' Cole says. 'Central command tries to stay under the radar. They usually don't get involved unless things are . . . *difficult*.'

'Well, things are most certainly difficult right now,' Dax says, shifting in the harness. He looks woozy, sweat dotted on his brow. 'We need to hide, and quickly. There's a location programmed into the controls . . .' He pauses as a *crack* sounds below us, loud enough to cut through the drone of the rotors. 'What was that?'

'Probably more goddamn fireworks,' Leoben says. 'Looks like there's a survivor camp down there.'

Dax's eyes cut to the metal shutter over the broken window and then to me, his face paling. 'Veer round it. Keep us a mile away.'

'You're not giving the orders around here,' Cole says.

'Just *do* it,' Dax says, his voice sharp. He coughs again, leaning forward in the harness, covering his mouth.

A chill creeps across my neck. That blast didn't sound like fireworks. The audio profile was all wrong. It sounded like the blasts Leoben and I heard back at camp. The Comox banks, veering to the left, and I stand and walk to the cockpit. Leoben is leaning forward, his eyes glazed, scanning the ground. The light is still dim, the forest painted in shades of blue and grey, but it's bright enough to make out the shadow of roads arcing through the trees. There's a camp below us – a dozen vehicles parked around a few squat structures. I scan the forest for a hint of fireworks or an explosion, but I can't see anything.

Dax coughs again. I look back at him, the chill on my neck spreading down my spine. He's still watching the Comox's broken window. He looked at it as soon as he heard the blast, and then he looked at *me*. There's air hissing through the metal shutter – it's not airtight, but that shouldn't matter. We don't need airlocks any more, not now that the vaccine is out.

'You OK, Dax?' I ask cautiously, walking back to him.

'I'm fine,' he says, swallowing, wiping his sleeve across the sweat on his brow.

'You don't look fine.' I drop to one knee beside him, searching his face. He's sweating, his eyes bloodshot, the bruise on his cheek purple and red. I reach for the collar of his shirt, but he grabs my wrist.

'Please,' he whispers.

'Don't *touch* her,' Cole says.

'It's OK, Cole,' I say. I slide my hand free of Dax's grip, reaching for his collar again. He closes his eyes, sighing in defeat, slumping against the harness.

I pick open the top button of his shirt and move down to the next. Dax doesn't smell great this close – he clearly hasn't washed properly in days, but neither have we. But it's more than that. There's something *off* in his scent. The collar of his shirt falls open as I unbutton it to reveal his pale chest, dotted with dark bruises.

It can't be what I think it is, but Dax's emerald eyes lift to mine, and a jolt of horror runs through me.

He's infected.

CHAPTER 6

'What's going on?' Leoben calls back. He looks over his shoulder at the bruises on Dax's chest, then drops the controls and stands from his seat. The Comox shudders, switching to autopilot. Leoben pushes past Cole, dropping to his knees beside Dax, his eyes wide with confusion as he takes in the bruises on Dax's face and chest. 'No,' he breathes.

Cole strides to the cockpit and leans forward, staring down through the windscreen. 'Are we in danger? Have we been exposed?'

'You're probably fine,' Dax says. 'We're high enough. The plumes aren't as big.'

'What plumes?' I ask. 'What the hell is going on?'

Dax leans back in his seat, closing his eyes. 'There's a new strain of the virus, and the vaccine isn't stopping it.'

Leoben just stares at Dax. I reach behind me for one of the Comox's seats and sit down blindly, the muscles in my legs suddenly weak. I *knew* it wasn't fireworks that we heard earlier. It was blowers. I close my eyes, seeing plumes on the horizon, bruised bodies detonating into mist. This world has been a living nightmare for the last two years, and even though Lachlan is still out there threatening us, part of me has been breathing easier knowing that at least the *virus* was dead.

But everything we've done has been for nothing. The vaccine isn't even *working*.

I think I'm going to be sick.

'What else do you know?' Leoben asks, one hand gripping the side of Dax's seat. 'How long has it been spreading?'

Dax pulls back the grimy left sleeve of his lab coat, tugging it over a cuff locked around his panel. It's a sheath of black metal, the same kind he was wearing when we went into Homestake, the Cartaxus bunker we stayed in. A row of blinking lights on the cuff's side grows brighter when Dax presses a button near his wrist, and a hologram splashes into the air.

The image wavers, a mess of glowing static resolving finally into a zoomed-out view of a survivor camp. It's somewhere cold, with snow scattered on the rocky shore of a beach, the ocean grey and still beyond it. A man is staggering towards the water, and a crowd of people are running from him, screaming. He drops to his knees in the shallows, his head snapping back.

He shudders, then detonates into a curling plume of mist.

The image changes to a woman's face. Scarlet hair and a steely gaze. Novak. The leader of the Skies. I've seen her trademark smile flash up on the jeep's dashboard each morning during the daily broadcast she and Dax have been sending out. They've been promising that everything is going well. That the vaccine is working, that the bunkers are getting ready to open again.

But this broadcast is different. Dax isn't in it – he's bruised and feverish beside me, and there's no sign of Novak's smile.

Dax cuts the feed off, switching to a map of the world with scarlet dots blinking across every continent, every island. 'The new strain has spread practically everywhere,' he says. 'We only detected it three days ago, and we've been able to keep it quiet so far, but our attempts to quarantine it have been useless. We're only seeing a two-per-cent infection rate, but that's enough to keep the virus alive. Cartaxus will be sending this broadcast out in the next few days. They're going to tell the truth – that we're at risk of losing the vaccine.'

The hologram of the map disappears and Leoben rocks back on his heels, rubbing his eyes. I lean against the Comox's side, swaying. I don't even know what would be left of the world if we lost this vaccine. After what Lachlan has done, we can't trust him to write another one. It could take us *years*. That's more years of plague – of bunkers, blowers, of choking down doses for immunity. There'd be no future, no running away to the beach with Cole. I don't even know if I could face it. The only way I made it through the outbreak was by distracting myself, protecting my heart.

But now I've had a glimpse of *hope*.

Every person on this planet has seen the vaccine's release and caught sight of a world without the plague. Every survivor, every civilian in the bunkers is still celebrating. They're riding high on a roller-coaster that's about to come crashing down. If we lose this vaccine, I don't know how they'll respond. There could be riots. There could be a war.

This could be the end of us.

Leoben stands and strides to the cockpit, leaning past Cole to flick something on the controls. The Comox shudders as we slow, dropping down to the forest.

'What are you doing?' Dax calls out, frustrated, rolling his sleeve back down over his cuff. 'Cartaxus is coming. We need to *go*.'

'We're not going anywhere,' Leoben says, staring back, his eyes blazing. 'You're *infected*. Jesus, Dax. We need to figure this out, and you need to get to a medical ward.'

We drop back through the flock of pigeons, sending them scattering, and descend into a dark, grassy clearing. The Comox groans, metal screeching somewhere below us as we touch down. Towering, slender pines stand around us, the three-peaked mountains looming in the distance. Cole leans his rifle against the Comox's side and sits heavily in one of the seats. There's still a pallor to his skin that tells me his tech is working hard on his injuries, but if the wound in his side is hurting him, he's not letting it show.

'We shouldn't be stopping. We're wasting time,' Dax mutters, buttoning up his shirt.

I look over the bruises on his face. My shock is fading, and my mind is clicking into gear, thinking of ways to fix this.

'Tell me more,' I say. 'How different is the strain?'

'*Very* different,' Dax says. 'It looks like a twelve-year mutation.'

'What?' I stand from my seat. 'Are you kidding me?'

Dax gives me a sad smile. 'I very much wish I was.'

I blink, staring at him, then pace to the back of the cargo hold. Mutations in gentech are classified by how long we'd expect it would take them to appear through natural evolution. A few genes change randomly in each new generation of any species, with the changes slowly compounding over time until the species is noticeably altered. The speed depends on the organism – a mutation in human DNA might take centuries to spread through the population, but bacteria can change within *days*. The longer the time assigned to a mutation for a given species, the more significant the change.

But the Hydra virus mutates fast – its infection period is just three weeks. A twelve-year mutation could be *radically* different. The plague has only been spreading for the last two years, and over that time the plumes grew taller, the detonations more powerful. If what Dax is saying is true, this new strain is what the virus could look like after another *ten years* of mutations.

'How could it mutate so fast?' Leoben asks, walking back from the cockpit. The roar from the rotors has dropped into a dissipating thud. He pulls down one of the seats from the Comox's side and sits opposite Dax, his body tight with tension.

'Genetic leaps like this have been known to happen,' Dax says. 'After the first vaccine failed, we started running simulations for all our code over a ten-year mutation range. The vaccine just wasn't built for a strain like this.'

'Could it be patched?' I ask.

'It can, quite easily,' Dax says. He meets my eyes, and I feel a flicker of the bond we used to have when we coded together. Two minds working in harmony, focused on nothing but the puzzle in front of us. 'My team drafted a patch the first day we got samples of the strain, but integrating it with the vaccine isn't easy, because it's not just the *vaccine* we're dealing with.'

'Shit,' I say. 'The extra code.'

Dax nods grimly. I tilt my head back, pressing the heels of my hands into my eyes. After the decryption, Dax said the vaccine was supposed to be five million lines long, but we sent out a version that had *nine* million. The implant in my head added the other four million lines – the daemon code that Lachlan used to launch the attack in Sunnyvale.

But the daemon code wasn't added as a block of text that could be easily deleted. I haven't been able to read much over the last week, but what I've seen showed that the decryption *blended* the daemon code with the vaccine. It's like cutting up two books and stitching their sentences into something new. It could take months of work to analyse each line and split them apart.

But without a copy of the *pure* vaccine, it's impossible to patch it. It would be like trying to design a replacement part for a machine you've never seen.

'Lachlan has done this on purpose,' I say, pacing back across the cargo hold. 'If the code were easy to alter, we might be able to block his attacks.'

'Yes,' Dax says, 'but it also means we can't fix the vaccine. My team has been trying to reverse-engineer the original code, but it could take us weeks to finish.'

'What about Lachlan?' Leoben asks. 'He could patch the vaccine for you. We could make a deal with him – he could even leave the extra crap in, as long as he makes it *work*.'

'What are you talking about?' I ask, spinning round. 'We couldn't trust anything he'd send us.'

'I'll take whatever Lachlan is offering,' Dax says, stifling a cough. 'I've already tried to contact him. I sent the patch to every account I could think of, hoping he'd update the code and send another version back, but he hasn't replied. He spent half his life working on this vaccine – I can't imagine him wanting to put it at risk. Cartaxus is desperate, and most of my team is infected too. We're running out of time. If Lachlan really has some grand plan to change the world, then this is the perfect opportunity to force Cartaxus to help him.'

Leoben's face darkens. 'How did your team get infected?'

Dax's eyes drop to the Comox's corrugated metal floor. 'It was an accident with a sample and a defective container, or at least that's how it seemed. But I'd checked every container multiple times. I think central command wanted to motivate us to work faster.'

I draw in a sharp breath. 'They *did* this to you?'

Dax gives me a tilted smile that doesn't reach his eyes. 'It's actually been quite effective.'

'No,' Leoben says, standing. 'They can't do this. You're their top researcher. It's madness to risk your life like this. I thought you'd be safe –'

'None of us are safe,' Dax says. 'That's why I'm here. Central command decided we're taking too long to reverse-engineer the code, and they're starting plans of their own. Orders are going out right now, and Brink is looking for you. I'm fairly sure he's planning a mission to go after Lachlan. But this isn't your fight. If

Lachlan wants to fix the vaccine, he can. None of you need to risk your lives for this any more.'

Something raw and fierce sparks in Leoben's gaze. 'Did you really think I'd *run* from this?' he asks. 'Is that why you didn't want us to know you were infected? Jesus, we've been planning to go after Lachlan all week. We were going to kill him, but I'd be happy to see him in a cell instead. If Cartaxus wants to send us after him, then I'm on board.'

'They won't send *you*,' Dax says, 'and they won't send Catarina. You're the basis for the vaccine, and Catarina is Lachlan's daughter. They don't know she's alive right now, but if they find her, she'll be a hostage. They'll probably infect her too.'

I stare out the window at the trees, chewing my thumbnail. Cartaxus still thinks Lachlan is my father, and I have no doubt they'd hurt me to get him to surrender, but Lachlan doesn't care about my safety. He turned the Wrath loose on thousands of people in Sunnyvale while I was there, unarmed and defenceless. He wouldn't give himself up if I was a hostage, but he *did* say that he needs me to finish his plan.

There's a chance I could help bring him in if I use myself as bait.

'What did you have planned, Crick?' Cole asks. 'Where can we run?'

'Cole –' I start, but he cuts me off.

'I'm not watching you get infected, Cat.'

'It's not as easy as just running,' Dax says. His eyes flick to the duffel bags and clear plastic boxes of gentech equipment stashed in the back of the cargo hold. The boxes are packed with vials of healing tech, bandages and empty IV bags. Cannulas are coiled in sterile pouches, stacked atop plastic jars of pale, jellylike cell scaffolding – the kind of thing they pack into severe wounds to speed up tissue regeneration.

'What's that for?' I ask. 'Surgery?'

But Dax isn't looking at me. He's looking at Leoben. 'You're recognizable,' he says. 'Both of you. There are ways to fake your DNA when it's scanned, but not your features. I know someone who can get you both into a bunker under false IDs, but there are still cameras.'

His tone makes me shiver. Most gentech apps aren't designed to *seriously* alter a person's appearance, but it's possible to do it. From what I could tell, that's how Lachlan made the puppet in the lab look like him. Most code takes months to change something like bone structure or the shape of the cartilage in your ears, but there are ways to speed it up. An app to change your skin works faster if your body is frantically trying to *regrow* your skin. An app to change your nose could take weeks to do it smoothly and safely, but it might only take a few days if it's broken.

I stare at the boxes of medical equipment. The bandages. The IVs. 'You want to change our *faces*,' I breathe.

Leoben's face pales. 'No, Dax.'

'It's the only way,' Dax says. 'You'll never get into a bunker otherwise.'

'I'm not going into a *bunker* to wait this out,' Leoben says.

'You might not have a choice,' Dax says. 'Brink refuses to lose this vaccine. He's preparing for flood protocol.'

A tense, cold silence fills the air. I look between the others, confused. 'What's flood protocol?'

Nobody answers, but the look on Cole's face sends a chill through me. I don't know what Brink could be planning that would save the vaccine – there's no way to protect it without patching it.

Unless . . .

I turn to Leoben, remembering the first conversation we had, back at the bunker we visited. Homestake. I told him I could never join a bunker and let myself be locked away, but Leoben said the people on the surface were the real jailers for keeping the virus alive. Without them, Hydra would run out of hosts and disappear.

There are *two* ways to kill a virus – you can beat it with a vaccine, or you can remove every possible host for it to infect, and it will die out on its own.

But Dax said this strain is all over the world. That makes *everyone* on the surface a potential host.

'Holy shit,' I whisper. 'They're going to kill us all.'

CHAPTER 7

I pace to the back of the Comox, numb with shock. There's cold air drifting through the metal shutter and into the cargo hold. There's grit in the creases of my palms, an ache in my calf where the dart hit me.

There are children and families still living on the surface. How can Cartaxus even *think* about killing them?

'They can't do this,' I say.

'They might not have a choice,' Dax says. He swipes the back of his sleeve over the sweat on his forehead, but the movement makes him sway. He's looking worse every minute. 'Cartaxus has three billion people in its bunkers to protect, and a vaccine that should be working. My team will be able to reverse-engineer the code eventually and patch it, but if this virus keeps spreading and evolving, the vaccine could be useless by the time we're done.'

'But there are millions of people on the surface –'

'I know,' Dax says, his voice low. 'Believe me, I want to stop this as much as you. My life is literally on the line here, but it's out of my hands. This is between Brink and Lachlan now.'

'We have to go in.' Leoben spins round, storming to the cockpit. 'If Cartaxus is planning flood protocol, we can't screw around any more. We need backup – drones, intel, soldiers. We have to find Lachlan. I'm not running away from this, and I'm not changing my goddamn *face*.'

His tone as he says the word sends a jolt through me – he's horrified, and not just at the thought of surgery. It's the thought of changing part of his identity. I know that's how he feels, because the same horror is rolling through me at the thought of changing myself. Lachlan's features stare back at me when I turn to my reflection in the Comox's triple-glazed window – his nose, his jaw – but they're *mine*, too. I've already been changed once.

I don't think I can handle the thought of doing it again.

'Lee, please.' Dax unbuckles his harness and half stands to follow Leoben, but he doubles over, coughing.

'You're *infected*,' Leoben says, wheeling on him. 'How could you think I'd hide in a bunker?'

'You have to,' Dax says, gasping for air. 'The vaccine is failing. They'll start the tests on you again.'

'I can deal with the tests,' Leoben snaps. 'I've been dealing with them since I was a child.'

'I know you can,' Dax says, falling back into his seat, 'but I'm their lead scientist now. If I survive this, they'll make me run those tests this time. They'll make *me* hurt you, every day, and I can't deal with that.'

I look between Dax and Leoben, confused. They're glaring at each other, but it's not just anger in their eyes. There's something more – a shift in the air. The same low power that rolled from Cole in the cabin's basement when I told him Jun Bei was alive. Leoben was Dax's bodyguard when they came to meet us outside Homestake. They travelled together, stayed together.

But they seem closer than that.

'This isn't just about you, Lee,' Cole says. 'Catarina will be in danger if we go back. We can land, I'll call the jeep. I can get her into hiding.'

'What?' I ask. 'No, Cole. Leoben's right – we can't do this on our own any more. This is bigger than us, and it's bigger than Lachlan. We need to go to Cartaxus.'

'Damn straight,' Leoben says, pushing through to the cockpit. 'If Brink is sending a team to the lab, we should go and meet them.' He sits heavily in the pilot's seat and flicks the controls. The Comox's rotors spin up, the cargo hold creaking.

Cole tilts his head back, his fists tight with frustration. We're going into danger – I know that. There's a good chance Cartaxus will hurt me to bring Lachlan in. They might find out the truth about who I am – that I used to be Jun Bei. They might lock me up in a lab. They might *kill* me.

But I can't run from this. I won't change my face, hide in a bunker and watch as Cartaxus kills everyone on the surface. If there's a chance I can help stop this, I have to try.

The Comox lifts from the clearing, tilting as we pass through the flock. Leoben turns us in a shuddering arc back towards the three-peaked mountains. The Zarathustra lab is in the middle of a valley, jutting from a wash of rain-streaked grass. Its windows are boarded, the ventilation turbines on the rooftop glinting in the morning's pale light. We've been camped an hour's hike from it all week, but I haven't seen it since the night we left. It's hovered on the edge of my senses every day, though, bringing back memories of locked doors and gloved hands. They grow stronger as we race closer, tugging at my senses. I see scalpels, restraints and barred windows.

I feel like I keep trying to leave this lab, but I still can't escape it.

Cole stands. 'They're here.' The lab's parking lot comes into view, a gleaming Comox standing on the grass, a row of soldiers lined behind it.

'I've hailed them,' Leoben says. 'They know we're coming.' He tilts the controls, bringing us into a descent.

'Are they going to punish you for coming out to find us?' I ask Dax, looking over my shoulder. He's slumped in the seat, his head tilted back, his forehead still glistening with sweat.

'I don't care,' he says. 'I'm already infected. I don't know what else they could do.'

Leoben's hands tighten on the controls. I don't know what's going on between him and Dax, but there's clearly *something*, though he hasn't mentioned it to me. It's hard to imagine the two of them together. Dax takes himself so seriously, while Leoben tries to turn everything into a joke. Still, the air between them feels charged, and I don't know how I didn't notice it when we were travelling together.

That was a dark time, though, and the only light I'd been able to see was Cole.

'OK, landing now,' Leoben says, guiding us towards the parking lot. The wind from the rotors sends ripples across the knee-high grass, the Comox's spotlights blinking on, lighting up the lab's cracked concrete walls. Its front door is open, a row of guards standing outside. They lift their rifles as we land.

Cole steps in front of me. 'Don't make any sudden movements. Try to let us do the talking.' He reaches back one hand and squeezes mine for a moment, then lets it drop.

I open my mouth to tell him that we'll get through this, and that I'm sorry for bringing him back here when he wants to run, but the Comox's door slides open with a hiss and the ramp folds down.

Cole and Leoben lift their hands, moving to the door. The soldiers keep their rifles trained on them as they walk down the ramp, but there are no shouted orders, no handcuffs, no bullets. Cole looks back at me, giving me a slight nod, and I follow him out, my hands raised, with Dax walking unsteadily behind me.

The grass is wet, the air cold, ringing with the cries of the pigeons. A figure is standing in front of a row of guards – a sandy-haired man in a grey military jacket. He steps forward, looking between the four of us, his eyes landing on me.

'Catarina,' he says. 'It's a pleasure to finally meet you. My name is Charles Brink.'

I straighten. Brink. The leader of Cartaxus's central command. I'm surprised to see him here in person. His voice is warm, but there's an edge to the way he looks at me, like he's trying to figure out how much I might be worth to him. He's tall, with a politician's smile and carefully constructed wrinkles around his eyes that lend him an air of easy credibility.

'At ease, Lieutenants,' he says. 'My team tells me you've both been dark for the last week.'

'We were injured, sir –' Cole starts, but Brink cuts him off.

'You were planning to go after Lachlan on your own.'

Cole's shoulders drop. 'Yes, sir.'

Brink nods, apparently satisfied. 'It's hard to blame you for that, but I'm glad you came back in. I see you've been taking care of Miss Agatta. We were concerned that something might have happened to her.'

He walks along the row of guards to stand before me. 'This must be a difficult time for you, Catarina. We've all been shocked to learn that Lachlan isn't the man we thought he was. I've known your father since we were boys, but I had no idea he was capable of this. I didn't even know that he had a daughter. He must have worked hard to keep you hidden all these years. Who was your mother?'

I shoot a nervous glance at Cole. If I say the wrong thing, Brink might figure out that I'm not really Lachlan's daughter. 'She died when I was little,' I say. 'She had hypergenesis.'

Brink's eyes glaze as he checks something in his panel. 'Ah, of course. The hypergenesis trials. Interesting. Well, I'm glad you've joined us now.' He steps back into the line of soldiers, and his elbow passes through one man's armoured torso.

He's not really here.

The man in front of me is just a VR avatar, sketched into my vision like the flash I saw of Jun Bei. Only, this feed isn't coming from a saved file in my panel. It's live, like a comm. Lachlan and Dax used to have conversations like this with other coders when we were at the cabin, but I could never see who they were talking to. There's a faint, pixelated fuzz around the edges of his image, but that's the only hint he isn't real. It's going to take me a while to get used to seeing people just *appear* like this.

'And Crick,' Brink says, turning to Dax, arching an eyebrow. 'I must say I'm surprised to see you here.'

'I sent him,' a voice calls from inside the lab. A figure strides out – a boy my age, maybe a little older. The guards part as he steps between them, clapping his hands as though dusting them off. His skin is pale, his shoulder-length hair dark and straight, hanging messily around his face. A rush of recognition rises through me as he steps into the light.

I *know* him.

I know his stance, his eyes, the planes of his face. Looking at him makes me think of code and coiled strands of DNA, but nothing rises in my memory. His clothes are black – ripped jeans, a leather jacket, and a T-shirt with a molecule printed on the front. Dopamine. A triangular piece of dark glass covers part of his forehead, sitting on his face like a second skin. It drops from his hairline to cover his left eye, arcing into a point on the edge of his cheekbone. It's a coding mask – a computer hooked directly into the net of electrodes lining his skull, connected through holes drilled into his forehead. A handful of leylines spill from the mask's edges, veering across his cheeks and down the sides of his neck, disappearing into his collar.

'I thought Dax might be able to bring in Catarina,' the boy says. 'Looks like I was right.' His eyes dance over us, a half-smile on his lips, and a low, trembling flame of fear lights up inside me. Brink doesn't frighten me, not really. He has the air of a businessman, and I know the guards surrounding us are just normal people beneath their armour and visors, but this boy is different.

He's a coder, and he's *smart* – that fact is clear from the piercing look in his eyes, the black glass on his forehead. The only reason to wear a mask like that is to code just *slightly* faster than you can through a panel. A mask doesn't need to use the cables in your body or your panel's memory, making every command just a fraction of a second faster. Anyone willing to drill dozens of holes into their skull for that shouldn't be underestimated.

'Ah, Mato,' Brink says. 'How's the lab?'

'Filthy,' Mato says, flicking the collar of his jacket to dust it off. He walks past Cole and Leoben, glancing briefly at them, then pauses beside Dax, looking at the bruises on his face before turning to me.

'Catarina Agatta,' he says, his gaze unnervingly intense. I can only see one of his eyes clearly, but the one beneath the mask is still faintly visible, his lower lashes catching the Comox's spotlights. 'I'm Somata Watson, but most people call me Mato. It's good to finally meet you in person.'

'We've spoken?' I ask, forcing my voice to stay level. I'm sure that Jun Bei knew this guy somehow, but he definitely shouldn't know *me*.

His mask clears slightly, the leylines on his cheeks exaggerating the lean, sharp angles of his face. He's beautiful in a cold, intelligent way, but there's an arrogant air about him. 'I was the one blocking the hacks you did with the Skies,' he says. 'You had decent – if rudimentary – attacks. You could be a good coder someday with training. That polyworm last summer almost made me break a sweat.'

I just stare at him. Is he seriously smack-talking me about my *hacks* while a mutated strain of the plague is sweeping across the world?

Brink clears his throat. 'Mato, the mission.'

A flash of frustration crosses Mato's face, his mask darkening again. 'Yes, the mission. I understand that Lachlan fitted you with a neural implant, Catarina. That's why we're here. I think it can help us.'

I exchange a glance with Dax. He's the one who discovered the implant during the vaccine's decryption. He said it was designed to suppress my memories, but then it added Lachlan's extra code to the vaccine. I've tried to check it a few times over the last week, but every test I've been able to run showed that it was blank.

'I think it was wiped,' I say.

'She's right.' Dax pushes away from where he's leaning against the Comox's side. It looks like he's having trouble staying on his feet. 'The output I saw from the decryption showed the implant being erased. Lachlan covered his tracks.'

'Yes, I *know*,' Mato says. 'I read the output too, obviously more closely than you. I have the same implant installed, and I know how it works. There's a trace in the log from Catarina's that I can't account for. It might help us find Lachlan.'

'Wait,' I say. 'What do you mean, *find* him?'

'I think your father put a tracker in it,' Mato says. 'It looks like it's pinging your location to him.'

My hand rises cautiously to the back of my head. One of the first things I did when my new panel was installing was have Leoben check my tech for trackers. If I'm as important to Lachlan as he made it sound, then he wouldn't have left me alone through the outbreak without a way to keep an eye on me. Leoben couldn't find anything in my panel, but we didn't think to check the implant. We figured I was clean, anyway, because Lachlan hadn't come after us.

It's been a week since Sunnyvale. If Lachlan needs me and knows where I am, why hasn't he come for me?

'I'd like to hack the implant,' Mato says. 'I might be able to follow the signal back to Lachlan. This lab is . . . outdated, but it has everything I'll need. We can try it now, if you'd like?'

It sounds like a question, but it's clear he isn't asking my permission. I don't know how I feel about this guy hacking anything of mine, let alone something in my *skull*, but if there's a chance it'll lead us to Lachlan, we have to try it.

'Yeah, fine,' I say.

'Good,' Brink says. 'Once we know where Lachlan is, we can bring him in. Franklin, we'll be wanting you in the extraction team.'

'Yes, sir,' Cole says.

'I'd like to volunteer,' Leoben says.

Brink shakes his head. 'Not this time, Lieutenant. You're too important to risk. I shouldn't have let Dax take you off-base in the first place.'

Leoben's jaw tightens, but he doesn't say anything.

'What about me?' I ask.

Brink turns to me, surprised. 'You don't have any combat experience. You'd be a liability.'

'If you want to bring Lachlan in alive to fix this vaccine, then you'll need someone who can talk to him. I can help you.'

Brink looks me up and down, considering. 'Maybe. Get us his location first, and then we'll talk. Why don't you wait inside? I need to brief Lieutenant Franklin.'

'Come on,' Leoben mutters, taking my arm.

'It was nice to meet you, Catarina,' Brink says as we step past his avatar. 'You're a smart girl. You could have a bright future at Cartaxus. You clearly have your father's mind, though you must have your mother's looks.'

I blink, exchanging a confused look with Leoben. I don't look anything like my *mother*. I'm the spitting image of Lachlan – everyone who's ever met me has said that. His DNA is coiled inside every one of my cells. I have his hands, his nose, the exact shade of his skin. 'Why do you say that?'

'Well, you certainly don't look like Lachlan,' Brink says. 'He never showed you pictures of himself when he was younger?'

I hold his gaze, unsure of how to answer. I don't know what he's talking about – what Lachlan looked like when he was *younger*. I know Lachlan's DNA better than anyone: grey eyes, a narrow nose, olive skin. The phenotypes are clear. There's no way he could have looked much different than he does today, which means there's a chance Brink is testing me. He said he's known Lachlan since they were boys. This could be a trap for me to reveal that I'm not who I seem to be.

But there's no reason for him to play games. I've already offered to let Mato run a hack on the implant in my head. He could easily run a scan on my DNA too.

'He wasn't really into photographs,' I say.

Brink nods. If he suspects anything, it doesn't show in his face. 'I thought he was just trying out a new look, but it makes sense having met you. It must have comforted him to see your features in the mirror while you were apart. A reminder of what he was working for, I suppose. Still, I always thought he looked better with his natural red hair.'

CHAPTER 8

Leoben guides me away from Brink and into the lab, leaving Cole and Dax behind us. I walk numbly down the hallway with the triangular fluorescent lights set into the ceiling, Brink's words circling through my mind.

I always thought he looked better with his natural red hair.

There's no way that Lachlan could have red hair. It would be obvious from his genetic profile. Lachlan's hair is dark brown, nearly black. He doesn't even carry a recessive copy of the red-haired gene.

I should know. The same DNA is in my cells.

Leoben pushes open one of the doors, leading me into a small laboratory. A set of shelves on the far wall holds a terrifying array of surgical equipment, a humming genkit beside it, a metal table standing in the centre of the room with plastic chairs stacked on top of it. The walls and floor are glistening white tile, a lab counter along one wall set with a row of sinks. A screen high in the corner of the room shows a silent mess of green and purple static.

No memories rush back to me as I step into the room – just blunt sensory flashes of pain, cold, and the fog of anaesthetic. I eye the shelves of scalpels and saws, probes and coiled wires. Cole said that sometimes memories aren't worth the pain they hold. Standing in this room, I'm starting to agree with him.

Maybe there are some things that I'm better off not remembering.

Leoben swings the door shut behind us. 'It's safe to talk in here.' He points to the ceiling. 'No cameras. They couldn't risk anyone hacking in and seeing what they were doing.'

I nod vaguely, pacing to the back of the room, rubbing a lock of my still-damp hair between my fingers. 'Lachlan's hair is brown, right?'

'As long as I've known him.'

'So what was Brink talking about?'

Leoben crosses his arms, leaning back against the counter. 'Maybe Lachlan used an app to turn it red when he was younger.'

I shake my head. 'That was before gentech. If he's using anything to change his hair, it'd be now, to make it dark. But he'd still be a redhead *underneath*. Gentech doesn't change your natural DNA. I'm the only one who can do that. I know Lachlan's genes, though, and they say his hair is dark.'

'Maybe he masks his DNA,' Leoben says. 'Dax was saying he could fake ours to get us into a bunker.'

I brace my hands against the lab counter, leaning over one of the sinks. It's possible. I've heard of apps that can trick a genkit into misreading your DNA. Genkits aren't foolproof – that's part of the reason I never realized who I was when I was at the cabin. If Lachlan really is a redhead, though, he's going to great lengths to hide it. But it doesn't make sense – Lachlan changed me into his daughter. He made me look like him.

Why would he make me look like a version of himself that isn't even *real*?

'Brink's probably just trying to mess with your head,' Leoben says. 'That's what they do. You saw what they did to Dax.'

I look up. 'Yeah – *Dax*. Anything you want to tell me?'

He looks away, kicking the heel of his boot back against the cupboards below the lab counter. 'There isn't really anything to tell.'

'Bullshit. Why didn't you say anything?'

He lifts an eyebrow. 'Maybe because he's your ex, and because the last time you two saw each other, he *shot* you and you bit his ear off.'

'Fair enough,' I mutter.

He tips his head back. 'I didn't even think I really cared about him, but now that he's infected . . . I can't think about anything else.'

I push away from the counter, ignoring the flicker of jealousy that coils through me at his words. Dax and I were barely even together back at the cabin, and we've been apart for the last two years, and I'm with Cole now. I should be happy for Lee, and I *am*, but that doesn't ease the sudden tension in my shoulders.

I lift down one of the chairs stacked on the table. 'How long have you been together?'

'We aren't *together*.' He follows me, grabbing a chair, lifting it down. 'I don't know. A year, maybe.'

I roll my eyes. 'A year? You guys are *totally* together.'

He grabs the last two chairs, one in each hand, and lowers them, his movements swift and graceful. 'Not all of us fall head-over-heels at first sight like you and Cole. It isn't anything serious. He couldn't understand the vaccine, so he ran tests to study me, and we got . . . close.'

Goose bumps rise across my skin at the thought of Dax experimenting on Leoben. I don't know how that could possibly have brought them *closer*. My eyes drop to the curled scars peeking from the collar of his tank top, and his hand rises self-consciously, following my gaze.

'Speaking of experiments,' he says, glancing at the shelves of medical equipment, 'I never asked – did Lachlan run tests on you when you were at the cabin?'

'I'm not done talking about Dax,' I say.

'Well, I am.' He crosses his arms. 'So, did he?'

I sit down on one of the chairs, the skin on my chest tingling in the place I once carried a map of scars like his. There's nothing there but smooth skin now, but there's still a tract of scar tissue running down my spine.

'No, he never hurt me, except for the code he used to stop me hacking my panel. It took off half the skin on my back when I tried to install an aesthetic suite.'

'I'd say that counts as hurting you. What an asshole.'

'Yeah,' I mutter, shifting uncomfortably at the instinctive urge to defend Lachlan. Somehow, despite everything that's happened, it's still hard for me to hear anyone else insult him. It's maddening. 'I just don't understand the whole charade of making me his daughter,' I say, 'especially if I don't really look like him.'

Leoben leans back against the lab counter, crossing his arms. 'What was he like as your father?'

I shrug, tracing my finger along a scratch in the metal table. 'I don't know – he was busy. He was nice whenever we coded together, but the rest of the time he was pretty distant. He was never really *affectionate*, but he was always protective, and I figured that meant he had to care.'

Leoben shakes his head. 'That's not love, squid. You need to unlearn that shit. You can't confuse protectiveness with love.'

My shoulders tighten. 'I know what love is.'

'I'm just saying, you fell for a guy who's pretty damn *protective* of you.'

I look up, my hands curling into fists. 'Yeah, well, you fell for a guy who was *experimenting* on you.'

Leoben looks away.

'Shit,' I say, 'I'm sorry, Lee, I didn't mean that.'

'No,' he says, staring at the table. 'I know it's screwed up, trust me.'

I let out a sigh, scrubbing my hands over my face. He probably has a point about Cole – I know I fell for him fast, and maybe it was partly his protectiveness. Maybe that's what I'd learned to think love was, like Leoben said. But there's more than that between Cole and me. Years more, even if I can't remember it. What we have is screwed up in a hundred different ways, but that doesn't mean it isn't *real*.

'I guess Lachlan screwed us all up pretty good,' I say. 'I'm sorry. I'm happy you guys have each other.'

He just nods, his eyes distant.

'Do you want to go check on him? I can wait here for the scientist guy.'

He looks up. 'You sure you're OK with him hacking something in your head?'

'Well, I'm not exactly thrilled about it, but if it'll help us find Lachlan, we have to try it. Go check on Dax. I'll be fine.'

He pushes away from the counter. 'I think I will. But I didn't *fall* for him, OK?'

I roll my eyes. 'Whatever, Lee.'

He gives me a ghost of a smile and pushes back through the door, leaving me alone with my palms pressed flat to the metal table. The shelf of medical equipment looms in my peripheral vision, tugging at my memory, though I don't want to remember what it might show me. I don't know if it's possible for *anyone* to come through a childhood like we had and not be screwed up for the rest of their lives. And yet, deep down, part of me is still reeling from the thought that I might not look like the man who did this to us. The man who still feels like my *father* on some fundamental level. I should be comforted that I don't share his true face.

Instead, I feel like another shard of whatever broken identity I've been clinging to has slipped away from me.

The door squeals open, and the dark-haired scientist, Mato, backs through it with a metal tray balanced in his hands. My heart speeds up as he sets it on the table and looks around the room. I don't know what the hack he wants to run on the implant involves, but something tells me it won't be pleasant.

And if he figures out who I really am, then there's no chance Cartaxus will let me go.

'This place is awful,' he says. He stands with his hands on one of the chairs, looking around. 'Cartaxus is so backward sometimes. Human testing like this is archaic. Brink's such an idiot, he doesn't realize what a dinosaur Lachlan is. No offence, of course.'

I swallow down another reflexive urge to defend Lachlan. 'Aren't you one of their scientists? Should you be talking like that?'

His eyes snap down to me, a cold smile spreading across his face. 'Oh, I'm central command. I can say whatever I want.'

He sits down opposite me, leaning back in his chair. I'm finding it tough to get a read on him. I came across a few hackers like him when I was working with the Skies – cocky, smart, but too sure of their abilities. The difference is, this guy is in Cartaxus's central command and something tells me he's cocky because he *knows* how good he is.

I still can't remember how Jun Bei knew him either. He's not the kind of person who'd be easy to forget, and not just because of his coding mask. He's the same height as me and, around so many towering soldiers, it makes him stand out. There are musculoskeletal apps most people start running in childhood to manage their posture and proportions, and practically everyone wants to be *tall*. Especially guys.

It's funny, most people thought gentech would destroy the relationship between biology and gender, and in a lot of ways it did. There are apps that construct a synthetic Y-chromosome, and others that inhibit its expression, as well as those designed to carve out presentations of gender across a spectrum. But the easy ability to change one's appearance came with the pressure to *do so*, and some gender stereotypes became even more entrenched. Height and silhouette. Eyelashes and jawlines, shoulder width and hand size. The ability to download traditional beauty standards became a temptation few could resist.

Back at the cabin, I thought I was short because I had hypergenesis. There were no apps safe enough to give me another few inches, to taper my square ribcage or lengthen my legs. But Jun Bei could have made herself look however she wanted, and for her to have kept the natural expression of her genes must have been a radical choice.

It's one that Mato made too, and it's starting to make sense as he holds my gaze, an undercurrent of razor-sharp intelligence glinting in his eyes. It feels like his height is making a statement – a way to intimidate people in the same way that I was frightened of Cole at the cabin when I saw he was unarmed. It sent the message that he could kill me with his hands if he wanted to.

Maybe Jun Bei's and Mato's size is a message that their real strength lies in their *minds*.

He slides a metal pen from his pocket and holds it between the thumb and forefinger of his left hand, flicking one end to spin it round, catching it again. 'You're lucky to have one of these implants. They're very rare.'

'What – the memory suppressant?'

He tilts his head. 'They *can* suppress memories, but that's not what they're for. Have you even seen what the implant looks like?'

I raise an eyebrow. 'I thought it was just a chip. It's in my skull, right?'

'Part of it.' He spins the pen again and lets his eyes glaze, a comm request with his full name blinking in my vision.

I accept it hesitantly, and a VR animation of a person's head appears above the table. I blink, staring at it. I'm still not used to just *seeing* things appear in front of me that look as real as this. I reach out for the image, and it rotates slowly as my fingers brush through it. The skin and skull on the head are both rendered in semi-transparent yellow so I can see through to the animated brain inside. A red oblong is attached to the inside of the skull, the size of my thumbnail. The skin on the back of my head prickles at the sight.

'That rectangle is the chip,' Mato says, spinning the pen again, 'and these are the neural wires.'

The image updates, a thick red line growing from below the chip, coiling into the person's spinal cord. Another dozen wires emerge, growing up and out like vines. They multiply, branching as they spread until they look like the limbs of a vast tree stretching through the brain.

The image seems to pulse in my vision, and the prickling skin on the back of my head rises into an ache.

There's one of these things inside my *head*.

'It's an amazing piece of tech,' Mato says, staring at the image, a gleam in his eyes.

I open my mouth, but I don't trust my voice. There must be a thousand wires digging through my brain. I've known all week that Lachlan found a way to alter my mind, but I've never really felt the horror of it until now. The *violation* of it. This wasn't some game where he tried to create a perfect daughter. This was an experiment. It was cruel, and sick, and the tools he used are still buried inside me.

I think I'm going to throw up.

I turn from the image, dragging in a breath, covering my mouth. The tiled walls seem to pulse, the room suddenly stifling.

'Oh,' Mato says, waving his hand. The image disappears. 'We can wait if you're feeling weak.'

I shake my head, trying to control my breathing. 'I'm *fine*.' I force myself to straighten, turning back to the table. Putting this off isn't going to make it any easier, and I don't want to look weak in front of this guy. 'What's the implant supposed to do?'

Mato spins the pen again, catching it cleanly, then passes it to his right hand. This time when he spins it, it clatters across the table. 'I'm better at this with my left hand than my right,' he says, his eyes on mine, 'but it's not from practice. It's from the implant.'

He spins the pen in his left hand again. A clean, perfect arc.

'You're telling me you're using *code* to spin that?' I ask.

'Precisely. It's just a mental command coded into the implant. Whenever I think of spinning it, my body responds.'

I frown as he spins the pen again. Code-controlled motions aren't new – that's how puppets work. They have a wiring system feeding impulses into their muscles and nerves. Some athletes have been caught cheating with similar tech. The sad reality is that machines are slightly better at almost any task than humans are. They still can't be programmed to move in all the ways that people can, but if you train a machine to replicate a single action – like catching a ball – it'll learn to do it faster and more accurately than the most talented person.

The controls aren't perfect, though. Even with wires in your muscles, your body would rather listen to your thoughts than to your tech. That's why puppets twitch.

But the implant doesn't send wires into your muscles. It sends them into your *brain*.

'The beauty of the implant,' Mato says, 'is that this skill would take up space in a normal brain, but I only have a few neurons dedicated to it. When I train a new movement into the implant, it sends the command directly into my spinal cord and suppresses that part of my brain until those neurons atrophy.' He picks up the pen with his left hand again, his eyes glazing, and tries to flick it, but he suddenly looks clumsy, like he can barely hold it at all. 'I'm using my brain right now, but the neurons that once controlled my hand are gone.'

His eyes glaze again, and the pen twirls round smoothly. Only, this time it doesn't just flick around his thumb. It rolls back and forth between his fingers, spinning seamlessly as he lifts his hand, never losing control. He's just showing off now, but the nausea I felt when I first saw the implant has subsided, curiosity taking its place.

'So you can't use your *hand* any more?' I ask. 'What if the implant glitches?'

He sighs. 'A coder with as much promise as you shouldn't be so limited in your thinking. If a machine can move my hand better than me, then why wouldn't I let it? A lot of our brain is dedicated to simple biological controls, and that's valuable real estate. After you suppress an action for long enough, the brain will reuse that space. The neurons that used to control my left hand can now be used for *better* things – thoughts, memories, calculations. This isn't a tool for controlling movements. It's a reorganization system for the human brain.'

I sit back, staring at him. The thought is completely wild: rewiring the brain and relegating movements to chips, reclaiming the space to become *smarter*. It's horrifying to think that Lachlan put this inside me against my will, but a hint of excitement flutters in my chest at the thought of using it. This is cutting-edge tech. Mato sets the pen back down and I find myself watching him, taking in the intelligence in his eyes.

I wonder just how much of himself he's given to the implant, and what he got in return.

'So no,' he says, rolling the pen back and forth on the table with his fingers, 'it isn't a memory suppressant, but it could be used to isolate the parts of your brain that hold your memories and quiet them. There are a lot of simpler ways to do that, though.'

I nod, shifting uneasily, my eyes following the pen as he rolls it across the table. There are a lot of simpler ways to do *everything* Lachlan has done to me. Hide me, change me, suppress my memories – even releasing the vaccine through me. But Lachlan has never been one to waste time and energy on something he didn't need to do.

There's a lot I don't understand about what he's done, and it's starting to frighten me.

'Are you ready to try the hack?' Mato asks. 'If you're too scared after seeing the implant, we can wait . . .'

I look up, narrowing my eyes, expecting a condescending look on his face, but instead his gaze is more like Leoben's during our sparring sessions. Fierceness in his eyes, the ghost of a smile on his lips, like he's pushing me into a place that's not comfortable but he knows I'm strong enough to handle it. I still don't know where Jun Bei knew this guy from, but something uncoils in me as I stare back at him. A voice, rising to his challenge.

'I'm not *scared*,' I say, leaning across the table. 'Bring it on. Let's do this.'

CHAPTER 9

Mato flicks his dark hair back from his face and stands from the table, unwinding two cables from the side of the genkit. One is a normal reader wire designed to burrow under the skin and connect with a panel, but the other is a bigger cable – a coiled black cord the thickness of a pencil. It's used to hook into the sockets that a person's panel grows inside them – in their knees, hips, shoulders and spine, controlling the infrastructure of wires that distributes their code.

'We'll jack in to your panel like normal,' he says, passing the slender reader wire to me. It's tapered to a needle point to dig through the skin, with a hollow tip to allow a stream of nanites through.

I take the wire, nerves fluttering through me at the thought of jacking myself in. If Mato decides to scan my panel, he'll find out the truth about who I am, and then I'll never make it out of here. I just have to hope he isn't feeling curious about my tech or my DNA.

I press the wire to the glowing stripe of my panel, and it lurches free the moment it gets near my skin, diving into my arm. I flinch, my panel flashing as it connects, the lab flickering momentarily out of focus. A green icon pops up in the corner of my vision, showing me a connection to the genkit on the wall.

'Clean link,' Mato says, his eyes glazing. It's a small note of respect for him to hand the wire to me instead of connecting it himself. It hurts to connect a reader wire – just a pinch, but it's enough to make most people afraid of it. Coders are used to it, though. Gentech coding sessions can be done over a wireless connection, but there's nothing as fast and secure as jacking yourself in.

'This one's more difficult,' he says, lifting the coiled black cable. He hangs the end over a hook on the edge of the table. 'We're going to have to connect directly with the implant, which means adding a socket there. You can take it out once we're done if you want, but I keep a permanent port to avoid having to reinstall it.'

I wince. He means to screw a piece of metal into my *skull*. 'You can't use the spinal node?'

'It needs to be closer.' He lifts a tool from the trolley that's shaped like a handgun with a wide barrel. A socket installer. 'You can do this yourself, but it's probably easier if I do it.' He steps closer, but I lift my hands.

'Just slow down,' I say. 'I don't understand how you're going to find this tracker if the implant was wiped.'

Mato sighs impatiently. 'The tracker wouldn't have been wiped. I think Lachlan hid it in the implant's power controls. I should be able to see it if I can get the implant to reboot. I really thought you were smarter than this.'

I sit back from the table. 'You don't have to be so rude.'

He shoots me a strangely disarming smile. 'You'd actually be surprised by how much it helps in my job.' He lifts the gun. 'Now, are you doing this, or am I?'

My chest tightens at the sight of the socket installer. 'I . . . I think you'd better do it.'

'Of course.' He walks round the table, gesturing for me to lean forward. My shoulders tense, but I press my hands to the table's surface and lean my face into them, letting him pull the hair away from the base of my skull.

'This will only hurt for a moment,' he says. The barrel of the gun presses against my skin and something whines, shaving away a circle of my hair. My heart rate kicks higher in anticipation. I walked into the lab of my own volition, but now there's a wire in my arm and a gun at my head in the hands of a member of Cartaxus's central command. I'm rapidly losing control here.

But there's no walking away now.

I close my eyes, digging my fingernails into my palms. Mato shifts the gun slightly, the metal cold on my skin, then it *clicks* and something smacks into the back of my head.

He lied about the pain. It crashes through me before dipping, but it doesn't fade away.

'Goddammit,' I spit, scrunching my eyes shut. It feels like a spike driven into my head, making my vision swim. I sit up and bring my shaking hand to the back of my head. A circle of cold metal is lying flush with my skin, the flesh around it slowly turning numb.

'OK, let's check it,' Mato says, stretching the cable round to the back of my head. It locks into the new socket with a click of metal that echoes through my skull. 'Clean connection. I think we're set to run the hack. I've invited Crick in to monitor your panel and make sure you're OK as we go.'

The screen in the corner of the room blinks to blue, showing a spinning white icon. A circle with a jagged slash through it, like a snake eating its own tail.

'That logo is from the implant,' Mato says. 'It was designed by a hacker called Regina. Do you know of her?'

'Of course I do.' Regina is one of the world's most famous coders. Some say she's as talented as Lachlan, but she never turned her focus to commercial apps. She leads a commune of genehackers living in a city they built in the Nevada desert called Entropia. They created the passenger pigeons, and contributed plenty of work to the Skies' databases of code during the outbreak, but I haven't spoken to many of them. Regina's hackers tend to keep to themselves. I've never seen this logo before, but a flicker of recognition rises through me as it spins on the screen. 'I didn't know Regina worked on tech like this.'

'She's worked on everything,' Mato says. 'It's my job to monitor the Skies' servers, but I also keep an eye on Entropia itself. You'd be surprised how much of Cartaxus's technology started out as files that were stolen from Regina's vaults. Brink's biggest mistake was trying to develop a vaccine in-house instead of collaborating with her people.'

He looks up as the lab's door swings open. Dax walks through, supported by one of the soldiers. The bruise on his face has spread to cover most of his cheek. His green eyes run over the room – to the genkit, to Mato and to the cable in my head. He falls heavily on to one of the chairs. 'Are you OK?' he asks me.

'Better than you,' I say.

He smiles faintly. 'Indeed.' He looks up at Mato. 'Thanks for covering for me with Brink, Somata.'

'Next time you feel like stealing a copter, let me know in advance,' Mato mutters. 'He'd have locked you up.'

Dax coughs, his shoulders shaking. 'A prison cell is the least of my concerns right now.'

I look between the two of them. Dax is the head of Cartaxus's science team now, so I'm sure he deals with central command regularly, but it sounds like he and Mato know each other better than that. There's no chemistry between them like there is between Dax and Lee, but there is *something*. They're both arrogant, and they're both skilled coders. Maybe the two of them just get along.

'I think we're ready,' Mato says. 'Dax, you monitor her vitals while I watch the implant. If I'm right about the tracker, then it should send a ping out once we reboot it, and we'll be able to trace it to where Lachlan is hiding. Catarina, are you ready?'

I watch Dax, drumming my fingers on the table nervously. He rubs his eyes, blinking against the fever he's clearly fighting. I wasn't expecting him to be monitoring my panel during the hack. Dax has been on my side until now – he made it clear in the Comox that he doesn't think I should have to suffer any more for what Lachlan has done. I don't know what he'll do if he figures out that I'm not Lachlan's daughter, though.

'You *ready*?' Mato asks, annoyed to have to ask me again.

I shoot a glare at him. 'Yeah, fine. Let's do this.'

His eyes glaze. 'OK. The hack is starting in three, two, one.'

The cable in my head vibrates, my panel flashing suddenly. I brace myself for a rush of pain, but it doesn't come. There is no pressure in the back of my skull, no ache building up inside me. The spinning circle on the screen disappears, replaced by a report with a list of readings and numbers.

'This is a diagnostic from the implant,' Mato says, scanning the screen. 'It says you suffered some damage several days ago. That would have been during the decryption.'

I grip the table. 'Wait, do you mean *brain damage*?'

Mato tilts his head. 'It's more like a concussion. These implants can be dangerous, but I've run code that's hurt me far worse than this. You'll be fine, but you should rest while you recover.'

'Shit,' I mutter. I've spent *hours* fighting Leoben every day for the last week. I must have hit the ground a hundred times, and I've barely been sleeping. That's basically the opposite of what I should have been doing to recover from a concussion.

I watch the screen, waiting for it to change. I don't even know if the hack is running yet. My vision is still clear, my heartbeat steady, but there's an ache starting up inside my arm. It radiates out from my panel and down into my palm, like a steady stream of too-hot water poured across my skin. It grows stronger as I breathe – the pain rising until I feel the urge to clench my hand into a fist.

'My arm is hurting,' I say. 'Is that supposed to happen?'

Mato frowns. 'I'm not seeing anything on the implant's logs. Crick, what's happening with her tech?'

'I think I see something,' Dax mutters. 'I'm trying to figure it out.'

I swallow hard, trying to keep my arm still. This pain is slow and insidious, spreading across my skin, setting my cells ablaze one at a time.

‘Should we cut this off?’ Mato asks.

Dax shakes his head. ‘No, found it. It looks like there are some hanging commands waiting in her spinal socket. One is running in her panel, activating an app, I’m not sure what, but the other looks like a command to the implant.’ He turns to the screen, focusing, splashing pages of text across it. ‘I think these commands were supposed to run during the decryption, but it looks like they glitched.’

‘What do you mean?’ I ask, gripping the arm of the chair, breathing through the pain. It’s growing sharper, like an army of insects burrowing beneath my skin. ‘I thought you got the whole vaccine.’

‘We did,’ Dax says. ‘I don’t think this code is related to the vaccine. This is something else.’

Mato follows his eyes, scanning the text. The code on the screen shows two commands with error messages beside them from the day we ran the decryption. Dax is right – this code was supposed to run, but it crashed. But if these commands aren’t related to the vaccine, what the hell are they supposed to do?

‘The command for the implant is a configuration change,’ Mato says, his eyes narrowing. ‘It’s switching off a suppression module, but it looks like the suppressor was already offline. You cut out your panel before the decryption, didn’t you? I think that might be why the command didn’t work.’

‘I’m going to reboot the spinal node and see if I can clear the commands,’ Dax says. His eyes glaze, and the code on the screen flickers . . .

Then the lab disappears.

Gravity tilts, my stomach lurching. The world flashes to black, then grey, then into dazzling light. I’m suddenly lying on a metal table with white lights blazing above me. The air is warm, scented with jasmine. A window beside me shows scorched desert plains stretching into a line of hazy mountains. The walls are plaster, hung with plastic sheeting. This is a makeshift lab, complete with walls of vials of nanofluid and a humming genkit.

Lachlan is standing over the table, staring down at me.

I blink back into the lab, sucking in a gasp of air. The pain in my arm is licking higher, pushing past my elbow. The image of Lachlan's face burns in the darkness behind my eyes. It must be another of Jun Bei's memories.

But when was she in a *desert*?

'Catarina,' Mato says, grabbing my shoulder, a flicker of genuine concern in his eyes. 'The implant just glitched. Are you OK?'

I nod, gritting my teeth, clenching and unclenching my hand. The pain in my arm is leaching through my fingers, burning across the creases in my palm. Whatever command Dax just ran feels like it's whipped my memories into a storm. I can feel them heaving against my senses. 'Is the hack working?' I ask. 'Can you see the tracker?'

'Just a minute more,' Mato says. 'We're almost finished.'

The pain in my arm blazes across my skin, spots of light bleeding into the corners of my vision. I open my mouth to tell Mato to stop – that it feels like my arm is on fire – but the room suddenly blurs in and out of focus.

I freeze, not moving, not breathing. I feel like I'm on the verge of blinking into another memory, but I have just enough control to stay out of it. I can feel it pulling at me, though, and I can feel something else too. An edge in my mind. A barrier between my thoughts and Jun Bei's memories.

It feels like a *wall* inside me. Like it's splitting me in half.

I try to suck in a breath, but the pain in my arm spikes, rushing up my neck and into the base of my skull. Something *shudders* under my skin.

'Something's wrong,' Dax says, standing up, his eyes glazed. 'We should sto–'

But he's too late. My forearm shakes, my panel blinking as dozens of black wires burst through my skin with a spray of blood.

I clench my teeth, biting back a scream, and blink out of the lab.

A new memory kicks me through the wall in my mind, and this time there is no fighting it. I'm in the desert again, lying on a bed, a drip in my arm filled with a green, glistening fluid. There are bandages on my hands and the sticky tug of tape on my neck. A humming genkit stands on the far wall beside a pair of clear glass doors with dark storm clouds beyond it. The air flashes with lightning, tracing the silhouettes of a flock of white-and-gold passenger pigeons.

This is where Lachlan changed my DNA.

I can feel it in my skin, my bones. He didn't transform me in the cabin. It was in *another* lab. There are notes scribbled on the walls and piled in stacks across the floor. Lachlan is standing at the window, staring through it at the pigeons, his arms folded behind his back.

I blink back into the Zarathustra lab, my own scream echoing in my ears. I'm slumped across the table, with Dax standing over me, his green eyes wide with shock. The rows of wires that erupted from my forearm are wriggling back into my skin, leaving bloody punctures behind them.

'Princess,' Dax breathes, grabbing my shoulders, helping me up. 'It's over.'

I let out a gasp, my throat raw. Blood is streaming down my arm, dripping from my elbow. I don't know why dozens of wires just *erupted* from my skin, but they're gone now, and anaesthetic is surging through me, making me dizzy. 'Did it *work*?'

'Yes,' Mato says, the black glass of his mask flashing with faint, pale glyphs. 'The implant rebooted. I'm tracking the ping now. It's not just a ping, though. I think Lachlan is using the implant to track more than your location – he's checking that you're healthy. It's feeding him a full vital scan.'

I scrunch my eyes shut, clutching my bloodied arm to my chest, my head spinning from the blood, the anaesthetic, and now the thought that Lachlan has been watching my vital signs. He's not just tracking me. He's *studying* me.

I really am just one of his experiments.

'I traced the ping,' Mato says, his voice lifting. 'We got him. He's in Nevada. He's in *Entropia*.'

I blink, fighting the wave of dizziness from the anaesthetic. Entropia. The city run by the hacker Regina. That would match the pigeons I saw in the memory, the desert mountains on the horizon. Lachlan must have a lab there. If it's where he changed my DNA, it makes sense that's where he'd be hiding now.

'There's more,' Mato says. Text blinks across the lab's screen. 'This was on the implant in a hidden folder. I think it was attached to the code the implant added to the vaccine.'

I scan the text, the edges of my vision blurring. My arm is still aching, my blood pressure dropping. I should lie down. I should get some healing tech, but I can't move. I can't even breathe.

There's a message from Lachlan blazing on the laboratory's screen.

If you're reading this, it means I have won. This work will usher in the dawn of a new age and recode humanity into a better, stronger species. You cannot stop this change any more than you can stop the sun from rising. A new era for humanity has arrived, and the world will never be the same.

'Holy shit,' I breathe. 'Are you seeing this, Dax?'

But he doesn't reply. His hand is over his mouth, and he's staring at me. The screen changes to a report – the log from the ping that Mato just traced. It shows our location in Canada and a set of coordinates in the Nevada desert. Entropia. The hexadecimal ID from Lachlan's panel is printed beside his location on the map, and there's another ID shown beside mine.

But it isn't mine.

It's not the ID number Dax knows, at least. It's the string of hexadecimal digits that Cole read out to me back in the cabin when I was trying to locate Jun Bei for him. I found a signal with her ID, but it was masked – bouncing between cities, between servers, hiding her location. It proved that she was alive but didn't reveal where she was.

But it wasn't Jun Bei's panel that I found that day in the cabin.

It was the tracker Lachlan left in my own *skull*.

'Oh my God,' Dax says, his face paling. 'You're not Catarina. You're Jun Bei.'

CHAPTER 10

Mato steps back, an unreadable expression on his face. Dax is deathly silent, a look of horror in his eyes. He half stands from the chair, blinking . . .

Then he launches himself across the table at me.

'What did you do to her?' he shouts. He grabs my shoulders, dragging me off the chair, and slams me back into the floor. The wire screeches from my panel, the cable in my head disconnecting. My wounded forearm hits the concrete with a burst of blinding pain. 'Where is Catarina?'

I shrink away, gasping. 'It's me! Dax, it's me!'

'Don't lie to me!' His eyes are wild. 'Tell me where she is!'

'I'm n-not lying!' I gasp. 'I'm not Jun Bei. Not any more.'

'Get off her!' Mato grabs the back of Dax's coat, yanking him off me. 'I called the others. They're coming.'

Dax lets me go, stumbling away. I scramble back, sucking in a gulp of air. There's a trail of my blood on the floor, and the pain in my arm is strong enough to make my vision waver. Dax stands, heaving in a breath, my blood on his hands. The doors to the hallway fly open, and Cole and Leoben burst into the room, followed by a troop of guards. My vision flickers, and Brink appears beside them, staring down at me. I try to shuffle back, but there's nowhere to go.

No exit, no escape. This is what I feared would happen. They've found out the truth about who I am, and now they'll never let me go. But they have to – we know where Lachlan is now. I *know* I can help find him.

Leoben's eyes turn black as he takes in the scene. He grabs Dax, pulling him away. Cole moves for me, but the soldiers lift their rifles, shouting for him to stop, clicks echoing around the room. One of them yanks me to my knees on the floor, gripping my wrists behind me.

'Well, well,' Brink says. I can hear him struggling to keep his voice calm. He seems genuinely shaken. 'Jun Bei. It seems you've returned home after all. I should have guessed that you'd be a part of Lachlan's sabotage.'

'I'm not,' I say, struggling against the soldier's grip. Blood is streaming freely from my arm, trickling over the back of my hand. 'I had no idea what he was planning. I'm not Jun Bei any more – I thought I was Lachlan's daughter until a week ago. I didn't mean for any of this to happen. All I want to do is save the vaccine.'

Brink clicks his tongue. 'See, I find that hard to believe. You were the one who *added* the extra code to the vaccine. You're the one who let us send it out to everyone.'

'She's telling the truth,' Cole says. 'She's as much a victim of this as anyone. She doesn't remember her past.'

'It's true,' Leoben says, but Brink lifts a hand. Half the soldiers aim their rifles at Cole and Leoben, walking them back against the wall.

Brink turns to Mato. 'Did you find Lachlan?'

Mato looks around the room. His dark hair is hanging wild around his face, his eyes narrowed. 'Yes, I did. He's in Entropia. He must be working with the hackers there.'

'Good,' Brink says. 'But we may be able to save ourselves some time. If Jun Bei here was the one who added Lachlan's code to the vaccine, I'm going to wager that she'll be able to tell us how to patch it too.'

My eyes widen. 'I don't know anything about that, I *swear*. We have to go after Lachlan. I'm not the threat here.'

'We'll see about that.' Brink lifts a hand, summoning a soldier by the door. The soldier pulls a black telescoping rod from his belt, flicking it to extend it. He twists the handle, and the end of the rod glows with dancing cobalt sparks.

'What . . . what are you doing?' The soldier holding my wrists tightens his grip.

'Stop,' Mato says, his voice sharp. 'Brink, we can't hurt her, not any more than we already have. Lachlan is using the tracker to monitor her vital signs. If he sees us torturing her, he could set off another attack.'

Brink lets out a growl of frustration. He scans the room, his eyes landing on Cole. 'Fine. Use him instead.'

'No!' I shout, struggling against the gloved hands holding me locked in place. The soldiers drag Cole to the floor in front of me, and he meets my eyes urgently.

'Stay calm,' he says. 'Just keep telling them the truth. We're not the enemy here.'

'Stop it!' Leoben says, pushing past the soldiers. He grabs one of their guns, and for a heartbeat I think it'll be enough. He lifts the rifle, aiming the barrel at the soldier holding Cole, but Brink turns and Leoben's body shudders suddenly.

Leoben drops to his knees, his eyes black and glazed. He's still conscious, but he's staring straight ahead, not breathing, not blinking. The rifle falls to the floor. Leoben's arms are hanging at his sides, but his muscles are tensed.

It's like Brink just put him on *pause*.

'Wh-what did you do to him?' Dax stutters.

Brink shoots a curious look at Dax. 'He's fine. Black-out agents are useful, but central command doesn't create weapons we can't control.' He turns to me. 'It's up to you now, Jun Bei. You added code to the vaccine once before. Now you're going to tell us how to do it.'

'I don't know how,' I beg. 'Please, Brink!'

He crosses his arms and nods at the soldier holding Cole. The soldier lifts the crackling blue rod and brings it down on Cole's back.

The effect is instantaneous. Cobalt sparks of light crackle across Cole's shoulders. His head flies back, the tendons in his neck taut. He lets out a roar of pain, the skin where he was hit sizzling, turning black.

Dax flinches, looking away. Mato's gaze doesn't waver, but his fingers are digging into his arm.

'Stop it!' I scream, struggling against the grip on my wrists. 'Please – I can help you find Lachlan. He *needs* me. You have to believe me!'

'Again,' Brink says, lifting his hand, and the rod swings down on Cole again, more cobalt sparks crackling across his skin. He lets out a cry, his body shaking. The flesh across his back is blackened in two sickening lines.

'You're going to kill him!' I scream.

'Tell us how to fix the vaccine!' Brink shouts.

'I can't! It's *Lachlan's* code. I don't know anything about it!'

'Hit him again,' Brink snaps. The soldier lifts the rod, its tip crackling with blue lightning, and time slows to a crawl.

Cole is pale, his eyes unfocused, like he was after Leoben's jeep blew up. He can't take another resuscitation. His body is already swimming with emergency tech.

This blow could kill him.

The thought turns my focus inward, something inside me shuddering – the wall between my mind and Jun Bei's memories. It's cracking at the sight of Cole's injuries, and the memories are spreading, shattering across my skin. Jun Bei's past is rising, howling, memories slicing through me like knives. I see a blonde-haired girl beside me whispering in my ear, Cole standing in the rain, shouting at Leoben. I see a bald girl with paper-white skin curled into a ball on the floor. I can feel the sting of stitches on my chest, scars curling over my neck. The memories are a wave, crashing against me.

But there's more than just fragments of them now.

The images rolling through me aren't just flickers or blurred moments. They're deep and real. There's more of Jun Bei's past locked inside me than I thought. This isn't just a handful of snatched images. It feels like an *ocean* of memories locked in my mind, pressing against the cracks inside me, trying to get out.

I gasp, swaying under the weight of the memories. They feel like they're going to sweep me away, tugging at the slender threads of identity I still have left. For a second I hear Jun Bei's voice, like I did when I was fighting Lachlan.

And then, suddenly, it's gone.

The room snaps into sparkling focus. Cole is on the floor, the soldier's weapon coming down on him. I reach into my panel instinctively, grabbing the first virus that rises to my call. It's something from Jun Bei's files, hidden in the depths of her folders of code. My mind tilts and pivots, flinging it into the soldier's panel.

He drops the rod and falls to the floor before I realize what I've done.

Dax steps back, his eyes flying wide as the soldier's head hits the tiles with a *crack*. Cole looks round, woozy, at the soldier on the floor.

My heart stops. The soldier isn't just down. He's *dead*.

I just killed him with Jun Bei's scythe.

Cole stares at me, a look of horror in his eyes. 'What did you do, Cat?'

I blink, getting control of myself. The soldier's body is limp, sprawled on the tiles. I didn't know that the code I sent would kill him, but he was going to hurt Cole. I didn't have a choice.

'I did what I had to,' I say, my voice sounding strangely distant. 'Brink, you have to let us go. We know where Lachlan is. We can find him.'

Brink is watching me with a calculating look on his face. He doesn't look angry that I killed the soldier – he just looks *interested*. 'Lachlan really did this to you,' he murmurs, walking closer. His feet step right through the soldier's body, his brown eyes locked on mine. 'You must be worth something to him.'

'I am. He needs me to finish his plan. He'll let me get closer to him than anyone else. *Please*. Let me help you stop him.'

'She's right,' Mato says. There's a strange light in his eyes as he looks at me. 'Lachlan left that tracker in her, but it's also a way to find him. He wants her to go to him. I need her on this mission.'

'Since when is this *your* mission?' Brink asks.

'Since it's sending us to Entropia,' Mato says. 'I'm the only person who can get to Lachlan if he's there, Brink. And I need Catarina to do it.'

Brink's eyes glaze, and Leoben's fade to brown, his muscles jolting as he slides out from under Brink's control. Lee looks around, standing unsteadily.

'You might be right,' Brink says. 'It's a fair trade, I suppose. Catarina did just give us her scythe code. We've been trying to re-create it since she first escaped. Every Cartaxus soldier's panel has been fitted with an app since then to record all incoming attacks. This is going to make flood protocol *much* easier for us in case we have to launch it.'

I suck in a breath, horrified. I've handed Jun Bei's scythe to Cartaxus.

I just gave them a way to kill everyone on the surface.

'OK,' Brink says. 'I'll give you a chance, I suppose. I want Lachlan back under control, and you have three days to do it. That's as long as I'm prepared to wait and let this virus keep evolving. Mato, Franklin – Catarina is your responsibility now. I won't wait for you to return before launching flood protocol.'

'We need Leoben,' I say.

Brink shakes his head. 'Out of the question. He's too valuable.'

'I *need* him,' I say, forcing myself to straighten. 'He's coming with us, or I'll kill the rest of these soldiers.'

Brink waves a hand. 'Go ahead.' I can tell he's just calling my bluff, but the soldiers on the edges of the room stiffen.

'I can reach you too,' I say. 'You're connected to my VR chip right now. That connection goes two ways.'

Brink goes silent. I'm just bluffing again, and he probably knows it, but he still turns to me with that same appraising look in his eyes. I don't know if I'm becoming more or less valuable to him. I don't know what I'm becoming at *all*.

But I know I'm not walking out of here without my brother.

Brink's lips curl. 'Fine,' he says. 'You can take the Comox you came here in. You have three days, Catarina. You had better hope that Lachlan needs you as much as you think he does.'

'Come on,' Leoben says. He slings an arm round Cole and lifts him up, his eyes blazing as he looks back at Dax. Something passes between them – fierce and urgent – then Leoben staggers down the hallway, half carrying Cole.

Mato takes my arm. 'Come with me,' he says, his touch gentle, the arrogance in his voice gone. 'Let's go, Catarina.' I let him lead me away from the soldier's body, down the hallway, through the waiting room and outside.

The Comox we flew in on is waiting on the grass, its rotors already spinning. Leoben hurries up the ramp and inside with Cole. I jog up behind them with Mato, my hair whipping around my face, clutching my wounded arm to my chest. The door hisses shut, and I close my eyes, seeing the lifeless soldier on the floor. I can feel the rush of instinct that led me to Jun Bei's scythe, that let me fling it into the soldier's panel.

I can sense the vast ocean of her memories locked inside my mind.

We lift into the darkness through the glowing flock of pigeons and tilt south, racing away from the lab. We have three days to find Lachlan and force him to fix the vaccine. He hasn't patched it yet, and he hasn't come in to Cartaxus, but he *must* know about the strain. Surely he doesn't want the virus to keep evolving any more than Cartaxus does. Maybe he's waiting for me to go to him. Maybe he's still trying to finish his plan.

And now I'm on a Comox, racing through the night towards him.

Either we're going to stop him, or we're flying straight into a trap.

CHAPTER 11

It's morning by the time we make it to the northern reaches of Nevada, the faint penumbra of the Comox's shadow sliding across barren desert plains. There are no trees below us, just an endless expanse of wiry bushes in shades of olive and brown, intersected by the occasional pale stretch of road. A flock of pigeons is flying in from the east, their plumage black and cobalt, the roar of their cries barely perceptible above the rotors' drone. Flickers of recognition rise through me as I watch the landscape pass below us, but the ocean of memories that I glimpsed in the lab is locked back in the depths of my mind.

The four of us are silent. I managed to sleep for a couple of hours on one of the plastic chairs that fold down from the Comox's side. Leoben is in the cockpit, Mato is standing to look out the window, and Cole is beside me, his head tilted back against the seat, his eyes closed. He's not asleep, but he's not talking, either. His tech is keeping him stable, and I don't think he's in much pain, but ever since we left the lab, there's been a wall of silence around him that I'm afraid to cross.

Not that I'm in the mood to talk. My panel arm is cradled to my chest, a plastic pressure bandage wrapped around it. It hasn't stopped aching since we left the lab. I should scan my tech to figure out what caused the wires to erupt like that, or at least turn on an anaesthetic, but I can't bring myself to dive into my panel and dull the pain.

I *killed* a man.

The thought feels like a wound inside me – something I need to fold myself around and wait for it to heal. But it's been hours now, and the guilt isn't fading. If anything, it's growing sharper. It doesn't help that Cole's silence carries the same undercurrent of horror that I saw in his eyes in the lab. Which is ridiculous. He would have done the same thing to protect me, and it's not like I've never killed anyone before. I lived through the outbreak; I've *eaten* people. There's plenty of blood on my hands.

But it's never been quite like this.

Every time I close my eyes, I see the flash of commands, the soldier's head bouncing when he hit the floor. Part of me is afraid to even think about Jun Bei's scythe in case I somehow run the code again. It feels like a loaded gun inside my mind, and I don't know if I'm in control of the trigger. I killed that soldier on instinct, but the instinct wasn't *mine*. Nothing I've experienced in the last three years taught me to lash out with code like that. It was a behaviour Jun Bei learned.

Her past is bubbling into my thoughts, pushing into my actions, and I don't know if I like it.

I'm starting to understand how Cole must feel being a blackout agent, acting on commands and responses that are not his own. The difference is, Cole's protocol is controlled by his tech, but the instinct to kill that soldier came from my own mind.

'We're almost at the coordinates Cartaxus gave us,' Leoben calls back from the cockpit. 'Does Entropia have anti-aircraft missiles?'

Mato turns from the window, concerned. 'It's possible. *Why?*'

'Because I can see the city, which means they can see us.' Leoben tilts the controls, and the Comox dips. 'I'm gonna start a descent and get out of visual range.'

I stand from my seat, using my good hand to grip the camouflage netting on the ceiling, and step across the cargo hold. Cole stays seated, but Mato follows me to the cockpit's entrance. His hand grips the netting beside mine, close enough for me to feel the tension in the fabric. I still can't remember how Jun Bei knew Mato, but I've been hyperaware of his presence the entire time we've been flying, and I know he's been watching me too. Twice I looked over and found his gaze on me while I was trying to sleep, and each time it sent an uncomfortable jolt through me.

I can't quite place the way I feel when I look at Mato. It's something close to the way I felt when Dax and I used to work together. There are so few people who code as intensely as we do that whenever I meet one, it feels *important*, like two ships crossing paths in a vast and empty sea.

I know Jun Bei coded for Cartaxus when she was at the lab, so there's a chance that she and Mato worked together. Whatever their connection, I feel like it was deep.

But he still hasn't mentioned anything to me.

'There's the city,' he says, lifting his hand to point through the windscreen. The curved glass of his mask is dark now, almost opaque, obscuring his left eye and brow. I don't know if there's a reason it keeps changing colour, or why he even has it over his eye, unless he prefers it that way – as an intentional barrier between him and the rest of the world.

I follow his gaze to a smudge in the distance, letting my ocular tech sense the focus of my eyes. The horizon swells in my vision. The desert is barren, rocky and brown, but a cluster of steel and concrete towers juts from a patch of colour: green and scarlet, white and lemon yellow. Fields and rows of flowers and plants are spread haphazardly around the base of a small mountain, canals shining between them.

Entropia.

I first heard about the city from the news stories about the passenger pigeons, back when they were first released. It was Entropia's hackers who created the flocks, along with dozens of other strains of animals and plants that have spread out of control. The hacker Regina moved here and started a commune decades ago, and people have been coming to join her ever since, setting up homesteads in the mountains, taking over most of this corner of the state. When the government tightened its laws on genehacking, Regina declared the territory around the city a sovereign state with herself as its queen. She barricaded their roads, erected a border and cut off contact with the outside world.

Regina says they're a team of artists, scientists and gentech enthusiasts dedicated to reinventing themselves.

I always thought they sounded like a cult.

'I didn't know the city was this big,' I say as we draw closer. The buildings are constructed into the mountain's slopes – a mix of gleaming skyscrapers and tilted wooden shacks clinging to every inch of the rock. Narrow, dusty streets wind in zigzags between them, a haze of drones and pigeons filling the air.

It's a jagged pyramid rising from an oasis in the middle of a dead and sprawling landscape, and something clenches inside me at the sight of it. It's sprawling, wild and beautiful.

I've *definitely* been here before, but I can't remember anything about it.

Leoben turns the Comox, heading for a rocky mountain ridge, and I scan the desert around the city. Miles of barren rocky plains stretch out from the mountain's base, meeting a wide ring of dark, gleaming purple. It looks like some kind of natural border encircling the city. Razorgrass, probably. The serrated leaves are distantly related to wheat, and they're sharp enough to shred tyres and bleed trespassers to death. The border must have been Regina's way of keeping her city safe from infection, like the mile-wide wastelands that Cartaxus builds around its bunkers to keep the clouds from drifting too close. Two narrow roads are cut through the border from the city, leading to what look like busy checkpoints in the desert.

'Yeah, this place is huge,' Leoben says, spinning round in the pilot's seat. 'What's the plan? It could take days to search all these buildings.'

'I have a plan,' Mato says, 'but first we need to land, stock up and load into vehicles. Our coordinates are for a Cartaxus safehouse an hour's drive from the border.'

'How are we going to get past those checkpoints?' Leoben asks. 'Looks like they're armed.'

'I can get us in,' Mato says. 'I'm a resident of Entropia. This is where I grew up.'

I look over at him. 'You *lived* here?'

He nods, a few strands of his dark hair falling across his mask as he stares through the window at the hazy rise of the city in the distance. 'I was here until a couple of years before the outbreak. That's why Brink let me take over this mission. I can get us a meeting with Regina – I've worked with her and she respects me. She'll be a useful ally in helping us find Lachlan.'

'Are you serious?' I ask. 'Regina could be *working* with him. We should be trying to lie low. Can't we just go to the coordinates Lachlan is at?'

Mato shakes his head. 'That tracker is only accurate to within a few miles. It puts Lachlan in the city, but we'll still have to search for him. He'll already know we're here, anyway. Regina's a little out of touch, but I don't think she'd be part of a plan that would put her people at risk. She'll help us find him.'

I exchange a worried look with Leoben. Mato doesn't seem concerned about meeting with Regina, but the thought sends a flare of unease through me. We're walking a dangerous line – we need to find Lachlan and force him to fix the vaccine, but if we make a wrong move, I could end up back under his control. Then there'll be no stopping him. He could use my DNA to rewrite everyone's minds – turn the whole world into one of his experiments.

But Leoben's right – it could take days to search the city. If Regina can help us, meeting with her might be worth the risk.

'All right, I see the safehouse,' Leoben says. 'I'm going to set us down. Hold on.'

Cole's face stays clouded as the Comox starts to drop. I don't know if he's worried about this plan, or if he's still upset about what happened at the lab. I sit back down, buckling my harness carefully around my wounded arm, and lean against the Comox's side as we descend.

The windows show a view of the flat, rocky desert and a two-storey concrete building that must be the safehouse. It's painted the same pale beige as the empty scrub-covered land around it. The Comox's rotors kick up a cloud of dust and feathers as we land – black feathers with cobalt tips, like the birds that were at the lab. They must have covered half the country by now. I've never seen a strain multiply this quickly.

The Comox jolts, touching down. A blast of hot, dry air billows into the cargo hold as the door swings open and the ramp unfolds. The sunlight is blinding after the dim view through the tinted windows, but my ocular tech adjusts smoothly, bringing the house into focus. It's a mess. The windows are boarded, junk strewn around it. A broken floor lamp leans against the rusted remains of a burned-out car, and one side of the house is smudged with black streaks from a pile of charred tyres.

'This place is trashed,' Leoben says, unbuckling his harness. He steps through the cargo hold to the ramp, lifting his hand to shield his eyes.

'That's how it's supposed to look,' Mato says. 'It's to discourage scavenging. The equipment is hidden in the basement.'

'There'd better be food,' Leoben says, jogging down the ramp. 'I checked the Comox's inventory. There's nothing on this thing, not even water. We're gonna need clothes too – we can't show up wearing Cartaxus gear.'

'There should be plenty of supplies inside the house,' Mato says, following him. His mask darkens as he steps into the sun, taking on a matte texture, as black and dull as charcoal. 'It looked like there was a market near the checkpoint too. We don't need much for this mission.'

'I need a *meal*,' Leoben says. 'There'd better be something in here.'

They head for the house. Cole stands quickly, one hand rubbing his ribs. He starts after them, but I catch his arm. This might be our last chance to talk in private about what happened at the lab – the scythe, the soldier. The ocean of memories I glimpsed during the decryption.

'Hold up,' I say. 'I need to talk to you.'

'Can it wait?' he asks, avoiding my eyes. 'I could do with some food.'

'It's important.' I unbuckle my harness, standing with my wounded arm held against my chest. Leoben glances back at us when he reaches the front door, catching my eye, then pushes through and urges Mato inside with him.

'I don't trust that guy,' Cole says, watching the door swing closed. 'I don't trust anyone in central command, but Mato seems especially dangerous.'

'Is that why you're being weird?'

'*I'm* being weird?' he asks, his gaze finally meeting mine. 'Cat, I just watched you kill someone with a weapon that horrified you when you saw Jun Bei use it. Why didn't you tell me you still had it?'

'Because I didn't know it was still in my arm.'

His brow furrows. 'Then how did you *use* it?'

I look down at the Comox's scuffed metal floor. 'That's what I wanted to talk to you about. When that soldier was hurting you, I saw more memories. There's more of my past inside me than I thought.'

Cole's breathing stills. 'How much more do you remember?'

I kick at one of the rivets in the floor. 'That's the thing. I felt like I remembered a *lot* more, but now it's gone again. I think Jun Bei's memories are still being suppressed by the implant. They felt like an ocean when I glimpsed them – like they were going to sweep me away.'

Cole's face pales. 'What do you mean, sweep you away?'

'I don't know,' I say, looking back to him. 'There's just so much of *her*, Cole, and there's not much of *me*. I don't know who I'd be with those memories inside me. I feel like I've already changed so much with the glimpses I've seen, and this is *much* more than that. There's a wall holding it back right now, but I don't know how long it's going to last. I felt it cracking when the soldier was hurting you, and that's when I ran the code. I didn't even know what I was doing.'

His expression softens. 'You didn't mean to kill him?'

'No,' I breathe. 'I don't know if that's better or worse. It just happened on instinct – but it was *her* instinct, Cole. It was an instinct from before Lachlan changed me. I'm acting more like her, and I don't know if I can stop it.'

Cole brings his hand to my cheek, his eyes tight with worry. 'You have to lock that down, Cat. This is your life. It's your mind. You have to take control of this before it takes control of you.'

Something in his tone makes me take a step back from him. 'Do you mean take control of the scythe, or of Jun Bei's memories?'

He glances at the house. 'I think both of them could be dangerous. I told you Lachlan used to erase our memories all the time when he was running experiments on us. That's why we stored the VR files and kept our scars. Erasing memories is easy – but *suppressing* them is hard. Why would Lachlan suppress Jun Bei's memories rather than erasing them?'

'I . . . I don't know,' I say, 'unless he wanted me to get them back someday.'

'Exactly,' Cole says. 'But why?'

'They started coming back during the decryption,' I murmur, 'but not *completely*. Dax said there was a part of the procedure that didn't finish back at Sunnyvale – a command to the implant that glitched because I'd cut my panel out.' I look up suddenly. 'What if Lachlan *meant* for me to get my memories back during the decryption? What if that's what the code that glitched was supposed to do?'

Cole's eyes go distant, but he doesn't answer. I stare at him, my mind spinning. Most of Lachlan's plan has been brilliant – he faked his death, escaped from Cartaxus, and convinced us to send his code into every panel on the planet. But one thing hasn't made sense – the fact that he thought I'd *join* him. After everything he's done and everything I saw, he actually thought I'd help him.

The thought is ridiculous. So ridiculous that it's hard to believe that it was Lachlan's plan at all . . .

And maybe it wasn't.

'He couldn't have predicted that I'd cut my panel out, and that the code would glitch,' I say. 'He thought I'd have Jun Bei's memories when he launched the attack on Sunnyvale.' The thought makes my breath still. With those memories back, I could be a different person. I don't know if I'd be *Jun Bei* or if I'd still be me, but there's a chance I would have seen that night through different eyes.

I wouldn't have been as afraid, that's for sure. I have a scythe in my arm. When I faced Lachlan in the lab, he said that nobody in Sunnyvale posed a threat to me during the attack, and he was right. I could have walked through that crowd unharmed, leaving a trail of bodies behind me.

I look up at Cole, my stomach tightening. 'Does he think I'll *join* him if I get Jun Bei's memories back?'

'I don't know,' Cole says, his hand rising to my arm, gripping me. 'What I do know is that you have a choice. If there's a wall between you and those memories, it might be there for a good reason.'

I close my eyes. I can't imagine *any* memory that would change my mind so completely that I'd choose to work with Lachlan. His plan for the vaccine goes against everything I believe in. Personal choice. Freedom. The right to make up our own minds about our own bodies.

But I can't imagine a memory that would have made me kill another person as easily as I killed that soldier, either.

I open my eyes. 'Would Jun Bei have killed that soldier?'

Cole looks away, dropping his hand from my arm. 'It doesn't matter what she would have done.'

'It matters to me. Please. Would she have killed him?'

He turns back, his eyes rising slowly to mine. It doesn't feel like he's really looking at me, though, as much as searching. Hunting for the answer to a question I don't know. 'Of course she would have killed him,' he says, his voice low. 'She was protective of all of us, but especially of me. Jun Bei would have killed every person in that room, but not for hurting me. She would have killed them just to take the Comox.'

CHAPTER 12

Cole steps down the Comox's ramp and into the sun, squinting as he scans the desert. I follow him out across the cracked earth, the sun blinding overhead. I don't know if it's because of what Cole said about Jun Bei, or because I know it's true, but even *thinking* about the ocean of memories locked inside me is suddenly enough to kick off a flare of panic.

I don't want to live with walls inside my mind, but I don't want to lose myself, either. I don't know who I'll become if Jun Bei's past sweeps back into me. I'm already chewing my nails like she used to, and I never did that at the cabin. Her past might be leaching through me in more ways than I can recognize. Would I even know if I was changing? I might be like the fabled frog in boiling water – not realizing that I'm becoming someone else until it's too late.

'I've never been to the desert before,' Cole says. 'The colours are amazing.'

I look around at the barren, rocky landscape, but all I see is shades of brown. My mind drifts back to his sketchbook, still hidden away in his backpack. 'Do you still want to be an artist someday?'

The question seems to take him by surprise. 'Maybe. I want to make sure we have a *someday* to look forward to first.' He pauses, one hand rubbing the bandage on his ribs, and stares into the distance. 'Someone's coming.'

I follow his eyes. There's a vehicle heading towards us, kicking up a cloud of dust. 'I'll get the others.'

'Wait . . .' he says. 'I think that's my *jeep*.'

I squint, staring at the vehicle. It's dark, enveloped by the dust, but now that I'm looking for it, I can make out the familiar lines of a hulking black Cartaxus jeep. It's scuffed, the solars slightly too small. Definitely Cole's. We had to replace the solars Marcus stole when he cut the healing tech core out of my panel, and Cole couldn't find a proper replacement. 'Maybe Cartaxus sent it down for us.'

'No,' Cole says, a smile spreading across his face.

The door to the house flies open behind us, and Leoben runs out, a rifle in his hands. He slows as he sees the jeep. 'You've gotta be kidding me.'

'What is it?' Mato asks, following him.

'We've got backup,' Leoben says, grinning.

The jeep races across the desert, its engine whining, bouncing indiscriminately over rocks and shrubs. It skirts a patch of boulders and then screeches to a stop in front of us, kicking up a wall of dust. I shy away, closing my eyes against the cloud of dirt and grit, and the jeep's driver-side door swings open.

A girl my age steps out. She's tall, dressed in black tactical trousers and a Cartaxus tank top, her long blonde hair pulled back in a high ponytail. Her skin is tanned, a dusting of freckles on her nose and cheeks, her piercing eyes the same ice-blue shade as Cole's. Lean muscles flex beneath geometric patterns tattooed on her arms, and a jolt of memories runs through me as she strides across the desert.

It's Anna Sinclair. Zarathustra Subject Two.

'Hey, assholes,' she says.

Cole runs for her, and she launches herself at him, laughing, wrapping her arms around his neck. He hugs her fiercely, his eyes clenched shut.

'Cole, your *hair*,' she says, pushing him away, messing with his tousled curls. 'You look ridiculous.'

'Love the tats,' Leoben says, running to join them. Anna throws her arms around him, and the three of them sway in a tight embrace.

Part of me bends towards them as they hold each other, but I can't bring myself to join them. I feel frozen, watching them. They look so natural, so right together. A family.

I'm part of that family too, but I feel like I'm standing outside the sphere of their shared past, and I can't see a way through.

Anna runs a hand over Leoben's buzz-cut. 'And you're blond? Who let you guys make these terrible decisions?' She turns, her eyes narrowing as they land on Mato.

The smile drops from her face as her gaze finally moves to me.

'Holy shit,' she breathes. Memories rush through me as her ice-blue eyes hold mine. I see her young and frightened, crouching in a white lab with a hairless kitten clutched in her arms. I see her sitting with Cole on a grey bunk bed, laughing with him.

I see her lying on the floor, a pool of dark blood spreading from a cut on her neck.

The memories drag a twisted mix of shock, affection and anger through me. Seeing Anna doesn't feel the same as it did when I first remembered my past with Cole or Leoben. There is no locked door opening inside me, no sudden surge of love. I can tell that Jun Bei *loved* Anna, but it's more complicated than that. There was a divide between them – something cold and vast and violent – and I can feel it unfolding between us too.

'You look just like him,' she says, stepping closer. A thread of tension tightens in my shoulders as she approaches. She's a foot taller than me, lean and long-limbed, walking with the same lethal grace as Cole and Leoben. She's a black-out agent too. That's what Cole said, and I can see it in her stance and her movements. She doesn't have any leylines that I can see, but a low hum of danger still seems to radiate from her. Even when I've fought Leoben, I haven't felt as small or weak as I do right now with her standing over me.

'Anna –' Cole starts.

'I know who she is,' Anna says, her eyes never leaving mine. 'It came up on a spec ops feed from central command last night. I didn't know whether to believe it or not.' She leans closer, but not to embrace me like Leoben did when he and I first saw each other after I learned the truth. There's no warmth in the look she gives me, just distant curiosity.

Curiosity, and a barely concealed undercurrent of threat.

'You even have his nose,' she says, 'his *jaw*. But it's really you, isn't it, Jun Bei?'

My throat tightens. 'It's . . . complicated. We still don't really understand what Lachlan did, but my DNA –'

'Yep,' Anna says, straightening, turning back to Cole. 'That's Jun Bei, all right.'

'My name is Catarina.'

She turns back to me swiftly, her eyes wide. 'You're keeping the name *he* gave you?'

Her voice is hard, and I feel a lick of anger rising in response. It felt natural to hug Lee when I remembered our past together, and it was natural to fall into Cole's arms, but it's completely different with Anna. There's something between us that I don't understand. The only thing that feels natural is to cross my arms and return the glare she's giving me.

'I'll call myself what I want. I'm not the same person I was before.'

She cocks an eyebrow. 'You sure *sound* like the same person.'

'Whoa,' Leoben says, walking to my side, slinging his arm round my shoulders. 'You can call her squid. She likes that.'

'Dammit, Lee,' I say, but he grins at me and it somehow eases the tension in the air.

'She's telling the truth, Anna,' Leoben says. 'She's not the same. But none of us are really the same people we were back then, right?'

Anna looks between the three of us, then rolls her shoulders. 'Fine, whatever. Let's talk about this mission.'

'Yes, let's,' Mato says, stepping into the circle of conversation. He's been standing silently, watching us, a frustrated look on his face. 'Why are you here, Anna?'

Anna gestures to the jeep. 'This thing returned itself to my base last night. I looked up your mission specs and figured I'd come down and save your asses. I told my commander that any mission *you* were running was sure to be a shitshow, and you could use all the help you could get.'

'Do you two know each other?' Leoben asks, looking between Anna and Mato. 'Anna isn't usually this mean to strangers.'

'We spent five months stationed in Alaska together,' Mato says, his voice hard. 'Small base, tight quarters.'

Leoben nods. 'That'll do it.'

'We learned a lot about each other, though,' Anna says, crossing her arms, 'including the fact that Mato here has a price on his head if he sets foot inside Entropia. This whole mission is screwed.'

I turn to Mato. 'Is that true?'

He pushes a hand back through his dark hair, glaring at Anna, but he doesn't reply.

'That's just great,' Leoben says. 'Why the hell is there a price on your head?'

Mato blows out a breath, looking out at the desert. 'Because I started a resistance group here. We tried to overthrow Regina's rule, but we failed.'

I search Mato's face. He can't be more than nineteen now, but it sounds like this was years ago. 'How old were you?'

'Sixteen,' he says, 'but age doesn't mean the same thing in Entropia as it does in the rest of the world. Regina did some of her best work in her teens. You have to understand – Entropia's only currency is code. Regina's fortune is considerable, and that's given her enough power to rule for decades, but she hasn't been on the forefront of some of gentech's latest advancements. Her people were starting to question her, and I managed to convince some of them that I had enough potential to take her place.'

Anna snorts. 'Not enough of them, clearly. You had to run away to Cartaxus.'

'Thankfully I did,' Mato snaps, 'otherwise we wouldn't have a chance of finding Lachlan. It could take weeks to search that city. We're going to need help, and I'm the only person who can get it for us.'

Cole shakes his head. 'I'm OK with talking to Regina, but not if there's a price on your head.'

'I have a plan, trust me,' Mato says, frustrated. 'I know how to handle myself here.'

Anna rolls her eyes. 'You know how to handle yourself? You couldn't fight your way out of a bag. This mission is bullshit. You're going to get thrown into a cell –'

'Entropia doesn't have cells,' Mato says. 'You don't know what you're talking about, Anna. If we're caught, I'll be taken to Regina, which is the only way we're going to reach her. Once I'm taken to her, I'll be able to talk to her. Otherwise, we can stand around outside this city arguing for the next three days, and Brink will kill us all.'

Anna frowns. 'You *want* to get captured? That's your plan?'

'*Millions* of lives are at stake right now,' Mato says. 'I know you don't think much of me, Anna, but there's a reason that I'm in central command and you're a member of the military division that's sworn to follow our orders. The three of you can discuss tactics as much as you want, but the mission is going ahead. I'm going to find some supplies. We'll leave when I'm done.'

He turns and strides towards the house. Anna watches him leave, her hand clenched into a fist at her side. She lets out a groan when the front door swings shut behind him. 'I hate that guy,' she says. 'Does he still do the pen-twirling thing?'

'Oh yeah,' Leoben says. 'He's pretty good at it.'

Cole's eyes are distant. 'He's right,' he says. 'This plan is probably the best way to find Lachlan. It's risky, but I don't know if there are any safer options. We should load up the jeep.'

'On it,' Leoben says, his arm still round my shoulders. 'We'll scope out the supplies.'

'OK,' Cole says. 'Anna and I need to catch up.'

Leoben looks between them for a moment, but nods. 'Yeah, sure. Come on, squid. Let's get you some food.'

I let Leoben guide me through the front door into a messy hallway with dirt and sand tracked through it. The house looks as bad inside as it does outside, but that's probably the point. Anyone breaking in will see a dump, and they'll leave it alone.

Leoben heads for a hidden trapdoor set into the floor at the back of the house that reveals a staircase leading to a dimly lit basement. I follow him down into a concrete hallway with a massive storage room branching off it, lined with shelves holding clothes, blankets and toiletries. I look around for Mato, but he's nowhere in sight.

'You hungry?' Leoben asks.

I look down at the bandage on my wounded arm. I should eat to give my healing tech more energy to run, but the thought of food right now makes my stomach turn. 'No,' I say. 'Let's get some clothes.'

'Good call.' He heads towards the giant storage room. 'Can't believe Anna's here.'

'Yeah,' I say, following him into the storage room, weaving past piles of survival equipment, tyres and spare Comox parts. There's a table near the back of the room stacked with clothes. 'She doesn't seem to like me.'

'Oh, Anna doesn't like anyone except Cole,' Leoben says, reaching the table. It's piled with folded trousers and shirts, most of which are in the Cartaxus palette of black and grey, but some are in lurid colours, printed with patterns and animals. 'They're siblings. You remember that, right?'

I look up. 'Really? What, like genetically?'

'Yeah,' Leoben says, picking up shirts, tossing them on the floor behind him. 'They share an egg donor. Lachlan said it was a fluke – they made thousands of us with a whole bunch of donors, and we were the only five that survived.'

'That seems like something I should remember.'

'Well, you were the one who figured it out. You scrounged together a genkit from parts in the basement and used to run tests on us. I think you regretted telling them, though – you used to get jealous about how close they were. Cole always sided with Anna in every fight, and you and Anna used to *seriously* fight.'

'Apparently not much has changed there,' I mutter.

Leoben picks up a green shirt with a dinosaur on it, tugging it on over his tank top. 'She's just going to take a while to come around.'

'Do the rest of us know who our family is?' I ask. 'Genetically, I mean?'

Leoben tugs off the shirt and tries on another – pink with a walrus on it. 'Actually, I do. I'm a clone of a French guy who was immune to a bunch of viruses. He's dead now, and I guess Cartaxus couldn't resist making a copy of him. There might even be a few of us.'

'Wow,' I say. I'm not surprised that Cartaxus created a clone of someone its scientists found interesting, but it's illegal to use someone else's genes to make a child for exactly that reason.

Back in gentech's early days there were horror stories of a black market for embryonic clones, or pairings of any two people that buyers were willing to pay for. I don't know if the stories were true or just anti-gentech propaganda, but Cartaxus clearly had no issues with breaking those laws.

'Dax found out for me,' he says, pausing, his eyes going distant.

'I'm sorry I didn't try to bring him with us,' I say.

He shakes his head absently. 'No, he's better off there. They'll be able to keep him comfortable until we fix the vaccine. I just can't get over the fact that I'm the only person on this planet who's immune, and I can't do anything to help him.' He looks up at me. 'You're going to chew your hand off at that rate.'

I look down, dropping my hand. My thumbnail is bitten to the quick, a spot of blood welling in the raw skin around it.

'You could do with some sleep, huh?' Leoben asks, pulling off the walrus shirt. 'What was the last full meal you ate?'

I shrug. 'I've been busy. There's a lot going on.'

'Yeah, a lot going on.' He rolls his eyes. 'I know you're different from Jun Bei, but you're still a lot like her. Every time things got rough, she'd chew her nails down and go into problem-solving mode, throwing herself into some coding puzzle like the world depended on her solving it.'

'The world *does* depend on us solving this.'

'That's not the point. What I'm saying is if you don't take care of yourself, you're gonna break like she used to. Only, you're probably not going to hurt one of us when you do it.'

My hands tighten on one of the shirts. 'She hurt you?'

He looks up. 'We all hurt one another. Jun Bei protected all of us, and she took the brunt of Lachlan's tests as often as she could, but sometimes she'd snap. She never really hurt me, but she was vicious with Anna, and I even saw her turn on Cole a few times.'

My breath catches at the thought of hurting Cole. Leoben reaches out to take my hand, turning it so that my palm is facing up. The half-moon cuts from my fingernails have healed to faint pink lines, but there's still dried blood in the creases of my hand. 'I know you're worried about being like her,' he says, 'but this isn't something she would do. *You* hurt *yourself* when you're drowning. I get it. Jun Bei used pain too, but she always sent it out to someone else.'

He closes my fingers over my palm, covering my hand with his. 'I don't blame you for trying to shut that out. I guess I've wanted to be someone else too. Maybe that's why I've had a hard time dealing with this. I should be trying to make this easier on you, not harder.'

He slides his hands away, and I miss the warmth of his touch as soon as it's gone. 'Does that mean you're going to start calling me Cat?' I ask.

His lips curl. 'Not a chance in hell.'

I roll my eyes, pushing away from the table of T-shirts. 'I think I'm hungry after all.'

'Rations are down the hall, to the left. I recommend the risotto.'

I step to the door, then pause. 'Thanks, Lee.'

He gives me a wink, grabbing another armful of shirts. 'Anytime, squid.'

I head back down the hallway towards a set of double doors with what looks like an industrial kitchen beyond them. The rooms on either side of the hallway hold weapons, survival gear, and a cabinet full of nanosolution vials. One door is open to a dim walk-in closet holding what looks like technical gear – a stack of tablets, screens, and piles of twisted charging cables.

I pause, ducking inside. There might be a genkit here. Now that my wireless chip is running properly, I can use a smaller, sleeker machine than I'm used to, but I can't see any on the shelves. I reach behind me with my good hand for the light switch, flicking it on, and a set of screens set into the wall blinks to life.

It's security footage. I can see the upper levels of the house on one screen, the image cycling between multiple cameras. The Comox is on another screen, the empty desert stretching behind it. A third screen shows the basement, and a fourth shows the jeep. Cole and Anna are standing beside it, talking. My audio tech crackles, connecting to the feed automatically, patching the sound through to me.

'She's struggling,' Cole says. 'It's a lot to take in.'

I freeze, staring at them. They have to be talking about me. I'm out of their audio range – they have no reason to think that anyone can hear them. I shouldn't be eavesdropping on them like this. I take a step back, but Anna throws her head back, groaning, and I pause.

'You're not going soft on me, are you?' she asks. 'Jesus, Cole. You're hopeless around her.'

'I'm fine,' he says. 'My head is clear.'

'Better be, soldier. There's a lot at stake.'

'I know,' Cole replies, his voice low. 'Trust me, I haven't forgotten. I have her under control.'

CHAPTER 13

I stare at the security feed, panic wheeling through me. Anna is climbing into the jeep now, and Cole is heading for the house. I stumble back into the shelves, sending a plastic box clattering to the floor, spilling memory chips across the concrete.

'Shit, shit,' I whisper, flicking off the lights, killing the feed. I leave the chips scattered on the floor and push out of the room, slamming the door shut behind me. My heart pounds against my ribs, a hot-and-cold flush of horror spreading through me.

I haven't forgotten. I have her under control.

The words feel like a knife twisting, cutting into me. A cry escapes my lips before I can clamp my hand over my mouth, and I close my eyes, forcing myself to breathe, to think it through. There has to be an explanation that doesn't involve Cole *lying* to me. He's worried about us going into the city. He's worried about Lachlan. He's a trained bodyguard, and we're running headfirst into what *definitely* feels like a trap. Mato says he has a plan, but Lachlan has always been two steps ahead of us.

But none of that explains why Cole and Anna would be talking about me like that.

'Hey, squid.'

I spin round, my panic spiking. Leoben is behind me, carrying the shirts and a box of paper towels. 'Find the food?'

I just stare at him, stunned, until his question hangs awkwardly in the air.

'I-I'm not hungry,' I manage to stammer.

'Are you OK?' He shifts the box to his hip, peering at me, then looks up suddenly. 'Hey, Cole.'

I turn round, my heart lurching. Cole steps into the hallway, his skin flushed from the sun, a bandage plastered to the rippled muscles of his left shoulder. There's no sign that he and Anna were just talking about me – no guilt, no nervousness in his face. There's even a softness in his eyes as he sees me.

'Looks like you guys have been working hard on the supplies,' he says, eyeing the shirts and the single box of paper towels on Leoben's hip. 'We've cleared out the jeep. Ready to start loading when you are.'

I swallow, driving my fingernails into the palm of my good hand, desperate for a scrap of self-control. Cole seems so casual, but on the footage I saw just a minute ago, he was tense and cold. There's definitely something going on, and even with the pain in my hand blossoming through me, dragging my focus into a point, I can't find the words to ask him what it is.

I can't think of *anything* to say. For the first time since Cole arrived at the cabin, I can see him as everyone else must – not as my friend or my soulmate, but as the Cartaxus weapon. His leylines suddenly seem like shafts of darkness etched into his skin. He's probably listening to my heart rate. He probably knows I'm freaking out. He's a black-out agent, and somewhere along the way I let myself forget that. His eyes narrow, lingering on my face, and a surge of fear rises through me.

Do I need to be *afraid* of him?

That question would have seemed ridiculous if I had asked it just yesterday, but suddenly I can sense the threat he poses. His strength. His training. The lethal grace in his movements. His brow creases, a flicker of suspicion in his eyes as he looks between me and Leoben, and I know that I have to lie. He can't find out that I overheard him. Whatever he was talking to Anna about, I'm not prepared to defend myself against him if it comes to that.

'I'm fine,' I say. 'I was looking for the food.'

Leoben gives me a puzzled look, but he doesn't say anything. His eyes lift to the hallway, over my shoulder, and I turn, following his gaze. Mato is striding towards us, wearing a black jacket with sequins sewn into the shoulders like epaulettes, a grey T-shirt and ripped black jeans. His dark hair is back in a braid, and he's carrying a metal briefcase. The differences between what he was wearing at Cartaxus and now are slight, but they somehow radically change his image. He looks like a *hacker*, not a coder.

'Where did you find those clothes?' Leoben asks.

Mato nods over his shoulder. 'Printer in the back.'

'Oh,' Leoben says. 'Smart.'

Mato looks between the three of us. 'I need to have a word with Catarina, and then we'll leave.'

Leoben hands the box of paper towels he's carrying to Cole, but keeps the shirts. 'Take that up, will you? I'll get us some proper clothes. You sure you're OK, squid?'

'Yeah, I'm fine,' I mumble. 'Get me something in blue.'

Leoben nods, still worried, but he backs away. 'Sure thing. I'll be right down the hall.'

Cole looks between Mato and me, shifting the box in his hands. I can tell he doesn't want to leave me alone with Mato, and the irony almost makes me laugh. I would never have dreamed that I'd prefer to be alone with a member of Cartaxus's central command than with him.

But I never dreamed that I'd hear him say he had me under his *control*.

'I'll see you in a minute,' I say. 'I want to talk to Mato too.'

Cole looks between us again, the furrow in his brow deepening, then turns and strides back down the hallway, his boots creaking up the stairs. I draw in a shaking breath as he leaves.

Mato glances curiously after Cole, but if he noticed the tension between us, he doesn't say anything. 'Let's talk in here,' he says, heading for an open door that leads into a storage room lined with tents, sleeping bags and survival gear. There's an empty table in the centre of the room with a few chairs around it. Mato sets the metal briefcase down and pulls out a chair for me. I fall into it, numb, and he sits down beside me, pressing his hands to the briefcase, watching me patiently.

'How is your arm?' he asks. The black glass of his coding mask lightens slowly until it's almost clear. His left eye fades into focus, his brow arched beneath the glass. Rows of small black ports are lined across his forehead where the wires cut through his skull.

I look down at my arm, surprised. I'd forgotten about my panel, and the mention of it brings back a rush of pain. 'It's sore.'

He nods, then watches me for an uncomfortably long time, searching my face. 'Do you remember me?' he asks.

I open my mouth, but I don't know what to say. Seeing clearly through Mato's mask feels suddenly intimate somehow, like he's baring a piece of himself to me. 'I . . . I do,' I say. 'Nothing specific. I recognized you, and I know that she knew you, but that's all.'

'*She.*' He says the word slowly, as though listening to how it sounds. He leans back in his chair. 'Yes, she and I made contact when I was new at Cartaxus. I was reading through Lachlan's work and noticed that she co-wrote some of his files. I knew she wasn't in possession of an ordinary mind, so I tracked her down and begged her to code with me. We worked together on a dozen separate projects.'

I frown, curiosity bleeding through the haze of my shock about Cole. 'But she was at the Zarathustra lab. She was a prisoner. How did she talk to you?'

He waves a hand. 'She'd been able to get online for years. We met in VR sometimes, but we mostly just shared code. I didn't know where she really was – or even that she was a prisoner – until it was too late.'

I lean forward. 'Did you speak to her after she escaped?'

'She never wrote to me, no. How much do you remember?'

I look down, running my fingertips over the fresh bloody half-moons etched into my palm. 'Not much. It's all scattered, but those six months after she escaped are just . . . *gone*, and that's the time I need to remember most. That's when Lachlan changed me – when he started putting this whole plan into place. I feel like if I could just figure out what he did, and *why*, then we'd have a chance of finding him.'

'Well,' Mato says, flicking the clasps on the metal briefcase, 'there's a chance this will help.'

The briefcase opens to a padded storage compartment holding a sheath of black glass. It looks like Mato's mask, but in a smooth cylinder instead. A cuff. Designed to slide over a forearm, hooking into a panel. I've seen a few of them before, but never one like this.

'This is mine,' Mato says. 'I upgraded to a mask a long time ago, but I still carry it as a backup. It isn't the right size for you, but it should shape itself to fit.'

I lean forward, and the wires in my arm squirm beneath my skin, dragging a gasp of pain from me. Mato lifts the cuff as though it might shatter in his grip and opens it along an invisible seam running the length of it. It falls open, revealing rows of silver ports embedded in the black glass. I look down at my arm, peeling back the bandage to check the rows of raised, inflamed wounds dotted across my skin. They match the ports in the cuff perfectly.

'As soon as I saw those wires erupt, I knew they were for this cuff,' Mato says, sitting it on the table. 'The pattern is unique to this particular model. Jun Bei always said that she wanted one. I don't know why the wires emerged like that during the hack on the implant, but I'm glad they did. This cuff will be useful when we go into Entropia.'

I stare at the sheath of black glass, the barest flickers of memory brushing against my senses. Glass on my skin. Tech wired straight through my flesh. 'What does it do?'

Mato holds the cuff out to me. 'See for yourself.'

The wires in my wounded arm twitch feverishly. I lift away the rest of the bandage and take the cuff carefully. It's slightly too long for my forearm, but one end is tilted and flared, like it could fit over the back of my hand. I turn the glass, laying it open on the table, and hesitate. It's probably not a *great* idea to attach a piece of tech to my body from someone I've just met, but I want to know what the hell is happening to my panel, and this cuff might hold the answer. I draw in a breath and press my forearm into the curved black glass.

The reaction is immediate. The wires beneath my newly mended skin burst back through it, wrenching a cry of pain from me. The cuff snaps closed around my arm on its own, its surface shrinking, pressing up against my skin. Cracks form along my wrist, creating a segmented join between the stiff sections over my forearm and my hand. The pain from the wires crescendos before crumbling into cool, sweet numbness.

My vision flickers.

The interface of my wireless chip slides across my field of view, only now it looks different. Instead of seeing a list of wireless connections, I'm seeing them highlighted as I turn my head. A *pulse* ripples out from the cuff, stretching into the distance, sketching a faint glow around Mato's mask, another around his panel, as well as the controls of an air-conditioning unit built into the wall. I look around, seeing more points of light dancing from sources outside my wireless chip's usual range – the faint outline of cameras in other rooms, a bright light in the distance where the jeep is parked.

'It's a wireless extender,' I say. It makes sense that Jun Bei would want this cuff. She perfected the art of hacking into every network and panel she could get close to. With this cuff, she could stretch even further. I turn my head, seeing the jeep, the Comox, a wireless streetlight in the distance.

The furthest connection in my vision looks like it's a *mile* away.

'It *has* a wireless extender,' Mato says. 'But that's not all it does.'

I lift my arm, feeling the glass stretch on my skin. A menu flashes into my vision – not my panel's interface, but something new, showing me the apps installed in my arm, filtering the mountain of Jun Bei's code into folders and databases. The menu spins across my vision, offering scans on my DNA, suggesting upgrades to some of my apps. I focus on an icon with a loop of wire on it, and a silver wire slithers from the side of the cuff, coiling like a snake.

It's a needle-tipped reader wire.

'Holy shit!' I say. 'This is a *genkit* too?'

Mato grins. 'It should help you control the implant as well. Its software is more sophisticated than anything you can run inside your body.'

'This . . . this is amazing.' I curl the fingers of my panel hand into a fist. There's no pain from the wires any more – just the cool press of the glass against my skin. Something about it feels familiar, and impossibly *right*. It isn't like I'm wearing a piece of tech – it's like the cuff is a part of my body that I was born without.

'Jun Bei *must* have worn one,' I say. 'This feels so natural.'

Mato nods. 'I agree, but Cartaxus's records don't show her using one in the lab. It would have been after she left.'

'That six months,' I mutter, tracing my fingers across the seams in the glass over my wrist. 'They're just . . . gone.'

Mato flips the briefcase shut. 'It sounds like you were wiped.'

I look up. 'Wiped?'

He nods. 'Depending on how ERO-86 is used, it can either be a neural suppressant, or it can erase memories completely. Cartaxus does it to black-out soldiers sometimes. It works backwards, destroying the most recently created neurons in your brain. If you run it for a few minutes, you can erase weeks. Run it for longer, and you'll take away years. The fact that you can't remember anything for six months tells me that's probably what happened.'

I sit back in my chair. He's right – it does seem like those months were wiped. But why not more, or why not just *suppress* those months like the rest of my memories? And why the hell would Lachlan ever give me this cuff? If Jun Bei was his prisoner during those six months, he would have wanted to keep her under control.

So why would he give her a cuff that made her a better *hacker*?

'Those memories are likely gone,' Mato says, 'but if you've worn a cuff like this before, then it probably wasn't far from here. These cuffs can't be bought with money – only with code, and it happens that the person who designed them is the same person who designed the implant, and my mask.'

'Regina,' I breathe.

He nods. 'If you're looking for answers, she might have them.'

I hold his eyes, the wireless feed from the cuff buzzing in my senses. He's given me more clarity in one conversation than I've felt all week. And he's given me a *genkit*. I open my mouth to thank him, but footsteps sound in the hallway, and Cole pushes into the room. His face softens as he sees me, but I can't return his smile. I still don't know how to process what I overheard between him and Anna.

'The jeep is stocked,' he says, but stops abruptly when he sees the cuff on my arm. 'What's that?'

'A cuff,' I say. 'It's a genkit. That's what the wires that came out of my arm were for. I think Jun Bei wore one like this after she left the lab.'

Cole stares at the sheath of black glass wrapped around my arm. 'What do you need that for?'

'Are you kidding me?' I ask. 'I'm useless without a genkit. I can't fight unless I'm able to code.'

'Can't we find you one like the model you used to have?' Cole asks.

'I *like* this one,' I say, frustrated. 'It's just a cuff.'

He looks between me and Mato. 'Fine. It's not my arm. If you're both ready, then we can leave.'

He turns away and heads back down the hallway. I run my fingers over the cuff's black glass, turning my arm to look at it. I don't know why Cole was so upset to see it. This thing might be the best weapon we could have. I still have the scythe in my arm, and now I can reach a *mile* with it. It's not that I want to hurt anyone, but there's some comfort in knowing I can defend myself.

Apparently Cole doesn't see it that way.

'He's afraid of you,' Mato says, watching Cole leave. His mask has darkened to black again.

I drop my fingers from the smooth, warm glass. 'Why do you say that?'

'I saw it in the lab when you killed that soldier. He was frightened by what you could do. They were all afraid of you, even Brink.'

'And you?'

Mato shakes his head. 'No, I wasn't afraid. I know you don't remember, but you've been my coding partner for years. All I saw in that moment was something impossible becoming real. I felt like I was seeing you for the first time.'

My eyes lift slowly to his, something trembling inside me, and a white alert from the cuff blinks at the top of my vision. A background scan. Something detected in the distance. I lift my eyes and send a pulse out, the command already instinctive and natural, and outlines glow around me – cameras, microphones, a halo of open connections.

'What is it?' Mato asks.

I narrow my eyes, staring up at three glowing points of light superimposed on the ceiling above me. They're faint, small. Far above us, in the sky.

'Drones,' I say, standing from the table. 'Someone's found us.'

CHAPTER 14

Mato rises from his chair, a spot of light blinking on the corner of his mask. 'I see them too.'

I stare up at the glowing specks of light, urging my cuff to scan their wireless signals. There are three drones hovering far above us, but I can't tell what model they are or if they're armed. There's no clue to who sent them – Cartaxus, Entropia, maybe even Lachlan. The cuff offers me connection details in case I want to try to hack them, but I have no idea how to do that.

I've never even *thought* about being able to hack a drone while it's in flight.

'We have to warn the others,' I say. 'They're exposed.' I push away from the table and back into the hallway. The feeling of the cuff stretching on my skin is strangely reassuring. It has the same calming weight that Lachlan's rifle did when I slept with it at my side in the cabin. A weapon, loaded and ready. I can't help but wonder if that's how Jun Bei felt about it when she wore it.

I stride past the storeroom and jog up the sand-covered stairs that lead to the house's main level, sending another pulse out from the cuff to keep track of the drones. They haven't moved. They're locked in a triangle above the safehouse, circling slowly. Definitely watching us.

'This has to be Entropia,' Mato says, following me up the stairs. 'It looks like a scouting fleet. We *want* to be discovered and taken to Regina. This is all going to plan. They'll scan us and go back, and then they'll send someone out to look for us.'

'Maybe,' I say, reaching the house's main floor. 'I still don't like the others being out there.' My boots crunch over the grit blown into the hallway from outside. I reach the door and pause, looking out. Cole and Leoben are standing at the back of the jeep, and Anna is sitting on the bonnet, her face tipped back to the sun. None of them seem to notice the drones hovering silently above us. For a moment I don't understand how I could possibly notice them before three black-out agents did, but then I remember the cuff on my arm.

My wireless scanner must be even better than theirs.

'Guys,' I call out, standing in the hallway. I take a single step closer to the door, and one of the points of light from the drones streaks in a blur across my vision. Something whistles through the air from it and *smacks* into my hand. I stumble back wildly, clutching my arm to my chest, letting out a cry. Mato grabs me to pull me back into the house, his eyes flying wide, but another whistle cuts the air, and something hits his arm.

He shouts in pain, and we fall into the hallway together, landing in a heap on the floor. Whatever hit me doesn't hurt as much as *sting*, which is somehow even worse. There's a lump forming on my hand, a tiny puncture wound between my thumb and forefinger. I scramble back on the floor, trying to get into cover. Whatever we were just shot with, it wasn't designed to injure us.

It was designed to be *implanted* into us.

Cole's head snaps up, his eyes flashing to black. He looks around, wrenching open the jeep's rear doors for his rifle. I try to shout to him to get inside . . .

But the moment I open my mouth, the desert disappears.

I stare around, blinking, scrambling to my feet. Mato and I aren't in the safehouse any more. We're in a tall, circular room with no windows, its concrete walls covered in hanging plants and hundreds of metal cages holding animals – birds, snakes and lizards, their cries filling the air.

'What the *hell*?' I spit, my heart pounding. This feels like the flashes of memory that have been hitting me, only Mato is here.

'It's OK,' he says, standing, brushing himself off. A strand of his dark hair has slipped from his braid, falling across his mask. 'We're still in the desert. This is a VR simulation. Regina wants to talk to us.'

I look around, still gasping for air, my hand held to my chest. I reach an arm out to where the wall in the safehouse's hallway should be, and my hand hits a hard, invisible surface. I can feel grit under my boots, even though the floor beneath me looks like slick, glossy concrete. Everything looks perfectly real, the rendering smooth as I move forward, scanning the walls.

It's like I've just stepped through a portal and into a completely different place.

'Where are we?' I breathe, rubbing my hand where I was shot. The stinging has faded, but the lump between my thumb and forefinger is still swelling.

'This is Regina's lab,' Mato says, straightening his jacket. It isn't the one with the sequins sewn into the shoulders that he was wearing just a minute ago, though – this is a plain black jacket. I look down, scanning my body. I'm dressed in grey Cartaxus trousers and a fresh black tank top. The skin on my arms is smooth and clean, my hair hanging in neat waves, sliding over my shoulders.

This isn't a *recording* of me – there are no VR cameras around us in the safehouse to send our images to Regina. This is an *avatar* being generated by the panel in my arm, based on whatever information it can find about how I look. I turn, searching for a reflective surface, suddenly frightened that Jun Bei's features might be stored in the avatar from when she used this panel – but my own face blinks back at me from the glass door of a cabinet.

The sight of my features, and of Lachlan's face in them, is more comforting than I expected.

I turn back, scanning the room. It's vast, the cries of the animals echoing from the curved walls. There must be a hundred different types of animals here, including dozens of strains of pigeons. This is definitely a *lab*, but it's not like any I've seen before. Black counters curve round the outside of the room in a ring, complete with shelves of glassware and sample canisters. The floor is sloped slightly towards a dark hole cut into the centre of the room, like a massive drain. There's a steel platform hanging over it, suspended by a chain. It looks like the platform is designed to be lowered down through the hole to whatever's beneath us. One side of the room opens up to a wide hallway set up like a farm, with rows of raised garden beds dripping with water that flows in rivulets across the concrete, disappearing into the drain.

It's wild, bursting with life and colour, nothing like the sterile, cluttered labs that I'm used to. Across the room from us, a small shrine is set up beneath an arch of flowering vines, displaying red candles, gilded photographs and a bowl of fruit. There's a massive coding terminal in the wall that looks like it's a Cartaxus model, linked to a humming genkit and four cylindrical glass tanks filled with bubbling clear liquid.

The tanks are holding four human bodies.

'Holy *shit*,' I say, staring at the tanks. The bodies have mottled skin, their eyes open and unseeing. They look like teenagers – hairless and floating, dressed in grey pressure suits. 'Why does she have *bodies*?'

'They're not bodies,' a soft voice says from beside us. 'They're alive, and I like to think they're listening, so I'd prefer it if you'd speak kindly about them.'

I turn, stepping back as a woman walks into the room from the hallway, flanked by two guards. I've never seen her before, not even a photograph, but I have no doubt that it's Regina. Her skin is covered with glossy scales coloured in shades of forest green and black, with a pattern like an overturned crown across her face. Her eyes are as black as the scaled skin around them, her cheekbones ridged and angled, a silky emerald dress hanging from her shoulders, rippling where it pools around her feet. There are tiny dots of cobalt light studded between her scales like a constellation of stars twinkling across her skin. She's short – even shorter than me – with long, blue-black hair tumbling over her shoulders, topped with a crystal tiara. A white snake is looped around her neck, a raven perched on her shoulder.

She is completely and utterly magnificent.

Some of the hackers I met at the Skies base at Sunnyvale were seriously modified, but none of them compare to Regina. They all looked like *people* who were running apps, but she looks like she transformed herself into a brand-new species. Every alteration she's made is seamless and perfect – her scales are smaller around the edges of her eyes and mouth in a natural-looking pattern that must have taken months to code. The two guards flanking her stop by the entrance of the room as she walks in. They're wearing grey uniforms, but they don't look anything like Cartaxus's soldiers. One is a woman, covered in pale, tufted fur, with claws instead of fingernails, and the other is a man wearing a coding mask similar to Mato's, except it covers his entire forehead and both his eyes.

'Somata,' Regina purrs, walking over to us, her movements eerily smooth and graceful. 'It's so wonderful to see you again. But I hope you haven't forgotten that you're a wanted man in this city.'

Mato's face darkens. 'What did you shoot us with, Regina?'

'Nothing that will hurt you as long as you behave.' She walks to one of the lab counters and lifts the snake from her shoulders, easing it into one of the cages, cooing at it. 'The pellets are called *weevils*. Tiny things, but very effective. They're geographically activated – if you try to come into the city without permission, they'll kill you with a lethal dose of neurotoxin.' She turns, lifting the raven from her shoulder, balancing it on her wrist. 'I wouldn't try to remove them, either. It might be the last thing you ever do. As long as the weevils stay dark, you'll be fine, but if they light up, you'd better go back the way you came.'

‘We’re here to ask for your help,’ Mato says.

‘Always straight to the point with you, Somata,’ Regina scolds. ‘That isn’t how deals are made, my dear. And if you want to come into my city, then we may be able to make a deal. We’ll see.’ Her black eyes drift to me. ‘I haven’t even met Catarina. Is that the name you prefer?’

I exchange a glance with Mato. ‘That’s my name.’

‘I know who you are,’ she says, stroking the raven’s beak with one scaled finger. ‘I know more about you than you think. The Zarathustra Initiative and Lachlan’s work on you and the others is one of the cruellest things I’ve heard of – using people for experiments like that.’

I glance at the bodies in the tanks, and she follows my eyes.

‘Oh, they aren’t experiments,’ she says. ‘I *saved* them. Cartaxus created them, but the experiment went awry and these poor dears were born without proper brains. They can think a little – reflexes mostly, and they sometimes move to music, but they can’t do much on their own.’

A shiver creeps down my spine as I watch the bodies in the tanks. One of them twitches, its leg kicking out, and I look away, shuddering. I don’t know what kind of existence it would be to live like that – trapped in a glass prison, unable to move – but maybe it wouldn’t be so bad if you didn’t know any better.

Regina scratches the raven’s neck, staring absently at the bodies. ‘I find them to be a good reminder of why I founded this city. Cartaxus’s scientists love to experiment on other people, but they don’t like it when people experiment on themselves. Entropia’s philosophy is the exact opposite. Cartaxus wanted to use these children for experiments, so I took them with me when I left.’

'Wait, you worked for *Cartaxus*?' I ask.

Regina looks between me and Mato. 'Yes, of course. Somata didn't tell you? I joined straight out of college and worked with Lachlan for years.'

I look at Mato. He didn't mention anything about Regina *working* with Lachlan. If she's allied with him, then this plan is ruined. We've already lost. There are drones hovering above us and a lethal weapon buried in my hand.

We might have already walked into the trap I've been frightened of.

Regina takes in my shock, waving one hand dismissively. 'Oh, don't worry, child. I'm not part of what he's doing now. Lachlan and I fell out back at Cartaxus and haven't spoken properly in a long time.' She leans back against the lab counter, tossing the hair from her shoulder, shifting the raven back to it. It flaps its dark wings as it settles into place, fixing Mato and me with its small black eyes. 'I take it you're not here for the birds?' she asks.

Mato tilts his head. 'Birds?'

She beams. 'Haven't you heard? Homecoming's tonight. There should be a few million pigeons coming in – the lovely ones with the glowing feathers. We're holding a party to watch them. Everyone's dressing up, everything's *glowing*. They're the prettiest flock we've ever had, and we didn't even design them. They evolved the luminescent gene all on their own. Isn't nature marvellous?'

I exchange a glance with Mato, confused. He said Regina was out of touch, but I didn't think she'd be like this. She clearly knows something about Lachlan's plan, and surely she's heard about the new outbreak – but she's talking about planning a party for the *pigeons*.

‘We’re here because of the vaccine,’ Mato says. ‘We’re looking for Lachlan. It’s important.’

‘Then you should have called,’ she says. ‘It’s been years. I haven’t heard a word from you.’

‘You *banished* me,’ Mato says.

She turns to him. ‘You still could have called. I didn’t know if you were alive or dead.’

Mato sighs. ‘You knew I was alive, Regina.’

I look between the two of them, confused. They’re talking to each other like a mother and a child. ‘Are you two related?’

Regina’s head snaps to me, her eyebrows rising. ‘No. But I have known Mato since he was born. His parents worked with me, here in Entropia. They’re in a bunker now. I’m sure he calls *them*.’

Mato tilts his head back, closing his eyes in frustration. ‘Banished upon pain of death. Those were your words.’

‘Oh, you had to leave,’ Regina says, ‘and not just because of your little coup. There’s a reason we don’t allow children at Entropia, and I shouldn’t have made an exception for you. This city is a place of radical ideas, but its citizens have all chosen to embrace them. You didn’t get that choice, and it was a mistake to take it from you.’ She looks him up and down appraisingly. ‘It was important for you to leave and experience another culture.’

Mato scrapes a hand over his face. ‘Yes, yes, my personal development. I remember. Look, we need your help. There’s a new strain of the virus, and it’s resisting the vaccine.’

‘Yes, I’m aware,’ she says, turning to another one of the cages. She swings open the door and lifts in the raven from her shoulder. ‘I’ve had people trying to get a sample of it, but they haven’t been able to. The infection rate seems low. I’m not concerned yet.’

'But it still *has* an infection rate,' I say. 'That's dangerous. The virus could evolve if it can keep spreading like this.'

'You sound like Lachlan,' she says. 'And no, before you ask, I don't know where he is. I've been trying to patch the vaccine. I'd like to keep my people protected from this little outbreak too.'

'This *little* outbreak has gone global,' Mato says. 'Yes, the infection rate is low, but it's not being contained, either. Cartaxus has given us three days to find Lachlan and patch the code before they launch flood protocol.'

Regina goes still, her hand frozen on the side of the cage, then shakes her head as though shaking a thought away. 'Brink won't actually do that,' she says. 'And Lachlan would give him the code before he did, anyway. They're just old friends having an argument.'

'This is *real*, Regina,' Mato snaps. 'People are dying from this outbreak, and Cartaxus is serious about flood protocol. Brink has a *scythe* now, and he's planning to use it. You've been in your bubble too long.'

'Maybe you've been at Cartaxus too long,' she says, her voice growing sharp. 'This is obviously about the Origin code that Lachlan added during the decryption.'

'*Origin* code?' I ask. She clearly means the extra four million lines that were added to the vaccine – Lachlan's daemon code.

Regina nods. 'Yes, Origin code. A road map to the human mind. I've been working on my own version for years, but it isn't nearly as advanced as Lachlan's, from what I've managed to read so far. We've been altering our bodies for decades, but we've never had much of a chance to change our *brains*. I'm thrilled he's finally created code that will let us do it.'

I almost laugh. I have a cuff around my arm and an implant in my *brain* that were designed by Regina. She's leading a city full of genehackers who treat her like a queen. She has to be one of the most innovative engineers in human history.

But she also seems completely *oblivious*.

'Lachlan doesn't want to *let* us do anything,' I say. 'He added that code to the vaccine so that he could alter the minds of every person on the planet. It's not a tool for us to use. It's a weapon he's using to change us all because he thinks we're broken.'

Regina looks genuinely surprised. 'Are you sure of that?'

'Of course I'm sure. Mato, show her the note.'

Mato's eyes glaze, and a page of text hovers in the air between us. It's the note we found when Mato was hacking the implant in my head. The last line sends a chill through me.

A new era for humanity has arrived, and the world will never be the same.

Regina stares at the note for a long, silent moment before turning, pacing across the room. 'I know Lachlan well, and he's an idealist, but this is extreme even for him.' Her eyes go distant, turning something over in her mind. 'We'll have to figure out a way to contact him.'

'He's in your city,' I say.

Her head lifts. 'Why do you think that?'

'Because I have one of your implants in my head with a tracker in it, and we traced him back to here.'

She searches my face, her black eyes narrowing, then turns to the pale-furred genehacker at the door. 'Cambear.'

The hacker steps forward, a rifle clutched in her claw-tipped hands. 'Yes, ma'am.'

'Send drones to watch the entrance tunnels.' Regina strides to a cabinet above one of the benches, swiping her thumb over a black lens in the door to open it. She pulls out a steel box. 'Get me security footage from the city and scan it. He might have altered his facial dimensions again – make sure you're being thorough.' She swings open the box and pulls out a clip of what looks like ammunition. 'If you see him, try to hit him with one of these.'

'Yes, ma'am.' Cambear steps forward and takes the clip, then turns and hurries out of the lab.

'What was in that clip?' Mato asks.

'Weevils,' Regina says, closing the box, pressing her hands to the lid. 'Yours are programmed to keep you *out* of the city, but if we can hit Lachlan with one, then we can keep him *in*.'

'So you'll help us find him?' Mato asks.

'I didn't say that. *I'll* find him,' she says. 'I'm not convinced that any of this is the threat you think it is, but you've concerned me enough to look into it.'

'Let us in then,' Mato says. 'We can help.'

'You're still banished,' Regina says. 'I might be willing to come to an agreement for a temporary stay, though. For the right terms.'

'You're not in a position to *barter*,' Mato snaps. 'Flood protocol will kill you and your people too. Even if you don't believe me, you can't take that risk.'

'They're *my* people,' she says, crossing her arms. 'I'll take whatever risks I please.'

'Fine,' Mato says, sighing. 'What do you want? Comoxes? Code? I can get you practically anything by the end of the day.'

Regina lifts her head, thinking. 'I'll take Catarina.'

I step back, my elbow hitting the invisible wall of the safehouse. 'What do you mean, you'll *take* me?'

'Your DNA has fascinated me for a long time,' she says. 'I've been trying to design ways to change people's natural DNA for decades now.'

'I thought your city was founded on *not* experimenting on other people,' I say.

'Oh, it is,' she says. 'Not against their will, at least. You wouldn't be a subject, though. You would be one of the *scientists*. I've seen your code. I know you're perfectly capable of doing research on yourself. I'd merely be supervising and guiding your work. Come and work with me in my lab while your friends are searching for Lachlan. You'd all be welcome guests in Entropia. You might even like it here.'

'She's not a bargaining chip,' Mato says. 'She's part of this mission.'

'It seems to me like you don't have a mission if you can't get into the city.'

Mato throws his hands up. 'I'm not trading Catarina to get back into my *home* to save you. I'm sorry I tried to take over your city, but you're in danger right now – *all* your people are in danger – and if you can't see it, then you don't deserve to be leading them any more.'

A look of pain flashes across Regina's face before she turns away. 'Fine,' she says, crossing her arms. 'If that's how you feel, then you clearly don't need my help. You can go back to Cartaxus and tell Brink I'll fix the vaccine myself.'

She waves a hand, and her laboratory disappears.

CHAPTER 15

I blink back into the safehouse, my eyes slowly shifting into focus after the VR session. Cole grabs my arm to steady me, and I can't help but flinch at his touch. He draws his hand away, confused at my reaction.

Mato grabs the wall for balance, shaking his head as though trying to clear his vision. Leoben and Anna are standing across from us, watching him. They must have been here the whole time, listening to everything we said.

'That sounded like a shitshow,' Anna says. She lifts her arm, showing Mato a red puncture wound in the middle of one of her tattoos. 'Was it part of your *central command* plan to get shot and locked out of the city?'

'No,' Mato says. 'That wasn't what was supposed to happen. She's worse than she was when I left.'

'She offered us a way in,' I say. 'She wants to work with me and study my DNA.'

'Yeah, we figured that part out,' Cole says. 'I agree with Mato – you're not a bargaining chip. If she's working with Lachlan and he needs your DNA, then going into her lab would be the end of his plan. You can't seriously be thinking about doing that.'

I rub the puncture wound on the back of my hand, glancing at Mato. Part of me knows it would be wildly dangerous to agree to Regina's terms – if there's a chance she's working with Lachlan, then giving her access to my DNA would be the same as giving it to him. I've been worried about walking into a trap, and this is probably the most *obvious* trap I could imagine.

It's almost *too* obvious.

'I don't think she's working with him,' I say. 'She doesn't seem to have any idea what's going on. She's organizing a *party* right now. She wants to study my DNA, but I don't think she'll do anything against my will. Mato said Entropia's currency is code, and I think she's just making an offer in the terms she's used to.'

'You'd really consider her deal?' Mato asks.

'I guess so. I mean, I'm not thrilled about it, but she has drones, and guards, and cameras. She can help us find Lachlan.'

Cole shakes his head. 'She wants to make you an *experiment*. She'll hurt you, I promise. You can't trust these people. They're all the same.'

I pause, my finger still pressed to the wound on my hand. 'What do you mean – *these people*? Do you mean coders?'

Cole shakes his head. 'You know what I mean.'

But I don't know if I do. I'm a coder too, and it's starting to become clear that Cole doesn't trust me, either.

'It's Catarina's decision,' Mato says, an edge to his voice. 'She can protect herself. She made that clear when she used her scythe to get you and Leoben out of that lab.'

Cole looks between me and Mato. 'You can't really be thinking of making this deal. This is madness. I'm calling Brink.'

'Brink isn't accepting comms any more,' Mato says. 'Not after Catarina threatened him.'

'What?' I ask. 'Does he seriously think I could kill him with a comm? I was *bluffing*.'

'Well, it obviously worked,' Mato says. 'He's gone into lockdown, so I'm the highest-ranking central command officer you're going to be able to reach right now. I think we still have a chance of getting into the city without this deal, but if we can't, then it's up to Catarina as to whether or not she wants to take it.'

'How else would we get in?' Leoben asks, lifting his hand. There's a puncture wound in the same place as mine – the pad between his thumb and forefinger. 'I'm pretty into tech, but I have no idea how to remove one of these things.'

'I know someone,' Mato says. 'A skinhacker. She works at a market near the closest checkpoint. We can drive there and see if she can remove them. She's expensive, though. We might need to trade the Comox.'

'That's a hell of a deal,' Leoben says. 'I hope you know, it sounds to me like we're giving away a Comox because you wouldn't call your mom.'

'Regina isn't my *mom*,' Mato says.

'Oh, shut up, you guys,' Anna groans, pushing away from the wall. 'Let's *go*. I want to get this thing out of my arm.'

Leoben and Cole check the house over before we pile into the jeep and pull away, Cole driving, with Anna beside him in the passenger seat. Leoben is sitting cross-legged with his back against the rear doors, and Mato and I are opposite each other, leaning back against the jeep's sides.

None of us are talking, but Cole and Anna make small noises of amusement every now and then that make me think they're texting each other. I open my comm interface, but there's nothing waiting for me – no group chat – just a backlog of Novak's broadcasts from the Skies mailing list and a picture of a squid wearing sunglasses that Leoben sent me while we were flying. Whatever Cole and Anna are talking about, they're keeping it private.

I still don't know what to make of the conversation I overheard between them. They could be worried I'll do something reckless – I *did* blow up an airlock at Homestake, and I knocked Cole out when I went in to face Lachlan at the Zarathustra lab. I got Cole and Lee out of the lab by using lethal code I didn't even know I *had*, so I guess it makes sense that Cole might be worried I'll do something to jeopardize the mission.

But that still doesn't ease the pain of hearing him talk about me like that.

Mato sits up straighter, looking out the window once we hit the road that leads to Entropia's border crossing. Billboards for the market line the road, offering food and immunity, ammunition and freezepaks. The city itself – and the mountain it's built on – inches out of the haze, revealing metal spires twisting up from towering buildings, wooden houses leaning against their foundations, a flock of pigeons forming a cloud around the mountain's peak. The stretch of razorgrass encircling the mountain gleams in the sun, vast and deadly, the colour of wine.

'How are there this many people here?' Anna asks, leaning forward to stare through the windscreen as we approach the market. Dozens of tables piled high with goods to trade are set up in a loose semicircle around the checkpoint, red-and-white awnings stretched over them. There's a café with a seating area, and a handful of groups selling supplies in the parking lot from the backs of their trucks. There must be hundreds of people here. I haven't seen this many since we went into Homestake.

'Not all of Regina's people live in the city,' Mato says. 'A lot of them are out here in the desert. They use markets like this to trade tech and code. Most of this corner of Nevada is populated by genehackers.'

'Nevada can have them,' Anna says, wrinkling her nose. 'I don't know why you people want to turn yourselves into freaks.'

I can't help but roll my eyes. 'Should you really be calling people freaks, Anna? How many chromosomes do you have?'

'Forty-six,' she says, spinning round. 'I'm the only one of us who was born with the *right* number. You really don't remember anything, do you?'

'No,' I murmur. 'Not really. So what's special about your DNA? What was your gift?'

She stares at me for a second, then turns back to the front, exchanging a look with Cole. 'I don't know. Lachlan never told me.'

Her tone is light, but something tells me she's lying. I try to remember the paper file that Lachlan kept on her. There was nothing special mentioned – just a few notes about a problem with her skin. It was covered in tiny bumps, and there was a mention of build-up and overgrowth in a lot of her body's systems.

There are a lot of mutations that could lead to effects like that, though.

'You sure about going into this crowd, Mato?' Leoben asks as we pull into the market, slowing to a crawl when we reach the parking lot. The people milling around us glance at the jeep as we roll past, but not with any real curiosity. It's an unusual vehicle, but it isn't obviously from Cartaxus. Cole swings us into an empty spot with a view of the market.

'I can see the person we need,' Mato says. 'I'll go and talk to her. It might be easier if you come along, Catarina. Lachlan is something of a celebrity in Entropia, and you will be too after the vaccine's broadcast. It won't hurt to have you there to prove that this is important.'

'Sure,' I mumble, hunting through the bag of clothes Leoben printed, dragging out a blue cotton T-shirt to pull on over my Cartaxus tank top. I don't really like the thought of being a *celebrity*, especially after the vaccine's broadcast. Every word of that speech was a lie, and I only said it because I didn't think I was going to live to see the aftermath.

'I'll walk a patrol,' Anna says. 'We need eyes on the other side of the market, and Cole and Lee are obviously Cartaxus meatheads.'

'Gee, thanks,' Leoben says.

Mato shoots a glance at Anna. 'Honestly, you're probably going to stand out the most here. In Entropia you'd be called a *norm* – someone who's clinging to the traditionalist view of what a human looks like. At least Cole and Leoben have leylines. You look like you've just stepped out of a bunker.'

'Hoo boy,' Leoben mutters.

Anna's eyes flare. 'Listen, *freak*. Your rank isn't going to protect you for much longer if you keep talking to me like that.'

Mato just shakes his head. 'Hollow threats aren't becoming on a black-out agent, Anna.'

She grabs her seatbelt to unbuckle it and launch herself at him, but Cole grabs her arm.

'Hey,' he says, his voice low and firm. 'Just chill, OK? Lee, why don't you go and watch from the other side? Let's focus on getting these things out of us.'

'OK,' Leoben says, swinging open the jeep's rear doors. 'But you gotta call me back over if those two fight for real.'

He climbs out and heads through the crowd. I slide from the back of the jeep with Mato, swinging the doors shut behind us. A smile plays across his lips as we head into the crowd.

'Why do you rile her up like that?' I hiss. 'She'll kick your ass.'

He shakes his head. 'She can try any time she likes. They think they're better than us because of their bodies and what they've been trained to do. They have no idea how the world really works. They're never going to be in control of anything.'

I stop, grabbing the sleeve of his jacket, yanking him round to face me. The urge to defend the others is sudden and overwhelming. 'That's my *family* you're talking about. You can't say things like that. I care about them.'

Mato looks down at my hand on his arm, surprised. 'Do you?' he asks, but there's no edge to his voice. He sounds genuinely curious. 'Then why was Jun Bei in Entropia three years ago while they were locked up in a lab?'

I draw my hand back from his sleeve. 'Lachlan brought her here. He must have been keeping her prisoner.'

Mato steps closer. 'Don't play the fool, Catarina. You're smarter than this. We both know Lachlan didn't give Jun Bei that cuff on your arm. It's not the kind of thing you give to someone you're keeping prisoner. How else would she get it?'

I drop my eyes to the gleaming black glass around my arm. 'I – I don't know. I haven't figured that out yet.'

Mato peers at me, intrigued. 'Well, hopefully you can find out once we get in.'

He starts to head back through the crowd, waiting until I follow him. A couple of people stop talking as we walk past, their eyes pausing on my face in recognition. I slip the elastic out of my braid and unknot my hair, letting it hang in curtains around my face.

The crowd grows thicker around the market. Long tables are lined up below tarpaulin awnings, selling piles of produce and salvaged pieces of tech. Some of the people look like they've come from miles away – survivors on trailers, families with children – but there are plenty of wild-looking genehackers who look like they've come from inside the city. The air smells like burnt plastic, the scent wafting from a hulking line of solar printers. A group of people are gathered around the crush chute line, tossing in scrap plastic, pulling out freshly printed tools and components.

Mato walks towards a stall selling genehacked vegetables. Long, curled bean pods with strangely translucent skin are piled beside mounds of potatoes in various colours. A girl steps forward to meet us. She's clearly a genehacker, with brown, strangely smooth skin that glistens in the sun and forms narrow, straight folds around her joints. Her muscles are long and angular, her face exquisitely crafted. She looks like a doll come to life. A pendant hanging around her neck holds an ID glyph that my panel throws into the edge of my vision, offering me her public profile, pronouns and name. *Rhine*.

'Mato,' she says, smiling. 'I heard whispers you were back. It's been a long time.'

'News travels fast,' he says, pulling her into a hug across the table. 'Rhine, I want to introduce you to Catarina.'

'I *know* who she is.'

I hold out my hand. She shakes it firmly, her skin cold and smooth, like leather.

'I'm glad I found you,' Mato says. 'I was actually hoping to make a deal with you.'

'Oh yeah?' she asks, running her fingers across a block of something on the table. It shivers under her touch, and I flinch, staring at it. It is exactly what it looks like. A slab of pale meat, grown to the exact size and shape of the scratched plastic container beside it. Its skin is light pink and eerily wrinkled, dusted with the finest layer of gossamer blond hairs.

Rhine follows my eyes. 'We call them kilomeat. They're all vehicle, no driver, with the absolute minimum of nerve fibres. Portable protein.' She lifts the pale oblong up and turns it in her hands, holding it out for me to hold.

I back away. 'I'm OK.'

'You prefer the real thing?' she asks. 'You like your meals to come from something that had to die for you?'

'I don't eat meat,' I say.

Rhine grins. 'Like hell you don't. Where'd you get your doses?'

'Well, except for that.'

She flips the kilomeat between her hands. 'These can be infected with a syringe, but you have to be careful about making sure they get to second stage.'

I blink, staring at her. 'That's human?'

'Mostly.' She sets it back down on the table. It twitches, and I suppress a shudder. She looks back at Mato. 'So what do you need?'

He pulls back his sleeve to show her the puncture wound from the weevil, but pauses, looking over his shoulder.

I follow his gaze. The jeep is still parked at the edge of the market, but Cole is standing outside it, his rifle in his hands, watching a busload of people that has just pulled in. They're getting off slowly, carrying suitcases and bags, and one of them seems to be arguing with the guards at the checkpoint. They have gas masks and goggles strapped to their faces, which would normally be common in a market like this, but nobody else here is wearing them.

Cartaxus hasn't broadcast the news about the mutated strain yet. As far as these people know, they're vaccinated and safe.

I glance back at Cole. He's moving through the crowd now, heading towards us. Rhine's smile freezes as the shouting near the bus grows louder. She reaches beneath the table, sliding out a shotgun. Everyone in the market is stopping what they're doing, turning to the group, and Cole picks up his pace, his eyes flashing to black. My stomach clenches. People are surging for the checkpoint, running towards the group.

It takes me a long, confused moment to understand what's happening.

But then I see her.

A woman. Young, dark-haired, wearing a camouflage jacket and cut-off shorts, her hair pulled back. Black-and-blue bruises cover her face and the exposed skin of her legs. Her eyes are glazed, and she's shouting at the guards at the checkpoint, swinging at them, but the people in the gas masks are holding her back. They look like her friends or family – like they've brought her here to get help.

But instead they've just brought an infected woman into a *crowd*.

I suck in a breath, catching the barest whiff of sulphur, and clamp my hand over my nose. Suddenly the rising energy in the market makes sense. The raised voices. The people running for the group in gas masks. This is the *Wrath*. The woman's scent is drifting through the crowd. My fingers are pinched over my nose, but I can already feel the response rising in me.

It's *wrong*, though.

This woman is first stage, no doubt about it. The mottled black-and-blue bruises on her skin are unmistakable. They're the first sign of infection, and they always fade to yellow or green by the time the second stage hits. This woman shouldn't be carrying the scent right now. She shouldn't even be *walking*. She should be laid up with a fever, not fighting wildly with Entropia's guards. I glance back at Cole, grabbing Mato's arm, pulling him away from the group, but the crowd is thick on every side, and the Wrath is spreading fast. It's most dangerous in a crowd like this. The response can spread like wildfire, and a group of people this big can turn on one another instead of the infected.

If we don't get out of here soon, we might lose ourselves to it too.

'Come on!' I yell, dragging Mato back through the crowd, heading for Cole, trying to keep my hand locked over my nose. A man shoves past me, almost knocking me down as he bolts for the checkpoint. The screaming is getting louder, the energy of the crowd growing frantic. 'We need to get back to the jeep!'

Mato's hand is clamped on his nose too, but I can see him fighting back the response, shaking against the Wrath. Cole is running for me, shoving past people, shouting something I can't hear. I push past a table piled high with broken genkits, elbowing my way through the throng, when a woman grabs my wrist, fingernails clawing into my arm.

It's too late. The crowd is already turning on one another.

'Cole!' I shout, shoving the woman away. I have to drop my hand from my nose, and the scent that takes its place hits me like a wave. 'Nightstick!'

But I don't know if he can hear me. The woman stumbles, snarling, but more people take her place, grabbing at my face, my cuff, my shirt. I bring my arms up to shield my eyes, looking behind me for Mato. Across the marketplace, the infected woman breaks free from a snarling pack of people, her panel blinking, her body bitten and bleeding. There are gashes on her legs and face, a pulse of blood pumping from her neck.

She straightens, shuddering, and horror grips me as she throws her head back.

A roar rips through the air as she detonates.

CHAPTER 16

I throw myself on to the ground as the shockwave hits us. A billowing wall of steam slams into the market, toppling the tables. Food and broken pieces of tech go flying. Umbrellas rip free of their holders and wheel into the air, and the bus tilts and crashes on to its side. I bring my hand up, locking it over my nose and mouth out of instinct, but this cloud isn't the scarlet mist I'm used to seeing. It doesn't rise into a plume, a single finger of fine droplets stretching up for the wind to carry it.

Instead, it explodes *outwards,* in a spray of droplets, splinters and shredded meat.

My stomach heaves at the feeling of it splattering across my skin. I want to keep holding my breath, but my lungs are burning, and it's no use, anyway. I'm already covered in it. The infected woman had a panel in her arm, which means this is the mutated strain of the virus.

It's resisting the vaccine, and everyone here is covered in it.

I push myself shakily to my knees, my ears whining in the aftermath of the blast. The crowd is silent, held in a moment of collective disbelief. The woman nearest me scrambles to her feet, glassy-eyed with shock. A metal rod from the scrap table is jutting from her abdomen. She looks down at it, swaying, and lets out a scream.

The crowd's silence shatters like glass.

Screams rise around me. I drop my hand from my nose and heave in a lungful of air, choking on the hot, humid stench of blood and plague. The scent has shifted away from the crucial notes that trigger the Wrath, and people aren't fighting with one another any more. Now they're *terrified*, covered in infected blood, scrambling to get away from the marketplace. My eyes burn, my vision swimming with tears as I push myself to my feet. Cole barges through a group of people, his eyes black, and grabs the top of my arm to haul me up. 'Come on!' he shouts. 'We need to get out of here.'

I grab the side of a toppled stall for balance, turning to look for Mato. He's behind an upturned table, pushing aside boxes of cables and wires to get back to the jeep. A stampede is starting – hundreds of dirty bodies scrambling over each other to get away from the crater. The crowd is panicking. Everyone knows that blower wasn't normal. People don't carry the scent in the first stage of infection, and they certainly don't *detonate*. There was no proper cloud, no climbing mist. Just an assault of biological shrapnel sprayed across the market.

And it might have infected us all.

Cole drags me away from the stall and back towards the parking lot. Mato follows, and the jeep races closer, swerving through a stall, sending it toppling. The doors swing open, Anna leaping out of the passenger side, her rifle clutched in her hands. 'Get in!' she yells.

Cole breaks into a run, dragging me with him. Leoben is in the driver's seat, watching the crowd, his shoulders tight. We climb through the rear doors and into the back, scrambling in to make room for Mato. Anna slams the rear doors shut behind us, racing to the front, and we surge forward as Leoben floors the accelerator.

'What the hell?' he asks, whipping his head round. 'Are you infected?'

'I'll check,' I say, summoning my cuff's menu, trying to get it to give me a reader wire.

'Head for the city,' Mato says.

'We can't go there,' Anna says, lifting her arm, showing us the puncture wound from the weevil. 'Did you forget about these?'

'We don't need to get inside,' Mato says, 'just into Entropia's perimeter. Regina has a no-fly agreement with Cartaxus, but it doesn't extend out here.'

Leoben wrenches the wheel, turning us round, the jeep's tyres bouncing over a toppled stall. We speed back towards the scattering crowd, heading for the gates at the checkpoint. They're open now – vehicles pouring through. The screams from the market fade as we careen on to the road and join the flood of cars speeding along the dusty trail that cuts through the razorgrass border. But I don't know why everyone is running. If we're all infected, then getting away from the crater isn't going to help.

'Why do we need to get into a no-fly zone?' I ask.

'Because Cartaxus is quarantining the new strain,' Mato says.

My breath hitches. He means that *drones* are coming. I close my eyes, remembering the points of light racing across the sky before Cartaxus's drones blew Sunnyvale to hell. That's what quarantining means. Blasting potential threats into dust.

Cartaxus is going to do the same thing to the marketplace.

The reader wire slithers from my cuff. I grab it with my filthy hand, unfurling it.

'Here, this is faster,' Mato says, pulling the metal pen from his pocket. He flicks off the cap and jams it against his wrist, then passes it to me. A blue circle blossoms across his skin. 'As long as this stays blue, we're OK.'

I take the pen and jam it into my wrist. It pinches, hissing, a prickling feeling spreading across my skin. I press it to Cole's wrist, then pass it to Leoben.

'How long do we need to wait?' Cole asks.

'Not long,' Mato says. 'A minute at most.'

Leoben stabs the pen into his arm, though he doesn't really need to test himself, then passes it to Anna.

'What the hell was with that detonation?' she asks, pressing the pen to her wrist. 'Was that because of the new strain?'

'I don't know yet,' I say. 'That's what I want to check.'

I swipe the tip of the reader wire across my arm, picking up a streak of the foam. Dax said the blasts from the new strain were smaller than usual, but he didn't say they were happening to people who were *first stage*. That's unheard-of. Dax is first stage. He's probably as far along now as the woman in the market was. My eyes cut to Leoben. I don't know if he's realized what this means.

My vision flashes, returning the results of the scan on the virus, showing me a dozen charts and genetic diagrams. The infected woman was definitely carrying a mutated strain – it has *hundreds* of genetic variations I haven't seen before. Dax wasn't exaggerating when he said this strain was a serious mutation. It's practically a different *virus*. I don't understand how a strain like this could have evolved so quickly.

'It's the new strain, isn't it?' Cole asks.

'Yeah,' I say, 'but that doesn't mean we're in danger. The infection rate is still low.'

'Well, I'm clear,' Anna says, lifting her hand. I glance at the circles on the others, and on my wrist. All blue. I slump in relief.

'Well, that's good,' Cole says, leaning forward, 'but we've got company.'

Mato's head snaps round, looking through the window. A cloud of drones is racing up from the south, splitting as they approach the market. They're not forming a blast formation like they did over Sunnyvale, though. They're dividing into two groups. Four drones are heading for the marketplace.

And another set of four are coming after us.

'Shit,' Cole says, 'we need to hurry.'

Leoben floors the accelerator. We race across the desert, bouncing over the rocky ground.

'Can't you call Cartaxus?' I ask Mato. 'Tell them we're here. Brink doesn't want to kill us.'

'I already have,' he says, his eyes glazed. 'I called them from back in the marketplace. They're not listening to me.'

Leoben swerves round a stalled car, the jeep swaying with the movement. 'So what do we do? Are we screwed?'

'We need to make it to the no-fly zone,' Mato says, clutching the side of the jeep for balance. 'I don't know if we'll be safe there, but it's our best shot.'

'And where is that?' Anna asks, loading her rifle. She winds down her window.

'Just a little further,' Mato says.

I crane my neck to look through the windscreen. We're almost through the razorgrass border, just a minute away, but that's time we don't have. I turn back to the drones, my heart pounding. The four following us are dropping lower, chasing the stream of vehicles racing in from the checkpoint. Anna swings round in the passenger seat, aiming her rifle at the sky. She fires off a spray of bullets, but it's like shooting at a tank.

'Can we hack them?' I ask Mato.

'I'm trying,' he says. His mask has gone clear, his eyes closed in concentration.

I stare through the window at the drones, letting a pulse roll out from my cuff, bringing up their wireless signals in my vision. I have no idea how to hack them. I don't even know if it's possible, but there are four of them screaming towards us, and it seems like a good time to try flinging viruses at them. It won't do much good unless they're networked, though. We'll never be able to hack them all unless they're centrally controlled. Each drone would need a separate hack, separate commands and focus. I reach for their connections with my cuff, but there are dozens of layers of security around them, and each of their entrance points looks different.

'They're not networked,' I breathe. If I picked one drone, I might be able to take it down, and maybe Mato could too – but we can't possibly stop them all.

'We aren't gonna make this!' Leoben yells back. There's still a stretch of razorgrass ahead of us – we haven't hit the no-fly zone yet, and the drones show no sign that they'll stop when we reach it, anyway.

'I'm working on it,' Mato snaps. His mask grows brighter, but the drones switch formation suddenly, and the jeep's dash flashes red.

It's too late. They're readying to strike. A weapons warning blazes across the dash, and my heart lurches into my throat. Cole takes my hand, clutching it in his. I brace for the impact, for the shockwave that will incinerate us . . .

But it doesn't come.

'Holy shit,' Anna says, looking back at Mato. I follow her eyes, still clutching Cole's hand. Mato's mask is glowing *white*, his lips moving faintly, and in the sky beyond the window, the fleet of drones following us has stopped. They're hovering. Motionless. Mato's mask pulses, and they suddenly tilt and fall, tumbling through the air. Their steel bodies smack into the razorgrass border, exploding in thick clouds of smoke.

The breath rushes from my lungs. 'H-how?' I stutter.

That's impossible. I saw their controls – they weren't networked. I've never even *heard* of code that could do that.

Leoben slams the brakes, staring over his shoulder at Mato, the cars and trucks speeding down the road screeching round us. Back at the marketplace, an explosion flashes, light splashing across the desert, and a shockwave of sound and pressure rocks the jeep.

The other four drones just bombed the marketplace, and now they're tilting, pivoting to come after us.

'Another four,' Leoben says, 'coming up fast.'

Mato makes a grunt of acknowledgement, his eyes still scrunched shut, the tendons in his neck tight. The last four drones whine closer, and Mato shudders, a muscle in his jaw tensing.

His mask pulses again, and the last four drones twist in the air, spiralling down, falling like stones.

'Holy shit,' I whisper, staring at Mato.

My mind is spinning, Cole's hand still clutched in mine. I have no idea how Mato did that. Four simultaneous hacks, *twice*. It shouldn't be possible, even with a mask. Every drone should have taken all his focus. Maybe he could have handled two with years of practice, but not four. That's like singing four different songs at the same time, navigating four mazes simultaneously.

It's not something the human brain is capable of, but I just saw him do it. Something wavers in me as I stare at him. That was like nothing I've ever witnessed. Every arrogant thing he's said suddenly seems inadequate.

He's absolutely and utterly *incredible*.

'How did you do that?' I whisper, but he doesn't answer. His mask is black, his eyes still closed, his body rigid.

'Mato?' Anna calls back, wrenching off her seatbelt.

Cole drops my hand, grabbing Mato's shoulders. 'Guys, he's not breathing.'

CHAPTER 17

Anna launches herself out of the jeep and races round to the back, flinging open the rear doors. Smoke billows in from the wreckage of the drones. Cars and trucks are still racing in from the bombed-out marketplace, veering wildly round us.

'His heart's stopped,' Cole says, kneeling over Mato.

'Out of my way!' Anna says. 'I know what to do.'

I scramble back against the crushed boxes of supplies to give them space, pulling myself into the gap between the front seats. I don't understand how Mato's heart stopped from hacking the drones, but there's nothing else that could have done this – the circle on his wrist is blue. He's not infected. There are scratches on his face and streaks of blood across his skin, but no wounds.

He shouldn't be *dying* in front of us.

'It's the goddamn implant,' Anna says, climbing into the back of the jeep.

I blink, staring at Mato in horror. He said the implant was dangerous and that he'd been hurt before, but I didn't realize he meant like this – that it could be *lethal*.

Anna pulls a silver canister from her pocket, a scarlet light blinking on its cap.

'What's that?' I ask.

'Adrenaline,' she says. 'It needs to go into his heart. This happened in Alaska.'

Cole stops the compressions and pulls open Mato's foam-splattered jacket, tearing open the crinkled fabric of his shirt, revealing his chest. A circle of five black ports is built into the pale skin over his heart. Anna slams the canister down in its centre, hard enough to shake Mato's body.

His mask flashes white again, his body arching. He lets out a gasp, one hand hitting Anna's chest, throwing her back across the jeep. Her head smacks into the window, the vial flying from her hand, out into the desert. She grabs the side of the jeep for balance, dazed, but her lips curl in a smile.

'Welcome back, asshole,' she says.

Mato rolls over, coughing, curling up on the jeep's floor, one hand pressed to his chest. His jacket is twisted around his neck, his shirt hanging open, his eyes scrunched shut in pain. 'Jesus, Anna. You broke a rib.'

'I saved your goddamn life.'

'He saved all our lives,' Leoben says, staring back through the window at the wreckage of the drones. A pickup truck races in from the market, swerving round us, its back crammed full of people. They stare at us as they pass, their faces coated with blood and dust. I doubt that everyone survived the bombing of the marketplace, but a lot of us are still alive because of what Mato did.

'Now we need to call Regina,' Leoben says, his voice suddenly hard, 'and tell her to let us into this *goddamn* city. We can't waste any more time playing games. We need to find Lachlan tonight.'

'Lee –' Cole starts, but Leoben cuts him off.

'I saw that blower,' he says, his eyes blazing. He slams his hand against the steering wheel in frustration. 'She wasn't much further along than Dax is. He might not have much longer, and I'm not going to sit and wait here while he *dies*. We have a Comox. There are weapons in that safehouse. I could burn down half this city tonight on my own, and I'm ready to do it.'

The air around him seems to shimmer. I haven't seen Leoben like this before. I don't think he's kidding about attacking Entropia.

Mato shakes his head, his cheeks flushed, coughing. 'Regina still won't let us in.'

'You called her?' Anna asks.

'She called *me*,' Mato says, his eyes glazed. 'She wanted to check if I was OK, and then she hung up.'

'I can arrange for you *not* to be OK again if it's going to help,' Anna says.

Mato closes his eyes. 'If taking down those drones didn't convince her to let me come home, then I don't know what will.'

Come home. The words echo in my ears. I look between Mato and Leoben. This isn't just about finding Lachlan and fixing the vaccine for either of them. This is personal. Leoben said he wasn't in love with Dax, but now he's threatening to burn down a city to save him. Mato says this is his home, and it'll be destroyed if Brink launches flood protocol. I don't know what his past with Regina means – why she acts like his mother – but it makes me think of Agnes, and the thought tugs at my heart.

'Tell Regina I'll make the deal,' I say.

'Cat –' Cole starts, but I hold up a hand.

'Mato just *died* to save us. I think I can handle being someone's experiment for a little while.'

'Thank you,' Leoben says.

'I should have made the deal when she first offered it,' I say. 'I just hope this is enough.'

Mato's eyes glaze again. 'Catarina says she'll come in.'

His eyes stay glassy, smoke still curling from the wreckage of the drones behind us. All of us are silent for a moment until Anna lets out a yelp, clutching her arm. A bump is rising through her tattooed skin.

'Oh, thank God,' Mato says, pulling back his sleeve. A lump is forming on his forearm. I lift my hand, staring at the puncture wound, but it's not doing anything. Cole's tricep twitches as the wound on his skin swells, metal antennae unfolding from it, the weevil slithering out. Mato's falls from his arm at the same time, clinking against the floor of the jeep. Anna's and Leoben's slide from their skin.

But mine doesn't move.

'That . . . that is truly disgusting,' Leoben says, watching his fall.

'She's letting us back in,' Mato says. 'She's going to help us too.'

'About time,' Anna says, dragging off the elastic around her hair, fixing her ponytail. 'We just saved a ton of her people.'

'*We?*' Mato asks.

'What?' Anna shrugs. 'I just brought you back from the dead. Give me a little credit.'

'All right, all right,' Leoben says. 'Are we good to go in?'

I lift my hand. 'Mine hasn't come out.'

Mato's brow creases. 'Maybe it's dead.'

Cole just shakes his head. 'We need to start treating this like a goddamn trap already. It's not Regina who's in that city waiting for us – it's Lachlan, and this is all over if he gets to Cat.'

Mato presses his lips together, looking at me. 'What do you think, Catarina?'

I look down at the weevil in my hand and up at Cole. I can tell he doesn't like this. Neither do I, but we're all covered in foam from a detonation, and if we don't find Lachlan soon, Cartaxus is going to launch flood protocol. The best hope we have is working with the woman who rules this city, even if it means taking the risk that she's our enemy.

I rub my hands over my face, trying to think. I have foam drying on my skin and scratches on my arms. Part of me just wants to get clean, to get indoors and to regroup.

And part of me knows I have a weapon hidden inside my panel in case we need to get out.

'It's fine,' I say, dropping my hands. 'It doesn't change anything. Let's go in.'

Cole sits back, crossing his arms, his face dark as Leoben revs the engine, pulling us down the last stretch of the dirt road that cuts through the razorgrass border. Once we're past it, there's still a couple of miles of barren desert to cross until we reach the fields at the mountain's base. The city towers ahead of us, houses and skyscrapers bristling from the rocky slopes.

'This place is huge,' Anna says, staring through the windscreen.

'The buildings on the surface are just a fraction of it,' Mato says. 'Most of Entropia is actually underground, in a bunker. The desert gets too hot in summer to spend more than a few minutes in the sun without dermal hacks. A lot of that mountain has been hollowed out and rebuilt into living spaces. It's huge.'

'Who built it?' I ask.

'Cartaxus, actually,' Mato says, rubbing his ribs. 'This was one of the first bunkers they ever built, but they mistook the limestone beneath this mountain for shale. They hollowed out a core for the bunker, drilled maintenance shafts and built the steel frame, then poured most of the concrete before they figured it out. The lower levels started slowly sinking into the ground, and they decided to abandon it. Regina made a deal to move her people here a couple of decades ago. They got hold of a few drilling machines, and ever since, they've been chewing up the rest of the mountain, carving out new living spaces.'

Leoben raises his eyebrows. 'Cartaxus gave her a bunker? That's a hell of a deal. What did she trade for it?'

'She designed the first panel bud almost on her own thirty years ago,' Mato says. 'Honestly, I think they owed her.'

I blink, staring at him. I knew that Cartaxus made the first panel buds, but I didn't know it was Regina who created them. People had been implanting themselves with the precursors to panels for years before that, but they were bulky implants they had to cut themselves open to insert. Writing gentech code to create skin or bone tissue is easy, but getting the body to grow a piece of silicon is *hard*. There's no precedent in nature, no script to copy and adapt. The self-growing panel bud was a lightning strike that changed gentech's history, taking it out of hospitals and into ordinary people's arms.

No wonder Regina's people worship her. She didn't just design my cuff – she's the reason there's a bar of cobalt light glowing beneath it.

Mato zips his jacket over his torn shirt, leaning back against the side of the jeep.

'How did you do that, earlier?' I ask. 'Those drones weren't networked – I saw their controls. They all had to be hacked individually. Were you running some kind of code the implant helped with?'

Mato glances at Anna and Cole. 'It wasn't special code, but yes, it was the implant that controlled it. It's something you can probably learn to do.'

Anna groans. 'We don't need her dying on us too.'

'It's only dangerous when it's rushed,' Mato says.

'What's dangerous?' I ask.

'It's called fractioning. Here, I'll show you.'

Fractioning. A flicker of recognition tugs at me, but I don't remember what the word means. Mato's eyes glaze, and a VR request blinks in my vision. When I accept it, the brain animation that he showed me back in the lab appears again, with the forest of scarlet wires curling through it from the implant.

'Every thought you have activates different regions in your brain,' he says. 'Your thoughts are a combination of your memories, your senses, and the brain's processing centres. Logic, emotion, mental models of the world. It helps to think about it as a computer with different apps running in different regions, all networked to help us navigate the world.' The image of the brain flashes with different colours – patterns of green and yellow spots glowing across it.

'Most of our thoughts are broad, though,' Mato continues. 'We might think of three or four things at once, but the signals from the different areas of our brain get blended, and our thoughts get jumbled too. It's hard to carry two separate thoughts in our minds without them merging into one. But with the implant, we can.'

The image changes. A red wall of light appears, cutting through the brain, slicing out from the implant. It looks like a barrier constructed inside the person's head – wavering and bright. The glowing colours on either side of it separate, forming two smaller patterns instead of one.

'When I say fractioning,' Mato says, 'I mean fractioning your *mind* – literally splitting your thoughts into two or more sections. The effect is based on research on people who had the two halves of their brains physically separated. Some of them were able to do two things at once effortlessly, like drawing a shape with one hand while writing a word with the other. Regina studied those experiments, trying to find a way to safely replicate them. She thought that maybe we could focus more if we broke down the noisy links inside our minds.'

The glowing wall inside the image of the brain seems to pulse in my vision. I can't help but think about the wall I've felt holding back Jun Bei's memories. I thought maybe it was psychological – something I could overcome if I tried to face my past.

But if it's coming from the implant, it might be a literal, physical *wall*.

'These barriers are created by weak electric fields,' Mato says. 'They make it difficult for the impulses of your thoughts to stretch between them, so the implant can allow you to temporarily isolate or split away any part of your mind. If you train yourself to think in a way that's aligned with the implant's wiring, you can learn to do two things at once. Or even four, or eight.'

'Or you could *die*,' Anna says. 'Don't forget to mention that.'

'Only if you rush into a fraction,' Mato says, 'or if you let a wall drop too quickly.'

I look up. 'How is dropping a wall dangerous?'

'It causes an electrical storm inside your mind – your neurons can overload when they try to reconnect.'

I stare at the image of the implant hovering in the air. When I sensed the wall inside my mind starting to split, I felt like I was going to lose myself somehow. I thought it was just the fear that Jun Bei's memories would overwhelm me, but if the implant is running like this, then there's a chance that breaking down that wall could be *physically* dangerous too.

'Is that what just happened to you?' I ask. 'You had a . . . a stroke?'

Mato nods. 'It was minor.'

'A *minor* stroke?'

'I'm fine.'

Anna rolls her eyes. 'That's the second one I've seen him have. Last time, in Alaska, he was out for three days. Nobody could figure out how to wake him up.'

Mato shrugs. 'It's easy to push yourself too far. Fractioning is addictive. It's hard to live in one dimension when you know how it feels to split your mind into as many as you want. It's a feeling that's impossible to describe.'

A rash of goose bumps rises across my skin. I look back through the window at the smoke rising from the ruined drones. Something inside me stretches, pressing against my senses, too blunt and shapeless to put into words. I feel like I've done this before – I've worn this cuff and used this implant. I've fractioned before, or at least Jun Bei has, and part of me desperately wants to do it again.

The strength of the urge frightens me, because I'm not sure the urge is *mine*. It feels like it's coming from the same part of me that makes me bite my fingernails and that killed the soldier in the lab. The ocean of memories locked inside me. Cole said I needed to take control of it before it took control of me, but I can already feel the reins starting to slip.

There's so much I still don't understand, though. It's becoming clear that both the cuff and the implant are *weapons*, and that it wasn't Lachlan who gave them to Jun Bei. Mato was right – the cuff isn't the kind of thing you'd give to a prisoner.

But if Jun Bei wasn't a prisoner during the six months after she escaped, then what was she doing here?

I glance through the windscreen at the city looming ahead of us. I don't know why Jun Bei was in Entropia, and I don't know how it relates to Lachlan's plan.

But I think I'm about to find out.

CHAPTER 18

Mato directs us past the edges of the sprawling farmlands and on to a heavily worn road that dips into a ridge between two hills. The city's buildings are sparser near the base of the mountain – most of them down here are wooden shacks built against each other, climbing up the slopes, their roofs a patchwork of steel and plastic. Skyscrapers rise above them, higher up on the mountainside, with winding streets cutting between them. The road we're following veers into a gap in the rock, entering a rough-hewn tunnel, wide enough for a truck, that dives into the mountain's side.

'Why are we going underground?' I ask. 'The lab I saw Lachlan in had a view of the desert. It would have been one of these buildings in the city.'

'Regina's lab is in the bunker,' Mato says. 'She's going to be expecting you there as soon as we get in. If she agrees to help us, then we can search the buildings on the surface this afternoon. She might even be able to give us vehicles, or people to help. But we'll need to see her first, and we might as well set up a base for the next day or two in the bunker. It's a communal living space – there are apartments we'll be able to use. It's a good central location.'

I watch the skyscrapers and buildings on the side of the mountain inch out of view as we roll into the tunnel, yellow lights sliding across the jeep's bonnet in a steady pulse as we drive. The tunnel branches off every few minutes to vast, fluorescent-lit parking lots blasted into the rock, filled with vehicles.

'Let's take this one,' Mato says, gesturing to one of the branching tunnels. Leoben slows the jeep, swinging us into a cavern filled with vehicles. Some are streaked with dust and foam from the market. We pull in beside a pickup truck with a crumpled door and shattered window.

Mato swings open the rear doors slowly, climbing out with one hand pressed to his ribs. I slide across the floor, grabbing my backpack, and follow him. The others climb out behind me.

'We need to go through the airlocks to get in,' Mato says. 'They're just showers, don't worry.' He gestures to a row of doors lined up along the wall with airlock symbols above them. They don't look like the Wash-and-Blasts at Homestake, though. They're smaller and far less complicated-looking. 'See you on the other side,' he says. 'I'll tell Regina's team we're coming.'

I sling on my backpack, heading for one of the airlock queues, but Anna grabs my arm. 'Really?' she asks. 'First thing you do in this place is go off on your own? You still have a tracker in your skull. Lachlan knows you're here. You need to be more careful.'

'Oh, right,' I say, letting her pull me along with her, unease curling through me. I look back at Cole and Leoben, but they're heading for another door across the other side of the parking lot.

'We'll wait till one of them gets through so you can meet them on the other side,' Anna says, joining one of the longer queues. 'You can't be alone while you're here.'

'Fine,' I mutter, swinging my backpack off, setting it down on the floor between my feet.

Anna looks around, crossing her arms. 'This place looks *old*.'

'It's a bunker, right?' I ask. 'It can't be that old.' Cartaxus only discovered the Hydra virus thirty years ago, around the same time that gentech was invented. Mato said this was one of the first bunkers Cartaxus built.

'I guess so,' Anna says. She runs her fingers through her long blonde ponytail, flicking away shreds of foam from the detonation, her nose wrinkling. The door to the shower slides open and a woman from the market heads into what looks like a small, gleaming white bathroom. The door hisses shut behind her. Anna looks me up and down, one eyebrow arched. 'I see you're back together with Cole.'

I scratch nervously at the foam plastered on my skin, avoiding her eyes. I still don't know for sure what I overheard her and Cole talking about, but she didn't seem happy about the idea of him and me being together. 'We're figuring things out.'

She groans, flipping her hair back over her shoulder. 'He has no logic when it comes to you.'

I narrow my eyes. 'What's that supposed to mean?'

She fixes me with a steely look that makes me want to shy away. 'You don't know how much you've already hurt him. You didn't see him after you left. I didn't know if he was going to *make* it. He barely ate, he barely slept. He told Lachlan to do whatever he wanted to him – cut him open, run experimental code. He didn't care any more.'

I drop my eyes. 'I didn't know it got that bad.'

Anna props her hands on her hips. 'Maybe that's because you didn't stick around to find out. You turned yourself into the only thing holding him up, and then you disappeared. Lee and I were with him every goddamn minute to make sure he stayed alive. Lee only joined the black-out programme so he could keep an eye on Cole – he should have been in the coding group, not in the field. But we had to put Cole back together after you left.'

I stand watching her, torn. She's unloading on me, and part of me feels like I deserve it, but it wasn't me who left Cole behind. I saw the footage of the night Jun Bei left. She wasn't trying to abandon the others.

She was trying to kill herself.

'Anna, that wasn't me –'

'How convenient,' Anna says, cutting me off. 'It was all someone else's fault, right? *She* ran away. *She* was the one who hurt us. *She* was the one who gave me this scar on my neck.'

She lifts her head, revealing a short, pale scar below her left ear. A jolt runs through me. A memory flashes back suddenly of Anna lying on the floor in a pool of blood, her eyes closed.

'She did that to you?' I gasp. Leoben said that Anna and Jun Bei used to fight – but the cut on Anna's neck looks like it could have been a fatal injury. It's right next to an *artery*. Fighting with the other kids is one thing – but this looks like a murder attempt.

'I can't believe you don't remember,' Anna says, smiling bitterly. 'That's so perfect. You just get to screw us all over and make a fresh start like nothing happened.'

I dig the fingernails of my left hand into my palm. 'Anna, I'm trying to figure this out too. Lachlan changed my DNA. He overwrote my mind.'

'Yeah, like you keep saying,' she says, leaning over me. I can tell she's using her size and her training to intimidate me, and I know she won't *hurt* me, but I still feel an instinctive lick of fear as she looks down at me. 'All I know, *Catarina*,' she says, 'is that you have a cuff on your arm right now, you're talking about screwing up your mind with Mato, and you seemed pretty willing to come back into this city even though Lachlan's waiting here for you. You might say that you're someone else, but it seems to me the person you are now is a hell of a lot like the one you used to be.'

The bathroom door swings open. Anna steps back, gesturing for me to go in. 'After you,' she says.

I pause for a moment, realizing that I'm shaking, then pick up my backpack and head inside. The door swings shut behind me, a shower starting automatically in the corner. I drop my pack and press the heels of my hands into my eyes, trying to get a hold of myself.

'Come on,' I whisper, forcing myself to breathe. I drive my fingernails into my palm again, drop my hands and look around.

The bathroom is small, scuffed but clean, with a chute for contaminated clothes on the wall and a UV box to disinfect bags and belongings. I slide my backpack into it and peel off my foam-streaked clothes, then dump them in the chute. I kick off my boots and add them to the UV box, then head into the shower and lean against the wall.

The water *burns* when it hits my skin – it's scalding hot and stinging with disinfectant – but I turn my face up to it and let it run through my hair, over the foam and blood dried on my body.

Anna's words are echoing in my mind. She obviously doesn't like me, and I understand why. Jun Bei almost *killed* her, and then she left all of them behind. It's looking more and more like Jun Bei escaped from the lab that night and came here to Entropia on her own. She must have got away from Lachlan somehow and made it through the snow. I know she was desperate that night – she went out there to die and ended up killing fourteen people, so it makes sense that she would have panicked and run.

But she never told the others that she'd made it out, and I still don't know why.

Part of me wants to go hunting for answers now, but I can't let myself forget why we're here. Lachlan is in this city. Cartaxus is going to kill us all if we can't bring him in. I need to keep myself focused on the mission – if we can't fix the vaccine, then getting answers about my past isn't going to help me.

The disinfectant in the shower washes off the dried blood on my arms and neck, running down to pool on the tiles, rolling in scarlet streaks to a metal drain. This place really *does* look old. The floor is covered with patterned ceramic tiles and grout, the kind you don't see much of any more. Modern tiles are usually variations on plastene and deposited ceramic, grown like coral, fitting seamlessly into complex patterns. But these are pre-gentech materials.

The whole bathroom seems dated, and a little strange. I don't know why a bunker that Cartaxus built would have *showers* instead of airlocks. I guess Entropia had no choice but to grow their razorgrass border and set up checkpoints if this is the extent of their airtight security. Virus particles can't survive more than an hour or so without a host, so the foam across my skin isn't really a *contagion* risk, but I don't know why Cartaxus would go to the trouble of drilling an entire bunker into a mountain without putting proper airlocks in it. It's almost like this bunker wasn't even designed for an airborne plague.

The shower shuts off automatically, a high-powered fan switching on in the ceiling. I squeeze my hair out, leaning to the side, looking around for something to dry off with. A panel in the wall hisses open, revealing a folded white towel and my clothes, washed and neatly stacked.

Only, they aren't my clothes. I pick up the grey T-shirt, stretching it between my hands. The top I dumped in the chute was low-tech cotton spun from genehacked crops, all-purpose and cheap. This top is made from a polymer thread, still warm from the printer that must have matched it to my clothes while I was in the shower.

At least, I'm *guessing* it's a printer, and it must be one with open-access controls, because there's a yellow squid stamped on the front of my shirt that wasn't there before.

'Goddammit, Lee,' I mutter. I grab my boots and backpack from the UV box, then scrub off with the towel and tug on the clothes, checking the bathroom over one more time before pushing through the exit. The door opens into a vast room with a row of elevators along the far wall. The floor is tiled, the walls and ceiling unfinished concrete. Cole, Leoben and Mato are waiting beside one of the elevators, and Anna steps out of the bathroom beside me, dragging her fingers through her long, tangled wet hair.

'That shirt is even better in person,' Leoben says, grinning.

I roll my eyes. 'Seriously, Lee. You're driving me crazy.'

'You ready to go in?' Mato asks, holding open one of the elevator doors.

I look between him and the elevator, suddenly nervous. Now that we're here, it's hitting me that I'm in the same city as Lachlan, and I've made a deal to walk right into the lab of a woman who might be working with him.

I should be frightened. I should be on the verge of panic. And yet all I can think about is what Jun Bei was doing here after she escaped. Who helped her get here – who sold her the cuff on her arm. I've felt something stirring in me ever since I glimpsed this city from the Comox, and it's rising into a buzz now that we're about to go into its depths.

It's not anxiety, though, and it's not fear.

It almost feels like coming *home*.

'Jesus,' Anna says, pushing past me to the elevator. 'Come on. Let's go and get this over with.'

CHAPTER 19

We file into the elevator. The doors are steel and modern, but the cab is a metal cage that looks like it was left over from the bunker's construction. A cold breeze rises through a metal grille in the floor, bringing up goose bumps on my still-damp skin. There's enough room for all of us, along with a man with silver circuits printed on his skin and a woman with a coat of coarse grey hair, like a horse. The doors slide closed, and we drop into the rock, the elevator's cables groaning.

'Should we book a room here, or something?' Leoben asks.

Mato shakes his head. 'That's not necessary. I know a place we can use, and the empty apartments belong to everyone, anyway. The city is a commune – it's shared. The food is bad, the power isn't reliable and the comm reception is spotty, but it's a pretty wonderful place.'

I glance at him, surprised by the warmth in his voice. He seems more relaxed here than he did at Cartaxus, and he definitely fits in better. His mask made him look like a freak around the

Cartaxus soldiers, but from what I've seen of Entropia's residents so far, his upgrades are relatively tame.

The elevator slows, and the doors ping open to a concrete hallway. I step out, looking around, scanning for something to trip my memory. A hint, a clue, to tell me if I've been here before. But *everything* looks familiar, because it has the same layout as the other bunker I've seen – Homestake.

The doors on either side of the hallway are missing, and I catch the same glimpses into the rooms as I did into the quarters there. Tiny apartments built of concrete and steel, only these are unfinished. Bunches of wires hang from unpainted ceilings, and holes gape in the walls where ventilation ducts should be. Some of them have bathrooms, some don't – some are empty, and some are overflowing with personal belongings.

Cole stays close to my side as we walk, his shoulder occasionally brushing against me. Part of me wants him to be closer, for his hand to be linked in mine, but another part wishes he would walk beside Anna instead. I don't have room in my mind to process what I'm feeling about him, but whenever I feel him brush against me, I remember what Anna said – that he stopped caring after Jun Bei left. He let Lachlan run whatever tests he wanted. Back in the forest, he told me he joined the black-out programme just a few months after she left, and that he let Cartaxus erase every VR clip from his childhood.

He must have been so hurt. Even though I'm mad at him, and I don't know if he's keeping something from me, it makes me want to hold him.

'So where's our room?' Anna asks, peering into one of the empty apartments.

'This way,' Mato says, leading us towards a hum of voices. 'It's through the park. You should get something to eat if you want. Regina texted me. She said she'll send someone down to get Catarina when she's ready, and for us to make ourselves comfortable.'

'Comfortable?' Leoben asks. 'What the hell is this, a social call? We should start searching for Lachlan. We don't have a lot of time.'

'You're quite a skilled hacker, aren't you?' Mato asks, glancing at Leoben.

He shrugs. 'I'm not into DNA, but I know a thing or two about tech.'

'I don't give compliments often, Lieutenant,' Mato says. 'I've seen your work.' He pauses in the hallway, his eyes glazing briefly. 'I just gave you access to Entropia's security systems – cameras, swipe doors, elevators. The firewalls are pathetic, in part because I was only eleven when I designed them. You could go and run around on the surface with a gun if you'd prefer, but this might be a more productive use of your skills.'

Leoben pauses next to Mato, his eyes glazing. When he snaps out of his session, he raises an eyebrow appreciatively. 'You were eleven when you wrote this?'

Mato shrugs, his lips curling faintly. 'I know a thing or two about tech as well.'

'Jesus, Lee,' Anna says, shoving Leoben's back, pushing him down the hallway. 'Will you please not flirt with every skinny nerd you meet? It's disturbing.'

Leoben rolls his eyes, heading down the hallway with Anna, but there's a faint blush on his cheeks. The rest of us follow, and

I shoot a curious glance at Mato. He's not blushing, but it looks like he's trying not to smile.

The hallway branches into a foyer leading to an open area the size of a city block, its concrete walls stretching up high above us. It's laid out like a park, with walking trails looping through groves of slender trees, a winding creek feeding a lake surrounded with picnic tables. It looks like a park I'd expect to find in a city, except everything here is the wrong colour, the wrong shape, the wrong luminosity. The grass is a shade of royal blue, sprinkled with glowing white flowers. The tree trunks are cobalt, their leaves yellow and white, shaped like stars. Bushes and shrubs in shades of vivid orange and gold line the walking trails, and a dozen species of different-coloured pigeons are looping through the air.

It looks like a living painting. The air is tinged with perfume, rolling from patches of purple grasses dotted across the lawn. Everything here is hacked – every blade of grass, every leaf, every flower.

And definitely all the people milling through the park.

I thought that Novak's team at Sunnyvale was extreme – but some of the people around the park make them look positively tame. One man in a top hat towers over the rest of the crowd with long, spindly legs and arms that stretch down to his knees. A group of three women at a table all have eyes twice the normal size and narrow jaws that make them look like living dolls. A couple walking along one of the trails have furred, prehensile tails that swing behind them.

I step out, staring at them, and lift my eyes. The park is a circle, ringed with walls of apartments rising up what looks like fifty floors. A giant circle of blue sky glows above us through a vast, circular opening, sunlight slanting through at an angle, falling across the walls of apartment windows. Every few levels, I can see a ring of jagged, broken concrete and bent steel jutting from the walls. It looks like there used to be more floors above us, but Entropia's residents broke through them, hollowing out a giant space in the centre of the bunker. It's completely open to the air – the pigeons are freely swooping in from outside.

There are absolutely no airtight protections at all.

'We call this the atrium,' Mato says, gesturing up at the empty space. 'There are blast doors at the top, but Regina likes to keep them open. It helps the plants.'

I turn slowly, scanning the atrium. Some of the apartment windows are sprouting with plants, vines snaking across the concrete. One section of the wall has a dripping waterfall running down it, bordered with moss and lichen, splashing down into a pool in the park below.

It's a wild underground city, and part of me loves it instantly.

The people in the park look like they're setting up for the party that Regina was talking about. Everything is in the same glowing shade of cobalt as the pigeons' feathers. A group of people are opening barrels of luminescent paste, dabbing it in patterns on their clothes and skin. Algae paste. It's probably hacked with the same gene that makes the pigeons' feathers glow. We step into the park, following one of the walking trails that cuts to the other side.

'I can't believe they just have those doors open,' Anna says, looking up at the giant opening above us. 'It's amazing they're not all dead yet. How did they make it two years without getting infected?'

'That's what the border is for,' I say, 'and there *are* doses.'

'Ugh, gross,' Anna mutters. 'This place is a freakshow.' She wrinkles her nose, watching a woman walk past us, a backpack on her shoulders with a breathing tube coiled out of it and plugged directly into her throat. 'I don't understand why people actually *want* to screw up their bodies.'

I look Anna up and down. Her legs are long, her muscles sleek, her skin so smooth it's practically shining, and there's no way that her face was always as perfectly proportioned as it is. She's *stunning*, and none of her upgrades are obvious, but she's clearly running a lot of aesthetic code. 'You're no different from them,' I say. 'Not unless you were naturally going to be a six-foot goddess.'

Her lips quirk briefly. 'Yeah, but I'm using *normal* apps, to look like a normal person, just . . . better.'

'So you share Lachlan's view on the human form, then?' Mato asks, plucking a leaf from one of the trees on the trail's edge. 'Interesting.'

She whirls on him. 'I don't share Lachlan's view on anything, asshole.'

'They're talking about gentech,' Leoben says, his hand sliding to Anna's shoulder. 'Dax talks about this shit a lot. Just ignore them and they'll stop.'

Anna rolls her eyes and picks up her pace along the trail, dragging Leoben with her.

'What about you, Catarina?' Mato asks me, folding the leaf between his fingers, smelling it. He flicks an annoyed glance at Cole, as though he'd prefer to be talking to me alone. 'What's your view on the human form?'

'I don't know,' I say. 'I haven't made my mind up yet.'

He's talking about the *craft hypothesis* – the question of whether the human form is good, or if it's just what we're used to. Most people fall on the *craftist* end of the spectrum, believing that weaknesses in our DNA should be patched as unobtrusively as possible. They're OK with upgrades like coloured hair and aesthetic tweaks, but they wouldn't like Regina's scales, or the tails on some of the hackers around us. Skin should be *skin*, they argue. Legs should be *legs*, with limits to the definition of the human form. They argue that people with a few years of coding experience shouldn't mess with the result of millions of years of evolution.

On the other side of the argument, the genehackers see human DNA as a starting point and their bodies as tools to change as they please. They think evolution has always been chaotic – it's just been slow, and now we finally have the tools to speed it up.

During the outbreak, the craftists focused their research on ways to upgrade the body's natural immune responses. That's how Lachlan cured Influenza X – by recoding human antibodies to hunt down the virus more efficiently than before. But the genehackers took a different view. They pointed out that since the virus was transmitted through breathing, the best cure was to remove everyone's lungs.

Simple, effective, and wholly alien.

'I take it you're on the hacker side of the spectrum?' I ask Mato.

He tilts his head, considering, the glowing flowers on the trees tracing arcs of light across his mask. 'Mostly. I think there were a billion roads that humanity's evolution could have travelled down, and that it's dumb luck that we ended up in a body like this. Two legs, two eyes, two ovaries. Our digestive system is a pile of nonsense. None of it suits the way we live, but we've built so much of our society around it that I don't know if we'll ever really be able to change.'

I nod, slowing my pace as we reach the edge of the park. I've never really aligned myself with either faction but I always felt drawn to the genehackers and their dreams of the future. They wanted to solve the world's resource crunch by shrinking the average human down to three feet. They wanted to fill our skin with chlorophyll so we could feed on sunlight. Part of me loves to imagine what humanity could become if we step past the constraints of our ancestry.

And yet Lachlan's plan to alter a single gene in humanity's DNA horrifies me.

'What about you, Lieutenant?' Mato asks Cole, a slight edge to his voice. I get the feeling he's trying to embarrass Cole – to get him to say that he doesn't know what we're talking about, and it makes the back of my neck heat with anger.

'I think I might be a naturalist,' Cole says.

Mato stops short, staring at him.

'Are you serious?' I ask. 'You don't think we should use gentech?'

'Not beyond medical code, no,' Cole says.

'That's . . . very interesting,' Mato says, looking between us.

'Can we get the hell out of here?' Anna shouts, leaning against Leoben at the edge of the park. 'I've seen enough freaks to last me a lifetime. Lee thinks he can use the cameras to flush the old man out.'

'Just *yell* the plan into the crowd, Anna,' Leoben says, throwing up his hands.

'It's this way,' Mato says, striding towards a hallway leading back into the bunker's walls.

I follow behind with Cole, glancing at him from the corner of my eye. 'Did you mean that, or were you just trying to rile Mato?' I ask him.

'I meant it,' Cole says, but his face is blank, a wall over his features that I haven't seen all week. 'It's too late for me, though. Black-out tech can't be removed.'

I reach for his arm, but he picks up his pace, walking just too far ahead for me to be able to ask him what he means. We wind through a series of branching hallways and up a flight of stairs to the apartment Mato is leading us to. There's a steel door with a programmable lock that blinks green when he swipes his panel over it, swinging open into an apartment big enough for the five of us.

Metal bunks are built into the walls, a bathroom in the back. There's only a plastic pipe jutting from a blank wall where the kitchenette should be, and the walls are covered with a genehacker's scribbled notes, but it's more comfortable than the back of a jeep, which is where I've been sleeping for the last week.

'We'll need to split up and search in a grid,' Anna says, pacing across the room. 'There's a billion more places to hide here than I thought.'

'The lab I saw was outside,' I say. 'If he's in the same place, it had a view of the sky.'

Anna nods. 'That helps, but we can't assume he's in the same place.'

'You can use network signatures,' Mato says. 'Wherever Lachlan is, he has a solid link to Cartaxus's satellite network – probably a hardwired mainline connection. He wouldn't be able to hook into people's panels like he's doing, otherwise.'

I walk across the room, taking in the graffiti scrawled on the wall. There are boxes of paperback books in the corner covered with a layer of dust, and a collection of metal pens in a glass jar on the floor.

'Was this *your* room?' I ask Mato.

'It was,' he says, smiling as though he's pleased I figured it out. 'I didn't live here, but it's a place I came to think and work. My first lab, in a way.'

Anna cocks an eyebrow, looking at the genetic diagrams covering the walls. 'What were you working on? Ways to change the *human form*?'

'No,' he says, watching her, a strange look in his eyes. 'Those are gene diagrams for the processes that govern ageing and cell death.'

I turn to the wall, scanning the scribbled diagrams. Almost everyone studies apoptosis and ageing soon after they start learning to code. Unravelling the mysteries of cell death is the holy grail of gentech. We can heal our bodies, cure our illnesses and change the way we look, but there's still no magical cure to keep people from dying. There's not even a scientific consensus on just *how* we die in the first place. There's decent work being done on anti-ageing, but it's only in its infancy, and hasn't been around long enough to test properly.

'Ugh, you nerds are so boring,' Anna says, scowling. She strides to one of the bunks and sits down heavily.

I lean back against the wall, staring at the diagrams a young Mato must have sketched. One is an analysis of the DNA of the only family of organisms whose cells don't age – tiny aquatic creatures only found in a few places around the world. Coders still haven't managed to figure out the mechanism that keeps them alive. I've seen the same analysis in some of Jun Bei's work while I was reading through the code stored in my panel, but I thought the files she wrote were about the virus when I first saw them. The name of the files was misleading.

Because the creature's name is hydra.

A knock sounds on the door. Anna jumps from the bed and paces to it, pulling it open. The pale-furred genehacker I saw in Regina's lab looks over the room.

'Catarina?' she asks, giving me a smile that shows a row of curved, sharp teeth. 'Regina will see you now.'

CHAPTER 20

The pale-furred genehacker leads me back through the park towards a set of stairs built into the side of the atrium. My stomach twists with nerves as we walk, even though I know I'm not alone. Cole and Anna are shadowing me at a distance, slipping through the crowd. They won't be able to follow me into Regina's lab, though. I'll be alone with her there. I don't know what she's going to want from me. A DNA sample? A scan of my body? A biopsy of my *brain*?

Suddenly this whole deal feels wildly dangerous.

The hacker and I reach the stairwell and start to climb. It's concrete, with metal railings, one side of the stairwell open to the park. As we rise, I can see that the walking trails and the trees have been laid out in a rough circle with a jagged line cut through it. It's Regina's symbol – the one I saw on the screen when Mato was hacking the implant in my head.

The hacker stops at a steel door with a security scanner built into the concrete beside it and swipes her panel across it. It swings open to a hallway that leads to the same room I saw in the VR simulation – the vast circular lab with plants and animals covering its walls. I pause on the landing outside it, looking out at the park, spotting Cole standing beneath one of the trees with his arms crossed. He gives me a nod, and I swallow and head into the lab.

'Welcome back,' Regina says, walking across the floor to meet me, spreading her arms. The raven is back on her shoulder, but not the snake that was looped around her neck. She moves with perfect, eerie grace, her dress rippling across the floor. She smiles at me, the scales around her black eyes crinkling. 'I'm *so* glad you're here.'

'Thanks for letting us in,' I say.

She waves one hand dismissively. 'Of course. Thank you for agreeing to my terms. I know it was unreasonable to ask for you as a trade, but I couldn't just let Mato back in, not after his little coup. Entropia is where he belongs, and one day he might be a good person to lead it, but he needs to earn his place here like everyone else.'

I raise an eyebrow. 'Does that mean you're not going to study me?'

'Oh, no,' she says, beaming. 'We're definitely doing that.'

She heads across the room to one of the lab benches. I pause in the entrance, my eyes drawn to the coding terminal built into the wall. It's definitely a Cartaxus model, and from the spinning icon on its screen, it looks like it has a connection to Cartaxus's network. I don't know why Cartaxus would give Regina that kind of access. I follow her, walking past the circular platform hanging in the middle of the room. It's holding a metal shelf full of cylindrical vats filled with a dark, viscous liquid. A cold breeze blows up from the foot-wide gap between the platform and the hole in the floor. It's hard to see what's beneath it, but I catch a glimmer of light on water somewhere far below us as I walk past.

'The platform's movements help,' Regina says, following my eyes, gesturing to the vats. 'We discovered that our mammalian samples grew faster when subjected to small motions like this. A more perfect re-creation of the *in utero* environment.'

I peer more closely at the vats. There are hints of pale, rippled flesh in the dark liquid. Lungs. There must be a dozen of them inside each vat, connected to one another by slender veins and snaking wires. Regina is probably growing them to test patches for the vaccine on.

'I still have that weevil in my hand,' I say. 'It didn't come out.'

Regina pauses, her eyes glazing. 'That's strange. I sent the ejection command. It must have destroyed itself inside your hand. It happens sometimes. Your own tech will clear it out eventually, don't worry. It's harmless now.' She walks to a lab counter on the far side of the room, a pattern of cobalt lights blinking across her skin. They're not just clustered in a typical panel formation, though. Her forearm holds the bar of light I expect, running from her elbow to her wrist, but there are also blinking LEDs set into her shoulders and across her chest, dotted across her cheekbones. I can just make out the faint glow of more lights flickering beneath her dress. I frown, staring, suddenly realizing what the pattern on her skin is for.

The black splotches aren't random like I thought. They're designed to hide the path of leylines travelling across her body. They're set into the pattern of her scales, low and flat, branching across her face and weaving down her back. There must be *dozens* of them. Hundreds, maybe.

'Do you like them?' she asks, following my eyes. 'Each of the lights is just a single core. Microscopic, really. It was only after I'd designed the original panel and seen it distributed to billions of people that I realized how limiting it was. One single object in your arm to control your body, using wires to transport nanites throughout your bones and muscles? It feels archaic even describing it. It was only later that I came up with the idea for these cores.'

I stare at the glowing cobalt dots on her skin. 'They're *panels*?'

'Single-function panels,' she says. 'Most only hold one or two apps. That's not what makes them special, though.' She smiles, lifting her forearm, turning it to look at a constellation of tiny blue dots on her black-and-green skin. 'Normal panels need a bud to begin, like a seed ready to grow a tree, but these panels are so lightweight that they can be grown with just a few synthetic genes. I could never have designed this kind of technology for Cartaxus, though.'

'Why not?'

She smiles. 'They'd be worried people would try to add it into the human germline.'

'You mean people could be born with these,' I say.

Her smile grows wider. 'Indeed. What a terrifying thought.'

She's being sarcastic, but the thought *is* unnerving. The one line most genehackers agree never to cross is the altering of their children's DNA. Gentech can't change your natural DNA once it's in your cells, but it's still possible to alter it and then grow a hacked person, like Cartaxus did with me and the other kids. But that hack would be passed down to their children too, and could make its way through the population over enough time. There are some minor approved genetic tweaks that people are allowed to use when they're having children, but they're mostly for health reasons. People don't tend to try it much, though, because a baby can just get a panel once it's born and use apps that are reversible instead.

'I'm interested in how you tracked Lachlan here,' Regina says. 'You said it was related to the neural implant? I'd like to analyse it, with your permission.' She opens a cabinet, touching a few boxes before sliding one out, then flips it open, revealing a small black nub. 'This is a processor that should fit in the port in your head.'

I shift uncomfortably. The last time the implant was analysed, I ended up with wires bursting out of my arm. 'I thought you wanted to look at my DNA.'

'I do,' she says. 'This is just a passive scan. It's going to listen to the implant's output and tell me what it's doing.'

'I . . . I don't know,' I say. 'Mato hacked it earlier, and it wasn't a lot of fun.'

She sighs. 'My, he's very young, isn't he? Mato needs to learn to take a more delicate approach. He learned to fraction too young, which is my fault, but it means that he approaches everything with brute force. I hoped Cartaxus would put him with Lachlan when he joined. Lachlan might have taught him the value of care and patience, but Brink invited Mato into central command almost instantly.' She lifts the nub. 'This won't affect the implant at all. You won't even notice it. If you really do have a connection to Lachlan's panel, then I think there's a chance we can exploit it even more than simply tracking his location. But first I need to see what kind of tech this tracker is based on.'

She offers the nub to me. I take it warily. It's surprisingly heavy, made of a dull black metal with a silver port connector in one end.

'It's wireless,' she says, nodding at my cuff. 'You can run the scan yourself if you prefer. I'd just like to see the output.'

I turn the nub in my fingers, pulling up my cuff's wireless controls. The silver port connectors glow white in my vision, an access code beside them. I'm still not sure Regina can be trusted, and I'm not thrilled about the idea of putting anything in my *head*, but she's right – if there really is a link between the implant and Lachlan's panel, we might be able to do more than just find his location.

There's a chance we could use it to *hack* him.

I pull my hair to one side and slide the nub into the port, using my cuff to switch it on. The lab flashes for a moment and an image appears in my vision – the same one Mato showed me of the transparent human head. It still shows the implant in red, with the forest of wires coiling through the brain. Only, now the brain has a blush of blue stretching in a slender line between its two lobes, and a giant dark patch over part of the left one.

'You've been injured,' Regina says. 'This is a significant concussion, but it looks like you're almost healed.'

Goose bumps rise on my skin at the sight of the giant shadow. 'Mato said it happened during the decryption. Is that dark patch where I'm hurt?'

'No, the damage is the blue line,' she says. 'The implant keeps a map of your neural abnormalities like this. The dark patch is unusual too, though. It's an *orphan* – a part of your brain that's locked away from the rest of it. It usually happens after injuries, but they can be created with the implant.'

'Could it be memories?' I ask, thinking of the ocean I glimpsed inside me while Mato was hacking the implant.

Regina nods, a crease folding on her brow, crinkling the pattern of scales on her face. 'That would make sense. Lachlan might have created a cage using the implant to hide memories from you without erasing them. This is a *lot* of memories, though. Reabsorbing this amount of neural connections is dangerous, and so is wiping them. You'll need to learn how to control the implant either way.'

I blink, looking up at her. 'Do you mean that I could use the implant to *control* my memories?'

'Certainly. I can teach you how, if you choose to stay here. The implant is designed to reorganize our minds in any way we want – you could build a filing system for your memories if you really wanted to. Almost anything would be better than this, though. An orphan that size is a stroke waiting to happen.'

I stare at the image, torn between excitement and horror. Being able to control my memories would be perfect. I don't want to erase Jun Bei's past, but I'm not ready to reabsorb it, either. And yet the sight of the network of wires coiled through my brain sets my teeth on edge.

'It's so creepy,' I say.

Regina looks amused. 'The implant?'

'It's like an alien inside me, with tendrils controlling me.'

She tilts her head back and laughs. One of the birds in the cages above us shrieks in surprise, its wings flapping.

'How is that funny?' I ask.

'It's not,' she says, her laugh subsiding into a wry smile. 'You're just so young. I forget how much you have to learn.' She looks down at the image of the implant, then steps silently across the floor to stand beside me. 'Close your eyes and picture yourself.'

I give her a cautious look.

'Go on,' she says. 'I won't bite.'

I close them reluctantly, trying to conjure up a picture of my face. An image rises in my mind, stitched together from memories that blur and overlap, morphing constantly. My features in the mirror. A girl in a Cartaxus tank top lying beside Cole.

Jun Bei's eyes scrunching shut as she runs for the fence.

I open my eyes, blinking the image away.

'What did you see?'

'I – I don't know. I still don't really know who I am.'

'Then describe the first image that comes to mind when I say Catarina.'

Her prompt works. An image flashes, clear and brilliant. It's me, standing beside the Zarathustra lab after I realized Lachlan was alive. The moment I knew that I had no choice but to stop him. 'I see a girl who's been through a lot,' I say. 'Her fingernails are broken and there's blood in her hair, but she has a mission.'

A light smile plays across Regina's face. *'Wrong.'*

I shift uncomfortably. 'I don't know what you want me to say.'

'It's not what I want you to say,' she says. 'It's what I want you to *see*.' She reaches out and slides one obsidian-skinned finger across my cheek. 'You are not your face, Catarina. You are not this body, either. I could take either of them from you, theoretically, and you would still exist. You don't have blood in your hair or broken fingernails. You don't have any hair at all. The entirety of *you* weighs a little over four pounds.'

She waves her hand and the image of the implant changes, showing a transparent human body with the brain, spinal column and network of nerves shown in red. 'Does this look familiar?'

I blink, staring at it. It's just like the implant – a tight core with tendrils stretching out from it.

'That's what *you* look like,' she says. 'You are small, round, and you have a lot of tendrils that you use to control the body you're in. Everything else is an illusion. If you drive a car, you don't *become* a car. You're always just the driver. Don't buy into the vehicle of your own flesh. You of all people need to understand who you really are, because you can *change* yourself.'

There's a hunger in her eyes as she says the word *change* that makes me glance back at the laboratory door, wondering if it locks from the outside.

'I know about your gift,' she says. 'I've dedicated my life to understanding the human body and its brain, and the work is still so limited. If you were to work with me on researching how you can change your *mind*, then the possibilities could bring about the dawn of a new world.'

A shiver runs down my spine. That's the language Lachlan used in the note Mato found.

'Think of the possibilities,' she says. 'Imagine being able to control your thoughts like we control the apps inside our bodies. Imagine being able to stop distractions from barraging us every minute of every day. Our minds are natural and overgrown, like wild forests thick with brush that we have to fight through in order to stay focused, but one day, with your help, we may learn how to tame them into beautiful gardens.'

'Is that why you wanted to bring me here?' I ask.

'Partly.' She turns away, lifting the raven from her shoulder, settling it on her wrist. 'I wanted to make amends too – in whatever way I can. You and your friends have a place here in

Entropia if you want it. I wasn't lying when I said that the Zarathustra initiative was the cruellest thing I've ever witnessed. It's the reason I left Cartaxus.' Her eyes slide to the floating bodies in the tanks on the wall. 'I managed to get some people out with me, but I couldn't save the five of you, and I've regretted leaving you behind ever since. Lachlan and I tried a couple of times to get you all out, but we never succeeded.'

My chest tightens. '*Lachlan* tried to get us out?'

She nods, stroking the raven's beak. 'There's no way to excuse the things he did, but you have to understand how controlling Cartaxus is. It was different before Brink took over. The former leader was the woman we used to call the Viper. As sharp, and just as deadly. She had an incredible ability to manipulate people.'

I open my mouth to ask her how Lachlan was manipulated, and pause. Part of me doesn't want to know how he might have been controlled. I don't want to hear excuses for the years of torture he put me and the others through. But the part that still feels like his daughter is desperate for an explanation, *any* explanation for why the man I loved fiercely for three years would have done such awful things.

'I don't expect any of us will recover from what Cartaxus did to us,' Regina says, setting the raven in one of the cages on the wall. 'It's not an easy thing, healing. Not in a world like this.'

I lean back against the lab counter. 'What happened to you?'

For a moment I think I've asked too personal a question, but she doesn't seem to mind. She lifts her eyes to the cages on the wall. 'I tried to leave Cartaxus once, before I finally made it out, and the Viper nearly destroyed me for it. I fell pregnant by mistake – I'd been hacking myself and glitched my birth control.

I didn't realize the hormonal readings were real until I was a few months along.' She looks over at me, tossing the hair from her scaled shoulder, an embarrassed smile on her face. 'It was a silly mistake, and it didn't make much sense to have the baby – I'd never really wanted children before that, and the father was married, but somehow I just *knew* it was what I wanted. I decided to leave Cartaxus, but the Viper told me I couldn't. She said they'd keep the child in boarding school so I could keep working day and night. But all I really wanted was a new life with my baby.'

She lifts her hand to one of the cages, reaching through the bars to scratch at the neck of a lizard curled on a stick. 'I told the Viper I was leaving, and she threatened the baby. I ended up running in the middle of the night with nothing but the clothes on my back and the names of some genehackers who might take me in. I made it to the desert and had my little girl. She looked just like I did when I was a child, and for the first time I understood the appeal of natural DNA. But then the Viper found us. I don't know how. I'd thought about doing a postpartum confinement – I knew my mother would want me to – but I was never a fan of rules I didn't understand, so one day I went into town with the baby. She was just two weeks old. She came down with a fever that afternoon, and by midnight there were bruises.'

A chill sweeps through me. 'They *infected* her?'

She flattens her hands against the lab counter, leaning her weight into her palms. 'The Viper thought it would help me move past the barriers that had been stopping me from progressing on a vaccine. I had no choice but to go back to them, coding every moment with the baby held to me until the scent began to rise and I couldn't be around her any more. They had to keep her in a glass box, and she wouldn't stop crying.'

I cover my mouth, not knowing what to say.

Regina looks up, smiling bitterly. 'I almost did it, you know? I was so close – just another week and I might have finished it. The cure was written for *her* – it wouldn't have worked on anyone else – but it would have been more progress than any of us had made in years. But I ran out of time. They dragged me away before she blew, but I *heard* it. Every time I tried to work on the vaccine after that, I heard that sound again. I don't think I'll ever be as sharp again as I was in those two weeks. I gave everything I had, and it wasn't enough.'

I just shake my head, too horrified to speak. The thought of Dax's bruised chest flickers through my mind. He said they'd infected his whole team. He said it had been effective.

How can Cartaxus be so cruel?

'That wasn't even why I left,' Regina says. She tilts her head back, staring up at the wall of caged snakes and birds. 'I just gave up after that and let them keep me there. I woke when they woke me, worked when they told me to, slept when it was allowed. I tried to code, but I was empty inside, and my code was empty too. But the Viper saw another way to keep me motivated. She realized that she'd pushed me too far and thought she could make it right.'

A buzzing starts, low in my chest. 'What do you mean, make it *right*?'

Regina lowers her head slowly, turning her black eyes to me. 'The Viper thought of a way to give me a chance to start over again with my little girl. A clone. A copy of the child they took from me. I didn't know they'd added her to the experiment – I couldn't have foreseen it, or I would have left, or killed them, or burned the place to the ground. By the time I knew, she was already six months grown, her little legs kicking in a glass tank, wires stretching from her arm. They open their eyes when they're in tanks like that, you know? I saw her just the once, and I knew I had to leave or they'd do the same thing – let me fall far enough in love before they threatened her. She'd never be allowed a moment of safety.'

The air in the room shifts, the buzzing in my chest rising into a roar.

Regina turns her onyx eyes to me. 'You have to believe me. I left to protect *you*.'

CHAPTER 21

The room seems to fall silent – the gurgling of the water running down the walls, the screeching of the birds in their cages all dissolve in the wake of Regina's words, echoing through me.

I left to protect you.

The ocean in my mind pitches against the wall as I scan her face, tracing out the lines of her features through the onyx and emerald scales that cover her skin. High cheekbones, straight, elegant eyebrows. I can see an echo of Jun Bei's face in hers – but there's more than that. The curve of her shoulders, the intelligence in her dark eyes as she watches me. There's not a shred of Regina's DNA left inside my cells, but I can still feel it. A low, insistent tug.

'You're my *mother*?'

She doesn't answer, but steps closer to me instead, her fingers sliding over my shoulder, pulling me against her. I stand, stiff with shock, then let myself lean in to her, my head turning so her smooth, scaled cheek presses against mine.

'You're home now,' she says.

The ocean whips higher. There's something *familiar* in the smell of Regina's hair, the press of her cheek. I step away, blinking. 'Did – did I come to you before?'

'Yes, you came here. You matched your DNA to mine in a Cartaxus file. When you escaped, you made your way to Entropia and tracked me down. You stayed here for six months. You didn't live in the city, but you came in to see me regularly.'

I turn and brace my hands against the lab counter, my head spinning. I have a *mother*. I'm a *clone*, created as leverage against one of the world's greatest coders. The thought leaves me reeling, but there's more than that. This is proof that Mato was right – I left the others and ran away. I spent the missing six months of my life here. Coding, working. Living freely, away from Lachlan's control.

'I've lost you twice now,' Regina says, her voice thick. 'I left you in that lab, and then I let Lachlan take you while you were here. I couldn't save you either time, but I'm going to try now. I don't want to lose you again.'

I turn to her, pushing my hand back through my hair. There's a locked cage of memories inside me, a virus spreading across the world, and a vanishingly small amount of time to stop Cartaxus from launching flood protocol, but for the first time in weeks, part of me feels like I have something to stand on. Solid ground.

'I don't want you to answer me now,' she says, 'but I want you to consider staying here at Entropia. Your friends will have a place here too, and I can protect you inside this city. As long as you're within my borders, Cartaxus can't touch you. I have enough records of the things they've done to destroy their reputation forever. You can have a home here, and so much more than that.

I can teach you how to control the implant and your memories. We can unravel the mysteries of your DNA together.'

'We have to survive the next few days first,' I say. 'We need to find Lachlan.'

'Indeed,' she says, her eyes glazing. 'Speaking of which, the scan from your implant is finished.'

I draw up my cuff's menu to connect with the nub, and a report appears in my vision. It looks like a piece of paper hovering in front of me. I reach for it, swiping my finger, and the pages spill sideways like a deck of cards. It's filled with readings from the implant that I don't understand, but there are a dozen pages on the tracker. I scan the rows of specifications, timestamps, server logs, searching for any weaknesses that might give me access to Lachlan's panel.

But there isn't anything.

'Hmm,' Regina says, her eyes still glazed. 'I don't think the tracker is going to be much help, but I'll have a closer look at it after the party. It's almost time to go and begin the celebrations. There'll be thousands of people out in the desert tonight to watch the flocks arrive. The pigeons are only a few miles away now.'

'But what about Lachlan?' I say. 'We don't have much time.'

'I'll arrange for a search team to assist you,' she says. 'Your friends can have access to my security feed too. I'd like to find him as well, but I think he'll come to you. Any day now, probably.'

I push away from the lab counter, tensing. 'Why do you say that?'

'Because the concussion you sustained is clearly the result of an incomplete command. You said it occurred during the decryption, which means there was something else that was supposed to happen, wasn't there?'

Regina is sharper than I thought. 'I don't know for sure,' I say, 'but I think I might have been supposed to get my memories back.'

She tilts her head. 'Interesting. Well, whatever Lachlan is trying to do, it's been on pause for the last week. I think he's had to wait while you recovered from this injury. If he'd tried again while you were injured, there's a chance it could have killed you. But you're almost healed now, so he'll probably come for you soon.'

A shiver races across my skin. I've been wondering all week why Lachlan hadn't launched any more attacks of the Wrath. He could have held entire bunkers hostage to get me to go to him, but he didn't. He waited. I've let myself slip into a semblance of security, thinking he was waiting for me to go to him willingly.

But maybe he wasn't. Maybe he just had to wait until I was healed before he ran his code through me again.

And now I'm in the same city. Now I've almost recovered.

There's no reason for him to wait any more.

'You'll be safe inside this bunker,' Regina says, 'and that's where I recommend you stay. You're even welcome to spend as much time in my lab as you like – it might be the safest place in the city. I'll have people watch you, and I'll send a team to help your friends search for Lachlan tonight while the party is happening.'

'I was going to search with them.'

'That would be unwise,' Regina says. 'It should be easier for your friends to blend in and search the city while there's a crowd this large, but it would also be a good opportunity for Lachlan to take you.' She holds her hand out, and it takes me a moment to realize she wants the nub back. I reach behind my head and pull it out, and she drops it back into its box. Her hand slides to my arm. 'Think about my offer, Catarina. There's so much I want to share with you. Let's talk in the morning, after the party.'

She steps across the room to the hallway and waits expectantly for me. I follow silently, flinching as the guard at the entrance shifts her rifle between her clawed fingers to open the door.

'Oh, one more thing before you leave,' Regina says. 'You said Lachlan's Origin code was designed to alter our instincts. Was there anything else it was supposed to do?'

'Why?'

'I'm just curious.'

I shrug. 'He just said he wanted to use it to remove the Wrath from humanity, but I think it could probably be used to alter any instinct. He wanted to make us *better*.'

'Ah.' She tips her head back. 'Yes, the *Wrath*. He's always had a problem with it. He can't see that it's useless to cut us off from one of the most important instincts we have. We'd never survive without it.'

'Is that really what you believe?' I ask. 'That violence is part of our design?'

She smiles. '*Design* is a strong word to use in a place like Entropia, especially when it comes to our DNA. There are those who cannot look at this universe, with all its living creatures and humanity itself, without believing that it has been intelligently designed. As a scientist, I can't rule out the chance that they're right – in fact, that question is what drives me. I have looked closer into our foundations than anyone alive. I have gazed into each cell, into the very patterns of life that bind them, and all I can tell you is this: if there is a design that underpins us, Catarina, then it is cold, it is violent, and it is cruel.'

She gives me one last smile, her black eyes gleaming, then turns and strides back into the lab.

I wrap my arms round my chest as I leave, walking back down the concrete stairwell and into the park. The party seems to be starting – the trees are glowing, the air humming with the low, pounding bass of electronic music that sounds like a thunderstorm with a melody. The towering empty space of the atrium is filled with floating cobalt lights shaped like jellyfish that my cuff picks up as a swarm of decorated microcopters. There are crowds of people filling the atrium, lined up behind the elevator banks, queuing to get up to the surface to watch the flocks come in.

Cole pushes through the crowd, making his way to me. He pulls me into a hug, but steps away when he feels the tension in my body. 'Are you OK?'

'I'm fine,' I say, looking around. 'Where's Mato?'

'He went to talk to someone. Come on, the others are back inside.' He lifts his arm as though he might slide it round my shoulders to walk back to the room, but he decides against it and falls into step alongside me instead. We weave through the park and back down the concrete hallways, echoing now with a pulsing bass I can feel vibrating in my chest. The steel door to the apartment is open. Anna is sitting cross-legged on the floor with a towel spread out before her, oiling the pieces of her disassembled rifle. Leoben is lying back on one of the bunks with his eyes glazed, his fingers interlaced behind his head, but there's no sign of Mato.

'What did Regina say?' Anna asks, looking up.

I cross the room to one of the bunks, dropping into it with a sigh. 'She's organizing a team to help look for Lachlan tonight, during the party, and she said that we can all stay as long as we like.'

'What the hell did you give her for *that*?' Anna asks, setting a gleaming piece of her rifle down.

'Nothing.'

Cole sits down beside me. 'What's going on? Did she hurt you?'

'No, she didn't even run any tests on me. She just checked the implant to see if it could help lead us to Lachlan, but I don't think it can.' I scrape my hand back through my hair. 'She's my *mother*.'

Leoben sits up, snapping out of his session.

'What?' Anna asks. 'Like, genetically?'

I nod. 'She had a daughter that Cartaxus killed. They made a clone of her to try to keep Regina working for them. That . . . that was Jun Bei.'

'Holy shit,' Leoben says.

Cole stands from the bed, walking across the room, his face unreadable.

'She said she tried to get us away from the lab,' I say. 'A couple of times. She said Lachlan tried to get us out too.'

'Bullshit,' Anna says. 'That was Lachlan's lab. Cartaxus barely had any control over him while he was there. He could have let us out any time he wanted. Sounds to me like she's working with him.'

'What do you think, squid?' Leoben asks.

'I don't think she is,' I say. 'She really doesn't seem to agree with what he's doing. She's worried about him finding me – she said to stay in the bunker.'

'It's getting hectic out there,' Leoben says. 'There's a shit-ton of people coming to see these birds.'

'That'll make it easier to blend in,' Anna says, clicking the pieces of her rifle together. 'We can cover a lot of the city if we have a team helping. Are you sure we can trust this Regina chick?'

'I think so,' I say. 'She seemed like she was being honest. She wants to get to know me again. She's interested in the Origin code, but I don't think she wants to force it on anyone like Lachlan does. It's intellectual for her.'

'Sounds like Jun Bei's mother,' Anna says, clicking the last piece of the rifle on. 'She couldn't get you anything else to help us find him, though? We gotta search this whole place?'

'Yeah,' I say, shuffling back on the bed, leaning against the wall. 'We tried running another scan on the tracker to see if it could get us a connection to him, but it doesn't look like it can.'

I pull up my cuff's menu and bring up the report from the implant again. The pieces of paper appear in my lap, sliding through the air as I swipe my finger across them. The only thing the tracker has been sending to Lachlan is my vital signs and my location. If it was sending anything more – like packets of data – then we might be able to slide a virus into them and send it into his panel.

But there's nothing we can exploit. The only other communication the implant is making is with a cloud server for what looks like regular software updates, which is strange. I've never set up my tech for software updates. In fact, my old panel was strictly *prohibited* from updates in case any hypergenesis-unfriendly code made it into my arm. I would have noticed update settings like this in my panel.

But this report isn't from my panel. It's from the implant.

I straighten on the bed, logging in to the server the implant has been connecting to, pulling up a log of software updates that stretches back for three years. These aren't just updates for the implant, though – they're pieces of code. They're gentech apps.

The implant has been giving Lachlan backdoor access to my *panel.*

'Holy shit,' I say, staring at the log. The implant has been slipping these apps silently into my panel's background memory. I might have noticed if Lachlan hadn't made me promise not to touch my tech – if he hadn't burned the skin off my back the one time I managed to hack it. He did that to stop me discovering the truth about my DNA.

But it also stopped me discovering *this*.

'What is it?' Cole asks.

'It's . . . It's the implant,' I say, reeling. It's been giving Lachlan complete control over my tech for the last three years. He still has access now. He could install and remove apps whenever he wanted. He could tap into my *ocular* tech.

He could be watching everything I do right now.

'Shit,' I say again, standing, my heart kicking.

'What?' Cole asks. 'What's wrong?'

'I . . .' I trail off, not knowing what to say. Lachlan could be listening. He could be watching us all right now, spying through my own sensory tech. 'Nothing,' I force myself to say.

Cole's brow furrows. He knows I'm lying, but I don't *want* to. I just need to find out what the hell Lachlan has been doing to my tech.

I pace to the edge of the room, sliding back into my cuff's interface, bringing up the log of software updates. They're all pieces of custom code written by Lachlan. The earliest ones look like healing tech boosts, metabolism smoothers and a couple of antivirals. They're dated from the first few months of the outbreak, before Agnes arrived at the cabin. I was barely eating back then, barely managing to stay alive. A few months later, he sent me a bone-knitting app when I broke my finger. There are a handful of nutritional apps, and one to help me sleep.

I frown, staring at the log. It doesn't look like Lachlan has been spying on me.

He's been trying to keep me *healthy*.

A strange feeling tugs at me as I scroll through the list, remembering every injury I had over the last two years. Each one is reflected in minor updates to my tech to help heal me without ever alerting me to the fact that Lachlan was doing it. He must have been monitoring my vital signs *constantly*. A dozen files were added to my panel the day the dose blew in my stomach. There are updates for sunburn, for cramps, for the lice that bit me when I was in the caves. Everything he sent to me was medical code. Every single file . . .

Except the one that was added to my panel yesterday.

The room seems to pulse as I draw the file into my vision. It's a giant piece of gentech code, unreadable and vast. Over nine million lines. It's bigger than the vaccine, but only slightly, and it was installed in my arm just a day ago. That was when I heard the blowers in the distance – when the new strain hit the mountains.

I look up at the others, shaking. 'I think I have the patched vaccine.'

CHAPTER 22

Leoben stands from the bed so fast he's almost a blur. 'Give me the code.'

'Here,' I say, dragging the file from my panel, sending it to him in a comm. 'I don't even know if it's really –'

'Dax can check,' he says. 'He's second stage already. I'll send it to him.' He turns and strides from the room and into the hallway.

'Why do you think you have the patched code?' Cole asks.

'Because –' I start, then pause, pulling up the log of software updates again. I still don't know if it's safe to talk. I scan the list, checking for anything he could be using to listen in on what I say or see, but all he's ever sent me is medical code.

'Lachlan has access to my tech,' I say. Anna scrambles from the floor, her eyes wide, but I hold a hand up. 'It's OK, I checked for spyware. That's not what he's using it for. He's just been sending me medical code. I think he was trying to keep me alive through the outbreak. He sent me an updated copy of the vaccine just yesterday. I need to check it against one of yours, to see if it went to you too.'

Cole offers me his panel. I summon my cuff's interface, ejecting the needle-tipped reader wire from its side. Cole tenses at the sight of it. My mind rolls back to the night I jacked him into my little laptop genkit in the cabin. He was frightened by the wire. It makes sense now, knowing his past and what he's been through, and it also makes sense that he doesn't like the cuff on my arm. It's a genkit – the same machine that was at the other end of every moment of torture throughout his childhood. And now I'm wearing one wired right into my body. I've only had it for a day, but it already feels like it's part of me.

I don't know what to make of the fact that this cuff is my new favourite thing, and that it's something Cole's afraid of.

I place the wire near Cole's panel, and it wriggles out of my grasp, diving into his skin, clicking when it meets his tech. A Cartaxus login screen appears, but I know the password. It's my name – Catarina.

His eyes glaze as I navigate through his tech, searching for the vaccine. He has two – one from after the decryption, and the earlier encrypted copy that Lachlan gave him before he came to find me.

But neither match the version in my arm.

I look up at him. 'He sent me the patched vaccine, but he didn't give it to you.'

'How could he?' Anna asks. 'He doesn't have a way to broadcast it, right? Only Cartaxus can do that.'

'Yeah,' I say, 'but why would he give it to me and not send it to Cartaxus? Dax said he's been trying to get Lachlan to send him a copy of this for days.'

'Lachlan doesn't care about Dax getting infected,' Cole says, his face darkening. 'He doesn't care about anyone else.'

He doesn't say the words, but I still feel them hang in the air. Lachlan doesn't care about anyone else except for *me*.

I shake the thought away. 'I'm gonna give you the new version, OK?' I upload the patched file into his arm and kick off the installation, then start to log back out, but pause. There are a handful of texts floating unread in his inbox. They're from Anna, sent in the last few minutes, after I got back into the room. The urge to open one is overwhelming, but he'd know that I read it, and I don't want to violate his privacy. A chat history is collapsed behind the new messages – I can't read any of them, but there are hundreds of texts from just the last few hours.

Another one blips into his inbox while I'm watching, and I force myself to log back out and retract the wire. I *knew* they were texting earlier while we were driving here. It looks like they've been communicating nonstop since Anna showed up in the jeep. I know they're brother and sister, and I know they've been apart, but it's not like the two of them couldn't have just talked in front of us.

Maybe not in front of Mato, but surely Leoben, and surely *me*.

'You want the code?' I ask Anna.

'Panel's locked up,' she says, waving her arm. 'Black-out soldier, remember?'

'I can hack it. I did that for Cole.'

'I'm good,' she says, scrunching up the towel she's been cleaning her rifle on. 'If it's the real deal, then Cartaxus will send it out soon anyway.'

I wind the wire back into my cuff. Anna clearly doesn't like the idea of me getting into her arm, but that doesn't surprise me. She doesn't seem to trust me much at all. I pace back to the bed to sit down, and Leoben pushes through the door, his face clouded. He heads for his backpack.

'What did Dax say?' I ask. 'Is everything OK?'

'I don't know,' he says. 'I sent the code to him, and he was installing it while we talked. He said it seemed like it was working, and then the call dropped out.'

'Mato said the comm reception was bad here,' I say.

'That's just it. I found a spot where it's not so bad. I think it dropped out from his end.'

'Maybe his panel needed to reboot to get the code running,' I say.

'Maybe,' Leoben mutters. 'What's the plan? Are we gonna kill Lachlan now that we have the code?'

'What?' I ask. 'That's not the mission. We don't even know if that code is *safe*. We can't kill him. We need to get him back to Cartaxus and under control.'

Anna snorts, rolling her eyes. 'Of course you don't want to kill him. He was your *dad* until last week. He's been sending you medical code, taking care of you, making sure you don't get the *big bad strain.*'

'Anna, stop it,' Cole says.

'What?' she says. 'It's not like this is anything new. She was always his favourite. They were practically *friends* back at the lab.'

I stand from the bed. 'You have no idea what you're talking about.'

'Yeah? Well, why does he want you to get your memories back, huh?'

I look at Cole. 'You told her?'

'He tells me everything,' she says. 'And thankfully he does, because I seem to be the only one here who realizes you're a threat. Lachlan wants to work with you – he's literally *said* it. He wants his coding partner back. His little apprentice.'

'How dare you?' I say. 'He *killed* me. He changed my *brain*. I have more reason to want him dead than any of you.'

Leoben steps to move between us, bracing his hand on my shoulder. I realize with a shock that both my hands are in fists, my feet sliding instinctively into the fighting stance that Leoben's been teaching me all week.

'Then where were you for those six months?' Anna asks.

'Drop it, Anna,' Leoben says.

'No,' she says, striding closer. 'I want to hear the truth. You were here, weren't you?'

I glance at Cole. His face is tight, and it makes my heart twist.

'Regina said Jun Bei spent six months living in the desert,' I admit.

Anna throws her hands up. 'I knew it. You ran away, and he let you. He could have tracked you down, especially if you were here.'

'He *did* track me down,' I say, 'and then he wiped my *brain*. I wasn't the only one who got out, anyway. Ziana escaped, and he never found her.'

'Ziana doesn't even have a goddamn panel,' Anna says. 'Finding her is impossible. You really don't know anything, do you?'

The breath rushes from my lungs. I had no idea that Ziana was unpanelled. I barely have any memories of her at all.

Anna rolls her eyes. 'I don't even know why I'm bothering with you. I'm gonna go and find this team of Regina's that's supposed to be helping. We need to build a search grid. You guys come and meet me when you've got your shit together.'

'I'm coming with you,' I say.

'Are you kidding me?' Anna says, whirling on me. 'You're *compromised*. You just told us Lachlan can get into your arm.'

'I told you, there's no spyware –'

'And are you going to check that every few seconds? What if he installs something when we're out in the streets? You can't come with us. You'd be giving away our location as well as yours. You can't even be part of our planning, OK? You're off this mission, and I don't care what Mato has to say about it.'

She snatches up her rifle and storms out of the room. I shove my hand back through my hair, pacing to the wall.

'That went well,' Leoben says.

I throw back my head. 'Not now, Lee.'

'I'm serious,' he says. 'That was always coming, and there was a lot less blood than I expected.' He looks between me and Cole, then grabs his rifle and heads for the door, pausing to press a kiss to my temple. 'We're going to find him, OK? You stay safe, squid.'

'Yeah, sure,' I mutter.

Leoben looks at Cole. 'We could really use you.'

'I'll see,' Cole says, and Leoben heads out.

'Anna hates me,' I say, pacing across the room.

Cole sighs. 'She's just angry that she never managed to escape. She had it hard, maybe harder than any of us. She really needed to get out, and she never could.'

I look up at him. 'What do you mean she had it harder? What's her gift? What was Lachlan doing to her?'

Cole purses his lips. 'That's between you and her. It's not for me to say.'

I tilt my head back, frustrated. 'I want to come with you tonight. I really don't think you can kill Lachlan.'

'We won't kill him,' he says. 'We all know he's worth too much. He needs to be put back under control, the way he always kept us. You've already done enough. You found the patched vaccine. That's huge, Cat. People are going to survive because of you.'

He makes a move towards me, as though he wants to pull me into his arms, but pauses as the door swings back open. Mato walks in, his black jacket streaked with glowing cobalt handprints. A buzz runs through me as I meet his eyes, but it's just another blare of noise in the static from the argument with Anna, from Regina, from Cole.

'I just heard from Brink,' he says. 'They're running tests on the code you sent, and it looks like the patch is working. Brink said they should even be able to separate the Origin code from the vaccine faster now that they can compare the two versions. We might just be a few days from having the clean code in our arms.'

'Does that mean they're going to send it out?' I ask.

'Maybe,' Mato says. 'People are dying, but the last time Cartaxus sent out Lachlan's code without understanding it, they ended up launching a drone strike on a city. Our orders are still to bring in Lachlan.'

I glance over at Cole. I know he won't want to leave me here, but Lee's right – they'll need him to search the city. If they find Lachlan, then three of them might just be enough to take him down.

'Regina said I could go to her lab,' I say to Cole. 'It's guarded. I'll be safe there. You should go with the others.'

'I don't want to leave you.'

'I'll stay with her,' Mato says.

'Lachlan might be coming for her. She needs to be protected.'

'I can do that,' Mato says, 'but Catarina is perfectly capable of protecting herself.'

I look between them. 'I'll be fine, Cole. I need to talk to Mato anyway.'

Cole glances at his rifle, torn. I know he wants to stay with me, but I also know he wants to be out in the city with Anna and Lee, hunting for the man who gave him the scars across his chest.

He reaches for my hand, squeezing it in his. 'I'll be back as soon as I can, OK?'

I nod, letting his fingers slip from mine. 'Good luck.'

He grabs his rifle, holds my eyes and jogs from the room.

CHAPTER 23

'Let's go,' I say to Mato, tugging on my jacket. I don't think I can stay still right now – I want to pace, to fidget, to find something to do. I know the patched vaccine isn't a real solution – Cartaxus still can't read it and figure out what Lachlan is doing with the code – but surely it means that Brink will hold off on flood protocol. Even if the vaccine is dangerous, it can't be as bad as killing everyone on the surface.

The only way we'll *really* be safe is once Lachlan is captured and stopped, but at least the threat of the new strain is probably over.

Probably.

I grab my backpack and head out through the steel door and down the labyrinth of hallways that lead to the atrium, following the sound of the pigeons. Mato follows close behind me, his hands in the pockets of his jeans.

'I was hoping you could help me learn to control the implant,' I say to him. 'I don't know how to use it at all. Lachlan has access to my tech through it, and I don't know how to shut that off.'

'Sure,' he says. There's something in his hair and on his clothes – like golden dust, but it's *glowing*. I didn't see anything like it in the atrium when I went through earlier. Everything there was glowing in shades of blue, not gold.

'Where have you been?' I ask, eyeing the specks on his jacket.

He dusts his shoulders off. 'I went to get something from the jeep. The elevators are crowded with people heading up to the surface to see the birds coming in, so I took a secret exit.'

I raise an eyebrow. 'Secret?'

He shoots me a grin. 'A maintenance tunnel. One of those things you find when you grow up in a place like this.'

We reach the end of the hallway and step out into the atrium. The park is packed full of people, the roar of the pigeons' cries drowning out the bass from the speakers. Some of the genehackers are carrying instruments, playing as they wait around the elevators. They'll all be heading up to the streets on the surface of the mountain to watch the pigeons come in.

The sky above us is dark, but cobalt bioluminescent paste has been streaked across every face, painted on clothing and pooled into lanterns carried atop long poles by the crowd. Instead of a mass of bodies, the glowing points of blue turn Entropia's people into an ocean of light splashing against the atrium's concrete walls. The air hums with their voices, layered over the hailstorm of the pigeons' cries.

Mato pushes into the crowd and I follow close behind, grabbing a fold of his jacket to keep from getting separated. The air is thick and humid with the breath and sweat of hundreds of bodies, tinged with the scent of the algae paste.

'How did things go with Regina?' he calls over his shoulder, dodging a man whose back is covered with porcupine-like spines.

I shy away from the man, tightening my grip on Mato's jacket. 'Did you *know*?' I yell over the music. 'About her being my mother?'

He looks back at me, his mask clearing so I can see both his eyes. 'Yes, she mentioned you.' A woman wearing a dress made of black feathers tries to cut between us, and Mato reaches his hand back for me. I grab it, and he hauls me closer. 'I didn't tell you because it wasn't my place,' he says, raising his voice over the crowd, 'and I didn't want to sway you to take the deal she offered.'

I can't decide if him not telling me the truth about Regina was thoughtful or reckless. I guess I can appreciate that he didn't want to push me into making a deal with her, but it makes me wonder if there's anything else about Jun Bei that he hasn't told me. We push out of the thickest part of the crowd and Mato drops my hand, heading through the park for the concrete stairs that lead to Regina's lab. My skin is slick with other people's sweat, smeared with cobalt paste, and my hand is warm from being in Mato's grip. The feeling sends a low, unwelcome jolt through me. I clutch my backpack straps and jog after him through the thinning crowd.

'So what's with you and Regina, anyway?' I ask, grabbing the stairwell's metal railing, climbing up after him. The stairs zigzag up through the side of the atrium, one side open to the air.

Mato shrugs, pausing at a landing, looking out over the park. 'There are no children allowed in Entropia. It's too dangerous for them here – hackers tend to get caught up in wild ideas like removing their stomachs or switching out their eyes, and they'd inevitably do the same thing to their kids. It's one of the only rules here, but Regina broke it to let me in. I think she paid extra attention to me to make up for not being around for Jun Bei.'

I pause beside him on the landing, catching my breath. 'Why did she let you in?'

He presses his lips together. 'Would you believe it was because I was an immensely talented coder even as a baby?'

I raise an eyebrow. His mask has darkened slightly, a cautious look on his face.

'Uhhh, sure,' I say. 'Talented baby it is.'

We climb up another flight of stairs to the steel door leading to Regina's lab. It's locked, the security scanner beside it glowing red. The pale-furred guard from before is standing outside it.

'Regina said I could be in here,' I say.

'She's out,' the guard replies. 'Nobody's allowed in.'

'She gave me permission,' I say, but the guard just shakes her head.

'Here,' Mato says, leaning forward to swipe his panel over the scanner. It flashes green, and the door clicks open. 'See? She gave me permission too.'

The guard doesn't look pleased, but she steps aside to let us into the hallway that leads to the lab. The lights are off, and the cages hanging from the walls in the circular room are silent. The four tanks holding the twitching bodies are lit faintly, casting a cool glow over the hanging platform and the jars of floating lungs. Mato holds the door open for me, then closes it carefully behind him, a smug look on his face.

'How did you do that?' I gesture to the door.

'I told you I wrote the security protocols,' he says. 'They're not very good, I have to admit. I thought Regina would have fixed them by now.' He glances at the tanks. 'Come on, there's a less creepy room upstairs.'

He heads for a staircase leading off the hallway, climbing past what looks like a storage room and into a vast room shaped like a steep pyramid, a pale green light set into its apex. The walls are metal, studded with DNA archive tanks, and a round white table takes up most of the floor. I dump my pack beside the table and walk to the archive canisters on the closest wall. There are old-fashioned photographs below each of them showing different strains of the pigeons – some pure white, some black-winged and some a brilliant gold.

'Is this whole room for the pigeons?' I ask.

Mato looks around. 'It looks like it. The birds came after my time here, but the city seems to love them. They've turned into a symbol for genehackers all around the world. I've always found them kind of disturbing, myself.' He leans against one of the walls, crossing his arms. 'So what did you really want to do here tonight?'

'I told you – I want to learn to use the implant.'

'That's not what you want to do,' he says. He pushes off the wall and walks over to me. The same uncomfortable buzz I've felt every time I've been around him is back, growing stronger as he steps closer. He leans against the slanted wall beside me, a low smile on his face. 'You want to learn how to *fraction*.'

The buzz grows stronger. 'I just need to block the access –'

'Fractioning will help with that,' he says. 'Any commands you can train into the implant will help you control it.' He slides the metal pen from his pocket and twirls it between his fingers. 'I can teach you, but it might take time. Would you like to try?'

I chew my lip, nerves fluttering through me at the thought. 'Yeah, OK.'

'Good.' He turns and looks around the room, then lifts two canisters at random from the archive tanks and sets them on the table. Two images suddenly appear in the air – VR animations of a green-feathered bird and a scarlet bird with purple wingtips. They hover above the table, still and silent.

'OK, let's see what I can do when I focus on each one individually,' Mato says. His eyes glaze, and the green bird responds. It suddenly flutters to life, flapping across the room, soaring in a circle above us. It's not really there – it's just a VR image, but I can't help ducking when it swoops past my head.

Mato pauses, and the green bird goes still. He does the same thing with the red one – sending it in a slow, lazy flight around the room.

He shoots me a smile. 'Pretty basic. Now I'm going to try fractioning.'

His mask brightens, glowing faintly as he stares at the birds. His eyes glaze, his body tensing, and the birds flutter to life again. Only now, both of them are moving. They soar in complex patterns through the air, dipping and banking on invisible winds. He's controlling them both at the *same* time somehow. He blinks, his mask growing dim, and the birds go still.

'That was a fraction,' he says. 'I was focusing on a different bird in two separate parts of my mind. Now it's your turn.'

'That . . . that sounds impossible,' I mutter, stepping round the table to stand where he was. I can barely even *imagine* how to do two things at once. I open my cuff's interface to connect wirelessly with the DNA canisters and look between the birds, one at a time. Each responds individually when I focus on it, urging them to move. The red bird swoops, then the green one. But when I try to focus on both at once, my eyes darting between them, they just fly in short, alternating bursts.

Mato moves to my side, standing so I can feel the fabric of his jacket against the back of my shirt. 'You're not trying to look at them both,' he says. 'You're trying to *think* about looking at them both. The images are responding to the net of electrodes in your skull, not your eyes. Try to hold the *idea* of looking at both in your mind.'

I let out a slow breath, staring at the birds, trying to conjure up the *thought* of looking at both of them. They flutter to life, moving faster, but they're still flying one at a time, and I don't *feel* anything unusual in my mind.

'Push harder,' Mato says. 'You can do this, I know you can.'

I press my fingertips into the table, trying to focus. At first, all I can think of is the two images overlaid across each other, but then the thought starts to blur in my mind. I can almost feel a wall rising like the one I glimpsed back at the lab, but pain blossoms in the base of my skull and I step back, shaking my head.

'I can't do it,' I say. It seemed like I was close to something there, but it felt like it was *hurting* me. Regina said I wasn't fully healed yet. I probably shouldn't be risking myself with a fraction right now. I rub my temples. 'Maybe I should wait. That felt weird.'

'You can practise anytime,' Mato says. 'It's easier after the first. Just don't go above two fractions. I didn't go above two for years. If you rush too fast into learning this, you can hurt yourself.'

I blow out a sigh. 'Everyone is so concerned with me hurting myself,' I mutter. My eyes drift across the room, landing on a canister for the glowing strain of the pigeons on an otherwise empty shelf. I pick it up and set it on the table. A VR image of one of the cobalt-and-black birds appears alongside pages of sequencing reports and gene diagrams that hover in the air. I scroll through them, curious about the birds' DNA. Entropia created the other birds, but Regina said that this flock had simply mutated on its own.

'What are you doing?' Mato asks.

'I'm just looking.' I scan through the gene report on the glowing strain, skimming over the mutations in its DNA. Most of it looks normal, but there are enough tweaks and quirks that I could spend years studying them. There are genes from rodents, from jellyfish, and even bacteria spliced into the birds' avian DNA. 'I just don't believe that this strain is a natural mutation,' I say, 'but I can't see any reason here why it wouldn't be.' I pull up the map of the glowing birds' spread. It looks like this flock first appeared in Canada. They've been thriving. There are millions of them, streaking across the country, crossing Alaska into Russia, across Greenland and into Europe.

'They're everywhere,' Mato says. 'All over the world.'

I nod, frowning, looking at the map, something tugging at my memory. A *crack* echoes faintly, making the canisters wobble on the table. It's followed by another, then a string of smaller, fainter explosions in the distance.

I look back at Mato. 'Fireworks?'

He tilts his head, listening. 'I think so, but those first two sounded *close*.'

'Could it be drones?'

'No, there's no Cartaxus activity near here. Those sounded like improvised explosives. Something small, but powerful. It's funny . . .'

I look up. 'What's funny?'

He purses his lips. 'They almost sounded like Hydra clouds. But they were too small.'

Another *crack* echoes faintly, sending a shiver up my spine, but Mato is right – it's too small to be a blower. It must be fireworks celebrating the arrival of the pigeons.

I draw my focus out of the DNA canister's connection, and the map of the glowing flock's population disappears just as its shape tugs at my memory. A jolt runs through me.

'Wait,' I say, throwing my hand out. The map reappears, hovering in the air. It shows scarlet lines streaking around the world, tracking the flock's spread. The population is getting bigger as they fly, breeding out of control.

But I've seen this pattern before.

Back in the Comox when Dax arrived at the lab, he showed me a map like this, only it wasn't pigeons he was tracking. It was the spread of the new strain of the virus. That was days ago, but the match is still uncanny.

'What is it?' Mato asks.

I grab my pack and push past him, pressing my shoulder against the door, jogging back down the stairwell to Regina's lab. Mato's footsteps echo above me, the door to the pigeon archive slamming shut. I hurry down the hallway as another *crack* echoes through the room, then pull open the lab's steel door.

The guard is gone, the music raging, a crowd still gathered in the park. I step across the stairwell's concrete landing and grip the metal railing to look out into the atrium. We're four floors up, high enough to see the people queuing for the elevators and the dark cylinder of the atrium. But it isn't really dark. The glowing flock is sweeping in from outside, painting streaks of light in the air above the park. The birds are circling, calling, swooping down into the bunker, their cries echoing from the atrium's curved walls.

A *crack* cuts through the music and my grip tightens on the railing. I lift my gaze, searching through the flock, spotting feathers puffing through the air. It looks like a glowing firework, sending streams of frantic pigeons racing away from it.

Mato reaches my side and looks up, confused, until another bird detonates in a glowing puff of blue. Screams rise from the crowds of people gathered in the park. Mato grabs my arm, staggering back, covering his mouth.

'Catarina, get *back*. We need to get inside now.'

'We've already been exposed,' I breathe. I can smell it in the air – sulphur and wood smoke. The unmistakable notes of plague. No wonder Cartaxus hasn't been able to contain the new strain of the virus. It isn't just spreading through *people* any more.

It's jumped to the pigeons.

Now there'll be no stopping it.

CHAPTER 24

The pigeons are a wild, swirling mess of cobalt light, circling down through the open blast doors and into the bunker's atrium. Their cries are deafening, echoing from the curved walls, and the people gathered in the park are scattering, fleeing through a slow rain of black-and-blue feathers.

I didn't know that the end of the world would look so beautiful.

Mato stands beside me, his face stricken, watching the pigeons arc through the air, the crowd below us fleeing for cover. But there's no cover any more, not really. There's nowhere left to hide.

If the virus is in the pigeons, then the vaccine may as well be dead.

I close my eyes, gripping the staircase's metal railing. There's no way to stop the virus from evolving any more. We could vaccinate every person on the surface and the plague would continue to thrive and spread like wildfire. It has *billions* of new hosts now, and it's just starting to move through them. No wonder the mutations in the new strain are so different. It's a species jump. We've been fighting this virus with the best tools we have – vaccines and doses, bunkers and quarantine strikes – and it wasn't even close to good enough.

Nature leaped forward on her own, and now she's laughing at us.

'We should go,' Mato says, taking my arm gently.

'Why?' I breathe. 'It's over. We've already *lost*.'

'No we haven't. Not yet. The patched vaccine still works.'

'For how long?' I laugh bitterly, gesturing at the birds. 'A week? A month? We lost Lachlan's first vaccine, and now we're going to lose this one. This is the end, Mato.'

'You haven't needed a vaccine to survive the last two years,' he says, his grip on my arm tightening. 'We're going to beat this. Lachlan isn't the only person who's capable of saving us.'

I stare into his eyes, the roar of the pigeons washing over my senses, his words circling through me. He's right. I survived the last two years without a vaccine, and this is no different. It's a new threat, but it's still just a virus. If the vaccine fails, we'll write another. Or maybe we'll get rid of our lungs, or alter our cells, or change our bodies in any of a thousand ways to beat this plague.

There's still hope as long as we're alive. There's a chance of a future.

Voices rise suddenly below us, near a bank of elevators on the edge of the atrium. People are streaming out of them, flooding down from the surface. They're dressed up for the party – smeared in glowing algae paste, but they're also covered with feathers, and one man is carrying a wounded woman in his arms. Regina said thousands had travelled here to witness the flock's homecoming, and they're all in the desert right now. It's going to be pandemonium up there, and they'll all be trying to get back down here.

This is going to turn into chaos, fast.

Mato's eyes glaze, glyphs flashing across his mask. He stiffens. 'Shit,' he says, 'we need to go. There's an elevator this way.' He turns and runs down the stairwell.

I tear my eyes away from the crowd streaming from the elevators and follow him, running down the stairs and into a tunnel that looks like it's been blasted into the rock.

'We should contact the others,' I say.

'They'll already be gone if they know what's good for them,' Mato says, reaching a concrete room with a steel elevator cage in its centre, a shaft cut through the floor and ceiling. He punches a button on it to call the car. 'I just received an alert from Cartaxus. They're quarantining these outbreaks. They'll be sending drones right now.'

'What?' I spit, grabbing the cage to catch my breath. 'That's madness. The virus is in the *pigeons*. Trying to quarantine them is like trying to quarantine the ocean. Bombing us won't do anything.'

'I know that,' Mato says, 'but I don't think Cartaxus will see it like we do. They have protocols to follow, and the one they're using now says to bomb an outbreak and kill as many of the infected as possible. They'll probably see this as a good opportunity to kill a lot of the birds.'

I draw my hand back from the elevator's cage, still gasping for breath. My skin is slick with sweat, a couple of soft, downy feathers plastered to my arms. The elevator cables sing as the car rises from below us. 'They can't bomb this place,' I say. 'There are thousands of people here.'

'Trust me,' Mato says. 'This is my home – I don't want this to happen any more than you do. We can try to stop it once we're out of here.'

The elevator doors swing open. The car is metal and wide, sized for cargo. Mato drags the iron grille aside, ushering me in. I lean against the wall, flicking the feathers from my skin, picking one from a fold in my shirt. Mato hits a button on the side, and we begin to rise.

'Will people be safe in the bunker if Regina closes the blast doors?' I ask.

'It depends what weapon they're planning to deploy. It won't be the smaller drones, not now they know I'm here. There are two kinds they could use that they know I can't hack – a nanite-weapon that should leave the lower levels unscathed, or destroyers with artillery. If they send in the destroyers, there's nowhere to hide. They carry payloads designed to destroy bunkers.'

'Why the hell does Cartaxus have weapons designed to destroy bunkers?'

Mato crosses his arms, his face dark. 'I think you know the answer to that question.'

The elevator rises, hurtling up through the rock, passing through open landings in a dozen higher levels. I close my eyes, trying to think, scanning through Jun Bei's code for anything strong enough to take down a destroyer, but I don't think it's something she ever thought to try.

An ache in my hand snaps me out of my session.

'Shit,' I whisper, looking down. 'Mato, we . . . we have a problem.'

I lift my left hand. A yellow light is blinking on the pad between my thumb and forefinger. It's aching, making the muscles in my hand twitch. It's the weevil Regina's drones shot me with. It was originally coded to keep me out of the city. Regina told me it was dead.

But it clearly isn't. She's recoded it to keep me *in*.

'Goddammit, Regina,' Mato snarls, looking up through the caged top of the elevator car. The shaft above us cuts all the way to the mountain's surface, a circle of cobalt light above us growing larger as we speed up through the rock. 'I can't get through to her. She isn't responding to my comms.'

'We have to be able to kill this thing,' I say, letting my eyes glaze, searching with my cuff for the weevil. A pulse ripples across my vision, lighting up Mato's mask and countless open connections around us – appliances and tech in the apartments around the atrium. A tiny dot in the back of my hand is glowing white.

A *thud* sounds against the top of the elevator, jerking me out of my session. 'What was that?' Another thud sounds, shaking the car. The weevil's light has turned orange, which I assume is a bad sign.

Mato looks up. 'Pigeons. They're in the shaft.' He narrows his eyes as though listening. A low roar is starting up in the distance, echoing from above us. 'I think there's going to be a crowd up there when we stop,' he says.

'Great,' I say, closing my eyes, trying to shift my focus back into my cuff. The weevil glows white in my wireless interface, and I try to hook into its controls, but it's not coded like anything I've seen before. It has more firewalls than most of Cartaxus's servers.

Regina hasn't designed her weevils to be easy to kill.

'Let's try it together,' Mato says. A request from him blinks in the corner of my eye, but it's not a comm. It's a shared coding session. A wall of text flickers into my vision when I accept it, commands from Mato's mask coming dazzlingly fast. He's joining my attempt to hack the weevil, but it isn't working. We're not even getting close. The light in the back of my hand is growing darker, pulsing a deep orange. The pain rolling from it rises steeply, feeling like a needle pressed into my skin.

I scrunch my hand into a fist, breathing through it. 'This isn't working.' I glance up. The roar of the crowd above us is getting louder. We're almost at the surface, and the elevator is groaning, slowing down. 'We have to be able to cut it out. It isn't that big.'

I sling my pack off my shoulder, flipping it open, digging inside it for something sharp. I've cut out my *panel* once before. This thing is smaller than a pea. My fingers slide over the files in my pack and I grasp the end of a slender medkit. I yank it out, leaning back against the side of the car.

'Wait,' Mato says, grabbing my wrist. 'She said not to remove it. I've seen tech like this that deploys a lethal dose when you try to cut it out.'

'So we cut around it,' I say, unzipping the medkit. 'There has to be a way to get this thing out.'

The elevator shudders to a stop at the top of the shaft, where a rocky cavern leads out to the winding streets on the mountain's surface. The cavern is completely packed with people, their voices frantic, their bodies pressed against the elevator cage. I jump away from the car's steel wall, slinging my backpack on again, moving closer to Mato. His eyes widen as he looks out at them. The air is humid and scented with sulphur, ringing with shouts and the cries of the pigeons. There are feathers plastered to the skin of most of the people in the crowd.

They could be infected. As far as I know, Cartaxus still hasn't updated the vaccine.

'Stay close to me,' Mato says, gripping my wrist, moving to the front of the car. The bell rings and the doors grate open. The crowd rushes in, hitting us like a wave of flesh and heat. Mato lurches out through them, shoving people aside, his hold on my wrist like iron. My backpack catches and tears on the hooks jutting from someone's implants, the crowd pressing so tight against us it's hard to breathe.

We make it halfway out of the elevator, but the crowd keeps coming, surging in, desperate to get away from the pigeons. But it's useless – they're just panicking. They're already exposed, and there's no safety from the virus waiting downstairs for them.

'Get out of my way!' Mato shouts, shoving a man aside. The crowd ahead of him parts just enough for him to push through with his shoulder, dragging me with him. We stumble to the edge of the cavern, the crowd thinning out around us, and Mato grabs the wall, heaving in a breath. His skin is soaked with sweat from the crowd, feathers plastered to his neck. The opening that leads outside is thick with people, but I can make out a circle of sky and glowing pigeons, like a wall of starlight beyond it. The weevil has turned red, the pain pulsing from it like a cigarette pressed into my skin.

'Shit,' Mato gasps, going still suddenly. His mask flashes with glyphs. 'Cartaxus has sent destroyers. I can feel them. I can't take these down.'

My blood runs cold. I look back at the crowd. Their voices are a roar of frustration and confusion. We should tell them to get out of here, but they're lost in panic. They're practically crushing one another to get into the elevators. The entire city will be in chaos.

I look down at the red spot on my hand. 'How much longer?'

'A few minutes,' Mato says. 'We need to get that weevil *out*.'

I drag my backpack off my shoulder and yank it open, searching for the medkit again. One of the pockets is ripped open, the fabric shredded by the hooks in the genehacker's skin. I glance back at the crowd, my stomach dropping. 'I can't find the medkit. It must have fallen out.'

'Are you sure?'

I nod, scrambling desperately through the backpack, yanking out clothes and nutriBars, dumping them on the floor. All that's left inside is a packet of wipes and a crumpled folder of Lachlan's notes. I shove my hand into the bottom, and my fingers brush the sharp end of a long, segmented strip of metal, and the breath rushes from my lungs.

The box of flash strips is still in here. Leoben used one to cut the cable holding down the Comox. I close my eyes, locking my fingers around one of the strips, my hands already shaking. I yank it out of my backpack. The black metal is scratched, but intact. My eyes rise to Mato's, a chill creeping down my spine. I've seen one of these things cut through steel chains.

It can definitely cut through my arm.

Mato's eyes flare. He looks back at the crowd, then nods swiftly. 'You'll need to get the top of the cuff off first. Go into your settings and unlock sections one through five.'

I fall to my knees, dropping the backpack, and close my eyes, logging into the cuff's settings, unlocking the wrist section. It shifts on my skin, a whirring noise cutting the air, and five sprockets around my wrist fly open, leaving the section of glass covering my forearm in place. I yank at the edge of the black glass, wincing as it pulls away from my skin. Wires tug out of the cuff, coiling back into a row of black ports that have grown across the top of my hand. Underneath the glass, the skin is pale and soft, the ports glistening with nanofluid.

And now my wrist is exposed.

I look up at Mato, wrapping the flash strip around my wrist, my hands shaking at the weight of what I'm about to do. This is no easy gentech fix. Reattaching a limb is possible, but repaired nerves grow differently – once neural pathways are disrupted, they'll never be the same again. I don't even know if we'll be able to save my hand. The weevil might kill it.

But if I don't do this, we're going to be trapped here when the destroyers arrive.

'We don't have much time,' Mato says, kneeling beside me. 'Do you want me to do it?'

I hold his eyes and shake my head, steeling myself, hearing the whine of jets in the distance.

The red dot pulses in the back of my hand, and I yank the flash strip's lever.

CHAPTER 25

A single heartbeat of time that feels like an eternity passes. I open my eyes and catch the starlight of the pigeons through the tunnel leading out into the city. Mato's shoulders are tight, his eyes locked on mine. Something tugs hard at my arm, and a flash of white light splashes through the air.

There is no pain. No sound. Just a sensation of *wrongness*, like I've made a choice that's wrenched the path of my life off course. A sudden desperate urge to go back and change my mind surges through me. I blink, swaying, and feel my cheek hit the cavern floor.

'Don't look. It's over now.' Mato's voice is calm above the screech of the pigeons, the shouting of the crowd, the desperate thud of my own pulse. My hand feels cold, my fingers are burning, and some part of me knows that they're not *there* any more, but the thought is still too foreign and violent for me to process it.

'You did it,' he says, grabbing my shoulders, turning me on the floor. His face comes into focus above me, flecks of cobalt feathers plastered to his cheeks. A group of people swarm into the cavern, screaming, rushing in from the city outside. Mato angles his body over mine protectively as they race past, shouting and stinking of infection.

He reaches out and picks something up, putting it in my backpack. Distantly, I know it's my hand. He grabs my shoulder, squeezing it. 'The weevil is out. It turned off when you severed it.'

I nod, trying to choke out a response, but all I can do is gasp for air.

Something clamps down on my upper arm. Mato jerks at something. His belt. A tourniquet. I glance down without thinking and my eyes dance over the wound.

There's nothing there. Charred bone and burned flesh. I choke back a sob, scrunching my eyes shut, turning my face into the floor.

'Shhh, you did good.' Mato lifts my head, gripping my face. 'You need to get up now. We need to get out of here. The destroyers are only a few minutes away.'

I try to reply, but my tech has sucked the energy from my muscles, trying frantically to heal my arm. My vision is rippling with warning messages. Blood pressure, infection, adrenaline. My panel wants to know where my hand is, if there's any way it can be reattached.

It's *gone*, I tell it, my thoughts fuzzy with shock. My hand is gone, and I don't know if it's coming back.

A pinching feeling starts up in my wrist as the tech in my arm responds, starting the process of closing the wound. Mato slings my good arm round his shoulder, lifting me. I struggle to my knees, but the rush of blood from sitting up has brought my nerves back to life, and the pain takes me like a bullet.

I gasp, doubling over. Mato tightens his grip on my wrist. 'Come on,' he says, grabbing the backpack, but his voice is tinged with static. The pain is a weight crushing down on me, and I can feel myself shifting beneath it, rearranging the pieces of my mind to escape its grasp. But it's more than just the injury. More than my glitching tech.

I feel something pulsing, tearing in the base of my skull.

'Come on, Catarina.' Mato heaves me forward, taking my weight, pulling me down the tunnel.

I swallow, trying to walk, but my legs just kick uselessly at the ground. My muscles are twitching, spasming. My nervous system is on fire. The crowd is still streaming in from outside – people screaming, plastered with feathers, trying to get down into the safety of the bunker. I should be telling them to turn and run, but my voice is gone, and my focus with it. Mato drags me through the crowd, weaving between the throng, and we stagger out into the street.

It's chaos. The pigeons are a constellation above us – impenetrable and infinite, their glowing wings forming an ocean of moving light across the sky. They're magnificent. My breath catches, and I feel Mato's catch too. We jerk to a stop together, spellbound, staring up at the wild explosion of light.

The flock's cries are more than clicks and whirs – they are a symphony rolling through the night. Complex streams of percussive sound, layered and melodic, as beautiful as the waves of light rippling across the sky. The sight tugs at something inside me – a thread coming loose in my mind. Flashes of memory pelt my vision, rearing through the light of the pigeons. Jun Bei's face seems to ripple across the sky, painted by the glowing wings, and snatches of her voice fill my mind as Mato heaves me out into the street. Now that we're on the mountain's surface, the houses are sparse, wide roads cutting between them. We weave through the crowd, heading for vehicles parked in the distance. The people split before us, their faces doubled in my vision.

I strain to focus, but the outlines diverge further, splitting into separate, distinct objects.

Not overlapping. *New.* Like the world has been doubled in front of me, occupying a completely new dimension.

'Mato,' I breathe, gasping. 'It's happening.'

I know what this is. This is what I was trying to do earlier, but it's taken losing my hand and running for my life to push me to this place. The pain in my wrist has broken through my defences and the wall of my conscious mind, and beneath the horror and the shock, the shuddering of my muscles, a lick of pleasure surges through me.

'I think I'm fractioning.'

Mato turns his head, slowing his pace. I feel his focus push into the cuff, testing, and then retract. 'I can't tell,' he says. 'We need to keep moving.'

A pulse ripples out from my cuff unbidden, flashing across the desert and into the sky. The panels of the people around me glow in my vision and then fade. Vehicles hum in the distance. Entropia is a pounding, blazing fire of light behind me. My eyes lift to the pigeons, to the wash of cobalt light, and I pause.

There's something *strange* about this flock. I scan the birds, trying to pinpoint it, but my focus slides past them to four blinding points of white light in the sky. They're racing in from the north, high above the pigeons.

'The destroyers are here,' I gasp, stumbling alongside Mato as he hurries down the street. I let my mind surge past the flock, rising higher into the fleet. There are four destroyers, each with smaller drones whining in formations around them. My cuff locks in on their controls, their satellite interfaces, connecting seamlessly.

'I think I can hack them,' I whisper, feeling drunk.

'Not all of them,' Mato says, weaving us through a crowd of people. 'They have unique firewall protocols. If you take down one, the others will go dark. We need to find a vehicle and get out of here.'

Vehicle. The word echoes in the chaos of my mind and I drop my eyes from the fleet, letting another pulse roll out from my cuff. There are hundreds of vehicles around us, thousands of pieces of tech sketched into my vision, but somehow my eyes lock instantly on a racing point of light near the base of the mountain. It's streaking closer, heading for us.

Cole. The jeep. He's coming back for me.

'No,' I whisper, staggering to a stop.

'Come on,' Mato growls. A flash of something cruel and desperate passes across his face. 'I'm not dying tonight.'

'The others are coming back.'

'Let them,' he urges, dragging me forward again. 'They can see the destroyers too.'

'I can't let them die.'

'That's their decision. They've had time to get out.'

I shake my head, swallowing, fighting against his grip, but he has one of my arms, and my other hand is gone. The point of light that is Cole's jeep is growing closer.

I can't let them come back here for me and die.

I swing my gaze up to the destroyers, my mind splitting cleanly in two. A seam forms in my mind and I throw myself at it until the world doubles again.

Four skies. Four horizons. Four separate points of focus are burning in my mind, and I latch them on to the hearts of the steel destroyers. Their controls unspool before me – hard, but not impossible to break. I could only hack one at a time without fractioning, but I have four consciousnesses inside me now. I draw in a breath, hurling myself against the gaping seam inside me, and force myself through it like a battering ram against a cracking door.

Jun Bei's voice rushes back to me. My legs buckle, my vision wavering, but my mind is sliding into the destroyers' systems like a hand into a glove. There is not one of me – I am no single voice in the darkness. I am a chorus. A symphony of code and violence, driving a knife into each of their hearts.

A virus unfurls from me, air gasping from my lungs.

'Catarina –' Mato starts, then he falls silent, his gaze lifting upwards. The pigeons are splitting, their calls rising into a thunderstorm as the dark shapes of the destroyers hurtle through them from the sky. Their steel bodies arc and tilt, falling in curves to the desert, shattering into broken pieces when they hit the ground. Plumes of fire splash through the night, sending up columns of orange flame, forming gaping black whirlpools in the pigeons. I slump against Mato, my chest shaking, the scent of sulphur and smoke biting at my throat.

Mato lowers me to the ground. His hands grip my arms tightly, but I can feel that he's trembling. The jeep screeches across the street, its headlights splashing over me. The doors fly open before it's even come to a stop.

'Cat!' Cole screams, but I can barely see him. My vision is a blur of silver, the light of the pigeons shaking like a video on repeat.

But the sky isn't shaking – I am. I'm having a seizure. My chest convulses, my vision fading in and out. Footsteps pound across the street. 'Cat, what did you do?' Cole's voice breaks, his eyes wild. 'Mato, what did she do?'

'She saved us,' Mato says, kneeling beside me. There is reverence in his voice, but his gaze is an abyss.

I hold his eyes and tumble into them, letting the darkness swallow me.

CHAPTER 26

When I wake, my eyes are heavy, my vision still blurry with sleep. I'm lying on something hard and cold, my mouth dry and tasting of ash. I must be indoors, because the air is cool and humid, faintly stale, humming with the low murmur of hushed voices. The edges of my mind are a sea of dark and raging waters.

We're losing the vaccine.

The light of the pigeons feels like it's burned into my eyes, millions of them swarming through the air, carrying the plague. The patched vaccine might hold the virus back from infecting us for a while, but there'll be no stopping its evolution any more.

I force my eyes open. A bar of light shines above me, surrounded by a halo of what looks like floating specks of brightness. The fraction in my mind is gone, but I can still feel the echo of it – the seam to split reality along, the myriad dimensions I glimpsed when I brought down the destroyers. It feels like a new *sense* inside me, and the urge to pick at it and take myself back into that place is hard to resist, even though it must have almost killed me. Mato was right. I don't know if I can bear the thought of living in just one dimension again.

A murmur of pain in my left arm brings back the memory of the flash strip taut around my wrist. The blinding cauterizing lasers. I try to clench my fingers, but all I can feel is a low, tingling numbness. It tugs at a thread inside me, and I try to stretch my hand out, but there's only an ache in response. I force my head up, fighting a surge of dizziness, blinking against the light above me. Blankets slide from my shoulders. I'm lying on a creaking metal camp bed, a strap wrapped around my arm keeping it locked down to the frame. My heart rate kicks higher, and I shove myself up on my good arm.

'Don't try to sit up yet.' Cole's face comes into focus beside me. He's sitting on a folding chair beside my bed, shadows beneath his eyes, lines etched into his cheeks. 'You should try to sleep a while longer. You shouldn't be moving.'

I just shake my head, craning my neck to look down at my wrist. There's a crinkled silver blanket wrapped around my left arm, a cannula and genkit wire coiling out of it. The feeling coming from my hand is still wrong, but I can see through the folds of the material that it's been reattached.

I let out a shaking sigh of relief, rubbing my eyes with my good hand. We're in a vast, dim room the size of a basketball court. The low concrete ceiling is supported with pillars stamped with hexadecimal location codes. Metal camp beds like mine are lined around me in a rough grid, filled with the slumbering forms of Entropia's inhabitants. Some are bandaged or bruised, and some have family sitting beside them on chairs like Cole's. A makeshift hospital ward. We must have evacuated to a deeper level in the bunker.

There's a strange haze in the air – glowing flecks of dancing light, like fireflies, but smaller. They form clouds around the lights and are dusted over every surface, gathered in glowing pools in the folds of Cole's clothing, scattered through his tousled hair.

'You have nerve damage,' Cole says, looking at my bandaged arm, 'and some of your ligaments are severed. The bones are stitched, but they won't be fully healed for a while. Regina saved it.'

I swallow, shaking my head. 'Regina is the reason I had to cut it off.'

'I know,' he says. 'She said the weevil glitched, that it was an accident.'

'It didn't *feel* like an accident,' I mutter. 'Are the others OK?'

'They're fine. A lot of people here got infected, though. Hundreds are showing symptoms, but Regina is circulating the patched vaccine, and it's working on the people who've received it so far. It's curing the infection, but it's taking time to distribute. It needs to be manually installed on everyone's panel, like you did with mine.'

'Cartaxus hasn't sent it out yet?'

'No, not yet, and morale here isn't good. Everyone knows what this means for the vaccine.'

I nod, trying to clench my left hand, but the muscles don't respond. Unease prickles through me. I tug at the silver blanket wrapped around my arm. It tears off in pieces, revealing my dirty fingernails, a bloodstained bandage wrapped around my wrist. The cylindrical forearm segment of my cuff is still gleaming and unharmed, an IV tube jacked into it, curling from a stand beside me. There's a clean incision in the back of my hand where the weevil was removed, and a cross-hatch of scars across my palm and fingers.

My hand is swollen and bruised, but it looks intact. Still, something feels *wrong*.

I pull up my panel's menu, invoking a scan. The muscles in my wrist are still mending together, a carbon-fibre lattice knitting the edges of my bones. It'll take weeks to heal, and even after the nerves are repaired, it might never feel the same again. But according to my tech, the reattachment was successful, all traces of the weevil removed.

'I want to check my hand,' I say, pushing myself up on my side. 'Something feels wrong.' A waterfall of the glowing dust falls from my shoulders. It looks the same as the specks of light I saw on Mato's jacket when I met him in the atrium. 'What the hell is this stuff?'

'It's a fungus,' Cole says. 'One of Regina's designs. This is the bunker's basement level. It's supposed to be a backup bunker in case the top section is breached, but there's not much air circulation down here because they didn't finish building it. I think the fungus is supposed to be keeping the air breathable.'

I grimace, feeling tiny dustlike flecks coating the inside of my mouth. I reach for the strap around my arm to pull the reader wire from my cuff, but the movement makes my head swim.

'Whoa,' Cole says, grabbing my shoulder, steadying me. 'Wait a minute. It probably feels wrong because of the nerve damage. Just take it slow, OK? You've been through a lot.'

I let him lower me back in the bed, blinking against the spinning in my vision, my tech disoriented by the swirling clouds of dust. He looks exhausted, like the last few days have hollowed him out from the inside.

'Here.' He reaches for a canteen on the floor beside the bed, passing it to me. I lift my good hand to hold it, but my movements feel slow and staggered, my hand jerking wildly.

'Easy,' he says. 'I'll hold it.' He watches me as I draw in a long sip of the water, the liquid soothing my throat.

I swallow. 'How long have I been out?'

He sits back down on the folding chair. 'Almost a day.'

I blink. 'A day? Where are the others?'

'Leoben and Anna are out looking for Lachlan, and Mato went into the desert to try to contact Cartaxus. He thinks the pigeons might be interfering with our comms. We've been sending reports, but nobody is responding. They've gone quiet since you brought that fleet down.'

'What's Novak saying on her broadcasts?'

'She says there's a small outbreak, that it's under control. They haven't mentioned the pigeons, and there's no chatter about the updated vaccine. She's calling for survivors to come into the bunkers as a precaution while this outbreak is controlled. She said the bunkers will be locking down in the next twenty-four hours.'

I sit up. 'But flood protocol is off, right? This outbreak is in the *pigeons* – killing the people on the surface won't solve anything.'

'You're assuming Cartaxus is listening to reason right now.'

I shake my head. 'That's madness. They can't kill every *bird* on the surface.'

Cole's face darkens. 'I'm not so sure. The bunkers are designed to last for over a hundred years. They have triphase clouds they could use to scorch the surface of the planet and kill this virus if they have to. If there's no hope of creating a vaccine that will last, then they'll find another way to stop the plague.'

The breath rushes from my lungs. 'They couldn't . . .' I start, then trail off, because of course they could.

The bunkers are underground, their civilians kept under perfect control, but Cartaxus has never done anything to protect the surface – they've never guarded any territories, never staked out forests or rivers or kept the cities from burning. All they did was protect their bunkers and their exclusion zones. It's like they thought that protecting the surface would be a waste of time.

'They've always planned for this.' I close my eyes, seeing clouds of triphase crackling across the planet. Swallowing fields and mountains, chewing up every living thing and leaving ash and dust behind.

Erasing an entire planet's worth of creatures. Every flicker of life, every coil of DNA.

'They've prepared for it,' Cole says. 'It was always a possibility. It would take a long time to rebuild, but it's possible. They have seed vaults, genetic libraries. They'd know how to start again. At this point, I don't know if there's any way to *stop* them from using flood protocol.'

'What are you saying?' I ask.

He lets out a slow breath. 'I think we should go back to Cartaxus. We might be able to convince them to stop, and if we can't, then there's nothing we can do any more. Finding Lachlan won't help us. This has gone beyond our mission guidelines. I think it's time to check into a bunker.'

'What? How could you even *suggest* that?'

'I don't think there's any other solution, Cat. They've made up their minds.'

'No,' I say, yanking the strap from my arm. 'They can't scorch the goddamn planet.'

'We can't stop them.'

'Yes we *can*,' I say. 'They're not all-powerful. I've been hacking their systems for years. Lachlan is *still* hacking them. They're just people, Cole, and they have panels in their arms too. We can stop this.'

Cole's brow furrows. 'What are you talking about?'

'I'm saying that if flood protocol is still on, then Brink is the one we should be going after.' I pull the cannula out of my cuff and sit up, swinging my legs over the side of the bed.

'Just slow down,' Cole says.

'I'm fine,' I say, ejecting the reader wire from my cuff. It coils out of the glass, and I push the needle-tipped end into the back of my hand to kick off a scan. 'I just want to make sure there's no traces of the weevil left.'

'You're not *fine*.'

'You need to stop worrying about me, Cole.'

'You died.'

The glowing specks of dust floating through the air seem to still. 'What are you talking about?'

He steeples his fingers and presses them to his forehead, drawing in a long breath. There's a new line of tension in his shoulders – a nervous energy, like he wants to break something. Like he can barely keep himself in the chair he's sitting in. 'Your heart . . .' He pauses, tilting his head back. 'Your heart stopped after the fraction. You died for over a minute.'

I stare at him, not breathing.

'Your brain activity cut out,' he says. 'You were gone. Mato revived you, but you're definitely not *fine*, Cat.'

I shake my head, confused. Even with gentech, a minute is a *very* long time to die.

'You can't take risks like that,' Cole says, leaning forward in the chair. 'We almost lost you.'

His voice is rough. I can't tell if he's angry or hurt, but the intensity in his gaze holds me in place, guilt plucking at the edges of my thoughts. I knew there was a risk the fraction would hurt me, but I couldn't see another way to stop the attack.

'I had to hack the destroyers. I didn't have a choice.'

Cole's eyes drop. 'You didn't hack the destroyers. They were flying dark on manual flight controls specifically to *avoid* getting hacked.'

'But . . . but I hacked them,' I say, confused. 'I broke into their systems, that's how I took them down.'

Cole's hands curl into fists. 'No you didn't,' he says gently. 'You hacked the pilots.'

His words circle through my mind, taking my breath away. I grip the side of the bed with my good hand until my knuckles bloom white. 'How many?'

'Four. One pilot in each. Mato said it was the same scythe code you used in the Zarathustra lab. They were dead before they hit the ground.'

I swallow hard. Four lives. That's the second time I've unleashed Jun Bei's scythe code without truly knowing what I was doing. Horror grips me. It's not the act of killing that's rattling me – I took down those destroyers to save the city – it's the fact that I'm carrying a lethal weapon I'm not in control of. What if I launched it wirelessly without meaning to? With my cuff's range, I could kill everyone within a *mile*. I want to delete Jun Bei's scythe from my arm, to scrub it from my panel.

But I can't afford to throw away one of the only weapons I have. Especially not now.

I blow out a steadying breath. 'At least we know the code still works. I thought Brink might have found a way to block it after I used it on that soldier.'

Cole narrows his eyes. '*That's* your response? Don't you care that you killed them?'

The question is like a slap. 'How dare you ask me that! They were going to *bomb* us. I was trying to save you. Jesus, Cole. I lived through the outbreak – I'm not innocent, OK? If we're going to stop Cartaxus from launching flood protocol, there'll be a lot more blood on my hands by the time I'm done.'

He goes still, staring at me, his face blanking with the wall I've seen slammed down so many times, but I'm sick of it. Sick of his judgements, of him looking at me like I'm something he needs to control.

'You should go,' I say. 'There's no reason for you to wait here with me.' I pull up the cuff's interface. It's still scanning my hand, showing inflammation levels and details on the tech that's running through my cells.

'You don't even know where the others are,' he says.

'I'll figure it out. I just want to . . .' I trail off as the results of the scan running in my cuff flash up in my vision.

'What is it?'

'I . . . I don't know.' The results I'm seeing are comparing the DNA in my hand with that in the rest of my body. They match perfectly, but they're showing an error. I push my focus into the cuff, digging through the results. Every chromosome has been sequenced and matched, accounting for minor mutations and changes. There are no toxins in my hand, no lingering effects from the weevil. No foreign DNA hiding inside my cells, waiting to attack me. My hand looks perfectly normal.

Except for the fact that it has forty-six chromosomes, while my body has forty-eight.

'What's wrong?' Cole asks, his brow furrowed.

I shake my head, feeling like I'm going to be sick.

'Cat, what is it?'

I blink the scan away, swaying. 'This isn't my hand.'

CHAPTER 27

Cole goes very still. His eyes drop to my left hand, where bruised skin peeks out from beneath the gauze wrapped around my wrist. Dark crescents of dirt are caked beneath my fingernails, my thumbnail chewed down to the quick. There are familiar scars on my palm, a cut on my skin from where the weevil was.

But it's not really mine.

It looks like it, but it's missing two of my chromosomes.

'What are you talking about?' Cole asks, his voice low.

'Regina took my hand.' I close my eyes, seeing a sudden flash of the bodies in the tanks in her lab. The buckets of lungs. The twitching kilomeat at the market. They were all *grown*, not born. Built cell by cell in a tank. Anything can be grown with enough skill and time, and the right piece of code.

Even a hand.

'Regina must have grown it,' I say. 'It only matches my normal DNA – not the extra chromosomes. Not the part of me that lets me change myself.'

The thought drags up another surge of nausea, but I swallow it down. I don't even know how Regina could have organized something like this. Growing an entire hand would have taken weeks, even at the fastest rate. But weeks ago, none of this was happening. Cole hadn't showed up at the cabin, and Regina didn't know that Lachlan had turned me into his daughter. There was no reason for her to start growing tissue samples of me, and certainly no guarantee that I'd show up here and cut my hand off.

It doesn't make any sense. But clearly, it happened. The proof is sutured on to the end of my wrist.

Cole stands swiftly, his eyes cutting across the room to the door. He drops his voice to a whisper. 'Are you certain?'

I follow his eyes. There's a woman at the door with a gun in her hands. She looks away as soon as I glance at her, and the hair on the back of my neck rises.

'Yes,' I whisper back. 'I'm sure. She took my goddamn hand.'

A muscle twitches in Cole's jaw. He's been saying all along that coming here was dangerous. He said Regina would hurt me, that I'd always be an experiment to her. I didn't want to believe it, and I still don't. She's my *mother*. She cried when she told me the story about how I was created. She said I could make a home here.

But she also said she wanted to study my DNA, and now she has a sample to keep alive in one of her tanks.

'We need to find her,' I say, pushing myself up, standing shakily. I'm in my dirty jeans and crumpled T-shirt, now coated with a fine layer of the glowing dust. 'I want my hand back.'

Cole grabs my shoulder, steadying me. 'We're not going to find her, Cat. I'm getting you out of here. We'll get your hand back, I promise, but first we need to get you to safety.'

'I'm not going into a bunker.'

'That's fine,' he says. 'We won't go to Cartaxus. We'll find the others and regroup outside the city. Just let me get you out of here, *please*. I don't think you're safe.'

I look down at my bandaged hand, and then around the room. There are dozens of other people in camp beds around me, sleeping or talking in hushed voices. A row of tables on the far wall is piled with clothes and blankets, a few people milling around it with steaming mugs in their hands. The only guard I can see is the woman at the door, and she's talking to one of the other patients, gesturing to the blankets. I have no doubt she's watching me, but she shouldn't be hard to get past.

'How can we get out?' I ask. 'They're not going to just let me out through the main entrance. Regina wants me here.'

'The elevators are guarded,' Cole says. 'People aren't supposed to be leaving – they're trying to quarantine the infected. There might be another exit, though. I saw a maintenance shaft near the agricultural section, but I don't know if it leads anywhere useful.'

I frown, looking down at the glimmering dust on the concrete floor. When I met Mato in the atrium, he was dusted in the same glowing fungus. He said he took a *secret* entrance to avoid the crowds waiting for the elevators. A maintenance shaft, like Cole said. A tunnel drilled through the rock. It must have come from the basement levels.

'I think you're right,' I say. 'Mato mentioned something. He said he used a maintenance shaft to get up to the jeep.'

'Perfect,' Cole says. He glances at the guard and reaches for my backpack, slinging it on, then slides his arm round my shoulders. I'm still angry with him, but I don't know if I'm going to be able to walk without his help. I wrap my good arm round his waist for balance, leaning in to him. 'You ready?' he asks, dropping his head to whisper in my ear.

'Yeah,' I say. 'Let's get the hell out of here.'

The woman with the gun watches us as we leave the hospital ward, but she doesn't try to stop us. Her eyes glaze, though, like she's sending a comm. Cole pushes through swinging double doors that open into a vast, bustling room full of haphazard groups of people and piles of belongings. The space has almost the same footprint as the atrium in the bunker – it's giant and circular, but the ceiling is only a couple of storeys high. There are groups camped on the floor, some sitting in circles with humming genkits. Fenced-off pens along the closest wall hold sleeping animals. A dozen hallways branch out from the edges of the room, leading to what look like dormitories and bathrooms. It's a miniaturized version of the bunker, packed completely full of Entropia's citizens.

'The shafts were this way,' Cole says, guiding me towards a hallway to our left.

I let him lead me through the crowd, keeping my wounded arm lifted protectively against my chest. I'm feeling steadier now that I'm moving around, but I really shouldn't be walking like this. There are special precautions people take when they lose a limb to prevent damage that even gentech can't repair. If I move around too much before the nerves in my wrist are fully bonded, then my brain might stop listening to the nerves in my hand. Neurons could be lost and never fully regained. Mato didn't seem to think much of losing the ability to control his hand, but the thought makes me nervous. I'm not sure I like the thought of relying on an app to control the way I move any part of my own body.

The hallway branches into an open, cavernlike space. The ceiling is higher here, and there's a wide pool of dark water in the centre of the room, pipes creeping out of it to rows of floor-to-ceiling trellises heavy with thousands of purple-black pods. The air is humid and heavy, and the glimmering dust floating through it hangs thicker here, forming swirls around Cole's shoulders as he leads me past the pool. The water looks icy and deep, thin shafts of light cutting down from high above it.

I crane my neck to look up, spotting a curved sliver of light on the ceiling. There's a round hole cut into the concrete, a circle hanging above it.

Regina's lab. The hanging steel platform. It must be right above us.

'Back here,' Cole says, guiding me between two of the trellises. The wall beyond them is hung with plastic sheeting, but there's a cold breeze here that forms a dark channel in the floating clouds of dust. Cole slides his arm from my shoulders and pulls aside one of the plastic sheets, revealing a gaping entrance, a chain hung across it at waist height.

'This cold air is coming from somewhere . . .' he says, trailing off as footsteps echo in the hallway behind us. He turns, his eyes flashing to black for a split second, then he lifts the chain and ushers me through, gesturing for me to be quiet.

The tunnel is raw stone, roughly circular, the floor littered with pebbles and chips of rock. It's cold and dark, but my ocular tech sketches out a dark curve ahead of me, curling to the left, sloping gently upwards.

'Do you think you can run?' Cole whispers, slipping under the chain, letting the plastic sheeting fall behind us.

I nod, lifting my wounded arm with my good hand, pressing it to my chest. 'I can try.'

His arm slides round my waist to steady me as we break into a run, his panel held up as a makeshift flashlight. I keep my audio tech dialled up, searching for a hint of the footsteps behind us. Voices echo faintly and the plastic sheeting crinkles, but nobody seems to be following us.

The tunnel rises at an easy gradient, curving constantly to the left. It must be cut in a spiral around the bunker. It's big enough for a vehicle, partially blocked by the occasional rock fall or pallets of concrete mix and excavation equipment. The muscles in my legs feel weak, but my tech compensates, sending oxygen into my muscles, sharpening my reflexes. After what feels like an eternity of running through the dark, a yellow light glows ahead of us and the tunnel widens. Cole slows us to a jog as we reach a fork.

'Which way?' I ask, gulping for air, leaning against his side.

'That's where the breeze is coming from,' Cole says, pointing to the right. 'My tech thinks the parking lot should be that way too, but I don't have a map to check.'

I look up at him. 'Didn't Mato give you guys access to maps of the bunker and the city?'

He nods. 'Yeah, but this shaft wasn't on them. That's why I noticed it earlier. It wasn't in the search grids we've been using.'

A flutter of unease rolls through me. I look between the two tunnels, then send out a pulse from my cuff. It seems to run sluggishly, my tech focusing its energy on my wounded arm. Ripples of light splash across the tunnel's walls, sketched in my vision, but they're just a mess of reflections. Something's blocking the scan.

'What is it?' Cole asks.

I hesitate, staring at the wavering patterns of light. The scan is probably screwed up because we're underground. We don't have time to waste checking both these tunnels. Regina's people are already looking for me. 'Nothing,' I say, following the breeze along the tunnel to the right of the fork. 'Come on, let's get out of here.'

The last section of the tunnel rises sharply, the cold breeze growing stronger until we round a corner and step into a dimly lit room cut into the rock. There are crates stacked against the walls, along with a pile of scrap metal and a broken drilling machine. The air is humming with the distant calls of the pigeons. We must be getting close.

'The parking lots are this way,' Cole says, weaving through the crates to a hallway.

I follow him, breaking into a run. The hallway branches into the cavern we first drove into with the showers along one side, the rows of trucks and cars lined up behind them. The jeep is waiting in a space near the back, covered with dust and feathers, but it's there.

Cole jogs for the jeep, slinging off my backpack. The doors open automatically, the headlights splashing on.

'Where are the others?' I ask.

'They took one of Regina's vehicles,' Cole says. 'I told them to leave this here in case I needed to get you out.' He tosses my pack into the back of the jeep and pulls out his rifle. 'Let's hope they don't have barricades at the entrance. Come on, let's go.'

I climb carefully into the passenger seat, cradling my wounded arm to my chest. Cole climbs in, revving the engine, and swings us out of the parking lot and into the tunnel that leads up to the surface. It's empty, the fluorescents in the ceiling dim. Feathers are scattered across the floor, along with the occasional splash of scarlet from one of the pigeons detonating.

Cole slows the jeep as we approach the exit, the tunnel brightening, daylight slanting in from the surface. The roar of the pigeons grows louder until it's deafening.

'Shit,' Cole says, slamming the brakes. 'They've closed the gates.'

I follow his eyes to a lattice of steel bars locked over the mouth of the tunnel, blocking the exit to the surface. There are no chains or bolts holding the gates shut. They must be controlled by Entropia's security system. Cole grabs my headrest to twist in his seat, starting to reverse back down the tunnel, but I grab his arm.

'I might be able to open the gates,' I say.

He glances back down the tunnel, then nods. 'OK, but be quick. Regina's people are going to be here any minute.'

I close my eyes, slipping my focus into my cuff's interface. A pulse rolls from it instantly, lighting up the jeep's dash, Cole's panel and a row of cameras set into the ceiling. A security port beside the gate glows white in my vision, and I lock on to it, feeling my way into its controls.

Mato was right – Entropia's security is lax. A single firewall crumbles before me, yielding me access to the gate, the lights, to everything in the tunnel. I send a command to open the exit, and the steel bars let out a screech of metal as they roll back into the wall.

'Nice work,' Cole says, revving the engine. He starts to pull us forward, but brakes suddenly.

A rumbling starts up from outside. Shadows flicker in the light cutting through from the exit as people spill through the newly opened gates, rushing inside.

It's a mob.

Dozens of people are running down the tunnel from the surface, some armed with guns, some carrying bags clutched to their chests. They must have been waiting outside the gates. The jeep's headlights splash across them as they race down the tunnel towards us, blocking our path. They all look like they're in shock – their eyes wide and glassy. Some are staggering, clutching the walls, their skin covered with bruises.

They're all infected.

'Holy shit,' I breathe. There are thousands of people in Entropia – maybe tens of thousands, including those in the settlements outside the city, and they were all watching the pigeons come in last night. There are only a few dozen people here, but even if the infection rate is only a few per cent, it'd mean there are hundreds more out there. This crowd looks desperate, terrified. They must have come here for help from Regina. And she can give it to them – she has the patched vaccine.

So does Cartaxus, but obviously they still haven't sent it out.

'There has to be another way out of here,' Cole says, staring behind us, swinging the jeep back down the tunnel. The crowd is bolting after us now, yelling, waving for help. More are pouring in from the entrance, following the others. An engine sounds behind us, echoing through the tunnel. Regina's people have come to chase us down.

'Goddammit,' Cole says, slamming the brakes, turning back to the crowd.

We're trapped.

The crowd surges, surrounding the jeep. None of them are trying to hurt us, but they've formed a throng around us, making it impossible to move. Cole's eyes lift to the rear-view as fresh headlights splash across the tunnel's walls. His knuckles bloom white on the steering wheel. 'Get your seatbelt on,' he says, his voice grim.

'No,' I beg him. 'We can't just drive through them. Hit the horn, tell them to get out of the way!'

He slams the horn, but the crowd doesn't shift. A woman is knocking on my window, her eyes wide and glassy, bruises covering her face.

'They aren't going to listen,' Cole says. 'They're feverish and desperate. Regina's people are almost here. I need to get us out.' He jerks the jeep into gear. The tyres spin, the jeep pressing into the crowd. A man near the bonnet starts screaming, and I grab Cole's arm.

'Stop it!' I shout. 'We have to *help* them.'

He hits the brakes, staring at me. 'Help them? What are you talking about? What the hell do you want from me, Catarina?'

'I have the vaccine in my arm,' I say, staring through the windscreen as the crowd swarms around us, angry faces pressing against the glass. 'Maybe I can hack their panels and install it.'

'We don't have time for this,' he growls.

'Just give me a second.' I drag up my cuff's menu again, searching for a virus I can use to force the patched vaccine into these people's arms. The engine behind us is getting louder. A man slumps against my window, leaving streaks of blood across the glass. I flinch away. His face is swollen, slick with blood, gashes open on his cheek and forehead.

My breath stills as he looks in at me with glassy eyes, his body twitching.

'Drive,' I whisper to Cole, my voice shaking.

He snaps his head to me, confused.

'Drive,' I urge him. 'We need to go now!'

His eyes flash to black, and he slams the accelerator. The jeep surges forward, tyres screeching, but the weight of the crowd keeps us held in place. Cole slams the horn, flooring the engine, and the throng of people starts to part. Some tumble down beneath us, but the bloodied man is still beside us, shaking now, his body rigid.

'Get down!' I scream as the man's head flies back, but it's already too late.

CHAPTER 28

The man throws back his head, and it happens in an instant. A shockwave against my door, crumpling the metal. My window shatters, pelting me with a million squares of broken glass. Hot, choking air rushes in with a *crack* that throws me sideways against Cole, and a spray of scalding mist fills the jeep. Cole swerves wildly, his eyes black, staring behind us, but all that's left of the man is a crater cut into the rock. The crowd is scattered, bloody, reeling. Cole shouts something at me, but his voice is lost in the whining aftermath of the blast.

I cover my ears, curling into a ball as another *crack* sounds behind us. Another blower, their cells not even close to detonation. Instead of a plume of mist, they form a spray of foam and flesh, pieces of their body flying through the air.

'Drive!' I scream, huddling into the seat. 'I'm sorry! Please, just get us out of here!'

The engine roars, struggling against the tide of people, the jeep bouncing and rocking as they fall beneath the wheels. I scrunch my eyes shut, my hands pressed over my ears as Cole floors the accelerator, ploughing through the crowd. The jeep screams along the tunnel, smashing through the metal barricades at the entrance, and fishtails on to the road outside. The pigeons form a blanket of swirling lights above us, their cries like a hailstorm. Cole is a statue of fury beside me, the muscles in his forearms rigid.

My good hand is shaking, misted with drops of scarlet from the cloud. A hundred fine scratches from the broken glass are traced across my skin like paper cuts, beading blood, but I can barely feel them over the pounding in my chest. We screech down the road, veering off it to follow the trail that cuts through the razorgrass border, heading out of the city.

'Are you hurt?' Cole asks, his teeth gritted.

'I'm OK.' I look down at my new hand, trying to pull my fingers into a fist. They twitch, curling slightly. My tech is in emergency mode, working hard to knit the nerves back together. But I don't want these nerves – I want my real hand back. I force my eyes away from it, looking back over my shoulder at the city.

There's a crowd of people who've been infected by the flock grouped near the entrance to the tunnels. They must be coming here for help, trying to get into the city, but Regina is keeping them away. There are hundreds of them – desperate and frightened. Regina will give them the vaccine, but that won't save the people who already blew in the tunnel.

'I'm sorry,' I say. 'I shouldn't have stopped you from driving through that crowd. I don't know what I was thinking.'

Cole doesn't reply. The wall of silence is back around him, bricked higher than I've felt it so far. Part of me wants to kick it down and force him to talk to me, but he's covered in blood, fine cuts from the shattered glass seeping streaks across his arms. We both have the patched vaccine, so we shouldn't be at risk of infection from the foam streaked across our skin, but the scent is stifling, turning my stomach. We need to clean off, to regroup and to figure out what we're going to do. I draw in a long, slow breath, leaning back into my seat.

We drive far enough for the cries of the pigeons to fade to a distant roar, the road winding through barren desert valleys and steep rocky hills. Signs posted along the highway advertise residential developments that must have been half finished when the plague broke out. This whole corner of Nevada has been dominated by the genehackers for decades, but most of them don't seem like the kind of people to buy into packaged land developments. The advertisements are faded and torn, showing illustrations of pretty gated communities. Bubbles of normalcy in the middle of Regina's wild kingdom.

Cole pulls us off the road, heading for one of the developments. 'I told the others to come and find us here. Lee and Anna are picking up the Comox. I can't get through to Mato. Let's find somewhere to regroup and figure out what to do.'

We wind down a concrete road into one of the half-finished suburbs. Dozens of houses in various stages of completion line a grid of cul-de-sacs, the bare dirt of their yards still stacked with building equipment and piles of gravel and sand. Some of the houses look finished, with solars glinting on their roofs, and a creek bed winds through the rocky scrub behind them, shining in the afternoon sun. Power, shelter, water. It's a good place to stop.

We roll along the road, past faded FOR SALE signs in front of the houses. The walls are all intact, the doors closed. Nobody's blown inside, but Entropia's people have probably been through here and ransacked them. Cole parks the jeep outside a finished-looking house and reaches into the back to grab some fresh clothes and a towel. He climbs out, pausing to uncoil a gold chain from his shirt. It's not his, but it's plastered to the fabric of his shirt with dried foam and shreds of flesh. There's a heart-shaped pendant strung on it, the kind that clasps together to hold a photograph, but it's hanging open, empty, the inside of the heart smeared with blood. It must have come through the broken window from one of the blowers in the tunnels.

Cole stares at it silently, then clenches it in his fist. 'I'm going to wash off in the creek,' he says.

He turns, heading for a path between the houses.

'Wait, I'm coming with you,' I say. I struggle to sling my backpack over my shoulder with my good arm and follow him out, jogging to keep up with him. The path grows narrow, following a series of switchbacks that take us down to the creek. The grass is thicker down here, a shock of green after days of endless desert. The creek looks shallow enough to ford, but deep and slow-running enough to bathe in.

'I don't know if I feel like talking right now,' Cole says, striding to the water. He drops the clothes on the ground and sets the necklace down beside them. He's wearing his silence like armour. I dump my backpack beside him and drop into a crouch on the water's edge to untie my bootlaces.

'That was horrible in the tunnel,' I say.

He doesn't reply.

'I'm sorry I tried to stop you driving through those people.'

He pinches the bridge of his nose, sighing, then unbuckles his shoulder holster. He drops it to the ground and hauls his tank top off, wincing as it rolls over the bloodied skin on his shoulders and arms. He tosses it down, still avoiding my eyes, and draws in a slow breath.

'I didn't *want* to do that,' he says. 'To drive over those people. I was doing my job. I *kill* people – that's part of being a black-out soldier.' He steps out of his foam-streaked cargo pants and strides into the water. 'But it's not trivial, taking a life. It's something I hate doing.'

I tug off my boots. 'I know that.'

He just shakes his head. I shrug out of my jacket and follow him into the water in my T-shirt and leggings, holding my panel arm up above the surface. The water is cold, but it feels good against my bruised skin.

'Cole, what is all this about? You've been different since I killed that soldier in the lab. What's going on?'

He bends over to dunk his head in the water, scraping at his scalp, then stands, letting out another sigh. 'I've been trained by Cartaxus since I was a child,' he says. 'We *all* were. But they should never have trained Jun Bei.'

A flutter of nerves kicks inside me at the mention of her name, the tightness in his voice as he says it. 'Why not?'

He swipes a handful of water over his face, rubbing his eyes. 'She was smarter than all of us – smarter than even Lachlan knew, and when they started training us, she blended what she was learning about violence with what she learned about coding, and it wasn't a good mix.'

I splash water over the dried foam on my chest. 'You're saying she should have been left weak? Untrained?'

'No,' he says, frustrated, 'I'm saying that it's dangerous to intellectualize murder – to make a science of it. That scythe in your arm is a nuclear weapon, and it's Cartaxus's fault that it exists, but it shouldn't. It's too dangerous.'

'I know that –'

'But you don't.' He closes his eyes. 'Anna and Lee and I are black-out soldiers. We've been trained to kill on instinct – it's what we chose. But Jun Bei could have turned her mind to *anything*. She could have changed the world, and so can *you*, but instead you're doing what she did. You're becoming a weapon.'

'Cole, I didn't *want* to kill the pilots, or the soldier. I took no joy in it –'

He shakes his head. 'That's how it starts. It's never good the first time. But then you did it again, and now you're talking about going after Cartaxus. Do you have any idea how many people we'd have to kill to take them down?'

'But the alternative is letting *more* people die!'

'That's the thing,' he says, turning to me. 'That's always the alternative. It's how these people stay in control. Nobody ever goes into battle thinking that they're going to be the annihilating force. It's *always* justified one way or another.'

I step deeper into the water, crossing my arms over my chest. 'Cole, I have to do whatever it takes to stop Cartaxus if they're going to kill everyone on the surface.'

'No, you *don't*,' he says. 'Dammit, Cat, you have to do *better* than that. You're smarter than they are, and it's killing me to see you using your mind like this. If you can't find a way to stop this without more bloodshed, then we may as well give up, because Lachlan is right.'

I stop, staring at him. He steps through the water. 'You're supposed to be better than me,' he says. 'You can't let yourself turn into a weapon. I'm past saving, I know that, but you don't have to be.'

My heart twists. 'You're not past saving.'

'I don't need comforting.' He turns away. 'I know what I am.'

'Cole, look at me,' I say. 'I know who you are too. You're a good person.'

'A good person?' He spins round. 'Cat, I'm a goddamn black-out agent. You can't be a good person and do the things I do, or the things *you're* planning to do. What do you need to hear to make you understand that this is something that will *change* you? You want me to say that I could have killed every person in that tunnel? That part of me wanted to just because they were slowing us down?'

My breath catches. 'Cole . . .'

He strides closer in the water, his eyes blazing. 'Do you need me to tell you how many people I've killed for Cartaxus? That I have dreams about walls of people between us that I have to kill to get to you, and that I *like* them? Do you need to hear that it's satisfying to me now? That I've turned into a monster? That I'm a goddamn *monster*? Is that what you need to hear?'

'You're not a monster,' I whisper.

'You don't know *what* I am,' he snaps. 'You don't know what they did to me after you left – what they *made* me do. I'm not going to let this happen to you too.'

'You're not a monster.'

He heaves in a breath, head tilted back, fists tight by his sides.

Tears prick at my eyes. 'You're not a monster,' I say again, stepping to him, pressing my hands to his chest. His body is like rock – tense and unyielding, resisting me as I slide one hand up behind his neck, pressing my face to his shoulder, breathing in the scent of his blood, of the water, of him.

Then his arms slide around me and his lips find mine, crushing me to him as he kisses me. The feeling of his body against me is a thunderclap of relief, and I sink with him into the water, my legs wrapping around his waist. Every nerve in my body is aflame. I kiss his lips, his cheek, his neck. There is nothing inside me but hunger for him. For the sound of his breathing, for the way our bodies fit neatly together.

This is the only thing that's felt right in days.

'I love you,' he says, his arm locked round the small of my back. 'I love you, Cat. I don't want to lose you to this.'

I coil my fingers in his hair, falling with him into the water, kissing him hard. He breaks off the kiss and pushes me back towards the shore, shifting his weight on top of me. His lips drop to my neck again, his stubble scraping fireworks across my skin. I rest my back against the shore and tilt my head back, the heat inside me sharpening into a pulsing, aching need. I want him. I want *all* of him, and the wildness of my desire feels like a creature waking inside me, its power so overwhelming that it takes my breath away.

His hands move down my body, tugging at the waistband of my leggings.

'What about the others?' I whisper.

'They're miles away.' He presses a kiss to the corner of my jaw.

I grab his hair and pull him up. 'Are you sure?'

'I'm sure.' His eyes are glazed, roaming over my body, rising slowly to my face. 'I love you, Cat,' he whispers again.

Something breaks inside me.

I don't know who I am, or who my memories belong to, but I know that I love him. One single truth. One constant in a storm of shifting identity. This isn't an echo of Jun Bei's feelings, and it isn't weakness or need. This is real, and it's *mine*. The fact that I love Cole might be the only thing I truly know about myself.

'I love you,' I whisper back, pressing a kiss to his lips. I reach my hand up to touch the scars on his chest, but they're not there. I draw back, blinking. His skin is suddenly pale, a circle of black ports set over his heart. My gaze rises to his face, and the water seems to freeze.

I'm not looking at Cole any more.

His soft lips are gone, replaced with a gleaming black mask over alabaster skin. Mato stares down at me, holding me locked in place. Deep down, I know this can't be real, but that doesn't stop my muscles from seizing. I blink again, and Mato's face flashes out of sight. Cole's ice-blue eyes return, the curving leylines framing his face, the soft curls of his hair.

'Are you OK?' he asks.

I just stare at him, forcing myself to breathe. Maybe my VR tech is glitching again. 'I – I'm fine,' I say.

He drops his mouth back to my neck slowly, kissing a line from the hollow at the centre of my collarbone all the way up to my hair.

'Mine,' he says into my ear, his voice hitting me like a shard of ice. Mato's voice. His lips on mine, his slender hands against my face. I can feel his breath on my skin, the coldness of the mask against me, the flickering of his wireless field pressing into mine. I close my eyes, willing him away, but when I open them, he's still there.

I can see the seams of his coding mask, the light playing on his hair. He leans down to kiss me, and something tears in my mind, like a stitch ripped from a wound.

This isn't just a glitch.

I shove Cole aside, scrambling from the creek, stumbling back in the water. My pulse is pounding, my vision wavering. Cole's face has returned, his features slack with confusion. 'Cat, what did I do? Are you OK?'

I just shake my head, swallowing against the nausea rising in me. Images are rushing back to me – indistinct and blurred.

But they're real. That wasn't a VR glitch of Mato I was seeing.

It was a *memory*.

CHAPTER 29

I stagger out of the water and spin round, my hand clutched to my face. My heart is pounding, my skin ablaze with the feeling of Cole's lips, his hands, the heat of his body. I can still smell him on me, feel his stubble grazing my neck, but when I blink, all I see is Mato.

The memory of his eyes meeting mine through the dark glass of his coding mask sends a flare of horror through me.

They were *together* – Jun Bei and Mato. I don't know if it was in person or just while they were meeting in VR, but I know it's true. I can feel it – a storm whipping up the ocean in my mind. I've spent the last few days with him, trusting him, working with him.

I can't *believe* he didn't tell me.

'Cat, what did I do?'

I spin round as Cole strides from the creek. He stares at me, water streaming down his face, clear rivulets flowing over the pale scars on his chest. He's trembling. I swallow hard, but I don't trust my voice, and I don't know what to tell him.

Finding out the truth about this would devastate him.

Whatever happened, it's clear that Jun Bei betrayed Cole – whether she was with Mato in VR while she was at the lab, or if she was with him at Entropia after she ran away. The ocean inside me is still raging, and I don't know how much longer I can hold it back. I'm exhausted, I'm shaking, and the bridge I've been trying to build between myself and Jun Bei is crumbling under the memory of Mato's smile. I feel like I'm standing on the edge of a cliff.

I need space, and silence, and time to clear my head.

'It wasn't you,' I manage to say. 'It's nothing you did.'

Cole grabs his towel. His wet hair is slicked to his neck, coiled and glistening, sending droplets flying across the rocks as he wraps the towel around his waist. 'What happened, then?'

'Nothing.' I force my eyes away from his, crouching on the shore to rip open my backpack. There's a towel shoved into one of the pockets, a few ration bars, a packet of wipes and a handful of reader wires, but the only clothes I have left are torn black leggings and a navy T-shirt with a squid on the front. I'm not even *clean*. There's still foam streaked across my neck and face. I need to wash it off, but I can't stay near Cole or I'm going to fall apart. I pull my tank top off awkwardly and tug the fresh shirt on over my wet bra. My healing tech has already closed the fine scratches on my shoulders and arms, but they still tingle with pain as the dry fabric scrapes over them.

'It isn't you, OK?' I say, wrapping the towel around my waist, shimmying out of my leggings. I yank the dry ones on over my damp skin, hopping on one foot to pull them on.

Cole scrapes his hand over his face. He looks like he's on the verge of tears, spots of colour blazing in his cheeks. 'You're just shutting me out? Cat, tell me what happened.'

'Nothing happened.' I unwind the towel from my waist and drop it on the shore along with my ruined clothes. Maybe one of the houses will have something I can wear. I sling my backpack over my shoulder with my good hand. 'I just need to be alone. I need to calm down.'

'Cat, talk to me.' He looks so lost and so bewildered that it's wrenching at whatever shreds of self-control I still have left. I want to cry; I want to break, to cross the space between us and step into the comfort of his arms. I want to give up the war I'm waging against my past. It's like fighting with a shadow. I'm trying to hold back a force I don't understand, and I'm so tired that part of me just wants to yield to it.

But I can't. Not yet.

Cole's words are echoing inside me, and they've taken hold. If we can't find a way to save ourselves without more bloodshed, then maybe Lachlan is right. There's no future for humanity if we can't find a way to live together. Cartaxus is planning genocide, and all I can think of is how to launch an attack against them first.

Because that's exactly what Jun Bei would do.

'I told you I had more memories inside me,' I say. 'That they're behind a wall.'

Cole nods, his face tight.

'Well, right now, that wall is cracking. I need to be alone, or I don't know if I can keep it together. If there is a way to save us, then I need to clear my head to think of it. Right now, all I can think of is what Jun Bei would do, and it involves killing absolutely everyone who might pose a threat to us.'

A shadow crosses Cole's face. 'Cat –' he starts, but I cut him off.

'The others will be here soon,' I say, forcing myself to take a step back towards the path. 'We'll need to figure out a plan, and I need to get my head straight first. I'm going to go check this house for clothes, OK? I'll see you soon.'

He searches my face for what feels like an eternity, then nods. 'OK. I'll be here if you need me.'

I turn, driving my fingernails into my palm, and stride up the path to the closest house, feeling Cole's gaze burning into my back as I leave.

The path winds through an overgrown garden to the house – a cavernous, majestic thing, with a wall of double-storey windows overlooking a leaf-strewn wooden deck. The front door is glass, the handle unlocked. I push it open, expecting the inside to be trashed, but it's spotless. The kitchen is white marble, opening up to a living area with black leather couches curving round a chrome coffee table. There's a sweater crumpled on one of the couches, an empty glass on the kitchen counter. It's creepy when a place is neat like this. Most of the houses I've broken into were ransacked and full of rats, or had a wall missing after someone detonated inside. This place looks like the owners just went out one day and never came back. Even their shoes are lined up by the door below a pair of jackets in matching beige.

I head for the stairs, trying not to think about the look in Cole's eyes when he thought he'd done something to shock me like that. Every time I force his face from my mind, though, I just see Mato instead. His smile. His lips at my ear. He and Jun Bei were definitely together. I don't know why he wouldn't have mentioned it to me.

What other secrets did Jun Bei have that I haven't remembered?

I climb the stairs, heading into the master bedroom. The bed is made, the closet open, holding two racks of women's clothes. Nothing in my size, but I grab a denim jacket, a T-shirt and a pair of socks, and head into the en suite. It's tiled in white, coated with a layer of dust but otherwise clean. I dump the new clothes on the floor and sit on the edge of the tub, pulling a packet of Cartaxus cleaning wipes from my backpack, then peel off my T-shirt and drag one of the wipes over the blood and foam plastered to my skin. It takes half the packet just to clean my shoulders and arms, but there's not much I can do with the foam in my hair. I rummage through the bathroom cabinet, pulling out a comb, and pause when I see a bar of lavender soap.

It's factory made, at least two years old by now, but the scent of it as I hold it to my nose brings back a rush of memories. Agnes and I made lavender soap in her basement last year. I spent days coding a hacked algae strain for her, designed to chew up soybeans from the farms near the mountains and create glycerin, and she gave me a stack of hand-cut bars in return. Violet, flecked with tiny purple flowers. I washed in the lake with one the next day, and it was the first time I'd felt truly *clean* in a year.

I set the bar down, sliding into my cuff's menu, pulling up my comm-link. There's a string of messages sent from me to her over the last two weeks, and then a rush of replies that she sent after the decryption. She was tracking Lachlan in Nevada. She said to follow the pigeons.

But I did, and she wasn't waiting there for me.

'Agnes?' I ask, opening a comm channel. Part of me knows it won't work – it hasn't worked in weeks, but I can't stop myself from trying one more time. 'I really need you right now, Yaya. I don't know what to do. I can't stop Lachlan, I can't stop Cartaxus, and the plague is out of control. I don't want to go into a bunker, and I don't want to give up. I just wish I could hear your voice right now.'

The comm bounces into Cartaxus's network. If Agnes is on the surface, she'll see it. She hasn't replied to me all week, and I'm not expecting her to now.

I just wish I could know if she's OK.

I drag the comb through my hair, flicking away the worst of the mess as an engine rumbles in the distance. A low thumping sound, loud enough to rattle the windows. A Comox, flying from the direction of the safehouse. The others are here.

'Hold it together,' I murmur. I look between the clean shirt I found in the closet and the squid shirt Leoben printed for me, and tug on the squid over my still-damp bra. I leave the cleaning wipes in a dirty pile on the floor and haul on my backpack with my good hand, then jog down the stairs and outside just as the Comox lands in the road. Its rotors kick up a plume of dust and dried grass. I hurry down the path from the house as the ramp extends.

Anna strides down it, a rifle slung over her shoulder. Her blonde hair is in a high ponytail, her skin smeared with dirt. She's back in Cartaxus gear – black tactical trousers, a grey tank top that shows off the lean muscles in her shoulders and the tattoos on her arms. The white scar on her neck gleams in the sunlight, and the sight brings me to a stop, guilt tugging at me.

Everything I've learned about Jun Bei just frightens me more. I don't know why she would have cut Anna's throat and jacked her into a genkit if not to torture her. No wonder Anna hates me.

I know how much it hurts to become someone's experiment when you think you're part of their family.

That's what Lachlan did to me, and it's what Jun Bei did to Anna in that lab.

'What the hell happened to the jeep?' Anna asks. She looks me up and down. Some of the anger from the last time I saw her seems to have faded. 'And what happened to you?'

'Crowd caught us in the tunnels while we were getting out,' I say. 'Some of them blew.'

She winces. 'It's bad out there. Hey, uh, thanks for taking down those destroyers.'

I look down, shifting my weight uncomfortably. 'Thanks for coming back for me.'

'Yeah, well,' she says, 'that was mostly Cole.'

'Thank you anyway.' I force my eyes back to her face. I don't know if the two of us have any hope of building a relationship again, but I'm not the girl who hurt her in that lab. I'm not the girl she grew up with, either, but there's still something between us that I don't want to lose. 'I'm sorry,' I say.

Her brow creases. 'For what?'

'For everything. For leaving you all behind.'

A shadow passes over her features. 'I thought you said that wasn't *you*.'

'It wasn't, but . . .' I pause. 'It's hard to explain. I'm just sorry, OK?'

Leoben strides down the Comox's ramp, shooting me a grin. 'Look at you two, huh? Bonding over blowing shit up. Why didn't you ever figure this out at the lab?'

'Shut up, Lee,' Anna says, shoving his arm.

'Where's Mato?' I ask.

Leoben motions over his shoulder at a dark speck in the distance on the highway we drove in on. My tech zooms in on it, focusing until I can make out the vague shape of a motorbike.

'He said he still couldn't get through to Cartaxus,' Leoben says.

'Do you know if Dax is OK?' I ask.

'He's still alive,' he says. 'I haven't been able to comm him – Brink is locking down communications everywhere, but I hacked into his lab's systems, and it looks like he's there. That's all I know. Regina said the patched vaccine is working just fine. I don't know why Cartaxus won't release it.'

'Because the last time they sent out code from Lachlan that they couldn't understand, they had to blow a whole city into dust,' Anna says. 'Lachlan is being an asshole. He needs to hand himself in.'

'It doesn't matter any more,' I say. 'Now that the virus is in the pigeons, there's no stopping it.'

'Sure there is,' Anna says. 'They just have to scorch the goddamn surface of the planet. Don't think Brink isn't planning to do that right now.'

'So what are we going to do?' Leoben asks.

'We go back to base, of course,' Anna says. 'This mission is over.'

'I'm not going in,' I say. 'I made it through two years without a vaccine. We can do it again. There has to be a way to stop this that doesn't involve slaughtering millions of people. I'm not ready to give up.'

'You and me both,' Leoben says, 'but this is a pretty big enemy, squid. Hey, how's your hand, anyway?'

I look down, tightening my fingers into a fist. 'It's not my hand. Regina switched it.'

Anna blinks, staring at me, then covers her mouth, stifling a laugh. 'Shit, I'm sorry!' she blurts out. 'Oh my God. It's really not funny.'

Leoben shakes his head. 'You're terrible, Anna. She's been through a lot. Give the poor girl a hand.'

She snorts, clutching her mouth.

I can't help but smile. 'Guys . . .'

'No, I'm sorry,' Anna says, catching her breath, fighting for composure.

'We have to keep it together,' Leoben says. 'This is serious. It's all hands on deck.'

'Lee!' she yells, smacking him in the arm.

He grins, slinging an arm round my shoulder, squeezing me. 'Don't worry, squid. We'll get through this. Any food inside that house?'

I glance back over my shoulder. 'I didn't check.'

He shakes his head. 'Rookie mistake.'

He presses a kiss to my temple and heads up the path and into the house. Anna runs her hands back through her hair, still breathing slowly, trying not to laugh. 'Is Cole OK?' she asks.

'Yeah, he's down at the creek.'

'I'm going to go check in with him.' She starts to head down the path to the water, then stops and glances over her shoulder at the highway, where Mato's motorbike is still just a speck in the distance. 'You waiting for Mato? He's not going to be able to change Brink's mind. If Cartaxus is still planning flood protocol, there's nothing we can do to stop it. You know that, right? They have bases all over the world. I don't care how many drones you can bring down, it won't be enough.'

'I know,' I murmur, watching the motorbike roll closer. She's right – we have no leverage and no plan. Part of me can even understand where Brink is coming from. He has three billion people to think about and protect. He doesn't need the people on the surface any more than we need Cartaxus.

We're just in each other's way.

'I'll go and look for food with Lee,' I say. Anna nods, heading down to the creek. I walk back along the path to the house's front door, pausing when I reach the porch to look back at the distant smudge of Mato's motorbike.

I don't know how to deal with him when he arrives – if I want to confront him or pretend I still don't know the truth. It seems ridiculous to even be *thinking* about something as trivial as him kissing Jun Bei while Cartaxus is planning to launch flood protocol, but I can't get the memories out of my head.

I can't talk about it with Cole, and I'm *definitely* not going to talk to Anna about it.

Lee might understand, though.

I push through the front door, looking for him. Packets of cookies and dried noodles are stacked on the kitchen counter, but there's no sign of Lee. A hiss is coming from upstairs, though – a shower. Leoben's voice humming a low tune. I let out a frustrated sigh. I didn't even think to check if the water was running.

I walk across the living room to the wall of glass at the back of the house. It overlooks the creek, where Cole is standing with his arms crossed, talking to Anna. He looks upset, but I can't hear what they're saying. All my audio chip can pick up is the shower and the distant murmur of their voices. I stare down at Cole, straining to hear him, my mind searching instinctively for something to sharpen my audio tech when a pulse ripples from my cuff unconsciously.

Cole's panel glows in my vision, Anna's beside him. I'm distantly aware of the Comox and the jeep behind me, Lee upstairs in the shower. A rush of sound patches into my ears – muffled and rough, but clear enough to make out Cole's voice along with Anna's murmuring reply.

But this isn't an audio filter I'm running.

I'm *hacking* Cole's tech.

Horror surges through me. I didn't even *mean* to hack his panel. I have no idea how I'm even doing this. Part of me wants to cut off the connection – it's one thing to strain to hear him through the glass, but it's another to break into his tech. Pain blisters at the base of my skull. This is wrong. It's a violation. The wrongness of it makes me want to turn away, but I can't stop myself from staring down at him.

'She's confused,' he is saying. 'She doesn't know what she's doing.'

'You just don't have it in you,' Anna says. 'You still love her. I can smell her all over you.'

Cole turns away, his face dark. 'That's why I have to be the one to do it. She's my responsibility.'

CHAPTER 30

I stumble back and out of sight. The echo of Cole's voice in my ears feels like a knife cutting through me. The room tilts. I double over, dragging in a breath, a wash of silver rising in my vision.

What the hell did he mean – *She's my responsibility*?

The words open up a wound inside me, and I can feel my strength folding in towards it, the pillar of my resolve swaying beneath me. This is more than concern. He's not just worried that I'm getting dangerous. He's actively planning to control me. To stop me somehow.

I have to be the one to do it.

I close my eyes, fighting the urge to throw up. There was no emotion in his voice when he said those words. Just steel and training. He held me in his arms just *minutes* ago and told me he loved me. I was ready to give myself to him.

Has he been lying to me this whole time?

A cry of betrayal rises through me, unbidden, but I clutch my hands over my mouth to stifle it. I can't let them hear me. Leoben is upstairs, and I don't know if he's in on whatever Cole and Anna are planning. My eyes cut to the door, the urge to leave singing through me. The jeep is damaged and strewn with foam, but I know how to control it, and it'll get me out of here.

I clutch my backpack to my shoulder, hurrying across the room and out the door. Every time I blink, I see Cole's face. The tears in his eyes after Sunnyvale, when he realized who I was. The way he held me to his chest and told me everything was going to be OK. My fear and confusion are coalescing, combining into a shimmering ball of rage.

All that talk in the creek about me being *better*. About finding a way to save us without more killing. He's been holding me back from my past, and for what? Because Jun Bei is slipping back through me? Because I'm becoming *dangerous*?

He doesn't know the half of it.

I make it to the driveway and break into a run. Past the Comox and over to the dented, foam-streaked jeep. I don't even know where I'm going, but I'll figure it out. I can't stay here, not any more. I yank open the driver's door, but a cold hand catches my arm.

'Are you OK?'

I spin round. Mato is standing behind me, the glass of his coding mask clear and sparkling. The motorbike is parked behind him.

'Let go of me,' I whisper, glancing back at the creek.

He steps closer, but his hand doesn't drop from my arm. 'What's wrong?'

I open my mouth but don't know what to say. Mato's been lying to me too, and I know I can't trust *him*, either, but some part of me is still stretching for him. All he's done since we've met is try to help me recover the strength I used to have, while Cole has spent the whole time trying to get me to turn from it. Mato hasn't told me the truth about him and Jun Bei, but he was honest about knowing her. Maybe he thought it would be too much to take in to tell me everything. Maybe it was nothing more than a single stolen kiss.

Or maybe I'm just lost and desperate, and terrified of leaving here alone.

'I – I need to go,' I whisper. 'I need to leave, right now.'

He glances back down towards the creek, his mask darkening. 'Are you sure?'

I nod. He watches me for a long moment, then drops my arm. He pulls open the jeep's door and gestures for me to get in. 'Come on, I'll drive.'

I glance back at the creek. Cole has probably heard us. I climb into the jeep, and Mato turns swiftly, walking over to the Comox. He slides something from his pocket – two small black squares. He presses one to the Comox's side, the other to the handlebars of the motorbike, then strides back to the jeep. The foam sprayed across the seats has dried, but the air still stinks of infection with a sour note of decay. Mato slides into the driver's seat and pulls the door shut behind him. Cole jogs up the path from the creek and stares at us, confused. Mato glances back once, his face expressionless, then floors the accelerator, sending us racing back along the driveway and up to the highway.

I hear Cole's voice calling my name over the whine of the engine. He's bolting up the driveway now, shouting after us. The look of confusion is gone – I see it click inside him. That he knows I heard him. He looks suddenly hollow, but his jaw sets, and he runs back to the Comox.

We skid on to the highway as Cole flings open the Comox's door and climbs inside.

'That thing you put on the Comox,' I say. 'It isn't going to hurt him, is it?'

Mato shakes his head, his eyes locked on the road. 'No, it'll just disable the engine.'

I grab the seat to turn round, staring through the foam-splattered rear window. Cole is climbing back out of the Comox, running down the road after us, shouting something I can't hear.

Something twists inside me as his silhouette shrinks into a smudge on the road.

'What happened?' Mato asks. We speed north on the highway, leaving the house and Cole behind us.

'I . . . I don't know if I can talk about it right now.'

Mato glances over at me, at my backpack. 'You look cold.'

I look down. My bare arms are pale, covered with goose bumps, even though the air is warm. 'I'm fine.'

He holds the wheel with one hand, shrugging out of his jacket. 'You look like you could use this more than me.'

He meets my eyes, and for a moment I think I might cry, but I pull the jacket on instead, swallowing. 'I don't know what to do, Mato. I don't know how to save us, but I don't want to give up.'

'I'm not giving up, either,' he says. 'Just relax. I know a place we can go.'

We drive for ten minutes in near silence through a flat landscape of rocks and twisted shrubs. I can't stop thinking about how I might have overreacted and misinterpreted what Cole was saying – how there might be some innocent explanation for what I overheard. But the explanation doesn't come. His name pops up on my comm – calling over and over, sending messages telling me to *come back*, but he doesn't say anything about Anna or what they were talking about at the creek.

He knows I heard him. He knows that's why I left.

And he can't think of a single thing to say to make me turn round.

Mato swings the jeep on to a dirt road. The hills in the distance are familiar, the low, rocky scrub stretching out for miles. A tingle of memory rises inside me – a low, insistent tug at my mind, like a scent in the air. Mato looks over. 'You don't have to talk if you're not ready, but I'm here when you are.'

I close my eyes, forcing out a shaking breath. 'I remember . . . I remember Jun Bei being with you.'

His hands tighten on the wheel, his eyes fixed on the road. 'I knew there was something different in the way you looked at me. How much do you remember?'

'Not much,' I say. 'Just flashes. Why didn't you tell me?'

He shifts his grip on the wheel, stretching his fingers. 'Lachlan gave you fake memories, didn't he? I have memories like that from my childhood too. They're a violation. Your own mind creates them when it's lost a piece of its past. People tell you a story with pieces of something that could be true and your mind fills in the details. Jun Bei made me promise once that I would never tamper with her past like that. I needed you to remember the truth on your own. I don't expect you to remember or understand, or even feel the same way as she did, but I always knew we'd find each other again.'

Something in his tone makes me suddenly nervous. I don't know how I feel about Mato – it isn't really attraction, but I do feel a connection. There was clearly more than a single kiss between him and Jun Bei – whatever they had was far deeper. I know they were coding partners, and that's a powerful bond. There's nothing else quite like the feeling of two minds working in harmony – two people building things together, solving problems as one, truly *seeing* each other. That's what kept me thinking about Dax for two full years after Cartaxus took him away, and it must have kept Mato thinking about Jun Bei in the same way.

But I'm not *her* any more, and I don't remember their bond.

'Where are we going?' I ask.

'You'll see in a moment – we're almost there,' he says, pulling the jeep down a dirt driveway. There are mountains in the distance, their profile tugging at my memory. The ocean locked inside my mind swells, the wall inside me trembling as we pull over a rocky hill and a steel rooftop appears in the distance.

The sight blazes through me like a flame along a fuse. Mato's eyes fix on the rooftop, a low smile curving across his face. We roll down the driveway, crunching across a rocky, barren plain, and my breath catches as the lines of the house draw into view.

I know this place. I know this valley, these mountains, this desert. I know the curve of the rocky driveway and the slope of the steel roof. The windows catch the sunlight like mirrors, and the house seems to burn as we draw closer, shimmering in my memory.

This is where Lachlan changed me. We've been searching for him in a lab in Entropia, hunting for a window with a view of these mountains, but it was here all along.

We've been looking in the wrong place.

I turn to Mato, suddenly terrified. 'Is Lachlan here?'

'No,' he says, pulling us in alongside the house. 'It's OK. Nobody's here.'

My heart is still racing as we roll to a stop in the gravel driveway. This isn't just a house – it's a *mansion*. Stucco and steel and glass, sprawling across the desert, folding out into a geodesic dome around an overgrown greenhouse. Pots of wild, purple-streaked grasses sprout around the front porch, a rainbow of cacti filling gravel beds alongside the driveway. It's beautiful. Wild and eccentric. It's a house that Escher might have built, coiled into the desert like a lizard curled upon a rock. The sudden urge to jump from the car and run to the front door rises through me.

And that isn't what I was expecting to feel when I saw it.

There is no rush of horror as I look at the house's windows, no flashbacks of torture and restraints. This is where Lachlan changed my face, but suddenly all I can remember is *happiness*. Bright days and long nights spent working and coding. I look over at Mato. His eyes are locked on mine, and I can *see* him here – sitting across a table, turning protein models in the air.

'You . . . you worked here together,' I whisper, 'didn't you?'

He nods as we roll to a stop. 'Yes, we did. This was our home.'

Our home. The words spin in my mind, whipping up the ocean locked behind the wall inside me. A hurricane of meaning in two little words.

Not a prison. A home.

'We started to meet in VR when Jun Bei was still in the lab,' he says. 'We were just kids. She never told me about the Zarathustra Initiative, not until after we met here. She'd known how to escape from the lab for years, but she was staying for the others. I understood. I have a brother, and we've been through a lot for each other.'

I stare at the house, my heart racing.

'But it was our work that connected us,' he says. 'We were so good together. She was so wild and brilliant, and I've seen that brilliance coming back in you. I knew you'd remember if I brought you here.'

He swings his door open and steps out. I climb from the jeep slowly, my boots crunching on the gravel driveway. A thread inside me tightens as I look over the house, drawing my past back to me. It feels like the building itself is trembling with memories, waiting to be unleashed. The scent of jasmine flowers wafts from a trellis on the porch, palm leaves swaying in the rocky garden.

This is the house where Jun Bei ended and I began.

'I need you to remember your past,' Mato says. 'It's time to let the walls down, Catarina. You need to bring back the girl you used to be. It's the only way to save us.'

'What are you talking about?'

'I spoke to Brink,' he says. 'They're launching flood protocol. Troops are going to raze every major survivor camp and bring as many people into bunkers as they can. They're going to try to kill the pigeons. The flocks aren't as scattered as they thought. Cartaxus has airborne weapons they can use to hunt them down. It might take years to get them all, but Brink has decided it's time to clear the surface of all possible hosts of the virus in order to protect this vaccine.'

'That's madness,' I say. 'They're birds – there's no way Cartaxus can kill *all* of them, no matter what kind of weapons they have. The birds will spread, they'll evolve. There'll be no way to stop them, and millions of people will die. We'll lose the vaccine *anyway*.'

'I agree,' Mato says. 'Cartaxus isn't thinking with reason right now. They're thinking with their *instincts*. Fear, survival, hatred. That's why I need your help to stop them.'

My breath catches. *Instincts.* He's talking about the Origin code. He wants to do what Lachlan has been threatening this whole time – to forcibly alter people's minds.

'You want to wipe the Wrath,' I say, shaking my head, stepping away.

Mato turns to me, the sunlight glinting off his mask. It's crystal clear, his eyelashes dark beneath it, a line between his eyebrows. 'I know you hate the idea of it,' he says, 'but I've been searching for a way to stop Cartaxus, and I believe this is the only way to save us. Without the Wrath, Cartaxus will see that there's nothing to gain from launching flood protocol. They'll see the only way to survive will be to work together to *defeat* the virus, not hide from it.'

I turn away, pressing my hand to my mouth, torn. I've never agreed with Lachlan's plan, and I still don't, but Mato's right – there might not be any other way to stop this. Brink wants to murder all of us because he's afraid of losing control. His base animal instincts might be enough to destroy the world.

'I couldn't help even if I wanted to,' I say. 'Lachlan is in control of the Origin code, and I don't know where he is.'

'We don't need Lachlan.'

Something trembles inside me. I turn to Mato. 'Wh-what are you talking about?'

'Do you really think that all this was Lachlan's doing?' he asks. 'Lachlan's work lives inside the body's cells, but he doesn't understand the mind. He's never worn an implant or rearranged his thoughts. He still uses a goddamn *scalpel*. Lachlan doesn't just need your DNA to use the Origin code, Catarina.'

He steps closer, and suddenly I can't breathe. The ocean inside me is raging, slamming hard against the wall in my mind.

Mato brings his hands to my face. 'Lachlan needs your *help* with the code,' he whispers, 'because you're the one who wrote it.'

CHAPTER 31

The air stills. I stare into Mato's eyes through the glass of his mask, feeling a crack in the wall inside me creak open.

The Origin code. *You're the one who wrote it.* The words sound impossible, insane – and yet they feel like truth as they settle inside me.

'No,' I breathe, pushing away from Mato, stumbling across the gravel driveway. I brace my hands on my knees, my vision spinning, seeing the Wrath sweeping over Sunnyvale, the crowd tearing one another to pieces. We've been hunting Lachlan down since the decryption to force him to remove his toxic code from the world's panels.

But he didn't even write it.

'Come inside,' Mato says, following me. He reaches for my arm, but I shy away, and he lifts his hands, stepping back. 'I know you're dealing with a lot, but we don't have much time. Brink is launching flood protocol, and I don't intend to let him destroy my home. We need to come up with a plan to stop him. Come inside, and we'll talk.'

I straighten, looking at the house. 'I'm not going to help you use the Origin code.'

'That's OK,' Mato says. 'It's your code. All I want is to save Entropia and stop this attack. I know that's what you want too. We'll figure out something together. Let's just talk, OK?'

I shove the hair from my face, drawing in a steadying breath and nod. Mato steps towards the house slowly, as though I'm a frightened animal that might bolt if he makes any sudden movements. He swipes his panel over a scanner beside the front door, and it swings open into a large, bright living area. I follow him inside cautiously, my arms wrapped round my chest. The living room has white couches arranged round a circular fireplace, with white-and-purple orchids painted on the ceiling. Everything about the house is *familiar*, but I don't remember it properly.

'This house is where Jun Bei wrote the Origin code,' Mato says, walking through the living area towards a slate-grey kitchen behind it. 'Well, it's where she finished it, at least. She started with a draft she'd written with Lachlan, but I don't think much of his original code remained in the final version. She'd been working on it with him for years at the lab. He noticed the instinct for the Wrath in Cole and saw a chance through her to build a suppressor for it, or even erase it permanently. He gave her a copy of it to keep working on when she left the lab.'

'She *talked* to him after she left?'

'Regularly,' Mato says, walking into the kitchen, testing the tap in the sink. It sputters for a moment before the water runs smoothly. He pushes back his sleeves and washes his hands.

'Lachlan was the one who got her out of the lab. She said she killed a group of guards, and then he walked her to the fire trail and called her a vehicle. He told her to come here, to this house – *Regina's* house – so she did.'

Regina's house. I look around, scanning the walls, pacing across the floor to a picture hanging near the kitchen. It shows a young woman who looks like Jun Bei, only she's in her mid-twenties, standing with a group of people. It must be Regina before she remade herself. The group is holding a giant snake stretched out, supported between them. She's laughing. One of the men in the picture looks like Brink, and another has a shock of red hair. His nose is different, his jaw is changed and his eyes look like they're *green*, but it's clearly Lachlan. Brink wasn't lying when he said he changed his appearance.

Mato steps up behind me and slides his jacket from my shoulders. 'Regina gave Jun Bei this house when she arrived. Jun Bei couldn't live in the city – it was too dangerous, and she didn't want to change her face, but she didn't want to be found by Cartaxus, either. So she stayed here. We'd been talking for years by then, so I started coming to work with her, and she quickly asked me to move in. She'd had four other people around her for her entire childhood, and she hated being alone more than anything.'

I turn to him. 'But she was *fifteen*. You were living together? How old are you?'

'I was sixteen,' he says, 'but it wasn't like that. We had a different connection. We were two minds working as one.'

'Mato, I remember kissing you.'

His cheeks redden. He turns away, folding the jacket. 'Well, I never said we didn't *kiss*.'

He sets the jacket down on the kitchen counter. 'Jun Bei became the person she was meant to be in this house. She began to heal from her childhood and she found a strength that even Lachlan didn't know she had. Her code was already spectacular, but it became truly extraordinary.'

I turn to him, walking to a stool near the kitchen counter, sitting down unsteadily. I'm still reeling, but my focus is drifting back to me. These are the answers I've been searching for ever since I learned the truth about myself. I draw in a slow, steadying breath, leaning my weight into my good arm on the counter. 'What happened to her? How did she end up as me?'

Mato leans back against the kitchen counter beside me, drawing the metal pen from his pocket, spinning it between the fingers of his left hand. 'I'm not entirely sure what started everything, but I think she went too far. We were rewriting our minds together here, learning to fraction, and building algorithms into sections of our brains nobody had touched before. Regina gave Jun Bei the cuff, but I installed the implant. I'd had one put in years earlier, but I hadn't made much progress in using it until I started working with her. Her mind was so flexible, and she always wanted to keep going – pushing to bigger and bigger parts of her mind, trying to dedicate more memory for fractioning.'

He looks around the room, wistful, as though remembering her here. 'There were almost no bodily functions she hadn't relegated to the chip. Breathing, digestion – every muscle control she could find an algorithm for. She even clipped her optic nerves and had her vision run through a VR chip for processing so she could free up space in her visual cortex. She was wonderful, but she was reckless too. She lost memories *constantly* when she was trying to organize them in her brain. Sometimes she'd forget what *trees* were, and there was a week when she had to listen to music in order to speak. I urged her to move her *essence* – her memories and personality – into a section of her brain that she could close off and protect so that she'd be able to recode the other side completely. But that was the mistake.'

A chill runs through me. Mato crosses the room, spinning the pen in his hand, staring out the window. 'I don't know exactly what happened the day Lachlan came. I was at the marketplace, and when I came home, she was in a coma. She was running code to erase her memories – she was *wiping* herself. I saw that she'd called Lachlan just before she started, but I don't know what he said to her. Whatever it was, it frightened her enough to make her erase every memory of the time she'd spent here. Everything in her panel was freshly encrypted, and she'd deleted every piece of code she'd written since she came to this house. I couldn't wake her, and Lachlan was on his way in a Comox. There wasn't enough time to get her to Regina.'

He drops his eyes. There's suddenly a hint of shame in his face – like he's begging me for forgiveness. But I don't even know what he's done.

He walks back to the kitchen, spinning the pen again. 'When Lachlan came, he said that what she'd done couldn't be reversed. He said the damage was irreparable. He was horrified by how much she'd done to her mind, even though he'd been altering her mind for *years*. You have to understand – I thought she was gone. I thought she was lost forever. He said that maybe she'd wake, but she'd be like a child, and that she'd wiped the core of her personality and all her memories. Maybe she wouldn't ever be able to speak or even communicate again.'

I grip the counter hard enough to send a pulse of pain through my wounded arm. 'You let Lachlan take her.'

He looks down, guilty. 'He said he'd take care of her, not back in a lab, but in the real world. He'd find someone to look after her body, and he'd work on bringing back her mind. I was so broken I could barely look at her. I knew I shouldn't have let her go so far. I didn't know he'd change her like this, though – overwrite her completely. Turn her into his daughter. I didn't know, I swear. I let him take you, and then I was lost. I tried to overthrow Regina out of anger and had to run. I joined Cartaxus, trying to understand the programme she'd come from, and threw myself into working my way up the ranks. I watched Lachlan from Cartaxus's satellites after he left the organization and bought that property. I watched for months, and then one day you stepped out of that cabin and walked to the lakeshore. You knelt and picked a flower, and I almost died.'

He closes his eyes. 'As soon as I saw you, I *knew*. You weren't her. You were someone else. When I realized she was gone forever, I nearly broke. After that, it hurt too much to see you. I ignored you and the cabin, and threw myself into neurocoding – trying to understand what had happened with the implant. I made more progress in a year than anyone had since Regina left Cartaxus, but it wasn't enough to tell me how to save the girl you used to be.'

He smiles bitterly. 'And all along, Lachlan was just suppressing your memories – suppressing who you really are. I thought you'd woken as a new person, that you'd been given a fresh start, but I should have known better. It was just another experiment. He was using the implant the whole time to hide your past from you – to hide *me* from you, and to keep your talents restrained. I could have come and taken you away any time, but I thought you were gone. When he told me the truth, I vowed never to make that mistake again.'

'What do you mean?' I ask, my head spinning. 'When did you talk to him?'

'When he came to me at central command to say that he was close to finishing the vaccine, and that it was time to release the code you'd written.'

I stand from the kitchen stool, adrenaline racing through me. 'You're *working* with him?'

Mato shrugs. 'He promised me the only thing I want – he said I'd get you back. Of *course* I'm working with him. Why do you think I came to the Zarathustra lab? To pick up the black-out agents? I came to find you and convince Brink to send us both here. You're the only one who can stop this. Lachlan doesn't even understand the Origin code – he can't figure out how to use it. You have to come back with me to run it yourself. You're the only one who knows how.'

I step away, shaking my head. 'I don't know how, Mato. I don't know that code at all. We have to find another way to stop Cartaxus.'

'There's no stopping this,' he says. 'Brink isn't going to turn back. If you don't use the Origin code, then we're all going to die up here.'

'If you can get through to him –'

'It doesn't *matter*,' Mato says, his voice sharp. 'There's no stopping him, because there's no stopping the virus any more, don't you see? Now that it's in the pigeons, it'll mutate into something new and more lethal every *week*. There's no way the vaccine will last more than a month. Brink wants to wipe the slate because he's thinking rigidly – all he can see is vaccines and viruses and traditional human DNA. He won't even consider the option of changing *ourselves* into something the virus won't affect. We've tried Cartaxus's approach to ending this plague, and it's failed us. It's time to give the genehackers a try. The Origin code will hold off the attack, and they can keep their bunkers for as long as they want. But the surface is *ours*. We can beat this virus together – you and I.'

I shake my head, backing away. 'There has to be another way . . .'

'Always a fighter,' he says, twisting the end of the pen he's been spinning between his fingers. A dull blue light glows at one end. A chill runs through me at the sight. Mato presses a button on the side, and the blue light blinks brighter.

I back into the kitchen counter, glancing past him at the door. He's blocking my exit. I don't know what the pen in his hands is supposed to do, but I don't think it's good. 'Mato, what are you doing?'

He tilts his head, spinning the pen back and forth between the fingers of his left hand. 'I'm making a gamble that you won't kill me for this once you return. This device controls the socket in your head. I had to prepare for the possibility that you would fight me on this. It's fitted with a tool to control the implant.'

My hand rises slowly to the tangled hair at the back of my head. 'Mato, please. Just stop this – let's talk. We'll find a way to contact Brink. We *have* to be able to convince him to see that this isn't a real solution. He's just panicking. He doesn't want millions of people's deaths on his conscience.'

'I'm through with Brink,' Mato says. He stops spinning the pen and holds it stretched between his hands, his fingers gripping the ends. He twists it slowly, and the back of my head *pulses*. I drag in a breath, my legs suddenly weak, clutching the kitchen counter for balance.

'I'm going to free you, Jun Bei,' Mato says. 'You're being held back by the very walls inside your mind that you built there. I'm going to help you knock them down. It's time for you to come back to me, and for us to work together to beat this plague the way we should have been all along.'

He twists the pen again, and the back of my head begins to ache. My lungs shudder, the edges of my vision growing blurry. I stumble back blindly, grabbing at the wall for balance. 'Mato, stop this,' I choke out. 'You're *hurting* me.'

'I know I am,' Mato says, stepping closer, his eyes shining. 'I've seen glimpses of you, of your *true* self coming back over the last few days, but only when you're wounded. I think I need to give you a little help to find your way back to me, Jun Bei.'

'I'm not Jun Bei, Mato,' I beg. 'She's gone. Hurting me won't bring her back.'

'Oh,' he says, tilting his head, twisting the pen again, 'I think perhaps it will.'

CHAPTER 32

Pain crackles through my head, arcing across my skull. I suck in a gasp, shaking, leaning against the wall.

'I would very much like to avoid this, Jun Bei,' Mato says. 'But the implant responds to your thoughts most clearly when you're fighting for your life. I've thought about every possible option, and I believe this is the cleanest way.'

'I'm not Jun Bei,' I say, looking around desperately for something to defend myself with. There are no weapons close to me, but there's a knife block on the other side of the kitchen. I throw an elbow into Mato's chest, trying to push past him, but he twists the pen again and a blade of pain cuts into the back of my head, sending me to my knees on the floor.

The world flickers to silver, then back again. I drag in a breath, trying to get up. The base of my skull feels like it's on fire. My nerves are blazing with pain. I try to stand up, coughing, my vision spinning.

‘You’ll understand soon,’ Mato says, walking over, his eyes locked on me. ‘I take no pleasure in this.’

I throw my hands up uselessly as he twists the pen again, and a wall of pain tumbles down on me.

My cheek hits the tiles, a scream tearing from my chest. My vision flickers, pixelating, flashing to black and white before refocusing. My legs draw in instinctively, my body curling into a protective ball on the floor.

‘Focus on your past, Jun Bei,’ Mato says, walking in a circle around me. ‘This may feel painful, but I assure you it’s perfectly safe. I even tested this code on myself to make sure I wouldn’t hurt you.’ He twists the pen again, burning a line of fire from my neck all the way down my spine. I scramble into a crouch, gritting my teeth against the pain, and launch myself at his knees.

He stumbles as I crash into him, and he falls back against the kitchen counter. He manages to grab hold of it and keep himself upright, but the pen clatters from his hands. It lands on the tiles beside me, and I throw myself across the floor after it, grabbing it desperately, snapping it in half.

Instantly, the fog of pain pulsing from the back of my head clears.

‘Impressive,’ Mato says, gasping for air. He straightens slowly, clutching his side where he hit the kitchen counter. He said Anna broke one of his ribs when she gave him the adrenaline shot outside Entropia.

I stagger to my feet, swaying, looking around wildly for a way out, but Mato is still between me and the front door. If I can’t escape, I’m going to need a weapon. My eyes cut again to the knife block, my training with Leoben roaring back through me.

Be aggressive. I launch myself across the room, bolting for the knives.

Mato's footsteps pound behind me. I force myself to run, urging every fibre of my tech-enhanced muscles to engage. I don't have to time to come to a stop when I reach the counter, so I slam into it, the grey marble lip hitting my stomach hard enough to knock the air from me. I have just enough time to grab a knife and whirl round, flinging the blade at Mato.

It hits him in the shoulder, embedding itself halfway. Deep enough to make him cry out and stumble back, clutching the wound. His eyes grow wide with shock as he looks down at the blade, then he yanks it from his shoulder and lifts it, blood streaming over his hand.

'I guess I'm going to have to hurt you the old-fashioned way,' he says.

Ice shoots through my veins. He lunges across the kitchen at me, the knife flashing, and I barely have time to throw myself out of the blade's path. He's still angling himself between me and the door, so I shove away from the kitchen counter and race down the hallway, searching for another exit. Past the dining room, past a bedroom with genehacked ivy clawing into the plaster.

I throw a glance behind me, seeing Mato with the knife in one hand following me with eerie calmness, his mask opaque and matte. A chill runs through me. I grab the wall for balance and throw myself into the room at the end of the hallway. There's a heavy-looking steel chair with legs that look like spikes, a small wooden table and a daybed with a linen cover and blanket draped over it. But no exits. The window is barred, looking out over the desert.

I've run into a trap.

'Shit,' I gasp, spinning round, but it's already too late. The glass door hisses shut behind me, its gleaming hinges locking with a click. Through the glass, Mato regards me with what might be a smile.

'I can't believe I didn't think of this earlier,' he says, his voice muffled through the door. '*Much* cleaner to keep you in here. I'll figure out a way to bring you back, Jun Bei, don't worry.'

I look around wildly for a weapon, a way out, and a dark smudge in the desert beyond the window catches my eye. A Comox is sweeping in from the south. It has to be the others. I spin back to Mato, but he's already turned away. He stalks back to the kitchen and runs the water in the sink, scrubbing the blood from his hands, then grabs his jacket from the counter and pulls it on carefully over his wounded shoulder. He slides one of the kitchen drawers open, lifting a handgun out, tucking it into his waistband at the small of his back. He closes the drawer and strides back through the living room to the front door as the Comox approaches.

He's going to hurt them. The Comox swings lower, dropping towards the driveway. I try frantically to send a comm to Cole, but my tech shows him as offline. He must have gone dark. The others don't know what they're walking into – Mato could *kill* them. He could torture them if he thought it would help destroy the walls inside my mind. Anna and Cole have been lying to me – for all I know, they've been planning to hurt me too – but they're still my family.

I can't let them walk into a trap like this.

'No!' I shout, pounding at the door.

The Comox lands in the driveway, sending up a billowing cloud of dust. I slam my hands desperately against the window as the ramp descends. There's no sign of Leoben, but Cole walks out, squinting, and Anna follows. They must have followed me here – found the house somehow. Maybe Cole could track the jeep. Anna's rifle is over her shoulder, but her other hand isn't near it, and she's half turned away from Mato to scan the desert as he walks out.

'No!' I scream, beating at the glass, but Cole doesn't even glance at me. Anna walks across the driveway towards Mato. Her lips part, but I can't hear what she's saying.

Whatever Mato says in reply, it seems to leave Anna satisfied. Her shoulders relax, and I don't know how she can't see that he's dangerous. He has a knife wound in his shoulder, a handgun in his waistband. And yet he holds out one arm, gesturing for Anna and Cole to come inside, and the two of them walk towards the house.

I turn from the window, my mind spinning with panic. I need to get out of this room. My eyes dance over the ceiling, the vents set into the floorboards, the sensor lock at the door. Nothing easy to hack, not enough time.

But there's also a wall of glass opening up to the living room, and *that* I can definitely get through.

I whirl round, grabbing the steel-pronged chair, swinging it at the wall. It bounces off the glass, but the sound echoes through the room, and Mato flinches. The movement sends a shock of pain up my wounded arm, but there's a fresh, gleaming chip in the glass. I grab the chair again, gritting my teeth, hurling it back again. This time, the chip becomes a crack. I let out a strangled cry, swinging the chair once more at the fraying glass, and it shatters.

Freedom. I lurch through the shattered wall, my newly mended wrist aching. White spots burn across my vision, my legs going weak. I push off the wall and race for the kitchen.

'Cole!' I scream.

The front door is open. The three of them are standing in the living room. Mato turns, regarding me coolly. Cole's eyes cut to me, taking in my face, but I can tell from his expression that he doesn't understand. He doesn't know that Mato's hurting me. Anna sees it faster – the situation, the threat. She reaches for her weapon. I lurch past Mato, drawing in a breath to scream that he has a gun, and time slows to a crawl.

Mato's hand shoots out and grabs my hair. Cole's eyes flash to black. The horizon tilts as Mato yanks me closer, dragging me in front of him. I stumble, trying to bring up one elbow to hit him in the face, but I realize too late that Mato is holding his gun.

Anna's rifle is out, but it's still at her side. Mato's is already up, microseconds faster. He lifts it in a clean arc, inhumanly fast, on a straight path to its target. I try to pull away from him, or throw out one arm to knock his aim off course, but it's too late.

A single shot echoes through the house as he shoots Anna in the chest.

CHAPTER 33

A scream tears from my throat as Anna flies backwards, her body jolting from the bullet. The sound of the shot echoes through me, saturating my senses. The gun in Anna's hands clatters away as she hits the floor like a doll, her head bouncing hard on the tiles.

'No!' I shout, sending an elbow back into the knife wound in Mato's shoulder. He gasps, his grip on me loosening just enough for me to break free. I scramble forward, launching myself at Anna. Her eyes are fluttering. Dark spots of her blood glisten on the tiles, her fingers tracing scarlet streaks on the marble as she reaches across the floor for her gun. I drop to my knees beside her and press my hands to the wound in her chest, scanning the room. There's still time to save her. She's a black-out agent. Her body is full of cutting-edge tech. I can get her through this if I can hack into her panel. I drag up my cuff's menu, but Cole lets out a cry of pain.

'Not so fast,' Mato mutters.

I look up. Cole is on his hands and knees on the floor, his muscles tense, struggling to breathe. His face is white, his skin beaded with sweat. He looks like he did when Leoben's jeep exploded – like he's hurt so badly it's crashing his tech.

But there's not a scratch on him.

Mato tilts his head and Cole collapses on his side, gasping in pain. Mato must be hurting him through his tech somehow. I press down harder on Anna's chest, trying desperately to stem the flow of blood. She's bleeding out. She's *dying*. Mato steps across the floor and kicks her gun away.

'Stop this!' I shout. 'Please, Mato!'

'You can save them both,' he says. 'This should be easy for you, Jun Bei.'

'No, please,' I whisper. I know what he's doing. He's trying to get me to fraction and split my mind to save Cole and Anna. He knows I'm on the edge, that it might bring down the wall inside me. I can already feel it crumbling, the ocean pressing against me. I'm on the verge of losing myself. Pushing my mind any further might break me.

But I don't have a choice.

I pull my cuff's interface into my vision again, sending out a pulse. Flickers of light blaze across the room – around Cole's panel, and Mato's. His mask, the jeep outside, Anna's arm beside me. I lock my focus on to Cole's panel, sliding into his black-out tech, but Mato beats me to it.

His response is immediate, deflecting my attack. Clear, swift, perfect code batting me away from Cole's tech. For the first time I can glimpse the true extent of Mato's skills. Even bent over, one hand clutched to his shoulder, his grip on Cole's tech is like nothing I've seen before.

He is killing Cole in more than one dimension – I can sense it, feel it prickling at those same corners in my mind. Mato's eyes gleam, the mask a slash of black across his face, and for the first time I can see what Cole must have when he saw me wearing the cuff. I understand what he was trying to warn me about when he said that Jun Bei shouldn't have been trained by Cartaxus – why you shouldn't mix science and death.

The perfect blend of those two powers is standing in front of me.

Mato is not entirely human any more.

He has become something else – something alien and dangerous, on a plane that humans should not be allowed to reach. The mask, the cuff, the implants in our skulls. They're a blurring of tech and violence – weapons we've added to our bodies, and I'm not sure we should have been allowed to.

'You can do better than this,' he says, straightening. His voice is still calm, the merest flicker of frustration crossing his features as he rolls his wounded shoulder. 'You're still so weak. This is why I'm trying to help you. It pains me to see you like this. You can be so much more, Jun Bei.'

Anna coughs. A wet, shallow sound. Her lungs are filling with blood. Every second that passes is going to make it harder to bring her back from this. I push my focus into her panel, but he's blocking that too – building firewalls around her tech to keep me from saving her.

'*Please,*' I beg. 'Let him go. Let me help her.'

Cole clenches his hands into fists, shaking. 'Leave . . . Anna . . .' he manages to choke out, but a tremor passes through him, and he lets out a roar.

I stare at Cole, suddenly confused. I don't know why he'd tell me to leave Anna. He mustn't understand how badly hurt she is. If I can't help her soon, she's going to die.

I dig my fingernails into my palm, stretching for the seam inside me, trying to split my mind into a weapon that can combat Mato's control. Anna chokes beside me, blood bubbling from her lips. A pulse in the side of her neck is fluttering, her chest shaking. Cole is motionless, his eyes wide and unfocused, but it looks like he's not in pain any more. It looks like he's *gone*.

I don't know what Mato is doing, or how I'll possibly be able to stop him, but I know I'm losing time.

I wrench open the barrier in my mind, aiming my focus at Anna's panel, but the instant the world begins to split, her eyelids flutter closed. The beat in the side of her neck ceases.

'No!' I scream. 'Please, Mato!'

The sunlight gleams off the silvery sheen of the dark blood soaking through her shirt. She's lying limp, not breathing, but I still can't get through Mato's defences around her tech. There has to be a way to save her. I can jump her panel. I can resuscitate her. She's only been dead for *seconds*. I push harder at the split inside my mind, but it's useless. The controls to her tech are locked down solid.

'Mato!' I scream, spinning to him. 'Let her go!'

'It's over,' he says, straightening, tossing a stray lock of hair back from his face. 'You were too weak to save her. I'm disappointed.'

Rage coils through me. I close my eyes, drawing up the scythe from Jun Bei's folders. I fling it at his panel, but it glances off like a stone skipping from the surface of a pond.

The merest hint of a smile crosses his features. 'Now,' he says, 'that's more like it.'

I growl, flinging the code again, urging myself back into the same space I slid into when I took down the drones. I know that this is what he wants, but I'm past reason now. There's a fire blazing through me, and I want him to pay for what he's done. The implant sends a spike of pain through the base of my skull, but I finally feel it stretching through my consciousness, splitting my thoughts like light through a prism. The world doubles, then doubles again. Four voices within me whisper, sending the scythe through Mato's defences. It's still bouncing off his firewalls, but now I'm sending it from four directions. Now eight. The world begins to shimmer, a buzzing starts up in my ears.

This is more fractions than I've tried before, but I feel like I'm getting stronger each time, and Mato's eyes are finally glazing with the effort of fighting back the attack. His control on Cole's panel is slipping. I tilt myself harder into the attack, flinging more viruses at him. Dozens of weapons are waiting inside my arm. My hands begin to shake, my control over the fractions fading, and I make a move for Anna's rifle, but Mato swings his gun at Cole.

Ice shudders through me. The chorus of death inside my mind falls silent. I look at Cole, still frozen on his knees. Defenceless. Wounded. Vulnerable.

I can't lose him too.

'Wait,' I beg. 'Please, Mato. I'll stop fighting you.'

Mato's finger hovers on the trigger, the gun aimed at Cole's head. 'I'm doing this for you.'

'No,' I say. 'Hurting him isn't going to help me remember who I was. All it's going to do is make me hate you.'

He shakes his head. 'You don't know what you need, Jun Bei. That's why I'm here. All I've done is help you, and I'm growing tired of being forced to explain myself. *I'm* not the one who's been planning to take away your freedom and your mind.' He throws out one arm, gesturing to Cole, dragging him out of his trance. 'Ask him, if you're so concerned with his safety. Ask him what he and Anna were planning. I've read their texts, I've heard their calls. Ask Cole why he was searching for you all these years.'

My heart skips. This is what Cole and Anna were arguing about at the creek. This is what I overheard back at the safehouse, what they've been talking about since Anna first arrived.

The reason Cole said that I was his *responsibility*.

'Cole, what is he talking about?'

Cole's voice is rough, his body stiff. 'It's not what you think.'

Mato stalks behind Cole, straightening his jacket, the mask on his face growing clear. His eyes are locked on mine, fierce and sincere. This isn't a game for him. This is deadly serious.

'I know what they were doing,' he says. 'Do you think he was searching for Jun Bei because he *loved* her?'

'I did –' Cole starts.

'Liar!' Mato snaps, and Cole bends over, letting out a cry of pain. '*I* loved her,' Mato shouts. 'I was the only one who ever understood her. Tell her the truth!'

Cole straightens, shaking. He's not even looking at Anna. Her pulse has stopped, and she's not breathing. We're running out of time to resuscitate her, but he doesn't seem to care.

'We were trying to stop Jun Bei from using the scythe,' Cole says. 'Killing those guards at the lab when she escaped was just the start. A few months after she escaped, sixty people died in a military base around a signal tower from what looked like lethal code. Cartaxus covered it up, and I didn't put it together until later, but her panel ID had been part of the attack. She wasn't going to stop, Cat. I don't think she could.'

I rock back on my heels, staring at Cole, the storm in my mind whipping into a gale. 'You think she *killed* sixty people and you didn't mention it to me?'

'You were barely holding yourself together,' he says. 'We had a mission. I didn't want to frighten you, and I don't even know if it's true. But I know you're not that person any more.'

My head spins. 'This is why you freaked out every time I used the scythe, isn't it? Were you seriously afraid I'd snap and commit *genocide*?'

'I didn't know –'

'You didn't *know*?'

A presence stirs on the edge of my senses, darkening now with rage. Cole and Anna were hunting me. They thought I was a threat – something that needed to be controlled. I should never have trusted them. My fists tighten, code that promises pain and control sliding through the shadowy recesses of my mind.

'You were going to kill her,' I say.

'No,' Cole gasps. 'No, I could never have done that. I wasn't going to hurt her. I was going to talk to her, and if it was true, I

was going to convince her to remove her panel. She was too powerful. She couldn't keep going like she was. Every time she lashed out, she was taking people's lives in her hands.'

'And when she refused?' I spit. 'What then, Cole?'

His face tightens, and lightning crackles through me. There is shame and guilt and something darker – something *worse* – in his eyes. 'We were going to erase her memories and remove her panel,' he says, 'but I was going to have the same done to me. I was going to start again with her – both of us, together. It was the only way.'

I just stare at him, pain slicing through me – but it isn't in the base of my skull. It's in my *heart*. Cole was kissing me just hours ago. He told me he was in love with me. The storm inside me keeps whipping higher, the ocean rising in my mind. He's supposed to be my soulmate. My friend and guardian. He and I were supposed to run away to the beach together.

But he wanted to remove my tech. To wipe my memories.

He was going to do the exact same thing Lachlan did to me.

'No, Cole,' I whisper, my legs growing weak. The pain in my heart feels *real*, wrenching at me. I don't know how much of a threat Jun Bei was, and I don't know what happened with that signal tower, but I do know that when she was here with Mato, she wanted to *improve* the human race. She wrote the Origin code – a way to erase our violent instincts. That's not something a person does before committing genocide. She was thinking about the future.

She was trying to *help*.

'You're just like Lachlan,' I say. 'Was it all a lie?'

'No,' he begs. 'But someone had to step in. That code in her panel wasn't just a risk to us. She was a risk to everyone on the planet. She could have killed them all without even really thinking about it.'

'You think she was just a cold-blooded murderer? Cole, she was a *child*. She was frightened. She needed to get out of that lab and heal, and that's exactly what she did until Lachlan took her again. She didn't want to hurt people. You don't understand – she was trying to make the world better. She *wrote* the Origin code.'

Cole's eyes are full of horror. He doesn't understand, because he's not *trying* to understand. He's already made up his mind about Jun Bei because she left him. She broke him, and it's easier for him to believe that she was a monster than a scared girl who ran away and was too afraid to go back.

I turn away from him, forcing myself to breathe. The storm in my mind is a gale, and the ocean of memories is raging. Mato stands watching me, his eyes alight. It's almost like he can sense how close I am to the edge of the cliff. How thin the wall between me and my past has grown. This is exactly what he wanted – to tear me down, and to bring back the girl he loved.

'I see it now,' Mato says. 'It wasn't hurting you that prompted your memories to return. It was him, and the others at risk. That's what's breaking through the barriers inside you.' He looks at Cole. 'If he dies, then your link to your past weakness dies too. You can finally be free. He's already admitted that he was prepared to *erase* you. You've left him once. Do it again. He doesn't understand you like I do, Jun Bei.'

I stare at Cole. I don't know if I can forgive him for what he was planning, for lying to me like that, but I know that I can't stand here and let him die.

'My name isn't Jun Bei,' I growl. 'Let him go.'

Mato flinches. He waves a hand at Cole. '*This* is what you want?'

'I love him.'

Mato closes his eyes. 'That's your weakness talking. You don't understand how much he's holding you back. You have no *idea* how strong you used to be. If you're not ready to kill him, then maybe I should do it for you.' He lifts the gun, raising it to Cole's head, and a single shot rings out . . .

But Cole doesn't fall.

I spin round, searching for the source of the shot. A woman stands in the open doorway, a shotgun in her hands. Wispy grey hair, keen eyes that lock on mine.

'Hello, Bobcat,' Agnes says.

CHAPTER 34

Mato stumbles back, clutching his stomach, blood trickling over his fingers. There's a blur of blood-streaked blond hair through the door as Leoben rushes through, knocking the gun from Mato's hands. Cole launches himself from the floor, a *crack* echoing as his fist connects with the side of Mato's mask, splitting it across his forehead.

Mato slumps to the floor, his head rolling back. I stand, shaking, staring at Agnes in the doorway. She's dressed in a tattered jacket, her hair pulled back, sand and grit caked into the creases of her face.

She's *alive*.

'Yaya,' I breathe.

'Come here, Bobcat,' she says, opening her arms.

I run across the room to her, wrapping her in a hug. She smells like lavender and ash, her skin damp with sweat. Memories rush into me at the scent of her – but they're *mine* this time, and the relief of feeling a memory of my own makes me want to cry. She's my *yaya*, my friend. My lifeline for the last two years. I step away, still clutching her shoulders, staring at her.

'I thought you were dead,' I gasp. 'Why didn't you answer my comms?'

'It's a long story,' she says, lifting the shotgun to rest on her shoulder. 'I'm sorry I wasn't there, but I'm here now.'

I just shake my head. 'How did you find me?'

'I went to the location you called me from. Your friend was there. I don't know where you keep finding these soldiers, but they're marvellous.'

'We're limited edition, ma'am,' Leoben says, stepping away from Mato. He shoots me a worried smile. 'You don't look so great, squid.'

Cole moves to Anna's side, but neither he nor Leoben is reacting to her being shot. She's lying cold on the floor, her blood spilled across the tiles. She must have some kind of tech to make it just *seem* like she's dead. But I still can't understand why neither of them are worried about the gunshot in her chest.

'What the hell is going on with her?' I ask.

'She'll be OK,' Cole says, stroking the hair back from Anna's face. 'She's not in danger.'

I just stare at him, confused. Anna clearly isn't breathing. Her panel is *off*. I cross the floor and kneel beside her. The wound on her chest is still closing up. Healing tech does that. It can keep running long after your mind has gone, healing your body, moving through your cells as though nothing is wrong. It can even restart your heart and preserve your body. You can lie in perfect health after death, your organs flourishing, your lungs breathing from emergency nerve stimulation.

But you won't wake up – not once the link between the body and the mind is severed. No amount of gentech can repair that. Something irreversible changes inside the mind during death.

Once the spark of your thoughts is truly lost, it can't come back.

So why do I feel like I'm still looking down at *Anna*, and not her body?

Cole straightens Anna's shirt, lifting her head gently in his hands. The scar on her neck gleams in the sunlight. The scar that Jun Bei gave her. An image flashes through my mind – Anna lying on the floor in the Zarathustra lab in a pool of her own blood. Anna said Jun Bei did that to her – she cut her throat – but I don't feel like it was while they were fighting. The memory is colder, quieter. Anna still hasn't told me what it is about her DNA that makes her special, but I think I'm beginning to see it.

Anna's lips twitch, a muscle spasming in the side of her face.

I kneel down beside her, a buzzing rising in my ears. There's colour bleeding into her cheeks, a pulse returning in her neck. This isn't a black-out app that stopped her heart – it was Mato's bullet. She's been lying here, dead. I *saw* her heart stop.

And now I'm seeing it start up again.

'She can't die, can she?' I whisper.

Cole shakes his head. 'Not permanently, no.'

I close my eyes, reaching my good hand down to the floor to steady myself. I thought my gift was special, but the ability to change my DNA is *nothing* compared to this. People would start wars to gain control of Anna's mutation. The world would change if they knew the truth.

If we could replicate Anna's gift, we could cheat death.

'She'll be OK,' Leoben says, dropping down beside me. 'Lachlan must have killed her a hundred times, and she always woke back up. But she said it hurts like hell.'

I cover my mouth in horror. I can't imagine the childhood she must have lived being literally murdered in that lab, over and over. No wonder she hates Lachlan. No wonder she was so angry at Jun Bei for escaping and leaving her behind. Anna would have hated her for being free while she was still a prisoner.

Or maybe she hated her because Jun Bei killed her too.

The memory of Anna lying in a pool of blood in the lab flutters back to me. It was Jun Bei who gave Anna the scar on her neck. Leoben said Jun Bei used to study all of them at the lab – so maybe she was *studying* Anna. Maybe she cut Anna's throat to try to understand her gift.

Somehow, that thought is even more horrifying than the idea of Jun Bei killing sixty people.

'We'd better get moving,' Agnes says. 'There's a cloud coming in.'

Leoben stands. 'Shit. Those things are fast. We barely outran one on the way here.'

I push myself unsteadily to my feet and walk to the window. There's a strange light in the distance, like a storm cloud with lightning streaking through it. But it's not in the sky – it's on the ground, rumbling across the desert. A crackling cobalt-blue cloud. It looks like the coiling ropes that made up the glowing fence around the Zarathustra lab, but this cloud is the size of a mountain. My ocular tech zooms in, sharpening the image, drawing into focus the blinking lights of drones above it, the twisting funnels of tornadoes at its edges. It's a *nanite* cloud, like the triphase Novak used to force us to go to Sunnyvale.

Only, this cloud is big enough to cut through an entire city, leaving nothing but charred earth and ash in its wake. A flock of pigeons is swooping ahead of it, their cries frantic.

Cartaxus is going to guide these clouds right over Entropia and every other settlement the pigeons are near. They're going to kill everything in their path.

'What is that?' Cole asks.

'It's Cartaxus,' I say. 'Mato said they had airborne weapons they were going to use to try to kill the pigeons. They're not waiting any longer. Flood protocol is starting.'

'We have to go,' Leoben says. 'Those clouds are everywhere. I don't like it any more than you guys, but I think it's time to turn ourselves in.'

'We could go to Entropia,' Agnes says. 'The basement levels will be safe.'

'Nowhere will be safe for much longer,' Cole says, kneeling to pick up Anna's body. She's still limp, her tech dark, but I see a vein pulsing in the side of her neck. 'They have the scythe. They're going to use it on everybody on the surface. There's a bunker near here that we might just make it to if we take the Comox.'

'No, we have time,' I say, looking at Mato's unconscious form. 'Mato said Cartaxus was going to round up as many people as possible. Brink is razing the settlements. That has to buy us time.'

'Time for what?' Cole asks. 'This is over, Cat. How can't you see that? If you stay out here, you're going to die with them.'

I look back at Mato. He wanted me to use the Origin code to stop this by doing what Lachlan has been planning all along. But I don't remember the code – I can't use it, and I don't think that's the right way to solve this, anyway. There has to be another solution. Something that isn't based on death or forcibly changing people's minds. If erasing the Wrath from Cartaxus's leaders is the only way to save us, then I don't know if humanity is *worth* saving.

'I don't know what to do, but I'm not running away,' I say. 'I want to go to Entropia. Maybe the genehackers have a plan.'

'You want to go back to Regina?' Cole asks. 'She took your hand, Cat. And Lachlan is there.'

'Then maybe they can help us *stop* this,' I say. 'Brink is *wrong*. He's not going to be able to control the pigeons, which means the vaccine isn't going to last. Mato said we need to move past the vaccine, and I'm starting to think he's right. We need to think of better ways to stop this plague, and Cartaxus's scientists aren't going to be the ones who'll invent them. They need bigger ideas – bolder ideas. They *need* Entropia. We just have to figure out how to make that clear to Brink.'

Cole sighs, frustrated. 'Wherever we go, we can't stay here much longer.' He heads through the front door, Anna in his arms, and strides out into the driveway to the jeep.

'I'm with you, squid,' Leoben says. He jerks a thumb at Mato. 'What about him?'

'Shit. I don't know.' Part of me wants to leave Mato here for the clouds. He was going to kill Cole, he shot Anna, and he tried to break my mind apart to bring back Jun Bei. But that doesn't stop something twisting inside me at the thought of leaving him here.

Jun Bei cared about him. Whatever he's done, I don't think I can let him die.

'Bring him,' I say. 'He's central command. He's useful as a hostage. Just make sure he doesn't wake up.'

'My pleasure.' Leoben picks up Mato and heads outside.

Agnes takes my arm as I follow them out on to the driveway. The pigeons' cries form a low rumble in the distance, and I can hear the crackle of the cloud's electricity as it rolls closer. Agnes takes my chin in her hand and tilts my face, peering at me.

'Bobcat,' she says, 'you look awful. Have you been eating?'

'Not really,' I murmur. 'I'm just so glad you're OK.'

'We have a lot of catching up to do,' she says. 'Come on. Let's get moving.'

There's a battered green pickup truck parked in the driveway that Leoben and Agnes must have brought here. The Comox Anna and Cole flew here in is parked in the dirt, its ramp extended to the ground. Leoben climbs inside with Mato. Cole is standing behind his jeep with the rear doors open, lowering Anna in.

I walk over and lift my pack from the passenger seat, reaching into the back to grab my holster. I shoot a glance at Cole. 'What are you doing with her?'

'I can't take her into Entropia,' he says, swinging the rear doors shut. 'I'll send the jeep back to a base.'

'You don't have to come –'

'I'm not leaving you,' he says. 'You have to decide for me too.'

I step back, shaking my head. 'That's not fair. Don't make me do that, Cole.'

'Whatever you want to do, we need to go,' Leoben says. 'This cloud will be here soon.'

I look at the horizon. The cloud is moving fast, already less than a mile away. It seems like it's coming straight for us, the drones above it glowing red, whining across the sky. I let a pulse slip from the cuff on my arm, just meaning to *scan* the drones, but my tech locks on to their signals automatically. Code scrolls across my vision. I stiffen, letting my backpack slide to the ground. Maybe it's what Mato did to me, or maybe it's finding out the truth about Cole, but I suddenly feel like I'm not in control of myself. I'm not the one launching these commands, at least not consciously. The ocean in my mind is surging, though, heaving against the splintering wall.

Code unfurls from my panel and out across the desert, my mind splitting seamlessly, fractioning into the drones – once, twice, three times, until their controls are a kaleidoscope inside my mind. I lift my hand, my cuff gleaming in the crackling light of the cloud, and send out a pulse in twenty-four dimensions into the hearts of the drones.

They halt, tilting in the air, then crash to the ground.

The cloud of triphase hangs for a moment before collapsing, spilling across the desert like a wave. It tumbles closer, cobalt fingers stretching across the plains towards us, diffusing into smoke.

'Holy *shit*,' Leoben says.

I draw my mind back into itself, folding the fraction closed, my reality shrinking down to a single universe, a single pair of eyes. The ocean inside me is still rippling, rushing over my senses.

And, for the first time, I know what it means.

I turn to Cole, barely breathing. He's staring at me, wide-eyed, the others behind him. They all look stunned by the drones on the ground, the collapse of the mountain of death, but none of them can see what I just glimpsed. They didn't feel the ocean inside me heaving or see the code unfurling from my arm without me consciously launching it.

They think I'm the one who brought down those drones.

But I don't think it was *me*.

'Cat, are you OK?' Cole asks.

I just shake my head, backing down the driveway, keeping my distance from him. He reaches for me, but I slide my gun from its holster and level it at his chest.

'Stay away from me.'

His face goes white. He steps back, his hands lifted, staring at me. 'Cat, what are you doing?'

'Hey,' Leoben calls. 'Whoa there.'

'None of you come any closer!' I say, my voice shaking.

'Cat,' Cole begs. '*Please*. I'm sorry.'

There's a desperation in his voice that wrenches at me, but I can't tell him what I'm about to do. I haven't even made up my mind myself, and I know he'd talk me out of it if he knew. He'd run for me and try to stop me. He'd take the gun away.

But I can't let him.

Mato has done what he intended – he's brought me to the brink. I can see the truth now, but it's not the one he expected. I just fractioned to take down the drones, but it wasn't me who did it. Not my code, and not my mind. The virus that just spun from me wasn't a random scrap of commands – it was wielded like a blade. Clean. Precise. Sent by a hand steadier than mine. I close my eyes, seeing Jun Bei's face, seeing mist shrouding the three peaks of the Zarathustra mountains. Cole steps forward again, but I lift the gun, my hands shaking.

He stops, his hands raised. Agnes is watching me, her eyes narrowed, like she's trying to understand.

'Don't come any closer.' I step back, the gun still aimed at Cole's chest. Rocks crunch beneath my boots, skittering across the uneven ground. I don't have time to tell them everything, and even I don't really understand what's happening. All I know is that I'm out of plans, out of ideas, and this is the only option I have left. There might be just one sliver of hope. One person with a chance of stopping Cartaxus and saving us all.

But it isn't me.

'Cat, please,' Cole says, his hands raised. 'I won't move, I swear. Just tell me what you're doing.'

I shake my head, sliding back the gun's safety. I think I finally know why the ocean in my mind rises into a storm every time I've glimpsed Jun Bei's past or pushed myself to my limits. The answer is echoing through me – that Mato was *right* – the girl I used to be is still there, locked away inside me, and now I'm standing at the edge of the abyss he tried to push me into.

But I can see into the darkness now. There's more than memories locked inside me. There's a life. There's a *mind*, and it's calling to me. It's whispering in my senses, rippling across my skin. Breathing a truth that shudders against the walls inside me.

Jun Bei and I are not the same, and I'm not another version of her. I'm not a weaker copy – I'm not a *copy* at all. I'm something separate, existing alongside her like the two horizons I just glimpsed while taking down the drones. I can *feel* her now, and I can sense the force of her thoughts pushing against my own like a wave breaking against a cliff.

She's smarter than me, stronger than me. She's outsmarted Cartaxus before. She's the only one who has a chance of stopping this.

And I think I know how to bring her back.

My eyes lock on Cole's, my hands tightening on the gun. It's still stocked with custom bullets. Hollow-core, ceramic, filled with beads of healing tech. I still haven't calibrated them. I don't know if this will work, but the closest I've ever come to breaking through the wall inside me was on the point of death. This might hurt me just enough to finally crack the wall and set the ocean inside me free, or it might leave me bleeding out in the desert while Entropia burns.

But the fact that I don't know if I'll survive this is why it just might work.

'Cat, what are you doing?' Cole asks, his voice shaking.

'I love you,' I say. 'I want you to know that, just in case.'

His eyes widen. 'What are you doing?'

I look at Agnes, at Leoben, wishing I could explain, but there's no time.

'I'm sorry,' I whisper, then lift the gun to my chest and pull the trigger.

CHAPTER 35

For a moment there is only pain. A world of velvet blackness with no light or form – just the feeling of a bullet tearing through flesh and splintering bone. I clutch my chest, letting out a scream, and the darkness resolves into a vast, echoing room. Concrete walls and ceiling, a gleaming white floor. Dozens of screens hang dark on the wall opposite me, a cluttered lab counter beneath them. Triangular fluorescents glow above me, and a floor-to-ceiling window on the far wall shows the silhouette of three mountains in the distance. Heavy storm clouds hang over their jagged peaks, flashes of lightning illuminating the arcs of pigeons swooping through the rain.

I'm in the Zarathustra lab, in the room where I blew up the genkits, lying on the floor, shaking, blood pulsing from my chest. Two hands are pressed to the wound, a face above me, but it isn't Cole or Lee.

It's Jun Bei.

Her dark hair is back in a messy ponytail, the baggy sleeves of a grey sweatshirt rolled up to her elbows. The sight of her hits me harder than the pain lancing through my chest. There's a stripe of cobalt glowing along the inside of her arm, four leylines snaking from it into the sleeve of her sweatshirt. One rises up her throat, wrapping round the edge of her hairline, disappearing into the soft, downy hair at the nape of her neck. She's on her knees, leaning over me, trying to stem the flow of blood. Her hands are slick with it, strands of her hair sliding across her face.

'Of all the stupid things you've done, Catarina,' she says, 'this might have been the worst.'

A jolt runs through me as I stare at her. Her eyes are a pure, brilliant emerald, a furrow etched along her brow. This is no dream. No glitching flashback. This is as real as any moment I've lived before. I choke in a breath. 'You're still alive.'

'No thanks to you,' she mutters.

I stare at her, my mind spinning. This isn't just another side of my personality. She's another person. She's the dark space the implant sectioned off. It hasn't been memories that I've been glimpsing for the last week – it's been *her*.

Jun Bei is the ocean locked behind the wall in my mind.

'I can't believe you shot us,' she says, pressing the heels of her hands harder into my chest. Her face reddens with the effort, patches of scarlet soaked into her sweatshirt. Blood is still bubbling up from between her fingers, gushing from the wound.

But this can't be real.

I'm not in the Zarathustra lab. I'm lying in the desert with a bullet inside me. This is just a VR simulation, but Jun Bei's hands feel *real*. The tiles are cold and slick beneath me, pooling with my blood, pain lancing through my broken rib from the pressure of Jun Bei's hands. I know the best VR simulations are hard to distinguish from reality, but the level in this one is overwhelming. I scan the room, staring at the humming genkits, the mountains beyond the window. The air is cold and scented with disinfectant and blood. There is no hint from anything around me that I'm not really here.

I cough, scrunching my eyes shut. 'How come this feels so real?'

'Because this isn't just VR,' she says, her green eyes flicking to mine. 'This is a simulation I built years ago. It's linked with the implant, feeding back into our brain. You can feel it the way you feel your dreams. Your mind makes it real.'

'Then why are you pressing on my chest?'

'I'm trying to *save* us,' she says. 'I told you – your *mind* makes this real. Your tech can handle the wound in your body, but right now I'm more concerned with our brain.'

There's an edge of desperation in her voice, though I can't understand how stemming the flow of blood from a virtual gunshot wound could be so important. She lifts one blood-stained hand, looking around, her eyes locking on a tea towel hanging from a hook next to the lab counter. She blinks, and it appears in her hand.

'I think it's stopped,' she says, balling the towel up, shoving it down on the wound. 'Please don't do anything like that again. Here, keep pressure on this.' She lifts my wrist and presses my hand down on the bunched-up towel, then rocks back on her heels.

I just stare at her. I've thought for days that Lachlan kept a backup of my memories inside me, but this is something else. He kept an entire person locked away and created someone new alongside them.

'What the hell did Lachlan do to us?' I ask.

'I'm still trying to figure that out,' she says.

'But how do we both exist in the same brain?'

She wipes her hands on the front of her sweatshirt. 'There's plenty of brain for the two of us. The left frontal lobe is mine, and the right is yours. There's a wall between us, held in place by the implant, and it's imperative it remains there if we're both going to survive. As far as I can tell, the two of us can stay separate as long as the implant keeps up the barrier, but every time it's come down, we've both lost a little of ourselves to each other. I'd like to keep my personality intact, and I'm sure you would too. I think it's possible for both of us to survive this, but we're going to need to work together.'

I shake my head. I still can't believe she's real. She's been there this whole time, waiting. Trapped inside her own body.

Inside *our* body.

'What do you mean, *both* of us to survive?' I ask. 'We only have one body.'

'Oh, I'm aware of that.' She presses her hands to her knees, standing. 'I was less than thrilled to wake up and find you inhabiting it too. I thought you were a dream for a while. But it wasn't a very good dream, and then I realized that something serious had happened to my brain. I don't know where you came from, but we're both here now, and we have to figure out how to survive.'

'We can't *both* survive like this.'

She tilts her head back. 'You're still thinking so *rigidly*. Didn't you learn anything from Regina? Why should we restrain ourselves to the historical definition of humanity? We have two hands, two eyes, two ears. Why not two minds? I didn't like it at first, either, but can you imagine the research we could do? You and I are something *new* – something unexpected. We could spend years analysing the way our brain works, and I'd like to do that very much. But first we have to make it through the next few hours.'

I lift my head, watching her as she walks to the lab counter. The pain in my chest is fading fast. I don't know if that's because someone has given me healing tech back in the real world, or if it's like Jun Bei said – my mind is making this real, and now I'm making myself feel better.

'We're going to need to figure out a plan together,' she says, turning on a tap above a steel sink, washing her hands. I lift myself carefully up on one elbow, still pressing down on the bunched-up towel. I look around at the lab – the mountains outside, the wall of dark screens, the genkit. It's a perfect re-creation of the room where I killed the puppet.

'How long have you been in here?' I ask.

'Not long.' She grabs another towel to dry her hands. 'It took me a while to wake up properly, but the first thing I remember recently was lying on that doctor's couch after he cut your healing tech out of your arm. *Marcus*, wasn't it? Lachlan's code had been generating the ERO-86 until then, and it was keeping me asleep. I remember glimpses from when he was changing me into you, but before that, the last thing I recall was being at the Zarathustra lab.'

I sit up, lifting the towel from my chest. There's still blood soaked into my shirt, a hole torn through the fabric, but the skin where the wound was gaping just a few minutes ago is closed.

'What about Entropia?' I ask. 'Those six months?'

She sighs. 'Nothing substantial. Just fragments left over from the wipe. Those months are gone from both of us.'

I stare at her. She looks young – because she *is* young. When Jun Bei last walked in this body, she was fifteen years old. She hasn't aged, hasn't stepped outside, hasn't drawn a breath in three years now. The thought is horrifying, but it isn't like the last two years have been a good time to be *awake*. She hasn't had to live through any of the outbreak. The clouds, the doses, the horror of the plague.

The entire world has fallen apart, and she slept through it all.

'I've been figuring out what happened,' she says. 'Mato was right – I'm the one who wiped those six months from my mind, and I think I did it on purpose. All I have from that time is a handful of VR files I saved before I wiped those memories, and I've spent the last week piecing together what made me do that.' She turns back to me, a flicker of nervousness in her eyes, then walks across the floor, stretching one hand down to me. 'Come on. I'll show you.'

I take her hand cautiously, letting her help me to my feet. Her skin is warm and damp, her grip surprisingly strong. My head spins as I stand, and there's still a hum of pain in my chest, but my feet find their way across the lab as I follow her to the wall of screens. She seems completely unconcerned about the fact that she's talking to me while we're sharing a *brain*.

But of course she is. She's known about me for weeks. She's had plenty of time to process this if she's been awake inside this body since I woke up in Marcus's house. I'm the only one who's thrown right now, trying to take this in.

There's another person living in my *mind*.

'It took a long time to sort through the VR files in our panel,' she says. 'I must have encrypted them during those six months that I wiped, because I couldn't remember how to unlock them. I had to hack them all – it took days. Most of them were from when I was younger, but a few were from my time in the desert.'

She looks up at the screens, her eyes glazing. They flicker on, showing a mix of text files and 2-D footage. Novak's face is on one, still calling for people to go into the bunkers. Another shows what looks like drone footage of Entropia. There are black trucks gathered outside the checkpoint at the marketplace.

'I managed to hook into Cartaxus's satellite network through our panel a few days ago,' she says. 'I've been trying to keep up to date with what's going on out there.' One screen is dark, with a faint line of blurred light across it, like the view I'm used to seeing through half-closed eyes.

'Is that a feed from my ocular tech?'

'*Our* ocular tech,' she says. 'You're going to have to get better at sharing this body. I have audio too. Like I said, I've been trying to keep up to date. It was confusing to wake up in here and not understand what was happening.'

My stomach clenches. It must have been terrifying for her to wake up as a prisoner inside a body that she couldn't control any more. 'I'm sorry,' I say, though the apology feels inadequate. I've taken her body. She's lost everything.

She looks at me, surprised. 'You have nothing to be sorry for. Whoever's fault this is, it certainly isn't yours.'

She turns to the screens and pulls up a clip that I recognize – it's her fighting with Lachlan in the house in the desert. Her face is streaked with tears, her shoulders shaking. She's screaming at him, and his arms are crossed, his face dark. There's no sound, but it's clear that she's distraught about something.

'What were you arguing about?'

'The Origin code.' Jun Bei chews at her thumbnail, staring at the screen. Her shoulders are hunched beneath the blood-smeared sweatshirt. 'Lachlan wasn't really there. It was a VR call. I was trying to give him the code, but he didn't want to take it.'

The skin on the back of my neck prickles. 'Why would you give it to him?'

She closes her eyes, letting out a slow breath. 'This clip is from the morning I wiped those six months. Mato said it was a mistake, but it wasn't – not from what I can tell. I think I did something that I shouldn't have, and I freaked out. I tried to give the code to Lachlan because I was planning on erasing it from my panel and wiping every memory of writing it.'

My blood chills. From what Mato said, it sounded like the six months Jun Bei spent in the desert were the best months in her life. She was just starting to heal from her time at the lab – starting to unpack the trauma of her childhood and move past the anger she'd been bottling up for years. She was getting *better*. She was falling in love. She was writing code that could change the world.

What could be so awful that it would make her want to erase those memories?

'Jun Bei, what did you do?'

She doesn't answer. Just holds her arms tight round her chest, staring at the screen. She's young and frightened, and she's locked inside a body that's been taken away from her. She's woken inside a world full of detonating people, with no memory of how she got there. I can see in her eyes that she's struggling to hold herself together. Leoben said she always threw herself into a coding puzzle whenever she was overwhelmed, and that's exactly what she's been doing.

She's spent a week inside this room decrypting VR files, watching screens of the world outside, trying to figure out what happened to her. I can't imagine how frightening it would be to wake up in here like that.

I step over to her, taking her shoulder, trying to keep my voice gentle. 'You can tell me. What did you do?'

'It was a mistake,' she says. 'I was trying to test the code on a bigger population and see if I could distribute it wirelessly. It was just a test, but I miscalculated.'

My breath stills. The signal tower. The sixty people who died. 'Jun Bei . . . Did you kill those people?'

'It *reversed*,' she says, pleading. 'You have to understand – the code can switch instincts on and off, and it was meant to run the other way.'

I don't understand what she means about the code running the other way. Lachlan said the same thing after Sunnyvale – that the code could elicit the Wrath and also suppress it. But that doesn't have anything to do with sixty people *dying*. 'What instinct were you testing?'

'The only one that really matters,' she says, turning to me, a light in her eyes. 'The one *everybody* wanted to find. They never thought of it as an instinct, but I knew it was. I knew I could use the Origin code to suppress it, but then all those people died.'

The screens beside me seem to pulse. 'But instincts don't kill you.'

'Sure they do. When doctors tell people they're going to die, sometimes they do, even if the diagnosis was a mistake. Couples married for decades die in their old age within days of one another. Terminally ill patients will cling to life just long enough to see a loved one make it to their bedside. Those aren't just coincidences, Catarina.'

I step back, looking between her and the screens, shaking my head. 'No. Death isn't an *instinct*.'

'But it is,' she says. 'Don't you see? Our bodies know how to live, and they also know how to die. Death isn't just something that happens to us – it's something our bodies *do*. People are still dying because coders don't understand the problem. They're trying to save people by altering what's in their DNA, but that's only half of it. The reason coders still don't understand death is because some of its controls live inside our *minds*.'

I stare into Jun Bei's eyes, swaying as the realization hits me. She didn't mean to use the Origin code to kill those people – she meant to do the opposite. To keep them alive. She's done what every amateur coder has attempted since the first days of gentech. She's cracked the code that doctors have been working on since alchemists were trying to turn lead into gold.

She hacked Lachlan's work – his attempt to remove humanity's violent instincts – and turned it into a script to switch off death.

CHAPTER 36

I step back across the lab, shaking my head. 'This can't be possible.'

But it is. I've seen it with my own eyes. Anna was shot in the chest. She *died*. I saw her body, felt her skin cool and her heart stop, watched her panel flicker off.

And now her heart is beating again.

Anna is the missing link – the key to unlock the mysteries of why gentech can heal our bodies when we die, but not bring back our minds as well. Whatever the equation of life and death is, it's been solved inside Anna's cells.

And Jun Bei figured it out too. She found a way to wrap up immortality in four million lines of code.

'That's why I had to stop the bleeding in your chest,' Jun Bei says. She lifts one pale hand to her mouth, biting the edge of her thumbnail. 'It wasn't your body that I was worried about. It was your mind. There's an instinct for death coded into all of us, and I needed to make sure that ours wasn't triggered by that gunshot.'

'But how can it be an instinct?' I lean back against the wall, shaking. I wrap my arms round myself, glancing at the screens, the lab counter, the mountains through the window. 'I don't understand.'

'Instincts are *links* between the body and the mind,' Jun Bei says. 'Gentech can take care of our bodies, but it can't stop our brains from flipping the switch that's triggered when we die. There's a thread inside us, and it can't be knotted back together once it's severed. All the Origin code does is strengthen that thread. It's still one piece of the larger puzzle of immortality, but it's a very, very big piece.'

I close my eyes, tilting my head back. 'This will change the world.' There's almost no injury or sickness that gentech can't cure given enough time, but plenty of people still die while their bodies are healing – while they're bleeding out or desperately sick. This code could save them all. It could let them drift into death and wake them once their bodies are healed. It wouldn't save everyone – not people hurt beyond repair – but this kind of code would radically change us.

We'd be practically indestructible. And it's already been sent out to everyone as part of the vaccine.

'How can we use it?' I ask.

'That's the thing,' Jun Bei says. She reaches back for the elastic in her hair, tightening her ponytail. 'I don't remember. I wiped the code from my memories and my files. I've been trying to read it, but it's four million lines long and it's part of the vaccine – I don't know which pieces of code are which. It could take weeks to unravel the rest. I don't think Lachlan really knows how, either, otherwise he would have done it already.' She lets out a breath of laughter. 'He's sent the Origin code out to everyone, but he doesn't know how to use it. How ridiculous.'

I pace to the windows, rubbing at a chill on my arms. 'Do we have it? I mean – can we *die*? Cole said I died when I took down the destroyers, but then I woke up. I just shot myself in the chest, and I'm pretty sure I'm alive right now too.'

'I don't know,' Jun Bei says, following me to the window. 'It's not exactly something I'm keen to *test*. I probably had it installed before, back in the desert, but then Lachlan changed our DNA and I don't know how that affected us. I think Mato has it, though.'

I spin round to her. 'What do you mean?'

'Well, he seems quite reckless with his fractioning, and I probably would have tested the code on him when we were working together.' Her eyes soften for a moment, a faint blush colouring her cheeks. She notices me watching and turns away suddenly, striding back to the lab counter. 'His heart stopped when he took down those drones, and Anna said it had happened before. I don't know if he's even aware of it or not, but I don't think he can die. So now you understand what's at stake. I was frightened of what I'd created before, but I'm not any more. I made a mistake –'

'A mistake? You killed sixty people.'

'It was an accident!' she snaps. 'I paid for it dearly. I almost *died* paying for it. I lost my body and half my mind trying to erase that code from myself so I couldn't do it again. I don't know how else I can pay for it except by trying to make sure that I save as many people as possible now. That's why we need to work together. This code is going to change the world, but it won't be a very good world if Cartaxus is running it.'

'That's why I'm here,' I say. 'Brink is launching flood protocol right now. Do you know how to stop it?'

She shakes her head. 'All I can think of is hacking Cartaxus's systems and trying to force everyone out of the bunkers. That would stop the attack, but it'd be madness. The civilians would blame the people on the surface, and there'd be even more divisions. I thought about trying to use the Origin code like Mato suggested, but I really just don't know *how*.'

'No,' I say, 'we can't use that code as a weapon. You've created something to save people's lives and build a better world. That world begins today, and I don't want to start it off with forcibly changing people's minds.'

'Neither do I,' Jun Bei says, her eyes locking on mine. She smiles, and a tremor shakes the room – a low rumble in the floor.

'What was that?' I ask.

'That was the implant,' she says, frowning. 'It's going to get worse the longer you're here. I breached one of its walls to meet you like this. I don't think it'll hold for much longer. There might be another way for us to talk, but it's going to take time. We don't have long – we need to make a plan.'

'I was thinking of going after Brink.'

'I know,' she says, shooting me a grin. 'I like the way you think. I wouldn't mind seeing all Cartaxus's leaders pay for what they did to me and the others, even if I'm not the cold-blooded killer Cole thinks I am.'

I pause at the bitter tone in her voice when she says Cole's name. 'You said you don't remember those six months in the desert.'

She shakes her head, her eyes locked on the floor, but she doesn't respond.

'Your last memories were at the Zarathustra lab. You . . . you were still with Cole.'

She wraps her arms round her slender shoulders and lifts her gaze slowly, giving me a sad smile. 'I told you I thought you were a dream when I first woke up in here. But it wasn't a very good one.'

'Shit,' I say, looking at the screens on the wall. One is from my ocular feed. She was seeing everything through my eyes. Cole and I together. Talking about her. Kissing. Driving hand in hand after I realized who I was.

Cole and I fell in love while Jun Bei was locked in this body, trapped, unable to do anything about it.

'You didn't know,' Jun Bei says, as though sensing my horror. 'Neither of you did. I was upset, but then you met Mato, and I'm starting to understand. I don't remember the night I left the lab, and I don't know why I left the others, but it's clear that I did. I left Cole behind.'

'You were escaping,' I say. 'You were alone. It's not like you had anyone to help you.'

She shakes her head. 'I had the *scythe*. I could have got them out too. But I didn't, and I don't remember why. I went to the desert, moved in with a boy and learned how to rewrite my own mind. I must have chosen Mato – I must have *loved* him.' She pushes a hand back through her hair. 'There's still so much I don't understand.'

Another tremor shakes the room – and this time it rattles the sample vials on the lab counter. Jun Bei's face darkens. 'We don't have much time,' she says. 'Killing Brink might stop this attack, but not permanently. There'll be new leaders within days, and they'll launch flood protocol again. We need to find a way to convince Cartaxus's leaders not to kill us.'

I shake my head. 'Forget the leaders. They don't care about us, but Cartaxus has three billion people in its bunkers who don't know that flood protocol is happening. They're being lied to. I don't think they'll want this to happen in their name. If we can find a way to tell them the truth, they could stop this.'

Jun Bei nods, pacing back across the room to the window. 'Maybe. But what makes you think they'll care about us? They'll be terrified of losing the vaccine.'

'That's exactly why we need to get through to them,' I say. 'They need to hear the truth – that the vaccine is *done*. It's finished. Cartaxus put all their hope into Lachlan and his code, and it wasn't enough. This virus is too smart. Cartaxus has *failed*. It's time for us to stop fighting each other and come together to beat this virus – Cartaxus *and* the genehackers. That's the only way we'll survive.'

Jun Bei nods, a light in her eyes. 'You might be right.'

'So what do we do?'

She chews her thumbnail, glancing at the wall of screens. 'Bring me to a terminal with a satellite connection. Something hooked directly into Cartaxus's network. I think I might be able to stop this attack and send a message to the bunkers.'

'OK,' I say. The only terminal I've seen that looked like it had that kind of access is the one in Regina's lab in Entropia. That's the last place I want to go. She stole my *hand*.

But it might be the only way we can stop this attack.

Another tremor rolls through the lab, shaking the screens. Jun Bei strides over to me, gripping my arm. 'I'm going to break the connection we're using to talk. I might not be able to contact you for a little while, but I'll be trying to help you as much as I can. Try not to die for real, OK? I don't really like this body you've got us in right now, but it's the only one we have.' She lets go of my arm, then looks over at me suddenly, a strangely vulnerable look in her eyes. 'And don't kill Mato. I don't remember those six months with him, but I'd like to try.'

I nod. She takes my hand, her fingers gripping mine, and the room plunges into darkness again.

CHAPTER 37

The darkness spins me like a wave, hugging my senses, then spits me back into my body like a doll thrown against a wall. I roll to my hands and knees, pain shooting through the base of my skull and rippling down my spine.

Jun Bei is gone. There is no hint of her voice, no brush of her thoughts against mine. She's been tamped back into a prison inside my mind. I can't feel her presence, but I can sense the gap inside me now. A black void, warping the edges of my thoughts. She's locked inside me, caged and helpless in her own body. A body that's been twisted to look like someone else. She can see through my eyes and hear what I hear, but she's helpless. The horror of the thought is as real and urgent as the pain inside my skull.

I force my eyes open, battling the urge to throw up. I'm in the back of the jeep. We're tearing down a dirt road through the desert. I catch a glimpse through the window of another cobalt cloud behind us, and my stomach heaves. I scramble to the rear doors and fling them open, letting in a wave of dust and the roar of the cloud.

'She's back. Hold up!'

Anna is awake and kneeling beside me, her eyes wide, her face still pale, a bandage on her chest. There's an electrode pad humming on my ribs, and Cole is driving. He snaps his head back, meets my eyes and hits the brakes. I grab the side for balance, the rear doors swinging shut as we skid to a stop.

'Jesus, Cat.' He flings his door open and launches himself out of the driver's seat, running round to the back, yanking the doors open to stare in at me. 'You were dead. You were *gone* again.' His face is pale, the muscles in his neck tight. 'What the hell is happening to you?'

I cough, wiping my mouth. My throat is sore, flecked with dust. 'Water.'

'Here,' Anna says, holding out my canteen for me. I take it, my hands shaking, and gulp it dry. The roar of the cloud seems overly loud in my ears, my vision still swimming. I sit back, leaning against the side of the jeep, forcing myself to breathe.

Cole and Anna are both watching me. I can feel Jun Bei's presence more acutely as I look at them – trace the jigsaw edges of my consciousness where it meets the wall between me and her. Cole and Anna don't know that she's still alive. And I can't tell them yet.

I meet Cole's eyes, swallowing. He's worried for me now, but he doesn't know that the girl he was afraid of is still living inside of me. If we're going to have any chance of stopping Cartaxus, I'll need them to trust me.

They'll never do that if they know the truth.

'Where are the others?'

'They left for Entropia,' Cole says. 'Cartaxus is taking the genehackers, but Regina is putting up a fight. Her people are holed up in the bunker, but Cartaxus has sent troops to bring them out. Lee and Agnes went to help, and they took Mato with them. He's valuable to central command, just like Lee is. Brink won't threaten airstrikes if there's a risk he'll lose either of them.'

'I need to go there,' I say. 'I think I can stop this if I get to the satellite connection in Regina's lab.'

Anna narrows her eyes. 'What the hell is going on with you? You *shot* yourself.'

I tip the canteen back again, draining the last drops. 'I was trying to get my memories back. I thought, if I did, I could end this. I don't remember everything, but I remember enough. This attack can be stopped, but I need to get to a terminal with access to Cartaxus's network.' I look around. 'Where are we?'

'We just got on the road,' Cole says. 'We were going to go into a bunker. You were gone, Cat. I know you don't want to go, but –'

'Is that really what you want to do?' I ask. 'Lee's in Entropia. Were you just going to leave him there?'

'You and Anna are *hurt*,' Cole says. 'There's nothing we can do. Brink is going to use the scythe –'

'Not if I can stop him,' I say. 'I have a plan. I need to get to a terminal, though. There's one in Regina's lab – I think I can use it to stop this attack. I just need to get into Entropia.'

'She's right,' Anna says. 'If Lee's still fighting, maybe we should too. We can't leave him on his own.'

'We'll never make it to Entropia,' Cole says. 'The troops are surrounding the bunker. We can't get through. Leoben said he and Agnes almost didn't make it in, and that was hours ago. Cartaxus has fortified their positions around the checkpoints on the border. It's locked down. We'd need an army to get in.'

An army. My eyes turn to the sky, where the triphase cloud is rolling across the desert. It thrashes closer, its crackling blue energy slamming into the ground, leaving behind charred earth and gleaming pools of molten glass. Flashes of red in the air above it hint at the drones controlling it.

Jun Bei's voice whispers in my mind, and the drones tilt in the air, circling, moving towards us.

'What are you doing?' Cole asks, looking warily at the drones.

'I think I know how we can get in,' I say. I'm not the one controlling these drones – Jun Bei is, but I think I know what she's trying to do. 'We need to leave now. We're going to Entropia, and we need to drive *fast*.'

Cole looks between me and Anna. 'Are you sure? There are troops in Entropia. This is going to be a battle.'

'She looks pretty damn sure,' Anna says. 'Come on, Cole. The fight's out here. Let's go and help Lee.'

'We could *die*, Anna,' he says.

She shrugs. 'Speak for yourself.'

He shakes his head, dragging his hand over his face.

'I can do this,' I say quietly. 'Please. We have to try.'

Cole's ice-blue eyes hold mine – full of doubt and fear. There's an abyss of secrets and lies stretching between us. I don't know if he trusts me, or if he believes that I can save us, but he nods. 'OK, let's do this.'

He and Anna climb into the front seats, and Cole starts the engine, glancing back in the rear-view at the cloud. My ears are ringing, my vision flickering with static. The drones hover behind us, dragging the towering cloud with them, its edges crackling with blue lightning. It slowly picks up pace until it's moving beside us, far enough away for it not to be a threat to the jeep, but close enough for me to see the earth lifting away around it, the blue lightning arcing down through it, slamming into the ground as it moves. A line of scorched, blackened earth stretches behind it, winding across the desert.

Anna twists round, grinning as she looks through the windows. 'Oh, that's perfect.'

I keep my eyes locked on the cloud, guiding it ahead of us until we're following it. The jeep's tyres spin on the freshly scorched path, but the engine whines, compensating, surging us forward.

'Holy shit,' Cole says. 'You can't be serious. You really think you can control this thing?'

'I can handle it,' I say, crawling through the back of the jeep, leaning between the two front seats to stare out the windscreen at the cloud. Only, it isn't me controlling those drones. It's Jun Bei. I can feel her presence, hear whispers of her voice as she guides them, commands beaming from the cuff on my arm.

'This might not be enough to disperse the troops,' Cole says. 'I'm not familiar with this weapon. They might have a way to neutralize it.'

'It'll work,' I say. 'We're not trying to disperse them anyway.'

Ahead of us, the mountain of Entropia's city inches out of the haze hanging over the desert. The pigeons are still thick in the air above it, the flock stretching for miles, a rippling ocean of black and cobalt. Cartaxus's trucks have formed a perimeter around the city's checkpoints, blocking off the only paths through the razorgrass border. There's no way to get through them, but they're not protecting the rest of the border, because the mile-wide stretch of razorgrass is impossible to drive through.

But not for us.

The heaving blue cloud surges ahead of us, veering away from the checkpoint, heading for a clear space in the gleaming razorgrass. Cole's hands tighten on the wheel. 'You sure about this? Once we go in, the troops will come after us. I don't know if we'll be able to get back out.'

I nod, staring through the windscreen, Jun Bei's voice whispering in my ears as she controls the drones. 'Let's do this.'

The cloud races across the razorgrass, scorching a line of blackened ground through it, wide enough for the jeep, but only barely. I can hear the shriek of the razorgrass against the sides, scratching into the metal. The edges of the cleared path catch fire from the heat of the cloud, billowing thick black smoke into the air. The soldiers stationed at the checkpoint shout, piling into their vehicles, scrambling to respond as we blow past them and through the border. Their engines roar to life, bullets slamming into the side of the jeep, but they're too far behind to catch us.

'The tyres can't take this speed any more,' Cole says. We're almost through the border, the desert plains around the base of the mountain stretching out ahead of us. 'They're going to catch us.'

'No they won't.' I follow the cloud with my eyes, watching as it turns once it's finished burning through the grass.

'Nice,' Anna says, twisting in her seat to stare behind us as the cloud loops back, cutting through the border to block the path.

The trucks screech to a stop, stuck in the narrow path through the razorgrass. There are more of them barrelling down the road from the checkpoint, but we'll be in the mountain long before they catch us.

We race into the valley, tyres bouncing over the rocky ground, heading for the gap in the rock that leads into the mountain. I feel Jun Bei's control over the drones slip as we drive out of range. The jeep screeches down the tunnel and into a parking lot just like the one from our first visit to Entropia – with the disinfectant showers, the foyer with the elevators beyond them. One of the entryways has been blown apart, its bathroom strewn with rubble, the door on the far side open to the elevator banks beyond it. We skid to a stop and climb out of the jeep.

Leoben jogs through the destroyed shower, his rifle in his hands. His face is bloodied, streaked with chalky dust. 'Nice of you to join us!' he yells.

'Where's Agnes?' I shout back.

'She's down in the bunker,' he says. 'The troops are dragging out the civilians, loading them into trucks. Regina's holed up in her lab, and a bunch of people have barricaded themselves in the basement levels, but they can't hold it for long. I hope you have a plan.'

'I do,' I say, 'but I need to get to the terminal in Regina's lab.'

He grimaces. 'That's gonna be hell to get to. Come on, let's get down there.'

He jogs back across the parking lot, when gunshots ring out behind us. 'Get down!' Cole shouts, pulling me behind a car.

A truck swerves in from the tunnel, headlights splashing through the rocky walls of the parking lot, with an entire platoon loaded in the back. They spill out as it skids to a stop. Leoben and Anna dart for cover, lifting their guns, but one of the soldiers throws a canister into the bombed-out shower. It hits the rubble, a plume of scarlet dust exploding out, enveloping the parking lot, bitter and choking. Voices rise in confusion, bullets ricocheting wildly from the cavern's walls. I drop to my knees, coughing. The smoke is dense and thick, completely impenetrable.

'Stay in cover!' Cole shouts. 'I'm going to help them!'

'Wait!' I shout, but he's already gone. I spit, coughing in the smoke. A group of soldiers run past me and I scramble backwards, doubled over to stay hidden. We can't get stuck in a firefight here. We need to make a run for the elevators and try to keep moving. The soldiers are wearing black uniforms and mirrored visors, but a figure is moving through them, wearing an armoured jacket and helmet. His face is visible, his brow furrowed. Pale, freckled skin, green eyes. Dax.

He scans the parking lot, his eyes locking on a battered green truck. He points at it, shouting something to the soldiers, and they yank open the rear doors and lift out a body. Limp, unconscious. Dark hair hanging loose over a forehead studded with black ports. Mato. Cartaxus has come for him, and I can feel Jun Bei's presence tighten in response, but she makes no move to stop the soldiers.

Not after what he did to us. Whatever there was between Jun Bei and Mato, it's not enough to fight for him right now. Still, something twinges through me as the soldiers load him into the back of the truck, and I don't know if it's from her or from me.

Dax strides towards the truck, the soldiers piling into the back, and for a moment I think he's leaving. But then he turns, watching the smoke clouds clearing from the ruined shower as a figure steps through.

Dark skin, a shock of white-blond hair beaded with blood. Tattoos curling over his arms. Leoben's eyes are black, unseeing, his muscles rigid. He's moving mechanically, walking back through the rubble towards Dax.

My heart clenches. Lee's being controlled somehow with his black-out tech. Dax is trying to drag him back to Cartaxus. I launch myself from cover before I realize what I'm doing, and Dax's eyes cut right to me, narrowing.

'You can't take him!' I shout, running for Leoben. 'Let him go! Dammit, Dax, don't do this!'

One of the soldiers breaks away from the unit, sprinting for me, but Dax lifts a hand. 'Leave her. If she wants to stay here and die, she can.'

The soldier halts but lifts his rifle. I skid to a stop, raising my hands as Leoben reaches the truck. A group of the soldiers grab his arms, guiding him into the back. I try to reach for his tech with my cuff, but there are fresh firewalls around his panel. Even if I broke Dax's control, I don't know if we'd be able to get away from this many soldiers.

'I thought you said you didn't want him to live as an experiment,' I say to Dax. 'They'll make you hurt him.'

'I don't have a choice any more,' he says. 'At least he'll be alive.'

'He can live if you help us!' I yell. 'We need to stop Cartaxus – they can't kill us all! This is genocide. I know you don't want to be a part of this.'

'I don't have the luxury of making that kind of choice any more,' Dax says, backing towards the truck, looking at Leoben.

His hand rises to his jacket, and he pulls something small from his pocket and tosses it through the air. It lands in the dirt beside me. 'Hurry. You don't have much time.'

He holds my gaze for one long, burning second, then gunfire cuts through the fading clouds of smoke, and he climbs into the truck.

It pulls away and screeches up the tunnel, taking Leoben with it.

CHAPTER 38

'Cat!' Cole runs from the row of showers, coughing. 'Come on, the others are through – we have to go, there'll be more troops soon.' He staggers to a stop. 'Cat, are you OK?'

I shake my head, staring at the tunnel Dax's truck just drove through . . .

Taking my brother with him.

'They . . . They took Lee,' I whisper. 'I couldn't stop them.'

Jun Bei's presence is a furious, heartbroken force inside my mind. Her thoughts are growing clearer now – whole and distinct, almost as though I could hear her voice again if I reached out to her. She has access to my panel, though. To *our* panel. She hacked the drones we used to get into this city.

But she didn't stop Dax from taking Lee, and I'm sure she could have.

'Who took him?' Cole yells.

I fall to my knees on the rough stone floor, searching through the dust and scattered feathers for the object Dax threw to me. My fingers slide over a flat black disc the size of a coin. A memory chip.

The moment I touch it, Dax's Cartaxus login credentials flash up in my mind.

'Dax took him,' I say, grabbing the chip, looking up at Cole. 'He took Mato too. Brink has the people he wants now. There's nothing to stop him launching the scythe.'

'He wants Regina too,' Cole says. 'She has to be worth more to him than Mato, maybe even Lee. We still have time. You told me you could stop this.'

Jun Bei's presence rises, fierce and resolute. I stand, clutching the chip in my good hand. 'I can,' I say. 'Let's go and finish this.'

We run through the debris in the ruined shower and race for one of the steel-caged elevators at the bank on the other side. An engine roars behind us, footsteps crunching through rubble, and Cole fires a spray of bullets at another wave of soldiers pouring through from the cavern. The elevator's steel doors slide shut, taking their fire, and I clutch the memory chip in my fist, huddled against the side of the steel cage as we plummet into the bunker.

Cole looks over himself and me, his eyes glazed, and I realize he's checking us both for bullet wounds. He slings his rifle over his shoulder and paces back and forth through the car as we drop. 'There's going to be more fighting downstairs,' he says. 'Anna says they're in the atrium. The genehackers have holed up in the basement levels, and most of the troops will go after them, but some will stay behind to defend their position. Where do we need to go when we get down there?'

'Regina's lab,' I say. 'The door is up a set of stairs that leads off the park in the atrium.'

Cole nods. 'I'm going to cover you, but I might not be able to make it through. If we get separated, I won't be able to contact you. Don't come back for me. The best way to help everyone who's dying up on the surface is to stop this attack.'

I nod, wrapping my arms round my chest.

The elevator doors ping open to a concrete hallway lined with unfinished apartments. Anna and Agnes are waiting nearby.

'About time,' Anna says. She looks between Cole and me. 'Where's Lee?'

'They took him,' Cole says. 'He's alive.'

'Goddammit!' Anna snaps. 'We should have blown the tunnel behind us. Those assholes. Well, come on. Let's do this.'

'You OK, Bobcat?' Agnes asks me as we jog through the twisting hallways.

I shake my head, clutching at the newly healed wound on my chest. It's closed over, but my tech is straining, and I'm exhausted and aching. 'Not really.'

She reaches for my hand, gripping it in hers. 'We'll get through this, Bobcat. You'll see.'

We reach the lobby at the edge of the atrium, the royal-blue grass of the park stretching out beyond it. Half the trees are snapped, charred and smoking. Scorch marks lick across the atrium's concrete walls, some of the apartments blown into rubble. Craters from what look like grenades are dug into the grass, and the air is thick with smoke, ringing with gunfire.

'There are troops in the atrium,' Anna says, 'and snipers in the apartments above it. We'll be totally exposed getting to the lab, but we can probably use cover fire to get you there.'

'That's suicide,' Cole says. 'We'll have to find a way through these hallways.'

'This place is a goddamn labyrinth,' Anna says. 'I don't even have a map for it. Who's to say there aren't more troops in here than out there?'

'Give me a minute,' I say, turning my focus into my cuff, sending a pulse through the atrium. 'I think I can find the soldiers.'

I look up through the atrium as lines of light streak across my vision, sketching the inside of the bunker out for me. I can see the empty space of the park, and a brilliant light on the far side of Regina's lab where her terminal is. Countless dancing specks of light glow brighter as I push up the resolution of the scan. The panels of the soldiers. Genkits and tech left in the apartments around the atrium, rising in a cylinder that stretches up to the dark void of the sky.

But the sky overhead isn't entirely *dark*. Wild arcs of light are glimmering above the bunker, swooping down through the atrium. If my cuff is showing points of light like this to me, it means they're wireless connections.

But it looks like they're in the *pigeons*.

'What the hell?' I breathe, staring up at the flock. There's something strange about these birds that's tugged at me since I took down the destroyers. I push the scan on my cuff, staring up at them, at their black wings and glowing feathers, their toothed, clicking beaks.

But there's a flicker of a reading from the birds that I can see with my cuff. Something tiny, blinking. Flashing in an encoded signal. I turn my focus to one of the birds, zeroing in on it, and the breath rushes from my lungs.

They're *panels*.

Tiny, miniature panels built into the pigeons. They're Regina's design, the same as the single spots of light that glow across her skin. But there's no way people budded millions of pigeons with panels. These must have been in the birds since they *hatched*. Coded into their DNA, passed down to their offspring, their cobalt glow masked by the luminescent tips of their feathers. The signals blinking from them are faint, barely perceptible against the blazing light of Entropia, but they're just strong enough for me to grasp on to them.

Text spills across my vision. The panels have a simple, rudimentary operating system that's running a single app – a navigational tool, based on the birds' own impulses. It can be programmed to guide the birds to any location. Regina said the birds were coded to migrate back to Entropia once a year. I thought she meant that it was part of their DNA. But it looks like it was more – their movements are being *controlled*.

Which means that I might be able to control them too.

I draw in a slow breath, reading through the app's triggers, its controls, and alter the settings in my cuff to match them.

'What are you doing, Bobcat?' Agnes asks.

I blink out of my session. My vision is still a mess of light, painted across the atrium. 'I . . . I don't know if this will work. But don't freak out if it does, OK?'

Cole takes my arm. 'If what will work?'

Anna glances out at the atrium. 'Holy shit.'

A roar is rising in the air, echoing from the atrium walls. A hailstorm, growing louder, rising until it's deafening. Arcs of black and cobalt cut across the view of the park. The pigeons are swooping through the atrium, descending until the air is black with them.

'That'll do it!' Anna yells over the roar, gripping her rifle. 'Come on!'

Cole's grip on my arm tightens, his muscles tensing, and we rush out of the lobby and into the park. It's like running into a hurricane. The birds swerve and dart around me, feathers brushing my skin, beaks snapping past my ears, catching in my hair. I throw my arm up, pressing my forehead into the crook of my elbow, trying desperately to see through the flock to the ground, but they're too dense. Agnes grabs hold of the back of my shirt, but we're losing momentum, lost in the cacophony of the flock.

There are too many of them. We're completely blind. But I don't need to *see*.

I scrunch my eyes shut and push my focus back into my cuff.

The world goes dark, then flashes with light, the storm of pigeons tracing wild, glowing streaks through the air. Their signals are weak, though, and I can see through them to the glowing heart of the mainline connection in Regina's lab ahead.

'This way!' I shout, but my voice is lost. I scrunch my eyes shut, reaching out to grab Cole's arm, clutching Agnes's wrist, and lurch forward, boots crunching over rubble. Cole's body jerks, his muscles tightening as he grabs at Anna, dragging her into our circle, his arm looped round her waist. I see their panels glowing in the darkness behind my eyes, flickers of light blinking from their guns. We half run, half stagger through the birds to the other side of the park and into the stairwell beside Regina's lab.

There are pigeons in the stairwell, but they're sparse enough to see through. Agnes's face is white, streaked with blood, and I realize slowly that I'm hurt too. Nicks and scratches cover my arms and chest from the flock's razor beaks, but the tiny wounds are better than a sniper's bullet.

Something *booms* behind us, followed by a hail of gunfire. I can't tell if it's one of the pigeons blowing, or a grenade from the Cartaxus troops. The pigeons scatter, their cries rising into a roar that saturates my audio tech. Bullets hit the wall behind us, sending out flying chips of concrete.

'Run!' Cole shouts, pushing me up the stairs. We reach the landing with the door to Regina's lab, and he presses himself against the wall, dropping into a crouch. His skin is slashed, his hair beaded with blood. 'Anna, get them inside!'

More gunfire echoes behind us, voices cutting through the roar of the flock. Soldiers, racing for us. I glance back at the door to Regina's lab. Agnes is at the scanner beside it. The scanner flashes green, the door sliding open. I don't know how Agnes got it to unlock, but she did, and the soldiers will be here in seconds. We need to get behind those steel doors and close them, but Cole pushes me away.

'Go!' he shouts, shouldering his rifle. 'I'll hold this door.'

'I'm not leaving you!'

The soldiers round the corner at the bottom of the stairs, and Cole lifts his rifle, sending a spray of bullets down at them, forcing them back into cover.

'Anna, take her!' he shouts, firing another round.

'No way!' I yell. I can see the panels of the unit at the bottom of the stairs with my cuff. They're readying to strike again. 'We'll hold it from inside. I'm not leaving you behind.'

He shakes his head. 'Can't risk them getting through. We need to finish the mission. Stop flood protocol. That's the only thing that matters.'

I look around, my heart racing, reaching for Jun Bei's presence, for the scythe, for anything that can get Cole safely inside with us. All I can see is the wall of the pigeons, and Cole exposed on the stairs. Jun Bei could solve this, I know it. She could find a way to get him through, to guard the doors without leaving him behind. I urge my consciousness closer to her, trying to find a way to give her control now, to let her take over.

But it's too late.

A soldier at the bottom of the stairs lobs a smoke grenade up to the landing. White, bitter gas billows into the air. I double over, coughing. Cole growls, turning, slinging one arm round my waist, heaving me back towards the doorway. I keep stretching for Jun Bei's presence, hurling my mind against the wall between us. A spark runs through me, burning like fire.

'Anna!' he shouts.

'Just a minute!' I scream. 'I can stop them!'

But Anna's arms slide round me, wrenching me through the door, and Agnes slams it shut.

CHAPTER 39

The door takes the sound of the gunfire away, replacing it with dull thuds of bullets hitting the steel. I choke out a cry, straining against Anna's grip. Cole is still out there. He's completely exposed. There's no way he's going to be able to keep that many soldiers at bay.

'Why did you *leave* him?' I cry, shoving Anna away.

'He'll be fine,' she says.

I stumble away, wiping my eyes, coughing. The gas from the smoke grenade is sour in my mouth, stinging like acid in the cuts across my skin. 'How do you know that?'

'Because he's trained for this. He knows what he's doing.'

'Let's go, Bobcat,' Agnes says. 'Sooner we get this over with, sooner he'll be safe.'

I stare at the door, sending a pulse from my cuff, searching for Cole's panel, but the steel blocks my scan. He could be hurt out there right now, and I wouldn't know.

'Come on,' Anna says, reaching for my arm.

I snatch it away. 'Why didn't you stay with him?'

'Someone needs to be in here to protect you in case they make it through that door.'

'Why didn't you stay instead? He could *die*.'

Her eyes flare with the accusation. 'He chose to stay out there. It's not my job to protect him, and it's not yours, either.'

Another hail of bullets thuds against the wall.

'We don't have much time,' Agnes urges.

I clench my hands into fists, then turn and push past Anna, striding through the rows of plants in Regina's nursery.

The lab has been cleared out – by Regina or by Cartaxus, I can't tell. The cages are empty. Potted plants lie strewn across the floor, spilling drifts of dirt across the concrete. The wall of sample canisters is half empty, and the row of tanks along the far wall have been drained, the twitching bodies gone. Regina is standing at the massive coding terminal on the far wall.

She turns, her black eyes wide, letting out a sigh of relief. 'You made it.' She looks at Anna, a flicker of recognition in her eyes, and then frowns as she looks at Agnes, as though trying to place her face.

'You,' I say, striding for Regina. 'Where the hell is my hand?'

'You were supposed to stay *here*,' she says. 'I didn't think you'd actually cut it off. But I couldn't resist once you had. We thought we needed a living sample of your DNA.'

I stop. 'Who needed it?' But I already know. 'You're working with Lachlan.'

'I am *now*,' she says. 'I wasn't lying to you, I swear. I had no idea Lachlan was in the city until you told me. I was planning on helping you find him and turn him over to Cartaxus, but then Brink sent destroyers to my city to *kill* my people.' Her voice grows sharp. 'Lachlan found me, and we tried to stop the attack together. But then you did it all yourself, my clever girl. We've been trying to use your Origin code to stop flood protocol, but it's locked to your DNA. We haven't been able to get it to work.'

I look around, gripped with fear, expecting to see Lachlan, but there's no sign of him. He must be working from wherever he's been hiding. A crash sounds near the door, and Regina straightens. 'Quickly,' she says. 'We need to stop this attack, or this will all be for nothing.'

'You think we're going to *help* you?' Anna spits. 'You're working with Lachlan.'

'Yes,' Regina hisses, 'I'm working with him to stop hundreds of millions of people on the planet's surface from being slaughtered. This isn't about ideology any more, child. This is about survival. Brink is playing an end game here – don't you understand? He's just rounding up everyone he thinks could be useful to him before he deploys the scythe. He's already taken most of my people. We don't have much longer. I think I can stop him from deploying the scythe, but I can't get past their firewalls.'

I look down at the memory chip Dax gave me, then hold it out. 'I think this might help.'

Regina snatches it, striding back to the terminal. I start to follow her, but Anna pushes past me.

Her muscles are rigid, her eyes black. She lifts her rifle in a swift mechanical arc, and fires a clip of bullets into the terminal. It explodes with a *crash*, sending out a shower of sparks. Anna turns, swinging the rifle to me, her eyes flat and black.

Time seems to slow.

The *crack* of her rifle echoes through the air, its barrel aimed at my heart. I try to throw myself to the floor, but I'm too slow. I see the bullet coming for me, racing through the air, and a dark-haired figure blurs in front of me, straight into its path.

'No!' I scream.

Regina cries out, falling to the floor, scarlet blossoming across her chest, soaking through the emerald material of her gown. Anna aims her rifle at me again, but Agnes strides past me, holding her hand out.

Anna freezes.

Her eyes stay black, unblinking. Her rifle falls from her grip, and she slumps to her knees, falling sideways on the floor. She's not wounded – she looks like Cole did when Mato took control of his black-out tech. I turn to Agnes, my heart kicking.

'How did you do that?'

'Put pressure on Regina's wound,' Agnes says, her gaze still locked on Anna.

I look down and choke back a cry. Regina's eyes are wide with shock, her breathing ragged. I drop to my knees beside her and press my hands to the blood bubbling from her sternum.

'Why?' I gasp. 'Why did you take that bullet?'

'It's your time now,' she whispers. She lifts her hand, the memory chip clutched in the black-and-emerald spotted scales of her palm. 'I'm so proud of you, my daughter. I've spent my life working to create the keys to immortality, and then you did it at *fifteen*.' Her hand rises to my cheek, tracing blood across my skin. 'I'm sorry I won't get to see your world, but you already gave me more than I could ever have dreamed of.'

'No,' I say, pressing down on the wound. 'No, you have to hold on.' Her blood is bubbling between my fingers. I look up, scanning the lab for healing tech, for anything that might help stop her bleeding. There's nothing. It's cleaned out.

But Regina already has the code she needs inside her.

'Jun Bei,' I gasp, pressing down on the wound, trying to stem the flow of blood. 'Jun Bei, if you have any idea how to use the code, you have to try. We need her. She's our mother. Please, Jun Bei.'

The presence in my mind whips into a storm.

Code scrolls across my vision, lightning fast. Gentech commands interspersed with blocks of protein array and nanite instructions. I shove down hard on Regina's chest, blinking as the pages of text flicker in front of me, catching the briefest glimpses of meaning.

But there's so much of it. Millions of lines. It is a universe of logic and algorithms written by a girl who wiped it all from her mind. I can feel Jun Bei's frustration rising, her thoughts growing sharp and violent, the text flashing across my eyes whirling into a hurricane.

Agnes drops to her knees beside me and puts her hands over mine, pressing down on Regina's wound. Anna is still slumped on the floor, motionless.

'Your friend will be OK,' Agnes says. 'Her black-out protocol kicked in. Brink must have programmed her to stop us if we got close to hacking his systems.'

My vision is a storm of code and logic, battering my senses, my hands slick with the warmth of Regina's blood.

'There isn't much time,' Agnes says. 'You need to stop this attack now, Bobcat. It's up to you.'

Regina lets out a shaking breath, and the lights dotted across her skin blink off one by one – a dark patch around the wound that spreads across her chest. Her collarbones go dim, the starlight of panels in her arms flickering off as the code in her skin fades into darkness.

She's dying.

'No,' I gasp, pressing down harder on her chest. Jun Bei's presence roars inside me, the code scrolling frantically. Regina's black eyes drift closed, her breathing stopping, her head tilting back on the floor. Her blood is splattered on the concrete, soaked into my shirt, slicked across my hands. Too much blood.

Her body falls limp, and I feel something tear inside me.

She's gone.

Agnes's eyes grow steely. 'Get yourself together, Bobcat,' she snaps. 'You have a job to do. A lot more people are going to die if you don't hurry. You can't save her now, but you can save her people.'

I look down at Regina, at the dark stars on her skin, pain wrenching in my chest. I barely had time to meet her. I never got a chance to know her. The storm of code around me falls silent, Jun Bei's presence going mute.

I drop my bloodied hand to the concrete, picking up the memory chip that's fallen from Regina's hand, numb. The terminal on the wall is still sparking, billowing dark smoke into the air. I can't hack Cartaxus from here.

Agnes follows my eyes. 'There has to be another one,' she says. 'Lachlan must have been using one.'

'But he could be anywhere . . .' I trail off, holding her gaze. Mato was working with Lachlan – he said he spoke to him while we were here at Entropia. My mind flicks back to the glowing dust I saw on his hair after I met with Regina. He said he'd gone to get something from the jeep, but there was nothing in his hands. He'd been down to the basement levels, to the maintenance shaft cut into the rock.

The shaft that wasn't on any of the maps Mato gave us access to.

'I know where he is,' I breathe. 'In the maintenance shafts. I went right past it . . .'

'Can you get there now?' Agnes asks.

I look back over my shoulder at the door. The sound of gunfire is still echoing from the atrium, bullets thudding against the door. That means Cole's still alive and still defending us, but I can't go out there – I don't know how to get to the basement levels from here, and Anna said the troops were massing there.

But I saw a ring of light from Regina's lab when I was in the agricultural room with the underwater lake. I look over my shoulder at the floating platform at the centre of the room. It's stacked with glass tanks, hanging above the giant drain in the floor.

'I think I can get to it,' I say.

'Quickly, then,' Agnes urges. 'I'll get Cole inside once you're gone. Hurry, Bobcat.'

I rock back on my heels, but pause as I look down at Anna's slumped form. Agnes stopped her somehow, the way I've only ever seen Brink and Mato do. She was the one who unlocked the door to this lab to get us in here too.

'Who are you?' I breathe.

Agnes's blood-streaked face crinkles in a smile. 'I'm your *yaya*, Bobcat. I always will be. Now *go*.'

I scramble to my feet, my hands stained with Regina's blood, and run to the floating platform holding the glass tanks. It sways as I step on to it, a cold breeze cutting up from the darkness below. There's a chain strung from the centre, as thick as my arm, suspending the platform above the lake beneath it. But there's no lever, no lock to release it that I can see. I scan the room, then swing my backpack off my shoulders and dig through it, my fingers closing around a cold, segmented curve of metal.

The last flash strip. I see a sudden flash of charred bone and blinding light as I lift it out. I grit my teeth and wrap it around the chain, looping it twice, looking back at Agnes and Regina. I won't have time to cut the chain and run from the platform before it falls. I'll go down with it, into the lake. Then I'll have to make my way up the tunnel.

And then I'll have to face Lachlan.

'Bobcat, now!' Agnes urges, colour flushing her cheeks.

My eyes drop to Regina's body, my heart clenching. Then I yank the lever on the flash strip. The chain snaps with a sound like a gunshot, and the platform drops.

CHAPTER 40

The metal table in the centre of the platform screeches as it tilts, jars of pale, rippled flesh tumbling around me. They seem to float as we fall together, hurtling into the darkness of the cavern below. Time slows to a crawl, my hair rising in slow-motion tendrils around my face, my muscles tensing for the impact I know is coming. There's a flash of green as we reach the lake, a blur of lights above me, then the roaring shock of the water as the platform slices through it.

The sample jars smack against the surface, some hitting the edge of the platform, shattering with a *crack* that echoes from the cavern's shadowed walls. The water hits me like a fist, the weight of the platform dragging me down through a roiling mess of dark water and shards of glass. The edge of a broken jar kisses my ribs, a puff of scarlet billowing through the bubbles, and a wave of pressure thuds hard against my ears. I manage to keep my hand locked tight around the memory chip, but the instinct to stop breathing comes a moment too late.

A lungful of water burns my throat. I scrunch my eyes shut, choking, kicking against the pull of the sinking platform. My breath races away in a cloud of silver bubbles that float up in zigzags, converging an impossible distance above me. There's no pain from my ribs, but I can taste rust in the water. There's too much blood. The cut must be deep. I kick off my heavy boots and claw upwards desperately, when something moves in the splintered light cutting down from the surface.

Hands. Pale, slender, reaching down for me. Arms thrust through the water from above, urging me upwards. I reach for them but they slide away, and I break the surface, choking in a ragged breath of air, grabbing hold of the concrete lip of the lake.

My muscles are shaking, alerts blinking in my vision. The air is thick with the glowing fungus wafting in spirals around me.

Jun Bei is kneeling on the floor, soaking wet, staring at me through the clouds of glowing dust.

'Come on,' she says, her voice thick. 'We can't let her die for nothing. We need to *go*.'

'H-how –' I choke out, dragging myself up on to the concrete floor. My stomach churns and I collapse on my side, coughing up the gulp of water I breathed in. 'How are you here?'

'I figured out how to access our VR chip,' she says. 'We're hurt. Show me the wound.'

I swallow, still gasping for air, and look down at my side. Four inches of skin are sliced cleanly in an arc beneath my bra, my

T-shirt hanging open, its edges stained with blood. The sight makes my head swim, and I scrunch my eyes shut.

'I can't *see* it if you aren't looking,' Jun Bei says. 'We only have one set of eyes.'

'Shit, right,' I breathe, opening my eyes, forcing myself to focus on the wound. The flow of blood seems to have slowed, but it's deep. It's going to take days to heal. It should be stitched or stapled, bandaged up, but we don't have time.

I look around, scanning the room. We're in the hydroponics chamber with the rows of curling purple beans, a dark hallway on the far side of the room leading to the rest of the basement levels. I can see the plastic sheeting hung over the entrance to the maintenance shaft Cole and I ran up. It *has* to be where Lachlan is hiding now. Gunshots echo in the distance, an explosion shaking the floor.

We don't have much longer.

'Not a lot I can do with the wound,' Jun Bei says, standing up. A chill spreads across my ribs. 'I closed the veins and the nerves. Come on, we have to go.'

Voices echo behind us. Boots pounding, weapons clicking. I scramble to my feet, lurching for the rows of plants, but a hail of bullets slams into the floor around me. I spin, frozen, as four visored Cartaxus soldiers race through from the hallway, their rifles aimed at me. I cast about wildly for somewhere to run, but there's no cover – nothing near. Just trellises of beans and flowers, endless clouds of glowing dust. I'm unarmed, soaking wet and wounded, with nowhere to hide.

'Hands up!' one of the soldiers yells, cocking his rifle.

I obey, lifting my hands, but the soldier lowers the barrel. He's aiming for my leg. He'll shoot me so I can't run.

I'll never make it to Lachlan.

'I don't think so,' Jun Bei says, flicking her hand. A *buzz* passes through me, rippling from the base of my skull, and the soldier drops to the ground. The three behind him watch him fall, stepping back in shock. More voices echo in the hallway, footsteps pounding closer.

Jun Bei tilts her head, and two of the remaining three soldiers fall, leaving one standing on his own.

'Drop your weapon,' she says, her voice low and calm. 'They're not dead, but they will be – and you with them – if you don't do as I say.'

I blink, looking between Jun Bei and the soldier. He can see her too. She must be hacking his tech, appearing as a VR avatar in his vision as well. The soldier stares down at the other three and tosses his weapon aside, dropping to his knees, his hands raised. The voices in the hallway grow louder and a group of genehackers run in, carrying rifles they must have taken from Cartaxus troops. They stare at the kneeling soldier, at Jun Bei and me, and stumble to a stop in the entrance to the room.

'Good,' Jun Bei says to the soldier, stepping forward. She drifts into a blur of light, reappearing in front of him, tilting her head. The buzzing in my skull grows louder, prickling at the edges of my senses. Commands and scrolling output logs flash across my vision.

She isn't just hacking the soldier – she's using his tech to stretch back into Cartaxus's servers, sliding into their networks, taking control. The gunshots in the distance grow quiet, the explosions ceasing. She's stopping Cartaxus's assault all over Entropia. The soldier's connection to Cartaxus is only local – she can't stretch any further – but she's single-handedly stopped the entire attack in the space of a few seconds.

The breath rushes from my lungs. I knew Jun Bei was smarter than me, but this is something else. Something higher. She's taken down hundreds of soldiers, and she's only using *half* a brain.

I didn't know someone like her could exist.

She looks up, blinking out of her session, turning back to me. 'Brink will know I'm here now. I don't know if that will buy us time or cost it, but either way I don't think we have much longer. We're going to have to run.'

I shove the sopping hair back from my face. 'OK. I'm ready.'

Jun Bei looks back at the genehackers, who are watching her with wide, incredulous eyes, and gestures to the soldier. 'He's all yours.'

She turns and lurches into a blur of light, reappearing ahead of me, her dark hair flying out behind her. I drag in a breath and race after her, weaving between the trellises of beans to the far wall of the room where the plastic sheeting hangs over the maintenance shaft. I shove it aside and duck under the metal chain, wincing at a stab of pain from the gash on my ribs, then bolt up the curving dark tunnel and into the rock.

It's pitch-black, the air cold and musty. My clothes are soaked, my hair streaming down my back. The glow of my panel is muted through the cuff on my arm, but Jun Bei glances back at me, and a light blinks on the side of the cuff, splashing out across the tunnel.

'Thanks,' I call out, my lungs burning.

'Come on,' she shouts back, always staying just a few strides in front of me, urging me forward. We run for what feels like an eternity, the rocky floor jagged against the thin cotton of my wet socks.

A light gleams ahead of us, the tunnel branching. The sound of voices echoes from the path that leads to the parking lot, the scent of smoke and plastic explosives choking the air. I follow Jun Bei down the other tunnel, the one Cole and I ran past when we were here. Fear kicks inside me. If this really is Lachlan's lab, he might be waiting for me, holed up in there, trying to stop the attack on his own. I don't have any weapons. I don't even have shoes. I'm exhausted, aching, and out of time.

But I have Jun Bei.

We reach a door set into the rock. Steel, riveted, reinforced. There's a security scanner beside it, but it blinks green when I reach for it. I don't know if it recognized my panel and approved the ID or if Jun Bei hacked it, but I shove my shoulder into the metal and force it open, stumbling inside.

The room is small and cluttered. Messy, like the lab in the cabin's basement. Black counters wrap round the edges, stacked with glassware and nanosolution. There are papers pinned to the walls, sketches and notes, scribbled gene diagrams, and a coding terminal on the far wall with the symbol for Cartaxus's satellite network glowing on its screen.

Lachlan is standing behind a table in the centre of the room. He looks haggard and skinny, with shadows etched beneath his eyes. A chrome cuff gleams over his panel, and there's a body lying on the table in front of him.

A girl with a bandage around the stump of her left hand.

She looks *exactly* like me.

CHAPTER 41

I stare at Lachlan and the girl. She's unconscious, limp, her mouth slightly open. There's a black glass cuff on her forearm that looks just like mine. Lachlan's grey eyes cut to me, then move to Jun Bei, and a lurch of fear rushes through me.

This is no puppet. This is Lachlan – alive and in the flesh, waiting for me. He's holding a body with my face, my hair, my *clothes*.

I think I have her hand on my wrist.

'Darling,' he says, his eyes lighting up as he looks at Jun Bei. 'You made it here. I knew you'd survive.'

My heart is pounding, but he's not even *looking* at me. He's just watching Jun Bei's VR projection as she steps past me and into the room.

'*You*,' she growls, shaking with barely controlled rage. Her clothes are still wet, like mine, her hair soaked and slicked to her neck. There's a murderous glint in her green eyes as she stares at Lachlan. 'You did this to me.'

'I know you're angry,' he says, his voice eerily calm, 'but there isn't much time. Cartaxus will find this tunnel soon. They know you're here. You can stop this attack, but you're going to need to stay out of their control.'

I look from him to the girl on the table, reeling. She has my skin, my face, my hair. She's a perfect replica. 'Who the hell is *that*?' I ask.

'She's nothing,' Lachlan says, looking down at her. There's a strange tone in his voice as he talks to me, and it feels like he's avoiding my eyes. It makes me think of the walls that close down over Cole's face when he's in pain.

But that isn't how Lachlan sounds when he's talking to Jun Bei.

He *knows* we're two people. He's treating us as separate entities. But that means he must have known that Jun Bei was alive inside my mind.

So why the hell was he keeping her locked up in there for years?

Lachlan strokes the face of the girl on the table, brushing her hair back from her forehead. She's identical to me – right down to the pale scars etched on her cheek from when I fell out of a tree at the cabin. He looks up at Jun Bei. 'I had Regina grow this body as a decoy in case Cartaxus ever discovered you during the outbreak. Her people could have switched it for you and brought you into hiding here. This body doesn't have a proper brain – it's even using a chip to breathe. It has the same normal DNA as you, though, so when I'm taken by Cartaxus with it, they'll think they have you and stop looking. It won't fool them for long, but you'll have enough time to end this attack.'

Jun Bei tilts her head. 'You're turning yourself in?'

'It's the only way,' he says. 'I'm no help to you here. You need to use this terminal to stop flood protocol. I can't get the Origin code to run properly without your DNA. It needs to be activated through your body like it was in the vaccine's decryption. You coded it that way to control it, and I haven't been able to alter it enough to run it on my own. You're the only one who can stop this.'

Jun Bei shakes her head, stepping into the room. Her hip passes through the edge of the table. 'No, Lachlan. We're not using the Origin code to lobotomize the planet. That's not why I wrote it. It's a gift, not a weapon.'

'You don't understand,' he says, frustrated. 'Cartaxus won't just kill the people on the surface. They'll reverse-engineer the Origin code. They're almost finished. Once Brink figures out what it's for and what it can do, he'll come looking for you so that he can use it however he wants. They'll turn it into a weapon far worse than what I would use it for, and they'll keep you prisoner until they figure out how to run it without your DNA. I just want to erase the Wrath, but they'll use it to turn people into *tools*. You've seen how they treat their black-outs. Imagine if they could alter the minds of the civilians in their bunkers. Your code will let them do that, darling. It's time for you to assume responsibility for it, and take back control. You were supposed to wake and do this after the decryption, but you were hurt instead. I had to give you time to regain your strength for this plan to work.'

My heart stops. Regina was right – she thought that Lachlan was waiting to finish his plan while I healed from the concussion. But this isn't the plan I was expecting. He's turning himself in to Cartaxus to stop them from looking for us. He's leaving Jun Bei and me to stop the attack.

This all feels *wrong*.

'Is that what you want from us?' Jun Bei asks, striding closer. 'You did all this – changing my body, suppressing me, adding the code to the vaccine. What has this all been *for*? Was this all to erase the Wrath?'

Lachlan looks surprised. 'This has all been for *you*, Jun Bei. Can't you see that?' He looks at me, and then away again, and the hair on the back of my neck rises. There's a note of affection in his voice when he talks to Jun Bei, but not when he talks to me. I step into the room, staring at the body on the table, confusion whipping through me.

'It wasn't supposed to be like this, darling,' he says. 'The code at the end of the vaccine's decryption was designed to handle the transition for you, but that butcher cut your panel open and ruined everything. The walls inside your mind were cracked instead of brought down smoothly. I never meant for it to be this difficult for you to come back.'

Come back. The words roar through me. So Jun Bei really *was* supposed to wake up during the decryption. But instead, she was already awake. She said she woke up on Marcus's couch after he cut my healing tech core out.

'But *why* did you do all this?' I ask, swaying.

'I had to hide you, my darling girl,' he says, but not to me. He's talking to Jun Bei again. He's barely even acknowledging me. 'I knew the attack on that signal tower was a mistake, but it wouldn't go unnoticed. People were going to start looking for you, but you were hurt. You'd wiped too much of yourself when you erased your memories. You lost crucial patterns in your brain that had to be painstakingly regrown. I tried keeping you in a coma, but it was taking too long, and your neural pathways were beginning to atrophy. Your brain needed to be *working* while you recovered. That's why I created Catarina.'

A crack opens inside me. An abyss, dark and violent. I feel myself sliding towards it.

'What do you mean . . . *created* me?'

'It's not as difficult as it sounds,' Lachlan says. His gaze finally turns to me, but it's dark somehow, threatening. The abyss inside me grows wider at the cold look in his eyes. 'Seeds want to grow, hearts want to beat and brain tissue wants to *think*. The implant kept Jun Bei's essence locked in her left frontal lobe, but the rest of her brain was a mess of altered sections that I didn't know how to repair. So I overwrote it – I wiped it back to a clean slate and waited. It took you just two days to open your eyes.'

'You . . . you created me to help Jun Bei *recover*?' I whisper. I grip the edge of the metal table, feeling my blood draining.

'I had no choice,' Lachlan says. 'It was the only way I could think of to keep her alive.'

I close my eyes, my mind whipping into a storm. I want to be sick – to scream, to drop to my knees. I'm not an experiment. I'm a *tool*.

Lachlan created me just to save Jun Bei's life.

'There were teething issues,' he says. 'You had to learn to talk, to move your body. But that development was fast, and it wasn't long until you thought you had a past and memories. With you awake, the neural damage began to repair much faster. It took almost a year for it to heal completely, though. I had to keep you in the cabin in the woods, away from noises and people. I blocked the wireless signals – everything I could do to help you heal. I couldn't even let you use VR or it'd strain the fragile pathways that were being regrown inside your mind.' He lets out a breath of bitter laughter. 'And then, when you were finally ready, when I knew it was time to wake Jun Bei up, I got a call from Cartaxus. There'd been an outbreak in an Argentinian glacier that had spread through a group of tourists before they contained it. I knew there'd be more. I waited, and it took just three weeks for the global outbreak to begin.'

Jun Bei's hands are clenched into fists, her face pale. She looks like she's reeling from this almost as much as me. 'So why didn't you wake me up?' she asks. 'Cat was alone. She almost *died*. We could have made it through the outbreak more easily if we'd been together like this.'

Lachlan shakes his head. 'You don't understand, darling. You would have had to stay hidden from Cartaxus through the entire outbreak. You could never go back to them, not after you'd written the Origin code. They'd do to you what they did to me – recruit you as one of their scientists, and then they'd own you forever. If I'd woken you, you would have had to stay on the surface, but I knew it would be hell, and you'd already been through so much. Those two years would have mentally scarred you even more than your childhood did. I couldn't bear to wake you up just to leave you stranded in a world locked in the grip of the plague.'

'But you left *me* there,' I say, my voice breaking. 'I was there the whole time.'

'Yes,' Lachlan says. His eyes cut to me, and the abyss inside me creaks wider. 'You were there to live through it, but then, during the decryption, you were supposed to disappear.'

The room tilts, the edges of my vision blurring. I grab the wall beside me for balance. He wasn't just going to wake Jun Bei up. That was never the plan. He created me to help her heal, but then he didn't need me any more.

The command that glitched at the end of the decryption wasn't just to wake her up.

It was to kill me. I was supposed to die.

I double over, choking for air. My heart feels like it's being gripped in a fist. No wonder Lachlan never told me that he loved me at the cabin. No wonder he was never warm around me.

I was nothing to him. Just thoughts in a body. A tool to keep Jun Bei alive.

He made me into his daughter and made me *love* him just so that he could control me long enough to bring her back.

He was always going to kill me.

'No,' Jun Bei says, her voice breaking. 'How could you? You *monster*. How could you want to kill her?'

'She's not *real*,' Lachlan urges. 'This is *your* body, *your* mind. She was a placeholder. I didn't think you'd have this much trouble moving past her. You'd reorganized your entire brain when you were at Entropia. You were ruthless with your mind – it was clearly a tool for you to use. I assumed you'd understand.'

'*Understand?*' she spits. 'You made a person inside me and then you wanted my waking to kill her? Do you have any idea how horrible that would be for me?'

'You were never supposed to meet her,' he says. 'She was supposed to disappear right at the moment you woke. There'd be glimmers of memory from the outbreak, but you'd assume they were *yours* and that the vaccine had simply erased them. You were supposed to step back into your body and take it for your own. It should have been *easy* for you.'

'You used your own DNA,' she says, her shoulders rolling in revulsion. 'Do you know how violating that is?'

'Yes,' he urges. 'That was the *point*. I wanted to make it as easy as possible for you to become yourself again. To recode your body and your mind back into the girl that you're *supposed* to be. I couldn't think of anything you'd find easier to do than wipe the face of the man who tortured you for your entire childhood.'

I stare between them, unable to move, to speak. My chest is shuddering, my vision starting to waver. The man I thought was my father – the man I *loved* – is talking about me like I'm nothing more than a pawn to use and discard.

'She's a *person*!' Jun Bei shouts, seething. 'How can you even talk like this?'

'She's an abomination,' Lachlan yells, gesturing at me. 'You're supposed to *hate* her, not defend her. She wears my face and thinks with my DNA. She's a tool, and now her usefulness has come to an end. It's time for you to take back what's yours and assume your rightful place in this world.'

I drag in a breath, trying to wrestle myself back under control. Every word from Lachlan's mouth feels like a blade driven into me, but my pain is rising into anger. This man took everything from me. I look around the room for a weapon, but there's nothing – just lab equipment, shelves of paper and nanite vials.

But I have a scythe inside my arm.

'My time is over, darling,' Lachlan says to Jun Bei. 'It's been over for years, but this vaccine's failure just proves it. I've failed Cartaxus, and I've failed humanity. But you can do what I cannot –

I know you can. You are our greatest hope for ending this plague. I may have been part of the group who created gentech, but you were *born* from it. It's as much a part of you as the DNA inside your cells. We're on the edge of a new world – you've almost taken us there already with the Origin code, and I know you're only just getting started. But now you need to fight, Jun Bei. You need to use this code the way it was designed – to cut away the Wrath.'

I summon my cuff's interface, searching through my panel for the scythe. I've used it twice now, but I've never done so consciously. I don't even know what it's *called*. There are hundreds of folders of Jun Bei's code inside my arm. I scan through them desperately, searching for something I can use to hurt Lachlan.

'The Origin code is *mine*,' Jun Bei says to Lachlan. 'I didn't write it to erase the Wrath, and I won't use it on anyone against their will. I know better than anyone how it feels to have your choices taken away.'

Gunshots echo from the hallway. Lachlan stiffens, then slides his hands beneath the limp body of the girl. I still can't find the scythe. I cast around desperately, searching the shelves for a gun, a shard of glass, but there's nothing.

'I understand powerlessness more than you might think,' he says. 'Cartaxus will be here soon if I don't go to them right now. You can stop this attack, darling. I know you'll do what's right.'

He lifts the girl's limp body to his chest and strides for the door, but Jun Bei blurs across the room, reappearing in front of him.

'What do you mean – you understand powerlessness?' she asks. 'What did Cartaxus do to you?'

He doesn't answer. He just stands there with the girl's body clutched to his chest.

Jun Bei steps back as though suddenly afraid. 'Why did you change your face? You were born with red hair and green eyes.'

A sad smile crosses Lachlan's face. 'I had to hide my DNA, which meant changing my face. I knew you'd sequence my genes eventually, and I couldn't bear the thought of you realizing who I was. It would make it so much more painful for both of us to do the testing they forced me to do. It was easier for you to simply *hate* me and call me a monster, which I am. You're so much like your mother, Jun Bei, but your green eyes are mine.'

My blood freezes. Jun Bei steps back in shock, her lip trembling. Lachlan just shifts the body in his arms. 'I'll be doing what I can from the inside,' he says. 'I'm so proud of you, my daughter. I can't wait to see what you become.'

His eyes blaze, locked on hers before sliding briefly to me, a hint of something almost like pain in them before he turns and pushes into the hallway, the lifeless girl's body gripped in his arms. The steel door of the lab clicks shut behind him and Jun Bei turns to me, shaking, tears sliding down her cheeks.

Now that I'm looking, I can see the same lines in her face that I saw in the photograph – the curve of her lower lip, her hairline, the slope of her shoulders. Lachlan is there in her features.

He's her father. He's *our* father.

We're the children of a monster.

'No!' she says, her voice breaking. 'No!'

'Jun Bei –' I start, but she grips her hair in her hands, then doubles over, letting out a scream, and the genkits on the wall explode.

CHAPTER 42

I throw myself across the floor, diving behind the table. The room fills with a cloud of choking black smoke, broken shards of plastic and glass hurtling through the air. I land hard on my side, the wound in my ribs hitting the tiles, wrenching a cry of pain from me. I drag my shirt over my mouth, coughing, and crawl to my hands and knees.

'Shit.' Jun Bei's eyes are wide, staring at me. She's kneeling beside me, her hands pressed to her mouth. 'Cat, I'm so sorry. I just lost control.'

I cough, sucking in a lungful of smoke that blazes down my throat. 'You could have killed us.'

'I'm sorry,' she says again. 'But he's my father. The things he did to me and the others –'

'He's my father too,' I say. 'He's hurt us all. He's a monster, Jun Bei, but we've *stopped* him. Now we have to stop flood protocol.'

She nods, her eyes still wide. 'You're right. Come on, we should hurry.'

She stands and moves in a blur to the terminal, and I grab the table to wrench myself up. My ribs are aching, my eyes and throat stinging with the smoke wafting through the air.

'Brink won't wait much longer if he thinks he has us and Lachlan,' Jun Bei says, shoving the sleeves of her sweatshirt up to her elbows. 'We're going to have to work fast. I think I can stop this attack long enough to send a broadcast.'

I lurch across the room to the terminal, fighting back a cough, and press the memory chip Dax gave me to it. The interface pops into my vision and a map of the world springs up, showing bunker locations, drone fleets, the population centres on the surface. I can see the entire file system of Cartaxus's research division – files and project codenames stretch out in front of me. Hydra. Zarathustra. Gemini. This is the raw architecture of Cartaxus's network.

'I'll stop the drones that are controlling the clouds,' Jun Bei says, her eyes glazing. I feel a tickle in my mind as she dives into our panel's memory. Files spin across my vision – the viruses I coded when I was working with the Skies, along with a dozen pieces of her code that I don't recognize. She folds them together, weaving them into a single virus.

But before she can launch it, the terminal goes black.

She jolts out of her session. 'What happened?'

'I don't know.' My hand is still pressed to the screen, holding Dax's memory chip against it. The power cables at the back are intact, and I can feel the terminal humming, but it's not letting us into Cartaxus's servers any more.

'Did you think it would be that easy?'

I spin round. A sandy-haired main is standing with his arms crossed in the wreckage of the genkits Jun Bei blew up, watching me with an amused expression on his face.

Brink.

Cartaxus's leader steps across the room, moving cleanly through the metal table in its centre. He looks between Jun Bei and me appraisingly. 'I had a feeling the unconscious girl in Lachlan's arms wasn't really the one we were looking for. I had to come and see for myself what made you so special. Now I'm starting to understand.'

My fingers curl into a fist around the memory chip Dax gave me. Brink must have used it to track us somehow – there's no other way he could have found us so fast.

Brink's eyes drop to my clenched hand, and he lets out a snort of laughter. 'You shouldn't take memory chips from people you don't trust, girls. Crick was surprisingly easy to control. We have other copies of Leoben, none quite as special as him, but useful enough to make him expendable. Dax became quite cooperative when we explained this to him. His login isn't going to help you now, and I've added more firewalls to our network that even Mato wasn't able to penetrate while testing them. You've lost.'

I grip the edge of the terminal, my fist tightening until the edge of the memory chip cuts into my palm. I don't know how I could have been so stupid. I should never have trusted Dax. Now we don't have a chance of stopping this.

'You have to stop flood protocol, Brink,' Jun Bei says. 'That's all we want to do. You can't kill the people on the surface – it won't help you.'

'We need to protect the vaccine,' Brink says.

'You need to *forget* the vaccine,' I say. 'It's a dead technology. Even Lachlan admitted it – it's not the way to save us. If we have a future, it lies with the genehackers and people willing to think outside the limits of their DNA. That's the only way we're going to beat this plague.'

'You sound so sure of yourself,' Brink says, looking from Jun Bei to me. 'I'd suggest you remember that our systems and protocols have kept three *billion* people alive for the last two years. Your genehackers have been dropping like flies on the surface. They're chaotic where we're steady. It might take us a while to beat this virus, but I can assure you we'll do it. It's unfortunate that so many of your kind are refusing to see the light and join us.'

'The civilians in the bunkers deserve a voice,' Jun Bei says. She disappears in a blur of light, reappearing beside him. 'You can't keep leading them from the shadows. They should have the right to make up their own minds about something like flood protocol.'

Brink tilts his head. 'Civilians? We've housed and fed them for two years now. We've protected them and saved them from this virus. They're not civilians any more. They belong to us now, and Cartaxus isn't a democracy – it's a *shield*. We're the only thing standing between humanity and extinction. I'd like the two of you to join us, but you're not going to have long to make that choice. I'll be deploying the scythe in ten minutes' time. That's long enough for you to make it to one of the transports here. You have a place at Cartaxus with your father – both of you. I suggest you consider taking it.'

His image flickers and disappears. I slump back against the terminal, closing my eyes, letting the memory chip tumble from my hand. 'Goddammit,' I say. 'What the hell are we going to do now?' I open my eyes, expecting Jun Bei to be fuming.

But she's grinning.

It's a smile I haven't seen on her before, but I recognize it from Cole's sketches. Her eyes are alight with excitement. 'When you threatened to kill Brink at the lab through his comm, did you mean it?' she asks.

I straighten. 'No, of course not. That's impossible.'

'That's what I thought too,' she says. 'But then he went into lockdown and Mato said he stopped taking comms. I thought that was curious. Why would he hide if he thought it was impossible?'

A flicker of hope rises through me. 'What are you saying?'

Her grin grows wider. 'I've never tried hacking someone through a comm before. I didn't really know what I was doing. But he was right to be afraid. Cartaxus's comm system isn't as secure as it should be.'

'Are you saying you *killed* him?'

'No,' she says, throwing her head back, laughing. 'I couldn't have if I wanted to. He's set up a firewall to protect himself from the scythe – that's the only reason he felt safe enough to comm us. But he should have thought it through, because I got this from him instead.'

She lifts one hand, and an ID card appears above it, rotating slowly in the air. It holds the same information Dax handed to us on the memory chip.

Jun Bei just hacked the leader of Cartaxus and stole his login credentials.

'Holy shit,' I gasp.

'Come on,' she says, still grinning. She blurs across the room, reappearing at the terminal. 'It gets better.'

I press my hand back to the screen. It blinks on, asking for my ID, and Jun Bei's eyes glaze as she flicks the credentials to the machine. The same server interface we saw before unfolds again, filling my vision, only now I can see more – every file and archive and record. There are access protocols for the panels of the civilians in the bunkers. For the satellites. For the *airlocks*.

Brink's login has given us access to *everything*.

'This won't take long,' Jun Bei says, stepping up to the terminal, her eyes still glazed. I feel her mind slipping into the interface, skating through the military servers. She's calling off flood protocol with a single command. There's no need to hack the drones or the soldiers. Brink's more powerful than that. His access lets us alter entire structures within Cartaxus's systems *instantly*.

'I'm going to send out the patched vaccine,' she says.

I move beside her, letting my own mind slip into the servers. I know the architecture of Cartaxus's systems – I've hacked them countless times before – but I've never seen them as clearly as this. I can see Jun Bei moving through the science division's files, searching for the patched vaccine, triggering its deployment through the satellites. I'm following a similar path, but I'm hunting through the military division, skipping through code banks, scouring them for a weapon they shouldn't have.

It's hidden in a locked folder, but Brink's access lets me see it.

The scythe. A single command, and it's gone.

'That's smart,' Jun Bei murmurs. 'I sent the patched vaccine. We're almost done. We just have to take down Brink.'

'How?'

She grins again, her green eyes sparkling. 'I've changed his login credentials – that'll stop him for a few hours – but by that time it won't matter. I just sent this out to every screen in every bunker in the world and set it to play on a loop for the next twenty-four hours.'

Footage appears in front of me, hovering in the air. It's a VR clip generated from my ocular tech. It's Jun Bei talking to Brink, standing beside the terminal. She's telling him that the civilians in the bunkers deserve a better leader than him – that they should have the right to make up their own minds.

And he's replying that they're not civilians. He's saying they *belong* to Cartaxus now.

'Shit,' I breathe. 'You did it. You actually *did* it.'

'*We* did it,' she says, smiling, a lock of her dark hair slipping across her forehead. 'You and I make excellent coding partners, Catarina. I wish I could hug you.'

I smile, trying to lift my hand from the terminal to reach for her, even though I know I'll pass right through her, but my arm won't respond. I try again, but the muscles stay frozen.

I can't move it at all.

'What are you doing? I can't move my arm.'

'I'm not ready to let go just yet,' she says. 'This might be the last time I have access to Cartaxus's systems at this level. I can't leave them like this.'

Fear flutters through me. 'What are you talking about? We've done what we came here for. We've stopped the attack. We've even brought down Brink.'

She tosses the lock of hair from her eyes. 'For now, maybe, but they won't stop. There'll be another Brink. Do you seriously think that Cartaxus is just going to give up this kind of power? Can you imagine them letting their civilians file out of those bunkers with full control over their panels?'

Her voice grows sharp, and my resolve wavers. Of course I don't believe that Cartaxus is going to fall this easily. The outbreak has given them access to the bodies of every one of their civilians. Brink won't be the only one who sees those people as their property. There's no way Cartaxus will relinquish their power because of a single hack.

But I don't know what Jun Bei could be planning to stop them permanently.

'I only had to live through a few days of the outbreak,' she says, turning, 'but what I saw already scarred me. This outbreak is an open wound on humanity that we can't possibly move beyond. How can we heal and step into a new world after what we've done to survive?'

I try to lift my arm from the terminal again, but it still won't respond. 'People are resilient,' I say. 'We'll find a way to move past this. Break the connection, Jun Bei. Let me go.'

'No,' she shakes her head. 'I need to do this. I understand now. I never really knew before why Lachlan used to wipe our memories of the experiments. I thought it was to control us, but it wasn't – he did it to keep us *functioning*. He knew that after enough pain and enough misery, it would consume and define us. The pain of this outbreak is defining all of us now – we've lived through things that our species was not designed to experience. We've killed – we've *eaten* each other. How can we come back from this?'

Fear ripples through me. 'Jun Bei – whatever you're doing, *stop*. We can find a way to come back from this. We can't overwrite humanity.'

'I know,' she says, her voice distant. 'I don't *want* to overwrite them. I just want to take their pain away.'

The fear inside me grows sharper. I don't know what she's doing, but she has complete control over my body. I can't move, can't get my panel to respond to my thoughts. All I can do is speak, breathe and watch in horror as Jun Bei paces across the room.

'Please, Jun Bei, whatever you're thinking –'

'This world is barely surviving,' she says, ignoring me. 'Brink almost killed millions of people out of desperation – that's what this plague has done to us. That's not just the Wrath. It's years of pain layered over us, and I don't think we can find a way to live together if it isn't washed away. I can't give people the gift of immortality if it means living forever with the horror of the outbreak inside them. What kind of species would we be? We'd be bitter and violent *forever*. There's a new world waiting for us, but we need to wash ourselves clean of this one first.'

Her eyes glaze and the terminal blinks. She's linking up with the satellites – but she isn't running the Origin code. I don't know what she's trying to do – what commands she's running. I can't move, can't force my focus back into my panel or my cuff.

Her lips move silently, and code flickers across my vision – commands lifted from a piece of code that's stored in our panel. It's generating what looks like a memory suppressant.

No, not a suppressant. It's a chemical to *erase* memories. That's how she wants to take the pain of the outbreak away from everyone.

She's going to wipe them all.

'*No!*' I gasp, struggling against her control. 'Jun Bei, listen! You can't do this – you can't erase people's *memories*.'

'They're hurting,' she says, her green eyes glassy. 'I won't take more than I have to. Just the outbreak – just the pain. Once it's washed from them, we can start moving forwards again. We can fix this world. We'll go back to how things were before the outbreak.'

Jun Bei's voice is lifted and unwavering. I feel like I'm seeing her for the first time. She is Lachlan's daughter, truly – standing at a terminal and making choices for the entire world. Her brow furrows, and something flutters in my mind, rising into a storm. She's fractioning. I don't know how many splits she's reached, but it feels like a whirlwind. My vision flickers with text – network data from the satellites. Brink's credentials slide past every firewall like a blade.

She's sending code to erase memories into every panel in the world.

'Stop it!' I shout. 'This is *wrong*. Can't you see what you're doing?'

She's not listening to me. I have to find a way to stop her. I close my eyes, summoning my focus, trying to wrench my hand from the terminal, but it won't move. I turn my mind to my panel, but it's locked from me. No access to my files, my viruses, my cuff. I can't even form a single command.

She lifts an eyebrow. 'You think you can fight me?'

'I'm part of you, Jun Bei,' I say. 'I know you don't really want to do this.'

Her eyes refocus, locking on me, steely and cold. 'You don't know anything about me.'

Footsteps echo in the hallway outside the lab. Jun Bei's concentration wavers, and I surge my focus into my panel, trying to break her control. It *almost* works. Her attack halts, spinning in my vision, but I can't wrestle the focus I need to stop it completely.

'Cat?' A voice shouts from outside, and a figure pushes through the door, stumbling into the room.

Cole.

His face is smeared with ash, blood streaming from cuts on his shoulders, his arms, his neck. A patch of dark, wet blood is blossoming on his trousers above his knee. He's been shot. He grabs the wall to steady himself, looking up shakily.

His face goes white as he sees Jun Bei.

'C-Cole,' I choke out, struggling to speak. Jun Bei is fighting against my breathing now, wrestling to take full control of our body. She's like a wave against me, clawing at my mind, and I can already feel the cracks in my control spreading.

Cole blinks, staring between us, the gun loose in his hands. He's shaking, his pupils narrowed to specks.

'Jun Bei?' His voice breaks. 'You're *alive*?'

'Cole, y-you have to shoot me,' I gasp, barely able to form the words. 'She's trying to wipe people's memories. I can't hold her back much longer.'

His brow creases as he looks around the lab. 'I came here to . . . to . . .' He trails off, confused.

The memory code must already be running. We don't have much time. 'Please, Cole!' I shout. 'You have to do it! Shoot me, please!'

His finger tightens on the trigger, but something flashes in his eyes, and I realize with a sickening thud that he won't do it. He doesn't understand.

'Please!' I urge him. 'You have to stop me!'

But he just blinks, looking between Jun Bei and me, and something cracks inside me. The abyss that creaked open when Lachlan told me the truth about why I was created. I didn't fall then, but I can feel myself swaying now as Cole's eyes pass over me.

He's looking at me like I'm a stranger.

'Who are you?' he whispers.

'No!' I cry. The abyss inside me roars open, darkness tugging at my heart. I fling myself against Jun Bei's control, thrashing wildly against the steel of her mind.

'He doesn't know who you are any more,' she murmurs, stepping to my side. 'The wipe is already running – it's eaten away weeks of the outbreak by now. He hasn't known you long enough to remember you.'

'*No*.' My voice comes out as a sob, my chest shuddering. 'Please, Cole – you have to remember me!'

But I can see it in his eyes as he looks between me and Jun Bei. He doesn't know me. He doesn't recognize me. He loved me. He said he wanted to run away with me. Whatever there was between us was strained, but at least it existed.

Now it's gone.

Jun Bei has taken him from me like I took him from her.

'This was really Cole's idea,' Jun Bei says, leaning against the terminal. 'He was going to erase me to stop me killing people. He said sometimes memories aren't worth the pain they hold. He's right, and you know it. Humans weren't designed to live with this amount of pain. It will take us centuries to move past the outbreak if we don't forget it now.'

I choke back another sob, shaking my head. 'Then we'll *take* centuries,' I beg. 'Please, Jun Bei, I know you don't want to do this. You heard Lachlan – you're the one who's supposed to *save* us, not control us like him and Brink.'

For a heartbeat, her gaze flickers to mine, her mind brushing closer. I know she can feel what I do, because I can feel her emotions in the same way, stretching through the wall between us. She is desperate and wounded, lost and betrayed, but she is not a monster, and she knows that this is wrong. She can see the horror, just like I do. I let the feeling rise through me, swallowing me, taking me down into the abyss.

Horror at what has been done to her. At the people who mistook her strength for darkness, who didn't see the gifts she brought and tried to control her instead. Horror at the man who tortured her for years and somehow made her *love* him.

Her grip on me falters, and I fall to my hands and knees, gasping on the floor, dragging in a choking breath as my control surges back to me. Cole steps closer, and I feel Jun Bei tighten. She's not going to stop. She's too angry. And maybe she's right. Maybe humanity is too broken to survive, too monstrous to live forever. Maybe we need to change our minds, to cut away our pasts, to wipe the legacy of our brutal history from our very DNA.

But I'm not going to be the one to do it.

I won't become a weapon turned against billions of people. I grab at one of the cables coiling out from the wall and yank it from the terminal. It sparks, popping with electricity, and I pull it closer before Jun Bei understands. She screams, wrestling for control.

But it's too late.

'I'm sorry,' I say to them both, then press the sparking cable to the socket in the back of my skull.

CHAPTER 43

The darkness fades slowly. A single spark of light growing into an ember, blossoming and multiplying across the dark city of my mind. My senses crawl back to me – whispers of sound, air on my skin, and the steady thump of my own heartbeat deep inside my chest.

I'm awake. I'm *alive*. The thought rises like a flock of birds. My breathing is rough and foreign, but it's *mine*, sending a lurch of pain through my ribs with every inhalation. Dark fabric blinks into view above me, hot desert air drying my lips. I'm lying on a bed somewhere. I try to sit up, but the world sparkles into silver diamonds.

'Easy, now.'

A girl's face ripples into view. Smooth brown skin with segmented joints at her neck like a porcelain doll. The hacker from the market. *Rhine*.

I lift my head, looking around. I'm on a camp bed in a canvas medical tent, lying between rows of wounded, bandaged genehackers and soldiers. The tent's doors are open, letting in the distant cries of pigeons and the hot, dry air of the desert. There's something taped around my head. A plastic bandage, plastered over most of my face. I lift my hands to touch it, but Rhine grabs my arm, her fingers sliding over my cuff.

'I wouldn't if I were you,' she says. 'Your face has been all over those screens.'

I try to sit up, but my vision spins, nausea rolling through me. After a moment I manage to straighten, swinging my legs off the side of the bed. A screen is set up in the corner of the tent, Novak's face splashed across it. Video feeds are playing beside her – cobalt triphase clouds, drones swooping over cities around the world. One of the feeds is showing footage of Brink, another showing Lachlan being marched through Entropia's tunnels, an unconscious girl held in his arms. Her face looks just like mine.

'You've been out for a while,' Rhine says. 'Two days, by my count. I've been checking in on you.'

'What happened?' My thoughts are scattered and wild. I remember the hack, the electric cable, the blackness that followed the shock. I lift my hand to the back of my head to check for a wound, but there's a pad of gauze taped over the socket.

'You were hurt pretty good,' Rhine says. 'Took a few of us to stabilize you. We figured it was best to keep you hidden. Things are dangerous right now.'

'What's happening?'

'Well, we have a vaccine,' she says. 'Who knows how long it'll last – the plague is in the birds now – but the code's working on people as far as we can tell. That isn't stopping the bunkers from revolting, though. There have been attacks on both sides. They're calling it a war. Some people think this is all the genehackers' fault, and some think it was Cartaxus. Nobody trusts *anyone* any more, not after the wipe.'

'The w-wipe?' I ask, coughing. My throat is dry from the desert air, my voice shaking with the effort it takes to speak.

Rhine reaches for a canteen beside my bed, unscrewing it for me. I take it in one trembling hand and lift it carefully to my lips.

'I wouldn't be too concerned if you can't remember much from the last few months,' Rhine says. 'None of us can. I don't know who did it, but everyone with a panel in their arm just found out that they weren't as in control of their tech as they thought.'

I let out a slow breath, my focus still scattered and foggy. My memory is intact, but it seems like a bad idea to tell Rhine that.

'Where are we?' I ask instead.

'Amnesty zone,' Rhine says. 'An hour from Entropia.' She presses a black memory chip into my hands. 'This'll unlock the controls of a Comox waiting for you on the edge of this camp. I'd get into hiding quickly if I were you. You won't be able to wear that bandage forever.'

'Thank you,' I say, locking my fingers around the chip, trying to clear my thoughts. 'Why are you helping me?'

Rhine smiles sadly. 'I owed your mother a favour that I never had a chance to repay before she died.'

The words fall heavily inside me. I clutch my hands into fists, trying to quiet the ache that rises through me at the memory of Regina's death. I barely had time to get to know her. There was so much I could have learned from her, but I wasn't strong or fast enough to save her.

I won't let it happen again.

I look back at the screen. It's showing footage of a flock of pigeons soaring over the desert, leaving a trail of feathers below it. The virus is still wild, and there are billions of hosts for it now. I don't know how long we'll have before it mutates through the birds and finds its way back to us.

'Rhine,' I say, 'who made this strain of the birds?'

She looks at the screen. 'They evolved all on their own from another strain. That's what people are saying, at least. I worked on a few of the early flocks myself. Nothing this good, though.'

'Do all the strains have panels?'

She gives me a quizzical look. 'None of them have panels. They're *birds*, not people.'

'Of course,' I say, clutching the memory chip in my hand. I force myself to my feet, fighting a wave of dizziness. 'I don't know what I was thinking. Thank you again for your help.'

She stands with me and gives me a tight smile. 'Good luck.'

My footsteps are clumsy and slow as I weave between the beds in the tent, ducking through the flaps to step outside. The sunlight is blinding, and it takes my ocular tech a full second to respond, drawing the lines of the camp into focus.

A dozen more medical tents are spread out across a grassy plain, surrounded by a rough circle of vehicles and smaller camping tents set up on the ground. People are milling through the grass, walking in groups of two or three. There's a mix of genehackers and what looks like Cartaxus soldiers, but they're not wearing their visors or armour. They're dressed in black tank tops and trousers, bandaged and dazed. There are no weapons in sight, no drones hovering above us. A flock of pigeons circles in the distance, a shifting mass of cobalt and black.

I let a pulse slip from my cuff, sweeping across the camp. It traces light around the arms of the hundreds of people around me, around the vehicles and humming genkits in the medical tents. Every wireless connection within a mile is lit up in my vision, open and waiting for me to hack in and control it.

Including the pigeons soaring through the sky.

Someone gave them panels. Someone created them. They let them loose on the world, and now the birds are covering it, swarming over every continent. The most successful iteration so far.

And the pigeons happen to be carrying a mutated strain of the virus that's resisting the vaccine.

I draw my focus out of my cuff, forcing myself to turn away from the flock, scanning the edges of the camp for the Comox. My eyes slide across the battered trucks and cars, landing on a dusty black vehicle with badly fitted solar panels on its roof.

Cole is sitting on the bonnet of his jeep, a bandage on his shoulder. He's scanning the camp, his brow creased. A girl in a baseball cap is walking through the crowd towards him, carrying two plates heaped with rice. Anna. She says something to him, setting the plates on the bonnet of the jeep, and slides up beside him.

My hand rises to the bandage that's taped across my face. It covers my cheek, my forehead and most of my nose, but both my eyes are clear. Cole picks up one of the plates, and Anna's gaze drifts across the tents, landing on me, but she barely pauses before looking away. No flash of recognition flickers in her eyes. I'm bruised and bandaged, but there's a yellow squid printed on the front of my T-shirt.

She doesn't remember me.

Neither does Cole. He digs his fork into the plate of rice, shifting on the jeep's bonnet. I stare at them a moment longer, then turn and force myself to walk away, pushing between rows of cars to the edge of the camp where the Comox is waiting. My footsteps are growing steady, but my control over my body is still weak. There are millimetres of error in each of my movements. My feet drag, and my fingers hit my face when I try to push my hair from my eyes. I know it'll pass with time, but it still makes me feel uncomfortable in my own skin.

I press the memory chip to my cuff as I get closer to the Comox. The door hisses open, the ramp unfolding. The cargo hold looks empty. I have no weapons, no tools. Not that I need them. I escaped from the lab with less than this when I was just a child. I've survived everything this nightmare of a world has thrown at me with little more than the clothes on my back and the panel in my arm.

I stride up the Comox's ramp and through the cargo hold, heading for the cockpit. It's clean and empty. I sink into the pilot's seat and push my focus into the controls, engaging the autopilot. The door hisses closed, the rotors spinning up, sending a gust of wind rolling through the camp. Cole looks up, his eyes narrowing, setting the plate of rice down on the jeep's bonnet as the Comox lifts up off the ground. The medical tents flap, the grass flattening in a circle beneath me as I rise above the camp.

Cole slides off the jeep's bonnet, staring up at me. He doesn't know who I am, but he will soon. Something inside me swells as he watches me leave, but it's weak. I wrestle it away behind a wall inside my mind.

I turn the Comox northwards, heading for the city on the mountain. It doesn't take long for the gleaming razorgrass border to come into view. There are black streaks burned across the desert around it, scorched by the triphase clouds. Half the buildings on the mountainside are charred and smoking, the farmlands destroyed. I circle the Comox over the mountain and drop towards the open blast doors at the top of the bunker's atrium.

The pigeons are still thick in the air, but I alter my cuff's controls to push them away from me, sending them scattering. The Comox tilts as I descend through the blast doors and into the atrium. The wind from the rotors kicks up a cloud of leaves and ash as I land slowly in the middle of the park.

The genehackers emerge from doors and hallways. They step through to the charred, rubble-strewn park as the Comox's ramp unfurls. Hundreds of them. Auburn skin. Flashing neon eyes. Entropia's survivors – the ones who refused to be forced from their homes. They congregate across the grass – some short, some tall, some gliding in too-perfect strides, their movements algorithmically designed. I step into the Comox's doorway and lift my hands to the plastic bandage on my face, peeling at the edges, tugging it away from my skin. The crowd murmurs in confusion as it falls away.

I scan the crowd, lifting my voice. 'Cartaxus tried to destroy us once, and they'll do it again. They have more weapons and more soldiers, but they can't threaten us. We're stronger than them, and we're smarter. We're the ones pushing humanity forward. This world should be *ours*, and I'm here to take it. I can give you everything you've ever dreamed of if you'll follow me. I can let you change yourselves in any way you want. Join me, and I'll give you immortality.'

The shadows of the pigeons in the atrium slide across the crowd. More people are stepping from doorways, moving to balconies above me. They're hurt and confused, and their city has burned, but I can see a glint of steel in their eyes. They know the virus isn't our only threat any more. There's a battle coming between Cartaxus and the genehackers, between control and freedom. I'm starting to understand what Lachlan was trying to tell me, and why he worked so hard to keep me hidden. He was preparing me for the war he knew was coming.

There's a new world waiting for us – one where we can live forever.

But we're going to have to fight for it.

'My name is Jun Bei,' I say, looking out at the crowd, 'and I'm here to finish what I started.'

ACKNOWLEDGEMENTS

There are so many people who have made my debut year truly . . . explosive! I can't possibly name them all, but I want to wish a huge thank-you:

To my editors – Sarah McCabe and Tig Wallace. Your vision, understanding, encouragement, guidance and patience turned this difficult novel into one I am truly proud of. I am so lucky to be working with you both. To Wendy Shakespeare, Sophie Nelson, Marcus Fletcher and my proofreaders – you're brilliant, and any errors in this text are my own.

To the team at Simon Pulse, especially Liesa Abrams, Mara Anastas, Nicole Russo and Sam Benson, and to Ben Horslen, Francesca Dow, Harriet Venn, Ellen Grady and Zoe Bechara at Penguin Random House Children's for your continued support. You have made my dreams come true. To DongWon – I couldn't ask for a better agent, or a better friend. To the HMLA team and #TeamDongWon – you're all magical. Thank you to Caspian Dennis and Heather Baror-Shapiro for sharing this series with the world. To Michael Prevett – thank you for making incredible things happen for my work. Thank you to Breck and Vincent for your vision and support.

To a real-life queen, Regina Flath, for this incredible cover and for letting me use your name. To Jan Bielecki – for the stunning printed edges.

To the wonderful booksellers I've met and have yet to meet, for your passion and commitment. To Kristen and Len at Tattered Cover for making me feel like a star (I still wear that T-shirt!). To the Waterstones team – especially Kate and Florentyna. To the Powell's team – especially Beth. To Readings Books in Australia, and the University Bookstore in Seattle. To the teachers and librarians who have shared my work with such enthusiasm. Seeing my book on your shelves is a dream come true.

To Amie Kaufman – you're AMAZING. I frequently ask myself, 'What would Amie do?' and my life is better for it. To Fonda Lee – I hope we have many more road trips to come. To Veronica Rossi – thank you for letting me adopt 'fractioning'. To Laini Taylor, Stephanie Garber, Victoria Schwab, Kayla Olson, Shea Ernshaw, Rachel Lynn Solomon, Margaret Rogerson, Amal El-Mohtar, Elizabeth Bear, Jay Kristoff, Alexa Donne, Heather Kaczynski, Emily A. Duncan, Meagan Macvie, Caitlin Starling, Curtis Chen, Wendy Wagner and the incredible authors who have made me feel so welcome – thank you, thank you, thank you. As always, Lora Beth Johnson – you are my first pair of eyes, my first call, my dearest friend. I can't wait to see your book on shelves.

To the team at Ooligan Press: Alyssa Schaffer, Joanna Szabo, Elizabeth Hughes, Sadie Moses, Melina Hughes, Kristen Ludwigsen, Jessica DeBolt, Grace Evans, Taylor Thompson, Emily Hagenburger, Hope Levy, Michele Ford, Amylia Ryan, Lisa Hein, Katie Fairchild and little Joey – you all have a special place in my heart.

To the bloggers and readers who have reviewed my work, with a special shout-out to Aditi Nichani. To Erica Chan – I hope you like meeting Cambear! To Kailey at Enchanted Book Box, Daphne at Illumicrate, and Floricci at Wanderlust Reader for featuring my work!

To my friends and family – thank you for listening to me talk about writing for approximately eight years now. I love you all so much and couldn't do this without you. Thank you to Edward for being my hero, my rock, my best friend and soulmate. I love you more than words can ever express, though I intend to spend the rest of my life trying.

IN CONVERSATION WITH EMILY SUVADA

What's *This Mortal Coil* about?

This Mortal Coil is a story about a young girl called Catarina who is a hacker of both computers *and* of DNA. She's the daughter of the world's greatest geneticist, and she lives in a frightening world where a virus has devastated the population. The virus is airborne, and detonates its victims into clouds of infectious mist – so it's actually a person exploding on the front of the book. After Catarina's father creates a vaccine for the virus, she must team up with an enemy soldier to release it. But first she'll have to unravel secrets about the vaccine and about her father that will make her question everything she knows.

Can you tell us a bit about the world you've created in *This Mortal Coil*?

The world of *This Mortal Coil* is one in which people are able to re-code their DNA in any way they want. You can download an app for green eyes, for example, or you could hack your metabolism or grow striped fur like a tiger. All of these apps run through a *panel*, a piece of technology that's embedded in a person's forearm, which re-writes their DNA on the fly. I come from a science background – I studied mathematics and astrophysics at college, which is not a typical background for a writer, but it's one that set me up with a very science-focused and technical view of our future. In the world of *This Mortal Coil*, I let my imagination run wild, mixing ideas about DNA with coding, and hopefully this book lets your imagination run wild in that future too.

What compelled you to write the book?

I read that you should write the book you want to *read*. Growing up, I really wanted to read a book about a young, science-loving female character, especially because I always loved science and mathematics. In *This Mortal Coil* I created a really nerdy, unashamedly brilliant and science-loving character in Catarina. Her heroism in the book comes from her knowledge of science and coding, which for me is the most exciting thing about the book. Catarina doesn't use a weapon to solve her problems – she uses code. She doesn't always make the right choice; in fact she makes a lot of bad choices along the way, but she makes those choices as a scientist – with the best information that's available to her at the time.

If you could hack any of your genes, what would you change?

I'd love to try to hack the way I sleep. There's a good chance that our sleep habits are genetic and that it's possible to alter them. Some animals, like giraffes, don't need much sleep at all and get by with just a few quick naps each day. Others, like dolphins, are able to put just half their brain to sleep at a time, so they can keep moving around and swimming. One of the things every writer wants is more time – time to read, to write, to think about their stories – and having some more hours in the day to do that would be fantastic. It would be a complicated genetic hack, but I'd be up for it!

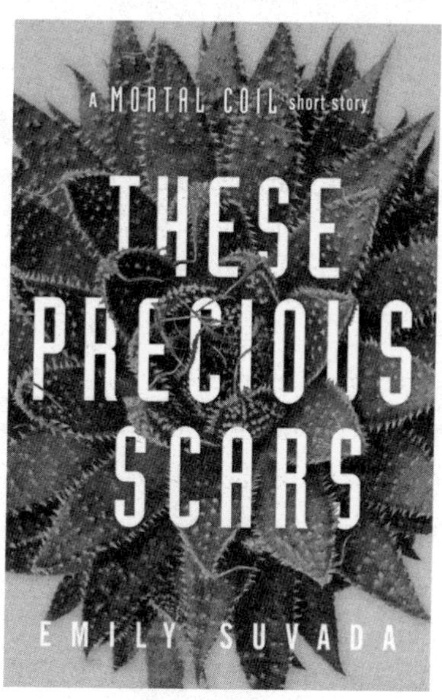

Jun Bei, Cole, Anna, Leoben, Ziana.
Five children with extraordinary potential.

They don't get many visitors at the remote laboratory where they live under the eye of legendary geneticist Lachlan Agatta. The man and woman who arrive are nothing like the others.

They're from Cartaxus and offer the children something rare and unfathomable: *escape*.

But freedom means different things to the five children. For one of them, getting what they want may mean betraying everyone else.

Free short-story ebook from Emily Suvada